BESTSELLING AUSTRALIAN AUTHOR

BARBARA HANNAY

Chosen

MILLS & BOON

CHOSEN © 2023 by Harlequin Books S.A.

ADOPTED: OUTBACK BABY
© 2008 by Barbara Hannay
Australian Copyright 2008
New Zealand Copyright 2008

First Published 2008
Sixith Australian Paperback Edition 2023
ISBN 978 1 867 28940 1

OUTBACK WIFE AND MOTHER
© 1999 by Barbara Hannay
Australian Copyright 1999
New Zealand Copyright 1999

First Published 1999
Fourth Australian Paperback Edition 2023
ISBN 978 1 867 28940 1

RANCHER'S TWINS: MOM NEEDED
© 2011 by Barbara Hannay
Australian Copyright 2011
New Zealand Copyright 2011

First Published 2011
Third Australian Paperback Edition 2023
ISBN 978 1 867 28940 1

This is a work of fiction. Names, characters, places, and incidents are either the
product of the author's imagination or are used fictitiously, and any resemblance
to actual persons, living or dead, business establishments, events, or locales is
entirely coincidental.

Published by
Mills & Boon
An imprint of Harlequin Enterprises (Australia) Pty Limited
(ABN 47 001 180 918), a subsidiary of HarperCollins
Publishers Australia Pty Limited (ABN 36 009 913 517)
Level 19, 201 Elizabeth Street
SYDNEY NSW 2000
AUSTRALIA

MIX
Paper | Supporting
responsible forestry
FSC   FSC® C001695
www.fsc.org

® and ™ (apart from those relating to FSC®) are trademarks of Harlequin
Enterprises (Australia) Pty Limited or its corporate affiliates. Trademarks indicated
with ® are registered in Australia, New Zealand and in other countries.
Contact admin_legal@Harlequin.ca for details.

Printed and bound in Australia by McPherson's Printing Group

CONTENTS

Barbara Hannay was born in Sydney, educated in Brisbane, and has spent most of her adult life living in tropical North Queensland, where she and her husband have raised four children. While she has enjoyed many happy times camping and canoeing in the bush, she also delights in an urban lifestyle—chamber music, contemporary dance, movies and dining out. An English teacher, she has always loved writing, and now, by having her stories published, she is living her most cherished fantasy.

In 2007 Barbara won the Romance Writers' of America RITA® Award for Best Traditional Romance with CLAIMING HIS FAMILY.

To catch up on all Barbara's latest news visit www.barbarahannay.com

Adopted:
Outback Baby

PROLOGUE

A SUMMER'S MORNING at dawn.

Nell and Jacob met at their secret place on the sheltered river bank, the only safe place for the boss's daughter and the hired help.

Arriving by separate tracks, they tethered their horses at opposite ends of the clearing. Nell was nervous and Jacob was on tenterhooks waiting for her news, but he came towards her proudly, striding through the misty morning light with his shoulders back and his head high, as if he owned the earth.

A metre from her, he stopped and she read the silent question in his serious grey eyes.

Too anxious to speak, she simply shook her head, watched the movement in his throat as he swallowed.

'You're pregnant then,' he said quietly.

Nell dropped her gaze to her clasped hands. 'I'm almost certain.' She heard his sharp indrawn breath and whispered, 'I'm sorry.' And she realised for the first time that she was a little afraid of this tall and ruggedly divine young man.

Suddenly, she felt as if she didn't really know him, in spite of the many stolen hours she'd spent with him here during the long, hot weeks of her summer holiday. Pregnancy changed everything, changed something precious and perfect into a shameful mistake. And it forced the two of them to consider a future they weren't prepared for.

More than anything, Nell was scared of what her father would do when he found out. His bad temper was beyond volcanic. He would never forgive her for this and she was certain that he would offer her only one option.

She trembled at the thought, drew a hasty breath for courage. 'My parents will want me to have an abortion.'

Jacob's frown was fierce. 'You don't want that, do you?'

No. She couldn't bear the thought of terminating a baby they had made. She shook her head.

'You mustn't do it then, Nell. Don't even think about it.' He reached for her hands, threaded his strong, work-toughened fingers through hers and she felt the familiar rasp of the callus on his right palm.

Beside them, the river chattered carelessly and the scent of eucalypts and sheoaks hung heavy in the air.

'I'm sorry,' she whispered again.

'Don't be.' Jacob gave her hands a gentle shake. 'Don't apologise.'

Tears stung her eyes. She knew apologies shouldn't be necessary. From the moment she and Jacob had met on that first afternoon, when she'd returned to Half Moon from university, the blame had been equally shared.

She'd seen him tending her father's horses and Cupid had started firing those dangerous little arrows. Their over-the-top attraction had blinded them to anything else, especially to common sense. They hadn't taken precautions that first time.

Now, Jacob gathered Nell in to him and his big hand cradled her head against his shoulder. She adored the smell of him—musky and warm and clean—and something very masculine that she couldn't identify.

He kissed her brow. 'Will you marry me, Nell?'

She gasped, feeling hot and cold with excitement. This was what she'd been longing for, the words from Jacob she'd been silently praying for, secretly clinging to the hope that Jacob would want her and his baby. It was the only way she could possibly face up to her parents.

With trembling fingers, Jacob traced the curve of her cheek. 'I'll look after you, I promise. We'll be all right.'

Oh, yes. They'd be all right. Nell had no doubts. Jacob was an excellent stockman, brilliant on horseback, with a deep love of the land. He would find work anywhere in the Outback. She wouldn't mind too much about giving up her studies and she wouldn't mind about being poor, not if she was with him.

Her parents were the only problem.

They were such painful, *painful* snobs. They'd only sent her to university to snare a rich husband and World War Three would erupt if Nell announced she was marrying their cook's son.

She needed to consider Jacob too, needed to be sure that he was being completely honest. He'd told her about his long-term plans to have his own cattle empire, but that was in the distant future. An early marriage hadn't figured in his scheme.

'Are you sure about this, Jacob?'

With his arms about her waist, he leaned back to look at her and he frowned as if this were a matter of life and death. 'I've never been surer, Nell. I know I don't have much to offer you. You deserve an educated husband, someone rich.'

It was exactly what her parents might say but, coming

from him, it sounded wrong. She opened her mouth to protest, but Jacob hurried on.

'I love you, Nell, I swear. And I promise I'll look after you. I'll work hard. I'll get two jobs. I'll make enough money for you and the baby and one of these days we'll have our own place. A big property like Half Moon.'

He was so determined and defiant and Greek god gorgeous he banished her fears as easily as the sun scattered mist.

He said again, 'I love you. You must know that.'

'Yes.' Smiling through happy tears, she wrapped her arms tightly around him. 'And I love you so much it hurts.'

Nell lifted her lips to meet his and they kissed deeply, hungrily. She clung to Jacob, confident that his hard, lean strength would protect her for ever.

'Everything's going to be wonderful,' she said and his face broke into a beautiful grin.

'So you'll marry me?'

'Oh, yes, please. Absolutely.'

'*Yes!*'

His sudden, joyful whoop startled a flock of finches in a nearby wattle. With another loud shout of triumph, he hoisted Nell high and their laughter mingled with the birds' cries as he spun her around and around in happy circles.

They were going to be married. With their baby, they would be a little family. No one would stop them. All was right with their world.

Jacob slowed before Nell got too dizzy and he let her back to earth, let her body ride slowly…slowly down his muscled length till she reached where he was hard and she almost burst into flames.

Again their mouths met, hungrier than ever. Nell poured

her heart and soul into the kiss, wanting him to be certain of how intensely, wildly, completely she loved him.

His hands slipped under her shirt and skimmed lightly over her skin, giving her exquisite shivers.

Abruptly, the stillness of the summer morning was broken by the sound of a cold metallic click.

They froze.

Nell felt Jacob's heart leap against hers as they turned.

Her father stood in the shadows, his face flushed with red fury as he shouldered a shotgun and took aim.

CHAPTER ONE

THE SERVICE WAS over.

Nell knew she must get up and walk outside, but she wasn't sure she could trust her legs to carry her. She had never felt so bereft, didn't know how to cope with the sense of loss.

It was so much worse today than twenty years ago, when they'd taken Tegan away from her. She had been in hospital then, too ill and medicated to fully understand what was happening. This week, a highway smash that rated a thirty-second mention on the six o'clock news had taken her daughter away from her for ever. Today there was nothing to deaden Nell's pain.

Her memories of Tegan were so few. And so cruel. The newborn bundle in her arms, the strong little limbs kicking against the tightly wrapped blanket, just as they had kicked in her womb. The little face and bright, dark eyes. The soft cap of dark hair, the tiny red mouth. The unique, newborn smell of her.

The memories cut into Nell and she wished she could gather her pain around her and disappear completely. It was a blessing, at least, that everyone's sympathy had been showered on Jean and Bill Browne, the couple who had adopted Tegan. Nell knew she must go and speak to them, just as soon as she regained her composure.

'Nell?'

Nell turned stiffly and saw Jean approaching the end of her pew, twisting a damp handkerchief as she peered at her anxiously.

'Jean.' With a hand on the back of the pew for support, Nell struggled to her feet. 'I'm sorry I haven't spoken to you yet.'

The two women—adoptive mother and birth mother—stood, facing each other. Jean Browne looked exhausted, her pale blue eyes rimmed with red, her short grey hair flat and lifeless.

'Please—' The women had met before, on the day after the accident, but now, unable to think clearly, to find the right words, Nell clung to formalities. 'Please accept my condolences.'

Jean's pale eyes swam with tears. 'This is hard for you, too.'

'Yes.' Fighting a dull headache, Nell gathered up her handbag and continued along the pew on unsteady legs. 'I've mentioned this to you before, but I want you to know that I'm very, very grateful to you and Bill. You gave Tegan a wonderfully happy home and—and everything she needed.'

Jean nodded, sent Nell a fleeting, watery smile, then her face crumpled. 'You were such a help the other day. I've been hoping to speak to you. About the baby.'

Nell pressed shaking fingers to her mouth. She'd broken down completely during the eulogy, when the speaker had mentioned Tegan's little son, born just a few short weeks ago.

'I had to leave Sam with a sitter today,' Jean said. 'But I

knew that you would like to see him again, especially as Mr Tucker's here as well.'

'Mr Tucker?'

'Tegan's father.'

If Nell hadn't been clutching the back of the pew, she would almost certainly have fallen.

Jacob Tucker was here?

Had he been here throughout the funeral?

An unbearable, thrilling, panicky terror gripped her as Jean flicked a sideways glance back down the aisle. Like the needle of a magnet, Nell whirled around and there was Jacob, standing at the back of the chapel, near the door, tall and stern, with his shoulders back.

His face was partly in shadow but there was no mistaking his chiselled features. All trace of the smooth-skinned boy had vanished, but his strong brows and nose, the handsome cleft in his chin, were still, after twenty years, painfully familiar.

He was wearing a dark suit but, despite the city clothes, the Outback clung to him like a second skin. It was there in the tan on his skin, in the hard-packed leanness of his body, in the creases at his eyes, in the way he stood, poised for action.

And there was a roughness about him now that was unsettling. Devastating.

Nell could still remember with perfect clarity the first time she'd seen him in her father's stables, remembered the shock of attraction that had startled her, enslaved her. She remembered, too, the awful morning on the river bank, the last time she had seen him.

Apart from the occasional photo in cattlemen's magazines—and yes, she'd scanned them regularly, hungry for any news of Jacob Tucker—she knew next to nothing about his life. He'd become a very successful grazier, but there had been no contact between them in twenty years so his private life was a blank.

'I've already spoken to Mr Tucker,' Jean said.

On cue, from the back of the chapel, Jacob offered Nell an unsmiling, almost imperceptible dip of his head.

Her heart pounded. Now she could see the expression in his eyes, the way he looked at her with a mixture of pain and contempt.

She tightened her grip on the back of the pew. With another despairing glance at Jacob, she turned back to Jean. 'I'm sorry. What were you saying?'

'I thought Mr Tucker might like to meet Sam. And I wanted to talk to you both, if possible. I have a problem, you see.'

A stranger, a woman in a green felt hat, bustled into the chapel. 'Oh, there you are, Jean. Sorry, we thought we'd lost you.'

'I won't be long,' Jean told her, then she turned quickly back to Nell. 'I can't talk for very long now. I've got to take Bill home and collect the baby from the sitter. But there's something I need to discuss with you. And Mr Tucker.'

'I—I see.'

Jean blew her nose and darted another glance in Jacob's direction. And now, as if he'd been waiting for some kind of signal, he began to walk towards them.

Nell's breathing faltered. She'd forgotten how big he was, how broad-shouldered and tall, and as his long strides closed the gap between them, she had to look up to see his face. She saw signs of strain in the bleakness of his eyes and in the vertical lines at either side of his grim mouth.

'Hello, Nell.'

'Jacob,' she managed, but her mouth began to tremble. She was exhausted and dazed and seeing his stern face was almost too much.

He said, 'Mrs Browne has kindly invited me to meet our grandson.'

Our grandson.

Nell wasn't sure which word shocked her more. *Our* suggested that the two of them were still united in some way. *Grandson* hinted at an intimate connection over many, many years, but they were strangers. And not yet forty.

'Maybe this is the wrong time,' Jean said, eyeing them both and sensing their tension. 'I—I have to go. But I couldn't let you both take off without speaking to you.'

'I'm so glad you did,' Nell said, clasping the woman's hand. 'And I'd adore seeing Sam again. That's very kind. We—' She swallowed to ease her choked throat.

'Perhaps you'd rather come separately?' Jean suggested, darting a glance of sharp-eyed curiosity from one to the other.

Nell felt her cheeks grow hot.

'I think we should come together.' Jacob spoke directly to Jean, as if Nell wasn't there. 'You won't want too many interruptions.'

'It would certainly be easier if I could discuss my problem with both of you.'

What was this problem that needed discussing? Nell wished Jean wasn't so evasive, but it certainly wasn't the time to challenge her.

'Would tomorrow morning suit?' Jean asked. 'Will you still be in Melbourne, Mr Tucker?'

'Yes, I'm staying for a few days.'

'At around eleven?'

'Eleven suits me fine.'

'And me,' Nell agreed.

Jean shoved her damp handkerchief into her handbag and snapped it shut as if, somehow, the gesture ended the matter. 'I'll see you then.'

With that she turned and scuttled out of the chapel, clearly relieved to leave Nell and Jacob alone.

Jacob stood at the end of Nell's pew, blocking her exit. She took two steps towards him, as if she expected him to be a gentleman and make way for her, but she was out of luck today. He'd been to hell and back in this chapel, saying farewell to a daughter he had never known, had never held, hadn't so much as touched.

No one here could have guessed or understood how he had loved and missed Tegan, without ever knowing her.

And this woman, whom he'd loved and lost in one short summer, had given their daughter away. So why was she here now, pretending she cared?

'I didn't expect you to be here,' he said between tight lips.

Nell shook her head and she was so close to him, he could smell her perfume, elusive and sweet and unbearably intimate.

'Why wouldn't I come?' Her voice was so choked he could only just catch the words. 'This is our daughter's funeral, Jacob.'

'But you gave Tegan away.'

'No.'

No?

How could she lie? Jacob wanted to confront her, to demand that she retract her lie, but, heaven help him, she looked so vulnerable and tired. Too pale.

Growing paler…

To his dismay, Nell swayed on her feet and sank down on to the pew, closed her eyes and hunched over, pressing her fingers to her temples. He stared at the top of her golden head and at the play of jewelled lights from a stained glass window throwing red and blue patterns over her.

Her hair was incredibly shiny and so much neater than he remembered. As a girl it had flowed in rumpled waves loose to her shoulders. He reached out a hand, but he didn't touch her. 'Are you OK?'

With her eyes closed, she nodded her head. 'Just tired and sad.'

A moment later, her eyes opened and she turned her head slowly, carefully, almost as if her neck were stiff, and looked up at him. Her blue eyes were lovely—even lovelier than he'd remembered. Looking into them, he felt punch-drunk.

'I really need to go home now,' she said.

Her weakness launched him into gallantry. The questions consuming him would have to wait. 'Of course.'

This time, when he reached down, he touched her sleeve at the elbow. 'Let me drive you.'

Pink stole into her cheeks. 'That's not necessary.'

'Did you bring your car?'

'No,' she admitted reluctantly. 'I came by taxi.'

'Then there's no argument.' His hand closed around her arm and he watched the colour in her cheeks spread. 'Come on.'

To his surprise, she didn't pull away from him, but rose obediently. Everything felt unreal as they walked together out of the chapel into sunshine and fresh air. The mourners had disappeared and the late model Mercedes he'd hired stood alone in the car park.

From a distance of ten paces, Jacob unlocked it. Its lights blinked and Nell gave a little mew of surprise.

'Nice car.'

'It's only hired.' He walked to the passenger's side and opened the door for her, watching every elegant movement as she ducked her head and sat, drawing her slim legs neatly inside. Grimly, he closed her door, walked around the car and got in beside her, wishing he could feel calm.

Keep your mind on the traffic. Forget that it's Nell. And don't think about the past. No sense in dragging her into an argument now.

'Where to?' Jacob asked, forcing cheerfulness into his voice. 'Would you like to go somewhere for coffee?'

Nell shook her head. 'I just need to get home, please.'

'That's in Toorak, right?'

'No.' She quickly donned oversized dark glasses that hid her expressive eyes. 'I don't live there now. I'm in Williamstown.'

Jacob frowned as he started the car and joined the steady stream of traffic. Williamstown was an attractive bayside suburb, but it didn't really make sense that Nell and her barrister husband had moved there. Why would they leave their exclusive address at Toorak, the Melbourne suburb synonymous with opulence and gracious living?

While he was musing over this she asked, 'Where do you live these days?'

'I'm based up in Queensland. Near Roma.'

'That should be good cattle country.'

'Yes, it is.'

'You've done well.'

Unsure if this was a statement or a question, Jacob didn't respond and he drove for some time in uncomfortable silence. Nell sat very straight and still with her hands in her lap, while he kept his gaze strictly ahead.

As they reached the Westgate Bridge arching high over the Yarra River, she asked, 'Did you know about the baby—about Tegan's baby? Before today?'

Jacob turned to her sharply. 'No,' he said. 'I had no idea. Did you?'

She nodded. 'Jean contacted me the day after the accident. She seemed to be struggling with it all and I went over to see if I could help. I saw Sam then. He's very cute.'

'I only found out about Tegan six weeks ago.' It was difficult to keep the bitterness out of his voice.

'So Tegan did write to you?'

'Yes. Quite a long and chatty letter.'

'It must have been a shock.'

He cracked a bitter smile. 'That's something of an understatement. It took me almost a week to recover before I sent my reply.' He paused. 'And then, two days ago, there was another letter from Jean.'

'About Tegan's accident.'

'And details of the funeral arrangements.'

'A much worse shock.'

'Terrible.' After a bit, he said, 'Tegan didn't mention that she was pregnant.'

'But I'm so glad she wrote.'

Jacob frowned. 'You sound as if you were involved somehow.'

Nell dropped her gaze to her handbag—genuine crocodile skin, if he wasn't mistaken. 'Not really.'

'Not really? What does that mean?'

She played with the handle of the handbag, running the tip of her forefinger over the stitching. 'Tegan wrote to me and told me she wanted to make contact with you. I told her what I knew, which wasn't much more than your name and your age. She did the rest. You know how clever young people are on the Internet these days.'

'But she'd already had contact with you?'

'Yes.'

'How? Through an adoption agency?'

'Yes.'

Jacob's hand clenched around the wheel. 'That doesn't make sense. Why couldn't the agency give her my name too?'

When Nell didn't answer, he lost patience. 'Why the hell did *my* daughter have to go to *you* to find out my name?'

'Jacob, be careful!'

A car horn blasted beside them and Jacob realised he'd swerved dangerously close to the next lane. Teeth gritted, he corrected the steering. And then he repeated his question. 'Why did Tegan have to ask you for my name?'

He sent another sharp glance in Nell's direction and, despite the obscuring sunglasses, he saw that her cheeks were flushed, her mouth contorted, embarrassed.

'That's because your name—' The stain in her cheeks deepened. 'Your name wasn't on the records. You—you weren't listed on Tegan's birth certificate.'

'What?' The word exploded from him, making Nell flinch.

Too bad, if he'd upset her. She'd upset him. Twenty years of physical exclusion and now the news that there had never been any recognition of his link to Tegan. *Father unknown.* Anger roiled through him, gathering force, an avalanche of emotion.

Beside him, Nell clutched her handbag against her stomach and sat very straight. 'Jacob, we shouldn't discuss this sort of thing while you're driving.'

She was probably right, but his only response was an angry hiss. Jaw clenched, he checked the rear-vision mirror, switched lanes in readiness for the Williamstown exit, and tension, as suffocating as smoke, filled the car's interior.

Five minutes later, Nell directed him into a quiet street a block back from the waterfront.

'My house is the little one over there with the blue door,' she said, pointing.

His anger gave way to bafflement as he pulled up outside a quaint but modest colonial cottage with a front hedge of lavender, a flagstone path and yellow roses over the door. It was the kind of old-fashioned cottage and garden his mother adored, but he'd never dreamed that Nell Ruthven and her husband would live in a place like this.

'Thanks for the lift,' Nell said quietly.

'My pleasure.' Jacob couldn't keep the brittle note out of his voice.

Her fingers sought the door catch.

'Shall I pick you up tomorrow morning to go to the Brownes'?'

After a slight hesitation, she said, 'Thank you. I suppose it makes sense if we travel together.'

'We should talk, Nell.' His mind was still seething with angry questions.

Her eyes met his and he saw a heart-wrenching mixture of sorrow and bewilderment and something deeper he couldn't quite pinpoint.

'After all this time, we have things to say to each other,' he said.

'I can't talk now, Jacob. There's no point in even trying to talk today. We're both too upset and tense.'

Although he was desperate to get everything out in the

open, he had to admit that he felt wrung out. And Nell looked far worse.

She pulled the catch, the door clicked open and the scent of lavender drifted in to him on a light sea breeze. In the distance he could hear a seagull's cry.

'It must be very pleasant living here,' he said in a more conciliatory tone.

'Yes, I love it.' She turned to speak over her shoulder, without quite looking at him. 'Why don't you come early tomorrow? We can talk before we go to the Brownes'?'

'Great idea. We can go for coffee somewhere in the city.'

'We can talk here if you like.'

Jacob frowned. 'Are you sure your husband won't mind?'

He was watching her profile carefully, saw her mouth curl into a complicated, off-kilter smile. 'That won't be a problem. There will only be the two of us. What time would you like to come?'

'Nine? Half past?'

'Make it half past. I'll see you then.'

Nell got out and closed the door behind her and Jacob watched her through the passenger window as she crossed the footpath and opened the front gate. A sudden breeze gusted up the street, shaking the heads of the lavender and, as she walked up the path, the wind teased a bright strand of her hair from its braid and lifted the collar of her jacket against her neck. Her high heels made a tapping sound on the paving stones.

Framed by cream and yellow roses, she stood on her front porch in her neat, dark suit and fished in her handbag for her door key, and she looked beautiful and citified and completely removed from the horse-riding country girl he'd known for two months of one summer twenty years ago.

Tomorrow.

Tomorrow he would be entering that house, talking to Nell at last, discovering the truth he both longed for and feared.

He flipped the key in the Mercedes's ignition so hard he almost snapped it in two.

CHAPTER TWO

TWO O'CLOCK IN the morning found Jacob awake in his unfamiliar hotel bed.

A picture of Tegan had been displayed at the funeral—his first, his only sight of his daughter—and it haunted him.

She'd been dancing on a sunlit beach and wearing a blue cotton dress that was a perfect match for the bright summer sky. Her feet had been bare and sandy, her tanned arms uplifted, her skirt billowing behind her in the wind. She'd been laughing and her long brown hair had streamed like a dark ribbon. Her eyes had sparkled with the sheer joy of being alive.

Jacob had been startled by how intensely and immediately he'd felt connected to her. The bond had gone beyond the uncanny likeness to his family in the darkness of her hair, the strong lines of her cheekbones, her straight, dark eyebrows. He'd felt it deep in his bones, in his blood, in his breath.

He had, of course, seen Nell in Tegan, too. She'd been there in the tilt of the girl's head, in the slender shapeliness of her long legs. And that led him to thinking about Nell Ruthven née Harrington, about their meeting today. After so long.

He'd been way too tense. Everything about it had been wrong.

So many times during the past twenty years, he'd imagined a parallel universe in which he'd met Nell again. He had never deliberately sought her out, not once he'd learned she was married, but he'd imagined a scenario where they would bump into each other quite by chance. They would drop whatever they had planned for that day and go somewhere just to talk.

They'd smile a lot and chat for ages, catching up. Their reunion would be so poignant that time and Nell's marriage to another man would become meaningless.

'I want to go on seeing you,' he'd say.

She'd smile. 'I'd love that.'

Problem was, this fantasy was based on the twenty-year-old assumption that Nell had been wrong about her pregnancy, that it had simply been a case of a late period. Jacob knew through gossip his mother had passed on that Nell's adult life had never included a child and he'd never dreamed their baby had been given away for adoption.

Tomorrow was going to be difficult. He had questions that demanded answers, but it would also be his one chance to enter that parallel universe, to reconnect with Nell's world. And, even if it was only for a day, he didn't want to get it wrong.

It would be easier to stay calm if he wasn't plagued by bitter-sweet memories of their amazing, devastating summer at Half Moon, if he couldn't still remember painful details of those two short months with Nell, right back to his first sight of her.

Home from university, she had been riding Mistral, a grey mare, and she'd come into the stables where he'd been working. Her cheeks had been flushed from the wind, her eyes bright and she'd been dressed like a glamorous, high-society equestrian in a mustard velvet jacket, pale cream jodhpurs and knee high, brown leather boots.

The fancy clothes had fitted her snugly, hugging the roundness of her breasts, cinching her waist and accentuating the length of her legs. Her pale hair had rippled like water about her shoulders and her eyes had been as blue and clear as icy stars. She had been beautiful. So incredibly beautiful...

But what had happened next was one of those unbelievably zany moments that should only have happened in B grade movies. Nell was leading her horse when she saw him and stopped. And instead of exchanging polite hellos, they'd stood there, open-mouthed, staring at each other, while Jacob's blood had rushed and roared and his heart had become a sledgehammer.

Looking back, he guessed they must have spoken, but the rest of that afternoon was a blur to him now. Much clearer was their meeting the next morning.

He'd gone to the stables just after dawn and noticed immediately that Mistral was missing. He'd guessed that Nell had taken her for an early morning ride and within a dozen heartbeats he'd mounted another horse and taken off.

Half Moon was a huge property and he had no idea where Nell was, but he'd been quite sure at the outset that he would find her, that she'd wanted him to find her. Perhaps the mysterious sixth sense that the gods bestowed on destined lovers had whispered that she would be waiting for him.

It wasn't long before he'd found her horse tied to a tree beside the river where white mist lifted in curling, wispy trails from the smooth, glassy surface of the water.

'Hey there, Jacob.'

Nell's voice seemed to come from a paperbark tree and when he peered through the weeping canopy he saw her sitting on a branch overhanging the water. She was wearing a blue checked shirt and ordinary blue jeans this morning, and dusty, elastic-sided boots. Apart from the golden gleam of her hair, she looked more like the everyday Outback girls Jacob was used to.

'G'day,' he called up to her as he tied his horse's reins to a sapling. 'Looks like you've found a good perch.'

'It's gorgeous out here. Come and see for yourself.'

He laughed and shook his head. 'I don't think that branch would hold the two of us.'

She bounced lightly. 'Oh, it's strong enough. Come on, the river looks so pretty at this time of the morning and I can see right around the bend from here.'

Talk about spellbound. There was no way he could have resisted Nell's invitation.

Knot-holes in the tree's trunk made it easy for Jacob to climb to her branch. He stepped on to it gingerly, pausing to test that it could take his weight. So far, so good, but the branch narrowed quickly.

Nell smiled, her blue eyes dancing with merriment, her white teeth flashing. 'Dare you to come right out.'

She was flirting with him.

And he loved it.

Arms extended for balance, he made his way along the branch. His extra weight sent the leaves at Nell's end dipping into the tea-coloured water, but she only laughed.

'No fancy jodhpurs this morning?' he asked as he got closer.

She screwed up her nose. 'They were a birthday present

from my parents. I only wore them yesterday to please them, but they made me feel such a poser.'

'You looked terrific,' he insisted, taking another step closer. 'You'll wear them to the picnic races, won't—'

A loud crack sounded and the branch exploded beneath them, sent them plummeting into the river.

It was summer so the water wasn't very cold. Jacob fought his way to the surface, looked about for Nell and panicked when he couldn't see her. Heart thrashing, he dived again into the murky green depths. Where was she? He prayed that she hadn't been hit by the falling tree branch.

Lungs bursting, he broke the surface again. Still no sign of Nell. Was she pinned to the river bed?

Once more Jacob dived, groped in the grass and the submerged branches at the bottom, desperate to find her, but again he was forced back to the surface, empty-handed.

'Jacob!'

Thank goodness. He turned to see her breast-stroking towards him.

'I've been looking for you,' she said. 'I was worried that you'd drowned.'

'I thought *you'd* drowned. I was looking for you.'

They swam to the bank. Jacob reached it first and, because it was steep and bare, he offered his hand to help her out. She accepted gratefully and they began to climb.

The bank quickly turned slippery beneath their wet boots and they had quite a scramble. As they neared the top, Jacob grabbed at a sapling for an anchor and pulled Nell towards him.

She came faster than he expected, bumped into him, in fact, and suddenly they were clinging together, her soft curves pressing in to him through their wet clothes. Her clear eyes and parted lips were mere inches from his and, despite the wet hair plastered to her skull, she was beautiful. Breathtakingly so.

She smiled. 'Now this is a new way of breaking the ice. My college social club would be impressed.'

He wasn't sure what she was talking about, but he understood very well the invitation in her eyes. And so he kissed her.

It wasn't a long kiss and it shouldn't have been a sexy kiss. Their lips were cold from the river and Jacob was clinging to the sapling's trunk with one hand while he held Nell to prevent her from falling.

But it was a kiss Jacob would never, to the end of his days, forget. From the moment their lips met, he adored the feel and the taste of Nell, loved her response—so feminine, so...*right*.

Too soon their wonderfully intimate hello was over and he boosted Nell up over the rim of the bank and came after her, tumbling on to the grass.

He might have kissed her again, but they were apart now and he lost his nerve, remembered that she was the boss's daughter and he was the cook's son.

Instead, they lay in the grass at the top of the bank and let the morning sun stream over them, and Jacob contented himself with admiring her breasts, gorgeously outlined by her wet shirt.

'So tell me about your college social club,' he said.

'Oh, they're always coming up with new ways to get everyone to mix.' Nell sat up and lifted her wet hair from the back of her neck. 'They've run a series of cocktail parties where girls and guys can meet, but we're only allowed eight minutes or so to chat with each person and to tell them about ourselves—just enough time to figure out whether people click.'

'Sounds…racy.'

Nell grinned coyly, leant sideways and squeezed water from her hair into the grass. 'Not really. It's only chatting, after all.'

Considering that he'd just kissed her, he supposed she had a point.

'So when you were at one of these parties,' he said, 'you would have said something like—I'm Nell Harrington, I'm nineteen and I'm studying Arts. I like horse riding, apple crumble with cream and sitting in trees.'

Her blue eyes widened. 'How did you know about the apple crumble?'

'My mum was asked to make it especially for your home-coming.'

'Oh, yes, of course. I like Maggie. My mother says she's the best cook we've ever had.'

'I'm not surprised.'

Suddenly the stupidity of this meeting hit Jacob like a smart bomb. What in blue blazes was he doing here chatting with Nell Harrington? Her father would have him neutered if he ever found out.

He jumped to his feet, grabbed his horse's reins. 'I have to get to work.' With luck, the sun and a fast ride would dry his clothes and no one would be any the wiser.

Nell smiled up at him, all sweetness and dimples. 'Do you think we should try for another date?'

That moment had been his chance. He should have told her, No, not on your Nelly, and changed the course of their history, saved decades of heartache. Should have got the hell out of there.

Now, twenty years later, Jacob winced as he remembered how crazily spellbound he'd been.

'I'll see what I can manage,' he'd said.

* * *

Nell studied her reflection in the bathroom mirror. Jacob would be here in five minutes and she looked a fright. The ordeal of yesterday followed by a sleepless night had left her pale and haggard, as dreary and limp as wet seaweed.

Dabbing concealer into the shadows under her eyes, she told herself that it didn't matter what she looked like. Jacob's regard for her had disappeared long ago, well before the turn of the twenty-first century.

Despite his controlled good manners yesterday, he'd made it painfully clear that he blamed her, probably despised her. She'd seen it in his eyes, had heard it in his voice and when he'd accused her of giving Tegan away, she'd been too stunned and numb to defend herself. Now he believed he had the high moral ground. For that reason alone she needed to gain some self control. And she needed to look OK.

Taking more than usual care, she lengthened her lashes with mascara, applied blusher to bring colour into her cheeks and selected her favourite lipstick. She ran her fingers lightly through her freshly washed hair, letting it fall loosely to her shoulders, took a step back from the mirror and drew a deep breath.

Her make-up and hair were OK and her floral top and blue skirt were cheery and feminine.

'You'll do,' she told her reflection. She actually looked close to normal now.

If only she *felt* composed. She was no more prepared to 'chat' with Jacob today than she had been yesterday after the funeral. She hadn't been able to stop thinking about him. About Tegan. About Tegan's baby, Sam.

Her mind buzzed like a bee in summer, darting frantically with no clear course. One minute she was drowning beneath the loss of her daughter, the next she was wildly, guiltily excited about the reappearance of Jacob after twenty years, and then she was sobered by the thought of her baby grandson and Jean Browne's mysterious need to discuss *something*.

Nell had telephoned the Brownes the day after Tegan's death. Desperately distressed, she'd needed to talk to them and she'd found comfort from being able to offer help. Bill Browne had suffered a stroke a few months earlier and poor Jean was carrying a huge burden, dealing with her grief while caring for him and the tiny baby, Sam.

Nell had done the little she could—a chicken casserole, help with finding a solicitor. She'd even minded Sam while Jean had dealt with the funeral directors. In a bonding moment over a cup of tea in the Brownes' kitchen, she'd told Jean the circumstances of Tegan's birth.

They'd cried together.

If Jean needed more help now, Nell knew she would be happy to lend a hand. She was less certain about Jacob.

Overnight, every forbidden memory of her youthful lover had shot to the surface—memories of the river, of the endless conversations she and Jacob had shared, of that first morning, sitting on the tree branch, falling into the water.

She and Jacob had even read poetry together. Fresh from her first year at university, she'd been mad about Yeats. She hadn't expected a rugged cowboy to be interested in poetry, had been gobsmacked when Jacob had brought a copy of Yeats that had belonged to his father. They'd read selections to each other and she'd loved listening to Jacob's deep voice rumbling sexily against a backdrop of chuckling water and softly piping finches.

Good grief. She shouldn't be remembering such things after all this time. But every memory of Jacob Tucker was alive and vivid in her head—his shy, serious smile, the sexy power of his body, his gentle hands.

When she closed her eyes she could still see him lying in the shaded grass, one arm curved above his head, throwing a shadow over his beautiful face. She could see him looking at her from beneath heavy lids. Could see the thrilling intensity of his grey eyes, feel the warmth of his lips on hers.

Nell forced her eyes open again, blinked hard, shook her head. It was both fruitless and painful to revisit the past.

She and Jacob had each gone down separate paths. She'd married Robert Ruthven and Jacob had acquired a cattle kingdom. They'd grown older, richer, wiser and had become very different adults.

Yet here they were, brought back together by the very thing that had separated them in the first place.

Their daughter.

The front doorbell rang and she jumped. *That will be Jacob.*

She wondered what they were going to talk about till it was time to go to the Brownes', and cast another frantic glance at the mirror.

Come on, Nell, you have to try harder than that. Chin up, back straight. Smile.

The smile was problematic, but at least her reflection looked a tad more determined as she hurried to open the door.

Jacob stood on her front doorstep. 'Good morning,' he said, smiling.

Nell's insides tumbled helplessly. 'Morning.'

Silly of her, but she'd been expecting him to look the way he had yesterday, all formal and serious and nudging forty. Today he was wearing faded jeans that clung low on his narrow hips and a navy-blue T-shirt that hugged his whipcord muscles. Apart from the fine lines at the corners of his eyes and the tiniest smattering of grey at his temples, he looked dangerously—way too dangerously—like the nineteen-year-old she'd fallen in love with.

'How are you feeling today?' he asked.

'Much better, thanks.' She almost confessed to not sleeping too well, but decided against giving too much away.

With an offhand smile, he held out a brown paper bag. 'Some comfort food from the bakery.'

'Oh, thank you.' As she took the bag his fingers brushed hers and the brief contact sent a strange current shooting up her arm. *Get a grip, Nell.* Now wasn't the time to become girlish and coy.

'Take a seat in here,' she said, indicating the cosy living room that opened off her front hallway. 'I'll make some tea. Or would you prefer coffee?'

'Tea's fine.' Jacob ignored her instruction and followed her down the hall and into the kitchen.

Flustered, Nell rushed to fill the kettle. It felt so strange to have Jacob Tucker in here, leaning casually against her butter-yellow cupboard with his long denim legs crossed at the ankles, arms folded over his strapping chest.

He looked about him with absorbed interest. Or was that *amused* interest? Was that a smirk she detected? What was so funny? Why couldn't he have waited in the living room, as she'd asked?

Lips compressed, Nell grabbed scarlet and yellow floral mugs from an overhead cupboard and set them on a wicker tray. She shot him a curious glance. 'Is something amusing you?'

'I was just revising my impressions of you. You haven't changed as much as I thought you had. Yesterday you looked so different in that efficient suit and with your hair all pinned up, but today you're more like the girl I used to know.'

His thoughts were so close to her own that she almost blushed. Her hand trembled as she reached for the teapot. *Don't be fooled. Remember, this isn't a proper reunion. Jacob's filling in time till we see Sam. Nothing more.*

She turned and fetched milk from the fridge, filled a small blue jug. 'I don't think the girl you remember exists any more,' she said quietly.

'I guess looks can be deceiving.'

I should remember that, too.

Nell selected a pretty plate and arranged the biscotti he'd bought at the bakery, set it with the other things on the tray. Turning to him, she said, 'Can you take this tray through to the living room? I'll bring the teapot in a minute.'

'Sure.'

As he left the kitchen, she drew a deep breath and let it out slowly. Behind her the kettle came to the boil.

One look at Nell's living room and Jacob knew that something very important was missing from Koomalong, his Outback homestead. He'd paid a great deal of money for a top Brisbane decorator to furnish his home and she'd gone to enormous trouble to give it a 'masculine edge'.

'A man like you needs an environment that screams alpha male,' the decorator had insisted.

He'd always lived alone, changing women as often as the seasons, so a 'masculine edge' had made sense. But, despite the expense and the Brisbane decorator's expertise, the so-called alpha male decor hadn't really worked for him. His place didn't feel like a home; it seemed to belong in a glossy city magazine.

The Ruthvens' cottage, on the other hand, felt very home-like indeed. There was something about Nell's living room, about the lounge furniture upholstered in muted creams and dusty reds, that invited him in. The slightly cluttered casualness, the deceptively careless mix of colours and florals and stripes enticed him to relax, to feel welcome.

No doubt the cosy effect was completed by the marmalade cat curled in a sunny spot among fat cushions on the cane sofa beneath the window.

Jacob set the tray down beside a vase of red and cream flowers on an old timber chest that apparently served as a coffee table. A thick paperback novel had been left there and, beside it, elegant blue-framed reading glasses.

Nell wears reading glasses now.

He knew that shouldn't bother him, but somehow he couldn't help being saddened by such a clear marker of the passage of time.

The cat opened its pale yellow eyes and stared at him as he selected one of the deep and friendly armchairs and sat. Almost immediately, the cat rose, stretched its striped orange back, then leapt daintily off the sofa and crossed the floor to jump into Jacob's lap.

As a general rule, he preferred dogs to cats and he eyed the animal dubiously as it balanced on his thighs, a small claw penetrating his denim jeans.

'Don't expect me to let you have this milk, mate.'

In response, the cat dropped softly into his lap, curled contentedly and began to purr, adding the final brushstroke to Jacob's impression of Nell's cottage as cosiness incorporated.

Unfortunately, he was particularly susceptible to cosiness. His childhood had been lonely. He and his mother had lived in a series of workers' cottages on Outback properties and he'd longed for the permanence of a cosy family home. There had been several times during the past twenty years when he'd been on the brink of getting married simply so he could enjoy the pleasures of a comfy home and family life.

But whenever he'd come to the point of proposing marriage, something had always held him back—a vital, missing *something*.

'Oh, heavens, Ambrose, what do you think you're doing?' Nell came into the room carrying a blue china teapot. 'I'm sorry about the cat,' she said. 'Shoo, Ambrose. You should have sent him away, Jacob.'

'I would have if he'd bothered me.' Jacob watched the cat return to the sofa, tail waving sulkily. 'Perhaps he's mistaken me for your husband.'

A strange little laugh broke from Nell as she set the teapot down beside the tray. 'No, I'm sure he hasn't. Robert and Ambrose never got on.' She looked flushed and avoided meeting his gaze, rubbed her palms down the sides of her skirt as if they were damp. 'How—how do you take your tea?'

'Black, no sugar.'

'Oh, of course, I remember now.'

As she said this, she looked dismayed and he was dismayed too, suddenly remembering the camp fires down by the river when they'd made billy tea, hastily putting the fire out as soon as the water boiled so that the smoke wouldn't give away their hiding place.

There was a tremor in her hands as she poured his tea and set the mug in front of him. She was nervous and he wanted to put her at ease.

'This is a lovely home,' he said. 'Did you decorate it?'

Nell nodded and concentrated on pouring her own tea, adding milk and a half teaspoon of sugar.

'You must have an artistic eye.'

'Actually, I do seem to have a way with fabric.' She smiled as she settled into the other armchair. 'I make quilts and I sell them.'

'You sell them?'

'Yes. There's quite a demand for my work, actually. It keeps me rather busy.'

Jacob swallowed his shock. But perhaps he shouldn't be so surprised. After all, apart from the gossip his mother gleaned from the social pages, he knew next to nothing about Nell Ruthven. He'd always supposed she was a carefree and idle society wife. One of those ladies who lunched.

But Nell Harrington, the girl he'd loved, had been crazy about poetry, an artistic soul.

'Your husband must be very proud of you,' he said cautiously.

Looking more nervous than ever, Nell picked up her mug of tea, then seemed to change her mind and set it down again.

'How Robert feels about my quilting is irrelevant,' she said quietly. 'He's not my husband any more.'

CHAPTER THREE

'WE'RE DIVORCED,' Nell told Jacob in her quietest, most matter-of-fact voice. Even so, she could see his shock.

'Why—' He lifted a hand to his neck as if he wanted to loosen his collar, but he wasn't wearing one. 'Why didn't you tell me that yesterday? I asked about your husband.'

With a heavy sigh, she said flatly, 'You would have wanted to ask more questions. I couldn't have coped just then.' Embarrassed now, and tenser than ever, she chewed at her lip.

'What about now?' Jacob demanded. 'Could you cope with questions now?'

Keeping her gaze fixed on the tea tray, she shook her head. 'Don't bother with the questions. I'll tell you. Our marriage didn't work. It was as simple as that. There was nothing nasty. Robert worked too hard and drank too much, but he never hurt me. We just drifted apart and I've been divorced for nearly a year.'

She tried to make light of it, but it wasn't easy to shrug off. She could hardly admit that after losing Jacob she'd married the wrong man, that too late she'd realised that Robert had simply wanted her as a trophy wife. He'd been happy to be seen with her at all the important functions around Melbourne but, in the privacy of their bedroom, their relationship had never really clicked.

'Robert had so many legal colleagues, we were able to settle things quite easily,' she said. 'It was all very straightforward and extremely civilised. The marriage might not have been a success, but the divorce was a triumph.'

'What do you mean?'

Lifting her chin, she tried to smile. 'I mean I'm now in charge of my life. For the first time ever, I'm independent and in control.'

Jacob nodded, but his eyes remained cold.

Embarrassed, she reached for her mug and took a long drink of tea. Her heart thumped and she held the mug with two hands so the tea didn't spill. Perhaps it was too much to expect Jacob to understand why she'd stayed too long in an empty marriage, that after losing her daughter she'd desperately hoped to avoid another failure.

'What about you?' She forced the question. 'Are you married?'

He shook his head. 'Never tempted.'

There was a glint in his eyes which she quickly avoided.

'I'm a well-seasoned bachelor,' he said.

Was he telling her that he was available? A wave of heat rolled over her. For heaven's sake. What on earth was the matter with her? Bending forward, she picked up the plate and offered it to him. 'Biscotti?'

'Not now, thank you.' Jacob's fingers drummed on the upholstered arm of the chair. 'So you've already seen Tegan's baby?'

'Yes, he's a lovely little fellow. He must be about seven weeks by now.'

'Seven weeks? They're still pretty small at that age, aren't they?'

She couldn't help smiling. 'Yes, quite small. Why?'

'Oh, I can't help being curious about what Jean wants to discuss. It's obviously something to do with Sam.'

Nell nodded. 'He must be a handful for Jean, especially when her husband's so incapacitated.'

'What's the matter with her husband?'

'He had a stroke last April.'

'Poor man. They are certainly going through a terrible time.' Jacob's eyes narrowed as he watched her. 'So will you be taking any interest in Sam?'

'What makes you ask that? Of course I'm interested in him. He's my grandson.'

His eyes were cold. 'You weren't interested in his mother.'

He couldn't have hurt her more if he'd tripped her, sending her flat on her face. 'How dare you?'

'It's the truth, Nell. You gave Tegan up for adoption.'

'Not me—'

Jacob steamrolled over her protest. 'And for nineteen years that poor girl was led to believe that I couldn't give a damn about her.'

To Nell's dismay, Jacob leapt to his feet and towered over her.

'You've deprived me of my daughter. Why on earth did you do that, Nell?'

'You know that's not fair.' Her hands fisted so tightly her nails dug into her palms. She wanted to leap to her feet too, but how ridiculous that would be. A sparring match. 'Have some pity,' she cried, looking up at him. 'You don't know what happened. You don't know what I've been through.'

He stood with his hands clenched at his sides, his jaw jutting at a stubborn angle.

With calm emphasis on each word, Nell said again, 'You don't know what happened.'

Jacob's mouth opened as if he was about to burst out with another angry accusation, but as he stood there, staring at her, she could see that her words were taking hold. The anger in his eyes lessened, confusion returned.

Sinking his hands into the pockets of his jeans, he looked chastened. 'I'm sorry. I was just letting off steam.' He returned to the armchair, lifted the mug of tea and stared at it. 'Can you tell me exactly what happened?'

Nell couldn't hold back a despairing sigh. 'I can't believe you think I could willingly give my daughter away.'

'Our daughter.'

'Yes, Jacob. Our daughter.'

He set the mug down. 'Until Tegan wrote to me, I didn't even know you'd given birth. Later, when I'd heard you and your husband referred to as childless, I assumed you'd had a miscarriage. Or an abortion. I thought there was even a chance that you'd never been pregnant at all, that you'd been mistaken.'

Nell swallowed. 'I'm so sorry you never knew.'

'Believe me, so am I.' He shifted forward in his chair, eyed her levelly. The muscles in his throat worked. 'I can't help feeling cheated.'

'I know,' Nell said softly. She'd felt cheated too—cheated out of motherhood. But at least she'd known where Tegan was, that she was safe and happy. '*I* didn't give Tegan away, Jacob. You must remember what my parents were like.'

He watched her with calculated wariness. 'I know your

father held a gun to my head. I know he forced my mother and me to leave Half Moon without collecting our wages.'

'And he sent me down here to Melbourne to a private Home for unmarried mothers.'

The hardness fell from Jacob's face. 'All the way down here?'

'Yes.'

'No wonder I couldn't find you.'

'Did you try to find me?'

'Of course I tried. I was desperate to find you. We'd planned to be married, remember?'

His eyes shimmered and Nell's heart stumbled.

'I couldn't find you either,' she admitted. 'I tried, but I wasn't allowed many phone calls from the Home. I tried again after Tegan was born. I rang everyone I could think of. Someone mentioned that you'd gone interstate, but no one knew where. You and your mother just disappeared into the Outback.'

When he made no comment, she felt compelled to ask, 'Do you believe me, Jacob?'

He nodded grimly. 'My story's much the same. I went to your university. I found people who knew you, but they couldn't tell me where you were.'

'I never went back to university.'

A shuddering sigh escaped him. He cleared his throat. 'So was Tegan born here, in Melbourne?'

'Yes. I won't burden you with details, but it was a difficult birth and I was in a bad way afterwards. They kept me heavily sedated.'

Jacob swore softly.

'When my parents gave me papers to sign, I didn't understand that I was giving the baby up for adoption.'

'But that's criminal.'

Choked by memories, Nell nodded again. She'd relived that day countless times. 'I thought I was just signing papers for the baby's birth certificate.'

It hurt to talk about this. A sob burned her throat but she stumbled on, needing to tell him everything. But, more than anything now, she wanted to share with him her precious memories of their daughter.

'Tegan was gorgeous, Jacob. When she was born, she was so tiny and perfect and cute. She had such a sweet face. Gorgeous dark eyes—a bit unfocused, of course. And her little pink fingers were curling over the edge of her blanket and she had the most perfect miniature fingernails.'

Avoiding the pain in his face, she closed her eyes. *Don't cry. It won't help anyone if you cry.* She drew a deep breath. 'I didn't know that was the last time I would see her.' She drew another breath for courage. 'They told me they were putting her in some kind of foster care until I was fully recovered.'

'Nell.'

'I broke down completely when I realised what I'd signed, but the nurse in charge just whacked me with more sedatives.'

'How could she?'

'It was twenty years ago. Anything could happen if someone paid enough money.'

A growl of rage broke from him.

'Afterwards, Mum and Dad whisked me back to Queensland and no one ever told me that I had thirty days to change my mind about the adoption. As soon as I was strong enough, I left Half Moon, but by the time I got back down here it was too late to reclaim Tegan.'

Hands fisted, Jacob sat very still, staring at her, his eyes dark with raw pain, his throat working overtime.

'As far as I'm concerned, my daughter was stolen from me,' Nell said finally. 'And there hasn't been a day—not a day—in the past twenty years when I haven't thought about her, when I haven't missed her.'

He nodded bleakly and Nell sensed that it was beyond him to speak at that moment. For quite some time he sat very still, his elbows propped on the arms of the chair, his profile showing no expression, his eyes downcast. The room seemed to hum with a thousand unspoken thoughts.

Finally, he asked, 'Is there any particular reason why you and Robert didn't have any children?'

His question was so unexpected that Nell blurted out the truth. 'Robert wasn't very interested in having a family. And I was happy enough to go along with that. Another pregnancy would have made me relive everything I went through with Tegan. I was trying to forget.'

'Forget?'

'Not Tegan. I certainly didn't want to forget her. But I had to find a way to move on.' When he didn't reply, she added, softly, 'I've wondered if you were trying to forget too, if that's why you've worked so hard for all these years.'

His eyes flashed with sudden surprise. 'How do you know I've worked hard?'

She laughed guiltily. 'I've read the occasional article in cattlemen's magazines.'

'You know they always exaggerate.' Jacob looked uncomfortable, glanced at his wristwatch. 'Hmm…how far is it to the Brownes' place?'

'Oh, it will probably take us about twenty minutes.'

'I suppose we'd better get going, then.'

'Yes.' As Nell gathered their tea things and stacked them on the tray, she felt unsettled. They'd spent the whole time talking about her and she hadn't learned anything about Jacob.

He said, 'We may as well take my car.'

'That suits me, thanks. I'll just pop these things back in the kitchen and get my bag.'

She was rather stunned to discover a huge bouquet of beautiful stargazer lilies on the back seat of Jacob's car and a brightly coloured, stuffed Humpty Dumpty.

'No prize for guessing which is for Jean and which is for Sam,' Jacob said with a sudden grin.

'That's very thoughtful, Jacob. I'm afraid I didn't think to get anything today.'

'These can be from both of us then.'

It was silly to feel so pleased, but she couldn't help it when Jacob smiled. 'The flowers must be from you,' she said. 'It will make Jean's day if she receives a bouquet from a handsome younger man.'

'Younger?' Jacob's eyes gleamed as he shook his head at her. 'I'm a granddad, you know.'

'Oh, yes.' Good heavens, they weren't flirting, were they? 'How could I forget?'

He opened the door for her but, before she could get in, his hand curved around the back of her neck and he turned her face towards him and kissed her, very lightly, on the mouth.

'Just curious to know what it's like to kiss a granny,' he murmured.

He rounded the car and slipped into the driver's seat as if nothing out of the ordinary had happened, but as they drove to the Brownes' Nell felt light-headed, almost dizzy.

Jean Browne must have been waiting for them because the door opened before they could knock. She looked terribly tired. Her grey hair hung limply and her dress was crumpled and there was a damp patch on her shoulder. Nell wondered if the baby had caused it.

When Jacob offered Jean the bouquet, her pale eyes welled with instant tears. 'Oh, how lovely.'

'I didn't want to come empty-handed,' he said. 'You've done so much for our daughter.'

Nell knew her heart wasn't supposed to flip at the way Jacob said 'our', as if they were still—had always been—a couple.

'Thank you so much. They're beautiful.' Jean buried her nose in the flowers and for a moment she looked quite girlish. 'Don't they smell wonderful? And how clever of you to guess that lilies are my favourite. Bill always buys them on my birthday.'

Her cheeks turned as pink as the lilies as she sent a fond glance back over her shoulder to her husband, who was sitting quietly in an armchair in the far corner. He was older than Jean, thin and balding with a fringe of white hair. His eyes were closed and he seemed to be asleep.

Lowering her voice, she said to Jacob, 'I didn't like to mention it yesterday, but Bill had a stroke five months ago. He's lost the use of his right arm and he still can't talk very well. He's a bit wobbly on his pins too, poor love.'

'That's very bad luck.'

'It's very frustrating for him,' Jean told them. 'He's always been such a wonderful help and now he feels as if he's a burden.'

'You must let me know if I can help,' Nell said.

'Well, that's exactly why I need to talk to you, dear. Come on in.' Jean stepped aside to let them enter. 'Sam's having a nap, but come and take a peek at him.'

As they followed Jean through to a back bedroom, Nell remembered the other time she'd seen Sam. She'd been expecting a replica of Tegan, had been on tenterhooks, ready for a mirror image of the baby she'd given up so many years ago.

But Tegan had been tiny and feminine, with a neat cap of soft, dark hair and tidy little features. Sam, by contrast, was chubby-cheeked and blond and his hands were plump and broad, making sturdy fists. He had been wearing a blue striped top like a miniature football jersey and he'd looked unmistakably masculine.

Now, as Nell stood with Jacob looking down at Sam in the old-fashioned, unpainted timber cot, she whispered, 'He's a bonny boy, isn't he?'

Jacob was standing very still, his gaze fixed on the sleeping baby.

Their grandson.

'He's *very* bonny,' he agreed at last. 'A real little bruiser.'

His voice sounded choked, but Nell heard unmistakable pride and when she looked up she was shocked to see the sheen of tears in his eyes.

On impulse, she reached for his hand and gave it a reassuring squeeze. His answering, shiny-eyed smile was so touching it sent tiny thrills flashing through her all the way to her toes.

'Sam looks like a lamb at the moment, but he isn't always as peaceful as this,' Jean warned them. 'There are times when he roars so loudly I swear he's a lion cub.'

They murmured their sympathy and tiptoed back to the front room. Bill was awake now and they were introduced. He offered them a crooked left-handed smile but, in spite of his stroke, his eyes sparkled with good humour.

Jean dropped a quick kiss on his forehead and gave him

an affectionate pat on the arm. 'Have you had morning tea?' she asked Nell and Jacob.

They assured her that they had and, as they sat, Jacob chose a spot on the sofa next to Nell.

Bill pointed to a photograph album on the coffee table and Jean picked it up quickly and handed it to them. 'We thought you'd like to see more photographs of Tegan.'

Nell knew straight away that it was going to be a battle to look at these snapshots of her daughter's life without getting tearful. Her hand shook as she turned the first page to a picture of the Brownes looking serious and middle-aged and almost frightened of their tiny newborn daughter, wrapped in a crocheted bonnet and lacy shawl.

Aware of Jacob sitting still as a rock beside her, she hardly dared to breathe as she turned more pages. Together they encountered pictures of Tegan as a small baby, as a grinning toddler, a lively little girl with her dark hair pulled into ponytails and predictable pink bows. Then there was Tegan in a striped swimsuit, her face covered in chocolate ice cream, in a school uniform, growing taller and missing teeth, frowning with concentration as she blew out birthday candles.

Nell felt her face begin to crumple.

We were never there for any of it, no part of our daughter's life.

She closed the book and took a deep breath.

'Tegan adored all the cards you sent for her birthdays and at Christmas, Nell,' said Jean.

Nell pressed her hands to her face. Any minute now she would be a mess.

Beside her, Jacob shifted uneasily. 'You said there was something you needed to discuss.' He spoke perhaps a little more loudly than he'd meant to.

Jean nodded. 'I'd like to explain our terrible dilemma.' She hesitated, as if she was sorting out in her mind what she needed to say. 'I'm Sam's guardian, you see. But we never dreamed that a young woman like Tegan could—' She had to stop and reach for a handkerchief, then dabbed at her eyes and blew her nose. 'Tegan was doing so well caring for the baby,' she said as she regained her composure. 'It never dawned on us that we would lose her and have to take re-sponsibility for raising Sam.'

'It must be very hard,' Nell agreed.

'Especially at our age. Sam wakes several times during the night and now, with poor Bill's stroke, we have so many trips during the day for his medical appointments. You wouldn't believe how many people we have to see—doctors, phys-iotherapists, occupational therapists, speech pathologists.'

Jacob leaned forward, elbows on knees, his gaze intent. 'You really need help, don't you?'

'I'm afraid I do. I love little Sam, but Bill has to be my first priority now.' Jean patted her husband's arm and smiled fondly. 'The thing is, it's not just caring for Sam while he's a baby that I have to think about. There's the long-term, too. Raising him through childhood, through school and beyond.'

It was a daunting prospect. And Nell couldn't help think-ing how stifling it would be for a lively little boy to grow up with an ageing grandmother and an invalid grandfather.

Jean lifted her hands in a gesture of helplessness. 'I feel torn in all directions, but I really don't see how we can be adequate parents for a growing boy. We were almost too old to adopt Tegan. And now—' She ran worried fingers through her thin hair.

'What are your options?' Jacob asked while Nell's heart began to thump as she guessed where this might be heading. Was Jean going to ask her to care for Sam on a permanent basis?

The thought awoke the hollow pain that had haunted her for many years after her parents had taken Tegan away. She'd eventually trained herself to put pregnancy and babies out of her mind, but now she felt stirrings of excitement, felt a leap of hope, like a rocket launching into a dark sky.

'I have two options,' Jean said. 'One is to hand over Sam to the state, but that certainly wouldn't be our preference. The other—'

Jean paused and Nell held her breath.

'I've had my solicitor check on the legalities of an alternative,' Jean said. 'And I can hand over my guardianship to a suitable person. It needs to be approved by a magistrate in a lower court, with the support of the child care authorities.'

By now Nell's heart was drumming so loudly she was sure everyone in the room must be able to hear it.

'Do you have someone in mind?' Jacob asked.

Every part of Nell tensed with anticipation.

Elbows on knees, Jacob leaned further forward. 'Have you considered Sam's father?'

Nell gasped. *Sam's father...* Good heavens, she hadn't given him a thought. Not a thought.

Who *was* Sam's father? Some scruffy teenager?

Good grief, already she was sounding as bad as *her* parents.

'We did quiz Tegan about Sam's father,' Jean said slowly, almost unwillingly. 'But she was a very determined, single-minded girl. So independent. She'd totally come to terms with being a single mother. When we pressed her, she said she would eventually let the father into their lives, but it would be very much on her terms.'

'But didn't she tell you his name?' Jacob persisted.

Jean shook her head. 'I got the impression that she might have regretted their encounter, that she didn't see him as long-term partner material.'

Jacob frowned. 'Hasn't anyone tried to trace him?'

'I'm afraid Tegan insisted on leaving his name off the birth certificate, so we have nothing to go on.' Jean glanced at her husband as if she wanted him to back her up, but he'd nodded off again.

Nell could understand that Jacob's sympathy would be with Sam's father, but she was selfishly glad that he wasn't in the picture.

The more she thought about taking care of little Sam, the more she loved the idea. She could easily imagine a baby in her life. She could picture herself giving him a bath, putting talcum powder and baby cream on him and dressing him in dear little clothes like the ones she'd bought as gifts for so many of her friends' babies.

It seemed very fitting for her to take care of Tegan's baby, almost as if the universe were making recompense for the baby she had lost. At night she could sit in her rocking-chair and cuddle Sam close. She'd give him his bottle and he would fall asleep in her arms while she rocked him.

'Our other problem is that Bill and I don't have any close relatives,' Jean was saying. 'Only older friends of our own age.' She gave a self-conscious little shrug of her thin shoulders. 'Poor little Sam doesn't want to be surrounded by a bunch of old crocks.'

The honesty of this silenced both Nell and Jacob.

Jean straightened her shoulders, looked resolute. 'It might come as a shock, but I assure you we've talked this through at length. Bill and I want to raise the possibility of you, Nell, taking over as guardian.'

Here it was. Out in the open. Nell pressed a hand over her thumping heart. She turned to Jacob, but her joyous smile was frozen by the cheerlessness in his face.

Oh, help. How selfish she was. Sam was his grandson too. And he'd already missed out on knowing Tegan. But how could they share Sam? Jacob lived in Queensland.

Jean was watching them nervously, waiting for an answer.

'I feel very honoured that you would trust me with Sam,' Nell said. 'It's a big responsibility. A little life in my hands.'

'We'd trust you, Nell.'

'But—but you know so little about me.'

Jean's eyes widened. 'I feel as if I've known about you for a very long time.'

'Really?'

'I've been reading about your charity work in the papers for years now. And you've been sending Tegan birthday cards since she was five years old. I've sensed it's been an effort for you to keep your distance, but you let us get on with our lives and we really appreciated that.'

Nell was gratified that Jean had understood.

'And then there's been this past week, since the accident,' Jean said, as if she were throwing down a trump card. 'I've really got to know you well and you've been so very kind.'

Nell wondered what Jacob was thinking about this, but his face was more composed now and it was hard to tell. She turned back to Jean. 'I don't suppose there'd be any difficulty getting the magistrate's approval?'

'Oh, I don't think there'd be any problem there. My solicitor tells me you're so well-known in legal circles, there's any number of people willing to give you a glowing reference.'

'Looks like you have it in the bag, Nell,' Jacob said dryly.

'There would have to be a kind of trial period,' Jean warned. 'To test the waters, so to speak. It will take about a month, I'm told, before the legal aspects are sorted out and you could have full custody. But we could place Sam in your temporary care any time.'

Nell nodded thoughtfully. 'And when were you hoping that might happen?'

'Well, I assume you'd like a little time to think about it.'

'I don't really need time. I—I'm perfectly free to take care of Sam. And I'd love to.'

'Oh, Nell.' Jean's eyes shone with tears, but she looked exceptionally pleased. 'Oh, bless you. That's wonderful'

'So you just have to name a day.'

Jean blushed and clapped her hands to the sides of her reddened face. 'This must sound terrible, but would tomorrow be too soon?'

'I know what you're thinking,' Nell said later, as Jacob drove the Mercedes back to Williamstown.

'What am I thinking?'

'That Jean totally overlooked the possibility that you might like to care for Sam.'

He gave a shrug that was anything but casual. 'It's not at all surprising. Jean doesn't know me from Adam.'

'But you still feel that the rights of fathers are too often overlooked.'

'It's a universal truth, isn't it?'

'Unfortunately, yes.' Nell watched the suburban houses flash past, their pointed rooftops looking like rows of red-tiled teeth. 'It's very difficult, isn't it? We certainly wouldn't want to start a custody battle and, as the mother, I—'

'You're the *grandmother*, Nell,' Jacob corrected, with a wry quarter smile.

She rolled her eyes at him.

'The truth is,' he said, 'we both have a claim, but the Brownes don't know me. And we can't split the poor little fellow in two.'

'Of course we can't. And, if you were honest, you'd have to admit it would be very hard for you to take on a baby.'

'Not necessarily.'

'Think about it, Jacob. Imagine trying to care for a little baby on your Outback cattle property.'

'It happens all the time.'

'Oh, yes? And how many single dads do you know in the Outback?'

He shrugged. 'I admit I don't know any personally.'

'Because it would be next to impossible to run an enormous cattle property and look after a baby at the same time. You're probably picturing Sam as a little boy, riding horses, but think about what caring for a tiny baby entails. All the bottles and formula, the nappy-changing, the sleepless nights.'

'Whoa there.' Jacob lifted a hand from the steering wheel.

'But I'm making valid points.' This was so like a man, to skim over the nitty-gritty domestic details.

He smiled gently, almost sadly. 'Keep your hair on, Nell. I'm not going to try to take Sam away from you. I'm actually delighted that you're going to care for him. You'll be wonderful.'

She released her breath with a sigh, realised she had been getting unnecessarily worked up. The thing was, Jacob might not be demanding his rights to Sam, but she knew he wasn't happy about being excluded again. What a sad, complicated state of affairs this was.

It was time to turn off the freeway and they let the subject drop until they reached her house. When they pulled up at her front gate, Jacob turned off the ignition but he remained in his seat, with one hand resting lightly on the steering wheel as he looked ahead through the windscreen at her neat suburban street.

Nell couldn't help admiring his profile—the high brow furrowed in thought, the strong nose, the attractive cleft in his chin. 'What are you thinking now?' she asked.

'About that photo album at the Brownes'. All those snapshots of Tegan's life. All those milestones.' His long tanned fingers tightened around the steering wheel. 'I was her father and I was never there. Not for one event, big or small, and neither were you, Nell. We were *never* a part of our daughter's life.'

Her throat was suddenly so choked she couldn't speak.

'I don't want a repeat of that with Sam.'

Eventually, she asked, 'What can we do?'

'I don't know,' he admitted grimly, but then he turned to her and the tiniest hint of warmth crept into his eyes. 'Let me sleep on it.'

'Sleep on it?'

'Bad idea?'

'Oh, in theory it's fine, I suppose. It's just that I haven't been sleeping very well lately.' She hadn't been able to sleep properly for days, not since she'd heard about Tegan's accident. Last night had been particularly bad. Seeing Jacob again had been enough to wreck her sleep, but now there was the excitement of Sam. It was like being pumped with mind-frying drugs.

Jacob got out and came around to her side of the car. As he opened her door, she wondered if he was going to kiss her again and her insides fluttered in anticipation. Heaven help her, she could still remember intimate details of how beautifully this man had made love to her.

'Here's a better idea,' he said when she was standing on the footpath. 'Why don't we talk about this over dinner tonight?'

'Dinner?' Nell repeated the word as if she'd never heard it before. The thought of dressing up and going out to a restaurant with Jacob Tucker messed with her head, stole her breath.

From the waterfront, a short block away, she heard the blast of a ferry's horn and the high-pitched screams of seagulls.

Jacob's eyes twinkled. 'You understand the concept of dinner, don't you? Two people go to a restaurant, sit at a table and enjoy a meal, usually an evening meal.'

She gave him a withering look. To go to dinner with him would feel like a date. A date with Jacob after twenty years...

'If you're going to take charge of the baby tomorrow, you should enjoy a night out,' he urged. 'Who knows what your life will be like after that? This might be your last night of freedom.'

'That's true.'

Smiling, Jacob ducked his head to catch the expression in her eyes. 'I'll take that as a yes, then?'

When he smiled at her like that there was no way she could refuse.

'I guess it's a yes.' Nell returned his smile shyly. 'Thank you,' she added, almost as an afterthought. 'But just for dinner.' It was important to keep this simple. No complications. 'I don't want a late night.'

'How about an Italian place on Lygon Street?'

Lygon Street, made famous after the welcome influx of

Italian immigrants, was one of Melbourne's best known restaurant precincts. She'd spent many a warm summer's evening there, enjoying the relaxing, friendly atmosphere and the wonderful food.

'Why not?' she said. 'Lygon Street would be perfect.'

CHAPTER FOUR

HANDS IN POCKETS, head down, Jacob paced Melbourne's central business district, hurrying along Spencer Street, Collins, King and Bourke Streets with little sense of direction or purpose. He passed some of Australia's finest department stores, many wonderful bookshops and cafés, but paid them scant attention.

He'd never liked the big smoke, with its endless streams of traffic, its towering concrete buildings blocking the sky, its dank and smelly back streets. He always felt sorry for the blank-faced pedestrians, dressed in dark suits all year round, always hurrying, constantly bombarded by advertisements urging them to spend, spend, spend.

After a few days in Sydney or Melbourne, he was itching to be back in the bush, with wide open spaces, the big sky, the smell of gum leaves and clean sunshine. Even the dust stirred up by cattle was preferable to the exhaust fumes of city traffic.

He would give anything to be able to spirit Sam away from the city and he thought it was rather one-eyed of Nell to wave aside any suggestion that Sam could grow up in the

Outback. She'd had a country childhood. She knew how good it could be.

Bush kids were fit and supremely capable. They learned to be self-reliant and to make their own fun outdoors, instead of sitting about, glued to television sets and video games. There was no better place for Sam to grow up.

But it wasn't going to happen. Jacob knew he couldn't stake a claim on the kid. Not now that he'd heard Nell's full story. Not now he'd spent a morning in her company, listening to her, watching her, discovering in the self-assured woman pleasing glimpses of the high-spirited girl he'd loved.

He had no doubt that Nell had earned this chance to be Sam's mother. But the looming distance between himself and Sam bothered him—*really* bothered him. Thousands of kilometres of separation. And once Nell had their grandson in her care, Jacob would only be able to visit him on her terms.

It wasn't, in any way, satisfactory.

Teeth gritted, brow fixed in a frown, he joined a group of pedestrians crossing Swanson Street at the lights and walked on.

At least Nell's husband wasn't in the picture. Jacob wasn't entirely sure how this made a difference, except that he'd kissed her on the strength of it...

And what wouldn't he have given to have let that kiss go on and on?

But that was fantasy. On the other hand, the issue of Sam's unnamed father was real. It was all very well for Jean Browne to act as if the father didn't exist, but there was a man out there, perhaps a young man of nineteen or twenty, who had a right to be consulted.

Fathers, and grandfathers for that matter, were important to boys. Jacob's own dad had died when he was very young and he'd missed the chance to get to know him. It had been damned hard for his mother to raise a boy on her own and Jacob had grown up with a deep-seated urge to be a husband and father, a tower of strength for his family.

But at just nineteen that dream had gone pear-shaped.

He continued, pacing all afternoon until serious-faced commuters began to bustle out of offices and on to trams and trains and it was time to head back to his hotel, to shower and change for dinner.

As he crossed the footbridge over the Yarra River to the South Bank, his disconnected thoughts suddenly fused and he made a decision. His plan of action would begin tonight.

Shortly before seven, Jacob walked up the path to Nell's front door. It was a beautiful evening and he took a deep lungful of air, laden with the scents of the sea and of lavender and roses. When Nell opened the door, however, he almost forgot to take another breath.

She was wearing a dark green dress with a ruffled top and a slim-fitting skirt and she'd threaded gold hoops in her ears. Her hair was swept up into one of those intriguing loose knots that looked as if they were on the verge of falling apart, so that a fellow had to keep watching, just in case.

There was something incredibly alluring and ultra-feminine about the soft fabric of her dress. The darkness of the forest-green made her hair more golden than ever, her skin smoother, her eyes brighter.

He wanted to gather her in to him, to hold her, to feel the softness of her skin against his, to taste her lush mouth again.

Too soon, he warned himself, but it was difficult to forget the eager way Nell had used to melt against him when they had been nineteen, the way she'd made him feel like a god.

The more time he spent with her, the more the memories flooded back, until it was hard to think about anything but lying with her in the sweet grass beside the river…undoing the buttons on her blouse.

'Have you had a busy afternoon?' she asked.

Jacob blinked, tried to rein in his thoughts by looking at her feet. She was wearing elegant sandals made from little gold chains and her toenails were painted an attractive berry colour. But what had she said? *A busy afternoon?* 'No, not exactly,' he managed. 'Have you?'

'Very busy.' Her smile broadened and he realised that she was glowing and bubbling with excitement. 'I've been shopping. It was so much fun. Come in and I'll show you. Actually, I need your help with something.'

As he followed her down the hall to a small room at the back of the house, he tried not to stare at her behind and the way her hips swayed in the neat green dress.

'I've put most of the things in here for the moment.'

Against the far wall, a single bed was piled with bags of disposable nappies, tiny infant clothes and a white wicker basket holding talcum powder, cotton wipes and tubes of baby cream.

'You didn't buy all these things this afternoon, did you?'

'I'm afraid I did.' Nell tried to look apologetic, but she couldn't hide her delight.

'That's quite a feat.'

'You have no idea how many gorgeous baby things there are. Look at this.' She picked up a pale blue garment that looked like a micro-sized boiler suit with rabbits embroidered on the front. Her eyes flashed brightly as she grinned at him. 'Have you ever seen anything so cute?'

'I don't suppose I have.' But he only gave the little suit a cursory glance before looking again into her lovely blue eyes.

Their gazes held.

And time seemed to stand still.

Nell's grin trembled and Jacob's throat constricted as the happy sparkle in her eyes changed to awareness. Breathtaking awareness. It was as if they were sharing the same memory, the same sensuous tug deep inside, the spectacular rush of mutual appreciation that they'd recognised and explored all those years ago.

It was over in a moment. Too quickly—way too quickly, Nell looked down and folded the tiny garment with extraordinary care.

Jacob scratched at his jaw. 'So what help do you need?'

'Oh, it's the cot.' She became businesslike at once, pointing to a room across the hall. 'I've assembled it in there, in my room, but I'm worried that I haven't got the wing-nuts tight enough. I'd hate the thing to collapse the minute I try to put Sam in it.'

The irony almost made Jacob smile. Right at this moment, there was nothing on this earth he wanted more than to follow Nell into her bedroom, but hell, he was getting sidetracked. This wasn't part of his plan.

'Aren't you jumping the gun?'

'What gun? What do you mean? I need to have everything ready.'

Ahead of him, she pushed open her bedroom door and he caught a glimpse of a king-size bed covered with an exquisite handmade quilt in shades of aqua, lavender and deep blue silk.

He stopped short of the doorway, averted his gaze from the bed. 'What's the rush to assemble the cot when we still haven't discussed what's happening with Sam?' Damn! That wasn't what he'd meant to say, but he couldn't go into that bedroom now.

Nell whirled around. 'I thought—I assumed—' Her eyes were round with worry. Her mouth opened and shut.

'Wasn't the plan to discuss Sam's future over dinner?'

She sagged against the door jamb. 'But I thought—'

She looked so disappointed that Jacob felt an urge to wave the whole matter aside, to say anything, do anything to make her smile again, to see her as happy as she'd been when she'd showed him the bunny suit.

But he curbed the urge. He had a plan and he didn't want to jeopardise it.

'Let's go to dinner,' he said gently. 'There'll be plenty of time to tighten wing-nuts tomorrow, before we pick up Sam.'

The restaurants of Lygon Street spilled out on to footpaths packed with crowded tables. Laughter and the happy chatter of diners filled the summer night.

Nell and Jacob, however, were shown to a table in a discreet alcove inside.

'I thought it would be easier for us to talk in here,' Jacob said, as soon as the waiter left them.

Nell nodded her agreement and wished she felt calmer about the impending conversation. Trying to share Sam was complicated, but that wasn't the only reason she was feeling tense.

There was the Jacob factor.

Jacob Tucker—gorgeous, passionate Jacob Tucker, the man who'd turned her world upside down—was back in her life.

In. Her. Life.

They'd gone beyond the chance meeting, beyond the chat

to fill the gaps in the past twenty years, and now Jacob was adding an unnecessary extra step by taking her out to dinner. Any way Nell looked at that move, it felt like a date.

And how was she expected to stay calm about that? The very thought…the tiniest possibility that she and Jacob might…

No, she couldn't let herself think about any kind of relationship with him. She'd had her chance when she'd been nineteen. Now she had to concentrate on Sam, on her responsibilities as a grandmother.

In a bid to calm down, she paid attention to their surroundings, to the whitewashed walls and trailing plants, terracotta floor tiles and red and white checked tablecloths, stout candles in amber glass covers.

She picked up the menu and studied it carefully, paying meticulous attention to every ingredient in every dish and then instantly forgetting what she'd read.

'I can recommend the mussels,' Jacob said. 'And the beef is particularly good.'

'So you've been here often?' she asked, surprised.

'A couple of times.'

Over the top of her menu, their eyes met and he smiled. *Oh, help.* His smile was sexy and slow and lit up his grey eyes and she was awash with girlish shivers and flutters.

Get over it. Remember Sam. His future is a serious matter.

'Would you like some wine?' Jacob asked.

'Thank you,' she said. 'You choose something.'

'Do you have a preference?'

'I like white.'

It seemed to Nell that Jacob only had to raise an eyebrow before the waiter was hurrying to serve them. He ordered the very best Semillon Blanc.

'You've changed,' she commented, remembering the raw country youth with his unassuming manner and shy smile.

'I haven't really.'

'You seem...worldlier now.'

Jacob shrugged, gave her an offhand smile. 'People don't change, Nell. I've moved on, that's all.'

Was he right about that? Nell had to admit that Jacob had always radiated an arresting born-to-rule quality, even when he'd been her father's lowly employee.

'You've done well, haven't you?' she said.

'Well enough.'

Her uneasiness gave way to intrigue. 'I read about your success a few years ago. How did you manage it, Jacob? You had to start from scratch with nothing more than a jackaroo's wage. And cattle properties are so expensive these days.'

'Don't you remember the strategy I planned?'

Nell found herself blushing. She and Jacob had had many long conversations on the river bank, but after twenty years she mostly remembered the lovemaking.

The waiter arrived with their wine and went through the ritual of removing the cork, offering the wine for tasting, then pouring.

After he left, Jacob raised his glass and smiled another of his melting-moment smiles. 'Here's to us and to the next twenty years.'

Gulp. What on earth did that mean? Nell wished her hand wasn't shaking as she lifted her glass to touch his. 'Here's to Sam,' she said softly. After all, it was because of Sam that they were here, wasn't it?

Jacob's response was a mere dip of his head.

Nell took a sip of wine to find it was crisp and dry and delicious.

She set her glass down. 'You didn't answer my question, Jacob. I'm still curious about your success. I remember your big dreams, but I was never sure how you were going to put them into practice.'

He gave her a considering look, as if he was weighing up the benefits of discussing his business with her. He took another sip of his wine, put it down and settled back in his chair.

'I got wise fast,' he said. 'I knew the banks weren't going to lend me much money, so I had to look at alternatives. I decided there was no point in trying to find cash to buy land when I knew that livestock brought the real returns.'

'So what did you do?'

'I bought the cattle and leased the land I needed.'

'And it worked?'

'Sure. City companies often lease their offices, so I looked for the best land leasing and agistment deals. I had to start small, of course, but whenever I had a chance to buy more stock I leased pastures in different parts of Queensland, so I got a good geographical spread.'

'That's clever. Thinking outside the box.'

He looked pleased that she'd recognised this.

'And it makes so much sense,' she said. 'Especially now, with climate change and the unpredictability of the seasons.' Absorbed by these ideas, Nell gave the stem of her wineglass a thoughtful twist. 'But that kind of farming would mean expensive trucking costs.'

'I solved that by buying my own trucks.'

'Good heavens. I thought those things cost the earth.'

'I got the first one for a song.' Relaxing with one elbow hooked over the back of his chair, he couldn't suppress a smile. 'I came across it one wet season, bogged in a black soil crossing on the Diamantina. The fellows who bogged it swam the cattle out, but they were going to abandon the truck. I made them a ridiculous offer.'

Nell laughed, imagining the scene—the squelchy black mud, the cattle in the river, the drivers' frustration. 'How did you get it out?'

'Mates with bulldozers. Only took them a matter of days to haul it from the river, but it took me six months to get the truck into working order.'

'Well, good for you.' She felt excited for him, and could imagine how satisfying his achievements must have felt.

Their entrées arrived—mussels in a Sicilian sauce for Nell and beef capaccio with lemon for Jacob.

She wondered when they were going to discuss Sam, but Jacob kept steering their conversation in other directions and she didn't object. But she hoped he wasn't waiting until she was relaxed with wine and good food before springing some kind of trap for her.

He encouraged her to tell him more about her quilt making, which she was happy enough to do. She could rabbit on for hours about textiles and colours and designs, but she didn't want to bore him.

Then he asked, 'Do you still like horse riding?'

Coming out of the blue, the question caught her off guard. 'I haven't ridden a horse in years,' she admitted.

But the seed had been sown in fertile ground and suddenly Nell was remembering her girlhood, when she'd thought there was nothing more fabulous than to set out on horseback in the early morning, over grass sparkling with dew, flying down the hill to the creek.

Nothing had been more exhilarating than the thrill of roaring along the river flats, losing her hat and not caring because the power of the beast beneath her was so magnificent.

'I've a beautiful bay mare at Koomalong,' Jacob said, watching her carefully. 'You'd love the country up there. We've had a good season. The creeks are running.'

'What is this, Jacob? An invitation?'

'Sure.'

'But I—' Nonplussed, she stared at him, while her heart galloped wildly.

The waiter arrived to collect their plates and Nell picked up her wineglass to take a sip, hoping it would calm her.

'You're inviting me to visit you at your place?' she clarified when they were alone again.

'You're planning a month to get to know Sam. Why not do that at Koomalong?'

Her mouth fell open. 'A month? You're asking me to stay for a whole month?'

'You'd enjoy it.'

'I—I—' She took another huge gulp of wine and tried to think straight. 'You're not serious, are you?'

'Why not?'

'You can't just drop out of the sky and into my life and say, Hey, come live with me, as if the past twenty years haven't happened.'

'I realise that.'

'What are you saying, then?'

His smile did wicked things to Nell's stomach. 'I'm saying that we're grandparents of a baby boy who needs us. We're both very keen to be a significant part of his life and it's damned difficult to do that if we're living thousands of kilometres apart. So my invitation makes good sense.'

Nell couldn't *think* what to say. How could Jacob make such a crazy suggestion sound logical and practical?

Their main courses arrived—fettuccini for both of them—

and she paid careful attention to her food, purposely avoiding his eyes.

He topped up her wineglass. 'Think about it, Nell.'

'Believe me, I'm thinking. But my brain's stuck in a groove.' She twirled ribbons of pasta around her fork and ate them before she went on. 'I'm stunned that you can treat this as if it's nothing more than a simple child-minding arrangement.'

'But it doesn't have to be complicated.'

She stared at Jacob. How could suddenly deciding to live together for a whole month after all this time be anything but complicated?

His grey eyes held hers and he smiled and, in spite of her bewilderment, she felt a delicious warmth spreading through her—warmth that had nothing to do with the wine.

She tried to concentrate on her food, but she was suddenly remembering another time when Jacob had simplified a very difficult and complicated situation—on the morning she'd told him she was pregnant.

Will you marry, me, Nell? I'll look after you, I promise. We'll be all right.

If her pig-headed father hadn't intervened she would have been able to marry Jacob then, to raise Tegan, to be that happy little family they'd dreamed of. She shivered, then gave a shake to dismiss it.

How amazing to think that now, twenty years later, there was another baby and Jacob was making another proposal. Making it sound so simple, so possible…

Part of her longed to mindlessly accept, to plunge in. After all, that was how everything had begun. She and Jacob had plunged into the river when the branch had broken and he'd kissed her as they'd scrambled up the bank.

'It's not such a crazy idea, is it?'

His voice snapped her out of her reverie.

Embarrassed that he'd caught her smiling dreamily, she became prickly. 'We—we hardly know each other now. We can't go back to the past and expect to take up from where we were at nineteen.' She hardly recognised herself as being the same person she had been back then. 'You know next to nothing about me now.'

'I know enough,' he said very quietly. 'I know you love the bush and I know you're a free agent.'

'But you're totally overlooking how I *feel*.'

A muscle worked in his jaw. 'That's true.' His eyes lost their amused sparkle.

She realised he was waiting for her to go on, to tell him exactly how she felt, to tell him that his proposal was audacious and impossible. There was no way she could live with him because...

Because...

To Nell's dismay, her mind wouldn't supply an end to that sentence. She gave a frantic shake of her head. 'Right now, I feel very, *very* confused.'

To her dismay, Jacob seemed satisfied with that.

Unsettled by the happy light in his eyes, she said, 'I have commitments here. Customers.'

'You can deal with them over the Internet.'

'How do you know that?'

'I found your website just before I came out tonight. It's very efficient.' He pressed his point home. 'Emotions aside, if you look at this practically, you could bundle up your quilting things and take them anywhere.'

She blinked. Jacob thought he had this all worked out, as if she were an object to be moved as easily as his cattle. But what he very carefully wasn't saying was that they would be alone together. There might be a baby in the picture, but they would be a couple living together and, even though she was a supposedly mature woman of almost forty, she didn't think she was ready to ask him what, exactly, that implied.

She chose a more oblique angle. 'You can't just look at this as if it's part of your business plan, Jacob. Another brilliant stroke of lateral thinking.'

But he wasn't listening, Nell realised. He was staring at some people who'd just come into the restaurant. They were behind her and she didn't like to turn around.

'What's the matter?' she asked. Jacob was frowning ferociously.

He didn't reply, but the newcomers were passing their table now, a well-dressed couple, the man in an impeccable suit—

Nell almost choked on her drink as she recognised the neatly bearded figure of Robert Ruthven, accompanied by a young woman in a very fetching red dress. A blonde, like Nell, but at least ten years younger.

They sat two tables away.

'Is that who I think it is?' Jacob hissed.

'Yes, it's my ex,' Nell admitted faintly. 'How did you know?'

'I've seen photos of him. My mother keeps an eagle eye on all the social pages.'

Nell wished she didn't feel so rattled. It wasn't as if this was the first time she'd seen Robert since the divorce. But she felt uncomfortable to be caught here with Jacob. If she'd been dining with a neighbour or a girlfriend, she might have remained quite calm. But Jacob was the man who'd taken residence in their marriage like an uninvited ghost. Worse, he'd just invited her to go off with him into the Outback.

'Nell!' Jacob's hand reached across the table for hers. 'Are you OK?'

As he watched her, Jacob's heart was tearing itself into shreds. He wanted to protect Nell, to rush her away, to save her from this embarrassment.

'It's OK, Jacob. I'm fine.' Nell had taken several deep breaths and was back in control, which was just as well, because at that moment Robert looked in their direction.

At first he looked shocked, but then, with the practised skill of an experienced barrister, he smiled, said something to his companion and stood.

'Well, well,' he boomed sonorously as he strolled towards them. 'Fancy seeing you here, Nell.'

'Hello, Robert.' She managed to smile very brightly as she held out her hand.

Jacob was on his feet and she said, 'You must meet an old friend of mine, Jacob Tucker.'

Until that moment, when the two men shook hands, she hadn't realised how much taller and more powerfully built Jacob was.

'Jacob Tucker.' Robert offered him a smile through gritted teeth. 'Of course, I've heard of you.'

'Likewise,' said Jacob grimly.

Robert sent Nell an eloquent roll of his eyes and there was no missing his message. *So this is the man you could never forget?*

A split second later, he was once again the smooth barrister. 'You have good taste, Mr Tucker.' For a moment he left the ambiguous comment up in the air, but when Nell and Jacob looked suitably puzzled, he smiled. 'The food here is excellent.'

He turned back to his companion, indicating to her to come over. 'You must meet Gabriella.'

Nell was certain that Robert puffed out his chest.

As she rose to meet the other woman, she noted with mild surprise that she didn't have any pangs of jealousy. She could smile at Robert's new girlfriend and wish her well without a qualm—with a marked sense of relief, actually.

Gabriella seemed quite nice, but rather shy, and the introductions were brief. Robert turned to Jacob and said with a hint of condescension, 'So you're down from the bush to kick up your heels in the bright lights?'

'Actually, I came to Melbourne to attend a funeral.' Jacob spoke quietly, but with a hint of challenge. 'And to deal with personal business.'

'Ah.' Robert took a step back. 'Nice to have met you. Enjoy your meal, Nell.' He looked, momentarily, as if he would have liked to keep on going, backing right out of the restaurant.

Seated again, Jacob said to Nell, 'Would you be happy to leave now, without dessert or coffee?'

'Yes, please. I've had plenty to eat.'

As he attended to the bill, she remembered that they hadn't finished their discussion about Sam. What would happen now?

On the footpath, Jacob said, 'We're going in opposite directions, so it makes sense to take separate taxis.'

So this was the end of the evening? 'You realise we haven't settled anything about Sam?' she said, feeling way too up in the air.

'I think we've made enough progress for one night.'

Had they? Jacob was being enigmatic when Nell wanted a black and white decision. She didn't want to admit it, but Robert's arrival had driven everything askew. It was so

strange. She'd known every intimate thing about Robert—
that he meticulously squeezed toothpaste tubes from the bottom up, that he liked to cut the corners off his toast and eat
them first, that he always slept on his back with his mouth
open.

She knew none of those things about Jacob and yet they'd
been parents, were now grandparents. And Jacob stirred her
in ways Robert never had.

The laughter of carefree diners floated around them as
they walked back along the footpath to the taxi rank. The
feeling that her discussion with Jacob hadn't finished properly, hadn't solved anything, bothered Nell, but there was a
cab waiting. Jacob ushered her forward. 'You grab this one.'

The evening was over.

'What about Sam?' she said in sudden panic.

'I'll come with you to the Brownes' tomorrow. We've
plenty of time to work everything out.'

'So we're going to sleep on this decision after all?'

An elusive emotion flickered in Jacob's eyes. 'I think you
know how this will pan out, Nell.'

Her heart leapt. What did he mean? She searched his face
and saw a tenderness that set a thousand yearnings stirring
inside her, spreading wings.

Oh, Jacob, don't look at me like that. I can't risk breaking
my heart over you again. I would never survive.

But she said, 'You're probably right. Things often make
better sense in the morning. Thanks again for a lovely dinner.'

She got into the taxi and Jacob closed her door.

Automatically, she lifted her hand to wave, but touched
the window instead. Jacob tapped the outside glass where

her fingers touched and the not-quite contact sent tendrils of warmth up her arms.

He smiled at her as the vehicle took off and she could see him standing on the edge of the footpath with his hands shoved deep in his pockets. Overhead lights caught the sheen on his dark hair, but she thought he looked very lonely as he watched her, as he waited until she turned the corner and was out of sight.

CHAPTER FIVE

I LET THAT turkey of a husband spoil our night.

Jacob entered his hotel room and let out a long, deep sigh into its darkened interior. He'd taken one look at that smooth barrister, that expensively dressed, silver-tongued ex-husband of Nell's, and his careful plans had flown out of the window.

But, in all honesty, he had to admit that the encounter had upset him more than it had seemed to bother Nell.

He showered, turning the taps on hard in an attempt to wash the tension from his body. Afterwards, he helped himself to whisky from the mini-bar in his room, tossing the fiery spirits down in two gulps.

In a final bid to get Robert Ruthven from his thoughts, he crossed to his suitcase and carefully retrieved an envelope from an inside pocket. Then he flopped back on to the huge hotel bed, reached above and snapped on the reading light. He opened a letter written in a round, girlish hand on sky-blue stationery trimmed with white and yellow daisies.

Lying in the pool of golden light, he read the words that he already knew by heart.

Dear Mr Tucker,

My name is Tegan Browne. I am nineteen years old and, shortly after my birth, I was adopted by the Browne family. My birth mother is Nell Ruthven, née Harrington, and I was recently given your name and told that you are my father.

I have no idea how you felt when I was given away. For years I was angry with both you and Nell, but now I'm nineteen I think I understand that decisions like adoption are complicated. I realise you might not even know I exist, so I'm sorry if this letter is a total shock, but I've decided I need to know more about you.

So here goes...

Hi, Dad.

Picture me smiling shyly as I say that, because it's weird to say hello after all this time, isn't it?

On the night I was told your name, I couldn't sleep. I kept saying your name over and over in my head... Jacob Tucker, Jacob Tucker, Jacob Tucker...

I could have been Tegan Tucker.

You have no idea how often I've tried to guess what you're like. When I was a kid, I looked at men on the train and wondered if one of them was you. Sometimes I'd choose a nice-looking guy and pretend he was my real father. But don't get me wrong, it's not because I've been neglected or anything. Bill and Jean Browne have been wonderful parents.

I searched for you on the Internet and I read that you're a bachelor still, which is none of my business, I guess, but it made me kind of sad. I could only find one photo of you on a website about cattle. You were on a horse and your face was mostly shaded by a big Akubra hat, but you looked really great.

You're a cattleman. Like wow! How cool is that? And you live in Outback Queensland. I guess you ride horses and catch wild bulls and walk like a cowboy. I think that's awesome.

I know our shared DNA might mean little to you, but I thought I'd tell you a few details about me. I'm 167 cm tall and I have dark hair and blue eyes and I'm divinely beautiful (joke). I'm no great scholar, but at school I loved art and music. I used to think about training to be an art teacher, but I took a year off when I finished school and I kind of bummed around and now, well, something's come up and I don't know what the future holds.

I like messing about in Jean's kitchen and I'm turn-ing into a pretty starry cook. You should try my blue-berry pancakes.

Anyway, I've rattled on for long enough for a first letter. I hope you write back. I would truly love to meet you.

Your very curious daughter,

Tegan

PS I think Jacob is a very nice name. It's on my list of favourite boys' names. And I have some other impor-tant news, which I'll tell you if you write back.

Jacob set the letter on the bedside table, switched off the reading lamp and lay in the darkness on top of the bedspread. He hadn't drawn the curtains so there was still a faint glow from the city lights outside and he could see red and blue flashes from a neon sign reflected on the ceiling.

Tegan's words played through his head.

Picture me smiling shyly...
...I read that you're a bachelor still, which is none of
my business, I guess, but it made me kind of sad.

The colours on the ceiling blurred and he was forced to
swipe at his eyes with the backs of his hands, but the damn
tears wouldn't stop. He'd read Tegan's letter a thousand times
and it always tore at his heart. The openness of her commu-
nication, the youthful informality choked him up every time.

His little girl. The precious baby he'd made with Nell.

Her letter, like the photos he'd seen at the Brownes' today,
was such a brief, tantalising glimpse into his daughter's personality, her life.

Jacob rolled onto his side and let out a painful sigh. Tegan
hadn't mentioned her pregnancy, but he was pretty certain
that the extra news she had been going to tell him was about
the baby. If there had been another letter, would she have
given him the name of her child's father?

What about that guy? It didn't seem possible that Tegan
could write such a touching letter to her birth father and yet
ignore the rights of her own baby's father.

Who was that young man? Where was he now?

It was something Jacob had to find out, no matter what
happened tomorrow when he went with Nell to collect Sam.

Lying with his hands folded beneath his head, he found
himself thinking about his own father and the photo that he
kept hidden away in an old album.

His father hadn't been a cattleman, but he had loved the
Outback and loved to ride horses and in the photo Jacob,
aged two, was up in the saddle in front of him.

As a boy, Jacob had stared at that photo so often it was

imprinted on his brain. That unfamiliar masculine figure on horseback had been his hero.

He could see the image now, could see his dad in a wide-brimmed hat that shaded his dark eyes, his straight nose and smiling mouth. His cotton shirt sleeves were rolled up, revealing strong, sinewy forearms. His hands were suntanned and long-fingered, one loosely holding the reins, the other curved protectively to hold the dark-haired little boy against him.

There were times when Jacob was sure he could remember that photo being taken, could remember that strong arm holding him close, could feel the texture of the rough cotton shirt against his back, the smoothness of the leather saddle beneath him.

He thought about Sam and felt an unbearable longing to have the boy in his life.

Tomorrow...

Jacob let out a soft groan. Had he ruined his chances?

He'd handled this evening so badly. He'd allowed Nell's ex to spoil their dinner and then he'd felt compelled to let the whole matter of Koomalong drop. Which meant he was no closer to his goal, and that was crazy.

Tomorrow was his last chance.

Nell dreamed of making love with Jacob, but she woke to a grim dawn, an empty bed and rain lashing against her bedroom window. She lay very still, enveloped by an overwhelming longing for her dream to continue, for Jacob's lips on hers, his arms about her, his body covering her.

Closing her eyes, she wished she could stay in the past. She wanted to be that reckless, careless girl again, longed for that time when her life had been focused on a single track, when her summer had been defined by her secret trysts with Jacob Tucker.

How resourceful she'd been back then, finding a sheltered glade inside a grove of trees on the river bank for their 'second date', sending a carefully coded message to Jacob via his mother, their innocent go-between.

She'd relished the danger and the secrecy.

'You know your father will sack me if he finds us,' Jacob said when he met her that second time. 'He warned me you were coming home, said there'd be hell to pay if I went anywhere near you.'

'Would you rather not come here, then?' she asked, disappointed.

He smiled shyly, pulled her in for a kiss. 'I don't think I can stay away.'

'That's settled, then.' She tried to sound calm but inside she was doing cartwheels. Already she was mad about Jacob. 'We should be OK at this time of the morning. My parents like to sleep in.'

'Yeah. Your father's the only cattleman I've worked for who isn't up with the birds.'

It was well-known in the district that her father was lazy, but Nell didn't want to waste time talking about him. She and Jacob sat together on a shaded patch of grass, their backs against the broad base of a gum-tree. 'It's your turn today,' she said. 'You have to tell me all about yourself.'

He grinned. 'I bet my mum's already told you everything you need to know about me.'

'Maggie's very proud of you,' Nell agreed. 'But in a nice way. She's not boastful, although I can tell she really loves you.' After a bit, she said, 'I've been wondering about your father.'

Good grief, she'd been blunt in those days.

Jacob's smile faded. 'My father died when I was two.'

'I'm sorry.' Nell could instantly tell how much this hurt him. 'That's so sad, Jacob. Do you mind—can I ask what happened?'

He shrugged. 'He was an engineer with the Main Roads and he was inspecting a work project on a road out near Longreach. There was motorist who didn't slow down.'

Jacob's eyes grew dark and she could see that his father's death had left an enormous hole in his life. Nell gave him a hug.

Jacob repaid her with a kiss. Cupping her face in his hands, he kissed her sweetly, tenderly, making her insides swoop and drop, as if she were riding on a Ferris wheel.

'What else do you want to know about me?' he prompted, as he continued to hold her close.

'Um—' Nell's head was still spinning. *Where did you learn to kiss like that?* 'Um—have you always lived in the Outback?'

'Pretty much. Mum and I have lived all over the place— Western Australia, the Northern Territory, Queensland.'

'And I suppose you've had lots of girlfriends?'

His face broke into a slow smile. 'None you need to worry about.' He cocked his head to one side and his eyes were breathtakingly serious as he sifted strands of her hair through his fingers. 'You're beautiful, Nell. I bet you've had hundreds of guys chasing you in Brisbane.'

'Hardly hundreds. And no one as nice as you.'

She was rewarded with another kiss and it wasn't nearly as gentle as the first. The intensity of it stole her breath, thrilled her, sent her blood racing. She'd swear she'd never been kissed with so much passion.

'About those college parties you were telling me about,' Jacob murmured huskily, close to her ear. 'What happens after the eight minutes of chit-chat?'

'Um—' Nell struggled to breathe normally. 'If people decide to hook up, it's—it's up to them what happens next.'

He wound a strand of her hair around his finger. 'If we were in the city, I guess I'd take you to the movies or to dinner or something.'

'Or something.'

He smiled again and his eyes revealed an unguarded warmth and emotion that sent Nell's heart thrumming. She longed for him to start kissing her again, knowing they were both burning up.

'No chance of movies or dinner for us.' His voice sounded hoarse.

'Then I guess that leaves us with *or something*,' she said bravely.

His smile turned shaky and his fingertips traced an electrifying line from her hairline down the side of her face to the little hollow at the base of her throat. Nell was on fire, almost bursting out of her skin.

Please keep touching me—please.

His fingers moved to the V at the neck of her blouse, and then to her first button, and Nell was drowning in a haze of heat. She willed him to undo that button, to undo all of them. She'd never offered herself to any man, but now she could think of nothing but how much she wanted Jacob, wanted his hands to touch her, to caress her intimately.

Looking back now, twenty years later, Nell was still amazed by the force of her youthful impatience. She could remember the way she'd thrown her arms about Jacob's neck, had kissed him hard, arching into him so that he could have no doubt what she wanted. And, in response, he'd attended to every one of her buttons and they'd made love.

She supposed that first time must have been more about passion than finesse, but she could only remember how blissfully happy she'd been.

There had only been one problem. They'd both been so carried away with the heady excitement of discovering each other that they hadn't waited till Jacob made a trip to the pharmacy in Roma.

'Morning, Nell.'

Nell was putting out the rubbish when her neighbour's cheery face popped over the fence.

Rosie O'Donnell was grinning at her from beneath an unruly mop of brown curls. 'I'm guessing you must be on top of the world.'

Nell tried not to look too surprised. 'Why would you think that?'

Rosie rolled her eyes to the pale morning sky. 'I've seen your visitor. Man, oh, man, Nell. Have you struck the jackpot, or what?'

'Which visitor?' Nell asked, playing dumb, as if she couldn't guess who'd put that silly grin on Rosie's face.

'Who else but the six foot plus, deadly handsome guy who's been calling on you?'

Nell dismissed this with an airy wave. 'Oh, that's just Jacob. He's an old friend from way back.'

'Old friend, huh? Every woman should be so lucky.'

'We were both at a funeral,' Nell added, hoping to dampen her neighbour's unwelcome enthusiasm.

Rosie simply shrugged.

And Nell tried to look just as nonchalant. She knew the

subject of her going to Koomalong would resurface today, but her feelings about it were as confused as ever.

Rosie's eyes narrowed as if she sensed Nell's troubled thoughts. 'These blasts from the past can be unsettling, can't they?'

'Sometimes,' Nell agreed, and then, because she wanted to deflect the conversation right away from Jacob Tucker, she added, 'I'm going to have another man in my life.'

'Well, you don't muck about.'

'This fellow's seven weeks old.'

There was a second's puzzled silence before Rosie shrieked, 'A baby!'

Behind her back, Nell crossed her fingers as she stretched the truth. 'I'm adopting a baby boy.'

'But that's fantastic, Nell. It's wonderful.'

'I'm probably going to need loads of advice, Rosie.' Nell had helped out with friends' babies, but she couldn't remember the last time she'd changed a nappy. Rosie, as the mother of three boisterous little boys, had to be an expert.

'Oh, honey, it's always a little scary when you first bring a tiny baby home, but you can count on me. I'd love to help and the timing's perfect as far as I'm concerned. I've been hopelessly clucky lately, but Fred won't consider another mouth to feed.'

'You'll have to come and cuddle Sam then.'

'I'd adore to. Sing out any time you want a hand.'

'You can count on it.'

'So—everything's fine, son?'

Jacob's phone rang just as he was finishing his morning coffee in a café on the South Bank.

'Really fine,' he told his mother.

'And the—funeral went—well?'

'Actually, yes. I'm glad I came down here for it.'

'That's a relief.'

Given that Maggie had urged him to attend Tegan's funeral, this reaction was puzzling.

'I don't suppose you knew anyone there?'

Ahhh...now his dear mother was fishing, and almost certainly she was angling for news of Nell.

Casting a hasty glance at the diners breakfasting nearby, Jacob rose. 'Hang on a sec.' He set money to cover breakfast and a generous tip beside his coffee cup, strode out of the café and on to the paved embankment beside the Yarra. 'Are you still there?'

'Yes,' his mother said eagerly and, before Jacob could utter another word, she asked, 'Did you see Nell?'

'I did.'

'And?'

'And she's well.'

'Jacob, for heaven's sake, you know you've got to tell me more than that.'

Yes. Jacob totally understood her need for details. His mother had suffered almost as much as he had when they had been forced to leave Half Moon two decades ago. But how did he begin to tell her about Nell without telling her about Sam? And once he began talking about Sam, how did he stop himself from telling her about his proposition that Nell should live with him at Koomalong, about the stalemate they'd reached?

There was no point in stirring her unnecessarily.

His mother, however, had her own questions. 'Did Nell tell you she's divorced, Jacob?'

He felt his jaw unhinge. 'Yes, she did. How long have you known that?'

'Not long,' she replied airily. And then her voice dropped. 'Be careful, son. It wouldn't be easy to walk away from Nell again.'

'I'm not a crazy kid any more. Don't start worrying about ancient history.'

Disheartening silence followed this and then his mother sighed into the phone. 'Don't—don't hope for too much. I couldn't bear to see you hurt like that again.'

'Not a chance.' Jacob watched a group of schoolboys laughing and joshing as they took the pedestrian bridge over the river. 'To start with, old Harrington's not likely to come after me with a shotgun.'

There was an annoyed huff on the other end of the line. 'You know I didn't mean that.'

'Don't worry, this is very low-key. Nell and I have talked. That's all. We had a lot to catch up on.'

'I dare say. So—when are you heading back to Koom-along?'

'Ah—soon. Possibly in the next day or so.'

There was silence on the other end. Jacob said, 'I'll call you as soon as I've settled everything here.'

'All right. But Jacob—'

'Yes?'

'Just remember that life moves on. It has to. You can't re-capture the past.'

How could he *not* remember that the past was lost to him? It was emblazoned on his brain in flashing neon lights. 'I'll remember,' he said.

Nell was grateful that her neighbour was a comrade in arms, but when she went back to her kitchen her optimism took a dive. She washed up the cereal bowl and mug she'd used for breakfast and confusion returned to settle on her shoulders like a ghostly blackbird.

Ambrose came into the kitchen and rubbed his silky flanks against her legs.

'What should I do, Ambrose?' She felt only a little foolish that she voiced the question aloud. 'Would I be horribly selfish if I stayed here in Melbourne and kept the baby to ourselves?'

Ambrose's mouth yawned wide in a silent miaow.

Nell sighed and told herself she was being sensible rather than selfish. She and Jacob could never recapture their youth. Their attraction back then might have been a spontaneous combustion, but it had been fuelled by the thrill of forbidden love, of youthful longing and secret trysts.

How different now—a practical arrangement between grandparents to facilitate caring for a baby. Nothing could be less romantic. There would be disappointment all round.

Anyway, it was arrogant of Jacob to assume that she could move easily, as if it were simply a matter of packing up her fabrics and sewing machine and abandoning her house and her friends for a whole month. His suggestion was preposterous. Was he really imagining that they could resume a relationship?

Nell closed her eyes and gripped the edge of the sink as a wave of heat rolled through her.

Help. This was what worried her most, wasn't it?

Jacob had given her one tiny kiss and she'd practically gone into orbit. She was as susceptible to Jacob's sexiness now as she'd been at nineteen.

But what if his proposed experiment at Koomalong didn't work out? She would be devastated and she couldn't risk that kind of pain again. And Sam might suffer too. Tiny babies were sensitive to their environment.

But then she remembered Jacob's disappointment yesterday. His pain.

We were never a part of our daughter's life.

As if that thought was the cue, a knock sounded on her front door. Nell thought she might cry as she hurried to answer it.

Jacob looked like heaven in blue jeans. 'Morning, ma'am. I believe you have a cot with dodgy wing-nuts?'

Each time she saw him she felt like a giddy schoolgirl— thumping heart, fluttering stomach, legs without bones. She gripped the door handle as Jacob held a pair of pliers high, like a trophy.

He was cool and relaxed, his manner almost flippant, and she didn't understand why or how that was possible. Yesterday, he had delayed this task because he'd wanted to settle everything about Sam. Last night they'd settled nothing and had parted uneasily.

So what did this apparent relaxation mean? Was Jacob putting on a brave face, or was he having second thoughts about Koomalong? Maybe he'd decided he'd be happy for her to care for Sam here in Melbourne. And maybe she had avoidance issues, but these weren't questions she wanted to ask.

'Come on in,' she said with a gesture for him to follow her down the hall.

With the purposeful lack of curiosity of a hired tradesman, Jacob headed straight for the cot in her bedroom.

Arms folded over her stomach, Nell leant a shoulder against the door frame and watched as he gave the cot a businesslike test rattle, then proceeded to tighten the wing nuts with the pliers.

She couldn't help admiring the way he worked. His hands were quick and efficient and she had a grandstand view of his back, so she could see the outline of his muscles rippling beneath his thin T-shirt and the breathtaking fit of his jeans. She concentrated on the back of his head.

But that was no help. His hair was dark brown, with no sign of thinning, and she liked the way it had been cut, making a neat, straight line—so *masculine*—across the back of his suntanned neck.

The job was done in a minute flat.

Jacob straightened and his grey eyes twinkled. 'The little fellow should be safe in there now.'

'Thank you.' Nell moistened her dry lips with her tongue.

Jacob watched her, then flicked his gaze to something beyond her left shoulder. 'How will you transport Sam? Do you have one of those special baby carriers for the car?'

'Yes. I tried to fit it yesterday afternoon, but I'm not totally confident I got it right. I—I wonder if you'd mind checking that it's secure?'

He nodded. 'Lead the way.'

Again, his readiness to help without question puzzled Nell.

'We still haven't sorted out where Sam's going to live,' she said when Jacob pronounced the baby carrier safe and ready for action.

He gave a slow shrug. 'You'll need a day or two to get used to him here. Let's take it one step at a time.'

'Just remember I haven't promised anything about coming to Queensland.'

'I know.'

'Jean might be very upset if she thought you were planning to take Sam all the way up there.'

Jacob nodded thoughtfully.

'As it is, she's going to be upset, handing over Sam.'

'You're right.' He looked sober as he considered this, but then he shrugged again. 'We'll soon find out, won't we?'

Jean's response surprised them both.

'Why not?' she said.

Nell stammered. 'W-we th-thought Queensland would be too far away from you.'

'But Tegan was very excited when she learned that Jacob was a cattleman. She loved the country. She went fruit picking after she finished school and I don't think she wanted to come back to the city. She actually told me once that she wished Sam could grow up in the country.'

'Really?' Nell's voice sounded as shaky as she felt.

'Oh, yes, dear.' Jean looked from one to the other and smiled knowingly. 'I'm sure Tegan would have loved to know you two were looking after Sam together. I forgot to tell you, Jacob. Sam's full name is Samuel Jacob.'

Jacob looked as stunned as Nell felt.

'And do you know what I think?' Jean asked them.

'What?' they replied in unison.

'Sam's a very lucky little boy. There was always a chance that neither of you would be interested in him. But to have both of you so keen to love him and take care of him—' Her eyes filled with tears, but she was smiling.

'Nothing's decided about Queensland yet,' Nell felt compelled to explain.

'Well, please don't keep Sam in Melbourne on my account. I know Tegan would have loved him to live in the Outback.' As an afterthought, Jean said, 'But if you went to Jacob's property, you'd keep in touch, wouldn't you? And you'd come back to sort things out with the courts?'

'Absolutely,' Nell and Jacob said together.

Over the next half hour, while they drank tea, Jean told them about Sam's milk formula and sleep patterns, his weight gains and immunisations.

Not wanting to forget anything, Nell took careful notes. But eventually Jean ran out of information.

'I'm repeating myself,' she said when she told them about Sam's weight gains for the third time. 'I think I've said enough. It's probably best if we make the handover quick and simple,' she said bravely. 'I'm not sure I could handle a prolonged farewell.'

Nell couldn't believe how suddenly nervous she felt, as if she were about to audition for a part in a play and had only remembered at the last minute that she hadn't learned her lines. Her heart knocked painfully as Jean extracted the sleeping Sam from his cot. She held her breath as he was handed to her.

Oh, how soft and warm and cuddly he was.

'Thank you,' she whispered, tears falling unchecked as she kissed Jean. 'Thank you so much. I promise I'll take good care of him and I'll definitely keep in touch.'

'Yes, dear. Feel free to ring me any time.'

Nothing felt real as they left the house and stowed a sports bag of baby clothes and nappies into Nell's car, plus another filled with formula and sterilising solution and bottles. Then they settled Sam into the baby carrier in the back of the car.

'Will you drive?' she asked Jacob. 'I'd like to keep an eye on Sam.' It was only half the truth. She felt too shaky and excited to take control of a vehicle and she had to get this right. Sam was such a huge responsibility.

'Sure,' Jacob said, smiling and holding his hand out for the keys.

As she snapped her seat belt, she spoke over her shoulder. 'We're taking you home, Sam.'

CHAPTER SIX

HOME.

Jacob turned in the driver's seat and his gaze met Nell. The unresolved question hung in the air between them. Where should Sam's home be?

Her throat constricted. When they got back to her cottage, they would have to finish their discussion, find an answer.

She looked down at her hands while Jacob started the car and they headed off, down the street.

'At least he's a good sleeper,' he said as they turned the corner.

'So far, so good.'

Right now, Sam looked angelic as he lay in his baby carrier on the back seat, his fine blond hair gleaming softly in the sunlight that streamed through the rear window and his pink mouth pouting a bubble of milk.

But they had hardly left Thornbury before he squirmed and pulled a face that made him look ridiculously like a very wrinkled old man.

'Sam's looking unhappy,' Nell announced nervously. 'He's squirming and moving,'

'I should think he would want to move.' Jacob smiled wryly as he took off at a green light.

'But he's turning red.' Nell didn't want to be nervous, but she'd had next to no practical experience with babies. 'I think he's waking up.'

'He has to wake some time.'

'But he shouldn't be waking now, should he? I thought babies were supposed to sleep in cars. Isn't something about the motion supposed to make them sleepy?'

As she said this, a tiny squawk emitted from the back seat. Scant seconds later, it was followed by a much louder wail. Then a full-bodied squawk. And another.

Oh, help! Was Sam missing Jean already? What should she do? He looked so distressed and sounded so miserable.

Nell wondered if she should ask Jacob to stop the car. They shouldn't just drive on, callously letting the baby cry, should they? Twisting in her seat, she watched Sam's small hand waving above him like a distress signal. She reached back and tried to catch it with her little finger.

'There, there,' she crooned as his fingers brushed the tips of hers. She dropped her hand lower and he clasped her little finger in a tight tiny fist.

It was lovely to feel him clutching her, needing her. 'You're all right, little man, don't cry.' How relieved she would be if she could pacify him.

Sam's wails grew stronger and louder, his face redder. He let go of her finger and his hand stiffened, fingers outstretched, imploring.

'He can't be hungry,' she said. 'Jean was quite certain that he doesn't need a feed for another hour or more.'

'Maybe it's wind,' Jacob suggested matter-of-factly.

How did he know about such things?

'Perhaps we'd better stop and see what the problem is.' Nell cast a doubtful eye over the busy lanes of traffic.

Jacob lifted his voice over Sam's cries. 'The Botanic Gardens aren't far away. How about I head over there? At least it will get us out of this traffic.'

'Yes!' Nell nodded gratefully. 'That's a good idea.'

Sam cries were ear-splitting by the time they pulled into the car park at the Royal Botanic Gardens. People getting into a car nearby turned to stare at them.

Nell flew out of her seat and fumbled with the straps binding Sam into his carrier. 'What's the matter, little man?'

Lifting him up, she felt his little body go rigid in her arms. It was like trying to cuddle a brick—a screaming brick. Nell tucked a muslin wrap around him and joggled him gently against her shoulder. She patted his back and when he didn't calm down she felt a shaft of real panic. She knew babies cried but she'd never heard one as upset as this.

What was wrong with him? He'd been fed, his nappy was dry. He couldn't have developed a dreadful disease in the short time since they'd left the Brownes'.

What if she couldn't calm him?

Jacob joined her and she shot him a frantic glance. He smiled, but she knew he must be thinking that her mothering skills were sub-zero.

'Why don't we take him for a walk?' he suggested.

'A walk? When he's screaming? Do you think it would help?'

'It's worth a try. You never know, it might soothe him.'

Nell directed a doubtful glare at the sweeping lawns, the majestic elms and oaks and the path circling the ornamental lake. The early morning rain had finished soon after breakfast and it was a lovely summer's day. Melburnians were out in force, enjoying their favourite parkland—joggers and parents pushing prams, toddlers entranced by the teeming birdlife—lots of babies, lots of small children. Only Sam was screaming.

Jacob didn't seem perturbed by the baby's uproar. He threw a protective arm around Nell's shoulders and she felt absurdly grateful for his reassuring presence. He clicked the remote control to lock the car doors and they began to walk, their footsteps in time as they crossed the gravelled car park to the path.

Sam kept yelling, but Jacob talked anyway.

'These gardens are my favourite part of Melbourne,' he said as the path led them down the slope towards the water.

'Let me guess—because it's full of trees and wide open spaces?'

'Absolutely. Being here is the next best thing to being in the bush.'

It was a not so subtle reminder. 'But parks are supposed to be tranquil places. Sam's disturbing the peace.'

'He's a tiny baby, Nell.'

She sighed. 'I know.' She gave Sam's back a firmer pat and hitched him higher on her shoulder. Almost immediately, he let out a huge burp.

And stopped crying.

'Goodness.' Nell lifted him away from her, so that she could look at him. 'Was that the problem?'

In the sunlight, Sam's fine hair was lit with gold. His blue eyes were still shiny with tears trembling on the end of dark lashes. He was staring at her with a look that suggested he was almost as surprised as she was that he'd stopped crying. He was absolutely gorgeous!

Nell smiled at Jacob. 'You were right. But how did you know he had wind?'

Returning her smile, he shrugged. 'I must have an acute understanding of infants.'

She wasn't buying that. 'Or you made a lucky guess.'

Grinning widely now, he snapped his fingers. 'Sprung.'

Nell laughed. And then she was instantly sobered by the realisation that this was the first time she'd laughed in ages.

Ages.

She remembered how often she and Jacob had laughed all those summers ago.

As she settled Sam back against her shoulder and walked on, her confusion about the tall, handsome man beside her returned. Jacob was slipping into her life with astonishing ease, but so far his role was hard to define. He was so much more than an old friend, more than a good egg lending a helping hand. He was almost a partner.

But the bottom line was that Jacob was Sam's grandfather. That was the reason he was here, taking a stroll through the park with her. That was why he wanted her at Koomalong.

Sam's grandpa.

She looked again at the tall, dark, not-yet-forty guy in blue jeans and almost giggled.

'What's so funny?'

'I was thinking that the universe has a perverse sense of humour, turning us into grandparents before we're out of our thirties.'

The skin around his eyes creased as he grinned. 'Don't worry, Nell. You make a very cute granny.'

She looked away and pressed a kiss to the top of Sam's head. He was warm and relaxed as he cuddled against her now, growing heavier as he snuggled in like a baby koala. The walk was indeed soothing him.

They passed a beautiful bright garden of massed perennials.

Jacob asked, 'Are your parents still living at Half Moon?'

Surprised by the question, but thankful for the change of subject, she answered readily. 'No. Haven't you heard? They had to leave.'

'How do you mean? What happened?'

'Dad, being the stubborn so-and-so that he is, wouldn't listen to all the warnings about global warming and drought. He overstocked and overgrazed and virtually ran the property into the ground. Then he couldn't repay his debts, so the bank foreclosed.'

Jacob let out a low whistle.

'My parents have moved to Rockhampton,' Nell told him. 'Dad works in the cattle sale yards now.'

She was rather grateful that Jacob made no comment. Heaven knew, he had plenty of grievances against her father and there were many things he could have said about how the mighty had fallen, but he probably didn't want to hurt her feelings.

'I've often wondered about your mum,' she said. 'How is she? Is she still living with you?'

'No way.' Jacob chuckled. 'She's married to a grazier in the Kimberley.'

'Really?' It was too late to hide her surprise. 'Wow, Jacob! That's wonderful.'

'She's got a beautiful home, a guy who's crazy about her, an extended step-family who adore her and she's as happy as a possum up a gum-tree.'

'I'm so pleased for her. I really liked her.'

It was the truth. Nell had genuinely liked Maggie Tucker and not just because she was Jacob's mum. Maggie was a handsome, fun-loving woman and a terrific cook. There'd been a warmth and an earthiness about her that Nell had found particularly appealing and strangely comforting. She'd spent many happy hours in Maggie's kitchen, in spite of her parents' disapproval.

'Maggie's teaching me to cook,' she'd told them. She could still remember the joy of learning from Maggie how to make perfect blueberry pancakes and scrumptious gingerbread. As for the chocolate pannacotta—yum!

'Your mother deserves to be happy,' she said.

'Yeah.' A fond smile warmed Jacob's face. He looked down at Sam. 'Speaking of happy—'

'Has he gone to sleep again?'

'Out like a light.'

'What a good little man.'

Speaking of happy...

Nell had never looked happier.

As they turned and walked back towards the car park, Jacob suspected that looking at Nell was a health hazard. She had always been lovely, but this morning, in the sunlight, holding the baby wrapped in a gauzy shawl, she was more beautiful than any Madonna painted by the great masters and Jacob had the pulse rate to prove it.

Nell's face had taken on a special tenderness, a mysterious sweetness that almost brought him to his knees.

With Sam in her arms she looked fulfilled and completely happy. And, like his mother, Nell was a woman who had copped more than her share of hard knocks, and she deserved this happiness.

What right did he have to put extra pressure on her by demanding that she make the huge shift to Koomalong? Could he really expect Nell to give up her cottage and her comfortable life here in Williamstown? She'd decorated the house with such care and made it her own. It was conveniently close to shops and the sea front and to pretty parkland.

He'd convinced himself that Sam would be better off in the Outback, but he couldn't deny that a seaside suburb had a lot of appeal for a small boy.

Now, looking at the expression of contentment on Nell's face, Jacob realised he had to back right off.

If he'd learned anything about women, it was that timing was everything and, right now, Nell's attention was tuned one hundred per cent in to Sam.

There was no point in trying to tell her that he still wanted her, as badly as he had when he'd been nineteen. Walking with her was not enough. Talking with her, watching the play of emotions on her expressive face, watching her holding Sam, was not enough. He needed her in *his* arms, needed the taste of her lips, the smell of her skin, her touch.

But there was every chance he'd totally scare her off if he tried to tell her that.

They reached the car park and Jacob pressed the central locking device. The car's lights flashed and the doors clicked. He opened the back door for Nell.

Nell, however, didn't move. She remained standing very still with Sam in her arms while she looked back at the green sweep of gardens, at the trees and the lake. And then she turned her attention to the street beyond the car park, to the busy lanes of jostling, honking traffic. Her gaze lifted to the skyscrapers—all glinting glass, concrete and metal—looked above them to a plane streaking through grey, smoggy clouds.

'Tegan was right,' she said quietly.

Fine hairs lifted on the back of Jacob's neck. 'What about?' His question was hardly more than a whisper.

'He likes open spaces.'

She smiled at him and he held his breath.

'And I think Sam needs both of us,' she said. 'Let's take him home and then we must talk about Koomalong.'

CHAPTER SEVEN

I THINK SAM needs both of us.

Nell couldn't believe she'd actually said that. She'd been so cautious, but now it was out and she was sure Jacob couldn't believe it either. He was looking at her as if she'd grown a third eye.

'Let's get Sam home first,' she said quickly. 'Then we can talk about it.'

Jacob sprang to life, moving aside so she could settle the baby back in the carrier. Luckily, Sam fell asleep and he slept all the way back to Williamstown. Jacob didn't press Nell to talk, for which she was extremely grateful. The enormity of what she'd said was sinking in and she was starting to feel the aftershocks.

When they reached her cottage, Jacob became business-like, carrying all Sam's things inside and stacking them in the back room.

'I think Sam needs a nappy change,' Nell said, feeling his damp rump.

Jacob's eyes twinkled with amusement. 'Will this be a first for you?'

'Of course not. I've changed oodles of nappies for friends' babies.'

'Great, then I can watch and see how it's done.'

Oh, good one, Nell. She was ridiculously nervous as she laid Sam on a fresh towel on the spare bed. Her hands were all thumbs as she unsnapped and lowered his pants and removed the nappy. It didn't help that Sam kicked his legs madly during the entire process, so that his little feet kept getting in the way.

'Hmm,' said Jacob, watching over her shoulder. 'Impressive family jewels.'

'All baby boys look like that.' Nell was annoyed with herself for being flustered. She thrust a packet of baby wipes at him. 'Here, you have a go.'

Jacob looked as if he'd swallowed a bug. 'What am I supposed to do?'

'Wipe over his nappy area with one of these.'

'Hey, I'm still learning. I'm happy to watch you. You're doing great. You're a genuine expert.'

She smiled at him sweetly. 'I've a better idea. Why don't you put the kettle on? We're going to have to heat up his next bottle.'

'OK.' Jacob was about to leave when he took a closer look at Sam. 'Nell, look. He has a birthmark just like yours.' He pointed to a tiny strawberry splash on Sam's ankle.

Nell gulped. After all this time, Jacob remembered the butterfly shaped mark on her hip.

'What about the kettle?' she said without daring to meet his eyes.

He accepted this task in good humour and headed for the kitchen, leaving her to fumble her way through changing Sam into a fresh set of clothes.

The subject of Koomalong was left until after Sam had been fed and carefully burped and put to bed in the little cot in Nell's bedroom. She decided to tackle it over lunch—tuna and mayonnaise sandwiches and cups of tea in the kitchen.

Nervously, she said, 'OK, I guess it's time to talk.'

'Whenever you're ready.'

His attempt at nonchalance didn't fool Nell. He was as uptight as she was.

She took a deep breath, then let it out noisily. 'The thing is, I agree that a cattle property is a great place for raising children, especially boys. But, more than that, I do understand how awful it would be for you to miss out on getting to know Sam.'

He nodded solemnly.

'But, to be honest, Jacob, saying that scares me. Half of me thinks it's a crazy idea.'

'But it would only be for a month to start with.'

'That's thirty days, Jacob.'

'What are you afraid of?'

'That you—'

'Yes?'

'That we—' The sudden amusement in his eyes made this conversation a hundred times harder. 'We can't expect to turn back the clock twenty years.'

'Is that a careful way of saying that you don't think we can resurrect our relationship?'

The kitchen grew suddenly hot and close. Nell wished she could fan her flaming cheeks. 'I—um—certainly don't think we should assume that a relationship would be the—um—likely outcome.'

Good grief. Were there lingering hints of regret in her voice? Had she ever sounded so flummoxed?

She tried again. 'It's going to be a very tricky situation. After all this time, we've probably romanticised the way we think about each other.'

Jacob's eyebrows rose and something disturbing in his expression forced Nell to study the remains of her sandwich.

'In reality,' she continued bravely. 'We've probably changed too much. I know I've changed and I'm sure you have, Jacob. And we only ever knew each other for such a short time. There's every chance that trying to live with each other won't work. We might be really disappointed. It could be a disaster.'

'That's always on the cards.' He spoke with annoying equanimity.

'So it's important to remember that I'd only be coming to Koomalong on a trial basis,' she said.

'There's no question about that. All three of us will be on trial. After all, we don't want to commit ourselves at this stage, do we?'

To her dismay, Nell realised that wasn't quite what she'd wanted him to say.

'It would be foolish to commit ourselves,' she told him.

Jacob smiled in a way that was both serious and gentle and he reached out and touched her cheek 'You won't regret this, Nell. You know how much you love the bush.' He traced a line on her cheek, creating a burning trail with his fingertips.

Nell struggled to breathe. Already he was breaking the rules! But, heaven help her, she was so vulnerable. Her skin was burning beneath his fingers. This one tiny intimacy was enough to launch her out of her chair and into his arms.

'Yoo-hoo! Anybody home?'

Nell jumped so quickly her chair fell backwards, clattering noisily on to the kitchen tiles. She saw her neighbour, Rosie, peering through the flyscreen door.

'Hi, Rosie,' she called, wincing at how out of breath and dizzy she sounded.

Rosie grinned and waved at her. 'I didn't mean to startle you, Nell. I was hoping I could take a peek at the new man in your life.'

Early in the evening, after attending to business in the city, Jacob returned to Nell's. As he pulled up, he could hear Sam's high-pitched cries and they grew louder as Nell opened the door.

'He's been grizzling like this for the past hour,' she said, gently rocking the unhappy fellow. 'The only thing that will keep him quiet is if I walk about and carry him. The minute I try to sit down he complains. But Rosie said her three boys were the same for the first couple of months.'

She looked apologetic. 'I hope you're not hungry. I haven't been able to do a thing about dinner.'

Jacob shrugged. 'It's a lovely evening. Why don't we take Sam for a stroll along the waterfront?'

'But don't you want to eat?'

'We can buy something, eat it looking out over the water.'

She beamed at him. 'I'll be ready in a jiffy.'

It was a beautiful summer's twilight. The sky was an extravagant lilac and scents from the gardens in Nell's street drifted slowly in the still air, blending with the smack of salt from the bay. Nell carried Sam, buttoned up in his warm little rabbit suit, and Jacob lugged the bag of essential baby things and more than one set of front curtains twitched as they passed.

In the row of shops around the corner, they bought fish

and chips wrapped in layers of butcher's paper, cans of lemon drink, a bag of fat purple grapes and a bar of chocolate.

They crossed the road at the lights and went through the parkland that rimmed the water till they found a spare picnic table right near the edge of the bay. A gentle breeze drifted in from the water and on the far side they could see the twinkling lights of Melbourne.

'Here, I'll take him,' Jacob offered. 'I can eat standing up.'

'I hope we're not spoiling him,' Nell said as she handed Sam over.

'You can't spoil them at this age, can you?'

'I don't know.'

'I'd rather eat standing up than sit in comfort while he bellows his lungs out.'

'That's how I feel, too.'

Nell tore off a corner of the paper, wrapped it around a piece of hot, crunchy fish and handed it to Jacob.

He bit into it and grinned. 'Nothing beats fish, fresh from the sea.'

'That's something you can't get in the Outback.'

'True,' he admitted. 'But then, only a select few can appreciate the hidden delights of life in the bush.'

'Because they're so hidden,' Nell said, but she smiled to show that it was her attempt at a joke. She looked at Sam, who was very peaceful now, with his head on Jacob's bulky shoulder, his eyes closed. 'Who do you think he looks like?'

Jacob twisted his neck, trying to examine him. 'I've no idea. He has your colouring.'

'Maybe he looks like his father. Tegan did.'

'Poor girl.'

'She was beautiful, Jacob.'

'Yes,' he said softly. 'She was.'

A seagull swooped low and stole a chip. Nell shooed it away before it could get another. 'I wonder what kind of boy Sam will grow into. Whether he'll be artistic or sporty or good at school.'

'He might be a philosopher.'

She laughed. 'He'll probably end up a cattleman.'

'Could do worse.' Jacob helped himself to another piece of fish.

Nell said, 'You seem to have a definite knack with babies. Sam looks like he's gone to sleep.'

'Are you sure?' Jacob turned to give Nell a better view of the baby's face.

'He looks sound asleep to me.'

'I might try sitting down, then.'

Sam snuffled and squirmed as Jacob lowered himself on to the long timber seat opposite Nell, but he quickly settled again, snuggling against Jacob's shoulder.

Nell thought how gorgeous the pair of them looked. She snapped the top of a drink can and handed it to Jacob. 'You'll need this after that salty fish.'

He took a long drink, set the can down thoughtfully and stared off into the distance.

'You're very pensive,' Nell said.

He continued to frown.

'Is something the matter?'

'I can't help wondering what would have happened if I'd stared your father down that day when he charged in on us.'

'But you did,' she cried, startled by the sudden turn of his thoughts. 'Don't you remember?'

'I was too upset to think straight.'

'I'll never forget that day. Dad was so angry his eyes were almost shaking in his head, but you more than stood your ground, Jacob. You pushed me to one side and started marching towards him like Achilles challenging Hector.'

'All I remember is that I didn't stand up to your old man the way I wanted to. I was afraid he would hurt you, or my mother.'

'You were as stubborn as he was,' Nell told him, smiling a little at the vivid memory. 'I was terrified you'd try to fight—that he might go into one of his violent tempers and shoot you. In the end, I was the one who told you to go. I ordered you away.'

'Did you really?'

'It seemed to take forever. You both just stood there, taking deep breaths and staring at each other.'

She shivered as she remembered the tension of it, the awful journey back to the homestead, the fearsome control of her father and her removal to Melbourne, how she'd cried for weeks.

'Don't think about it now, Jacob.'

'There's no point, is there?'

'None at all. It's ancient history. Here, try one of these grapes. They're so sweet and juicy.'

When they'd finished their meal, they threw the paper and empty cans into a rubbish bin and walked together back to her house.

'Perhaps I should take Sam now,' she said at her front gate. 'He might be less disturbed if we swap here, rather than inside with the lights and everything.'

They'd handed the baby to each other several times now, so Nell had no idea why, this time, it took so long and felt so incredibly intimate. Perhaps it was a matter of proximity.

Jacob didn't step away and neither did she. And her skin grew tight and her breathing faltered as they stood together in the dusky twilight. And then Jacob dipped his head and kissed her cheek. 'Night, Nell.'

'Would you like to come inside?' she found herself whispering.

'I'd love to.' He dropped a feather-soft kiss on her brow. 'But I'm not going to.'

Oh.

Her disappointment was silly. This was the first day of a month-long trial.

And she should be grateful that Jacob was much more cautious now than he had been when they were nineteen.

From the front seat of Jacob's Range Rover, Nell smiled when she saw a set of five-barred gates and a weathered timber signpost bearing the name Koomalong in dark green lettering.

Their vehicle rattled over the cattle grid.

'I'll get the gate,' she called, opening her door as soon as the vehicle came to a halt and jumping down, as eager as a child, home from boarding school.

She pushed the gate open and smiled again as she heard the musical squeak of its rusty hinge. Was there ever a gate in the Outback that didn't have squeaky hinges? She watched the dusty vehicle pass through, closed the gate and stood, looking about her, taking everything in.

Beyond the gate, a dirt track led up a gentle, brown-grassed slope and, on the brow of the hill, a magnificent old gum-tree stood clear against the blue blaze of the sky. The tree's solid trunk was silvery-white and its soft, grey-green leaves hung with a familiar tapering droop.

Nell sniffed at the air. The Outback smelled exactly as she remembered. She dragged in a deeper breath, absorbing with it the scents of dusty earth and cattle and the subtler notes of dry grass, of sunshine and eucalyptus.

She'd had occasional trips into the countryside during her marriage, but Robert had been uncomfortable away from the city so they'd never stayed long. Now, a kookaburra broke into laughter and a thrill of excitement rippled through her.

It was good to be back.

'Are you going to stand there all day?' Jacob called to her.

Turning, she saw the white flash of his teeth in his tanned face as he grinned back at her.

'Coming,' she called. And then, as she climbed back into her seat and pulled the door shut, she thought, *Jacob's right. This is my country. It's so good to be back in the bush.*

She turned to check Sam in his carrier on the back seat, happily cocooned between Jacob's dogs—a Labrador and a blue cattle dog which they'd collected from a boarding kennel in Roma.

There'd been an agitated few minutes when the dogs had first seen Sam and the tension had escalated when they'd located Ambrose in a cage in the back of the vehicle. But, after a quiet word from Jacob and a scratch behind the dogs' ears, they had settled down beautifully.

Now, as Jacob drove along bumpy tracks that crossed grassy paddocks dotted with cattle and gum-trees, Nell could make out the course of a creek marked by the wattle trees and melaleucas that lined its banks. Another burst of kookaburras' laughter sounded and, from the stretch of brown grassland, the piercing three-note call of a spur-winged plover.

She began to feel as if she'd come home.

Which was pretty silly, considering this wasn't exactly a homecoming. She had no actual right to feel so choked up and sentimental. She was moving into Jacob's home on a trial basis. Not the same thing at all.

Who knew if this experiment would work?

She wasn't sure what Jacob expected. He had reverted to being very practical and helpful. And Nell had been totally occupied with learning to cope with Sam while packing up. Any hint of romance had been dropped.

If the nineteen-year-old Nell had been told that she and Jacob Tucker could have spent so much time in each other's company without sharing so much as a kiss, she would never have believed it. Nell still found it hard to believe.

Secretly, she'd wondered if Jacob and she were complicit in a crazy mind game where they'd both pretended not to want each other. She had even indulged in the dangerous fantasy that once they got to Koomalong they would fall in love again and give up pretending. The horrible thing was, she knew deep down that if their experiment failed she would leave Koomalong broken-hearted.

So this was potentially dangerous territory and as the track turned a corner and a low, sprawling, white homestead became visible through a grove of shade trees, she had no idea what lay ahead.

The situation became crystal clear, however, the minute Jacob brought the vehicle to a halt at the bottom of the homestead's front steps and a figure uncurled with catlike grace from a cane chair on the veranda.

Nell swallowed her gasp of surprise as a young woman— a long-legged, green-eyed, Titian-haired girl in tight jeans and a low-necked blouse—sauntered confidently down the steps, her smile radiant as she waved at them.

'Who's that?' she asked Jacob.

He groaned. 'A girl from Roma.'

'A girlfriend?'

'No,' he said through gritted teeth. 'I met her once at a party.'

Nell's fingers trembled as she unfastened her seat belt and she chastised herself for not being prepared for something like this. Any woman with reasonable eyesight knew that Jacob was an attractive man. Chances were, he had quite a fan club and she would have to get used to it.

Slipping quickly out of the vehicle, she turned her attention to the dogs and to Sam, while behind her the young woman embraced Jacob with noisy enthusiasm.

The dogs, eager to be out of the car, bounded away clearly ecstatic to be free, darting about the garden, sniffing, lifting legs, exploring.

Nell unbuckled the straps that had held Sam safe, scooping him up. 'This is your new home, little man.'

He was delightfully drowsy and warm as she lifted him out. She kissed his soft, chubby cheek and cuddled him close, was overawed once more by how quickly and completely this darling little fellow had claimed her heart.

'Ooh, the baby!' the girl shrieked. 'Jacob's housekeeper has been telling me all about him. I've been dying to meet him. His name's Sam, isn't it?'

The redhead scurried around to Nell's side of the Range Rover. 'Hello.' She beamed at Nell and countless silver bangles tinkled as she offered her hand. 'I'm Katrina.'

Nell smiled carefully. 'Hello, Katrina. I'm Nell.'

Katrina pulled a face at Sam, screwing up her nose and pouting her bright lips. 'Aren't you the cutest button?' Straightening, she smiled more coyly at Nell, lifting a smooth eyebrow. 'You must be the baby's nanny.'

'Not exactly,' Nell said quietly and with necessary dignity. 'I'm his grandmother.'

Katrina giggled nervously and then she smacked a hand over her mouth. Clearly puzzled, she turned to Jacob, who had joined them, looking thunderous.

'So she's—' Katrina hooked a thumb towards Nell, her frown deepening. 'So if Nell's the baby's grandmother, then that must mean that you and she—' Looking flustered and red-faced, she shot another anxious glance Jacob's way and finished her sentence with a flap of her hand, setting the bangles jangling again.

'It was all a long time ago,' Nell said, taking pity on her. 'Water under the bridge.'

Jacob nodded, which she took to be approval. 'Come on inside,' he said. 'I'll show you around.'

'Just a minute. I need to fetch Sam's bag of tricks out of the car and I should rescue poor Ambrose from the back. Here, Jacob, you take Sam.'

Katrina watched with hawklike attention as Nell handed Sam to Jacob. Nell wondered if the other woman felt the same little swooning sensation she always felt when she saw tiny Sam cradled in Jacob's big, muscular arms.

With the nappy bag in one hand and Ambrose's cage in the other, she followed Jacob and Katrina up the steps, across the deep veranda and into his house.

It was a lovely house, quite old in the traditional Queenslander style, with a ripple iron roof, timber walls and a wide veranda running around all four sides. Generous-sized rooms with high ceilings opened on to the verandas and the central hallway, creating cross ventilation, so necessary in summer.

A classic timber archway separated the lounge and dining

rooms and all the walls were painted in pale tones, increasing the impression of light and space.

But the decor was very masculine and rather urban, with lots of dark leather and smoky glass and chrome, not quite the cosy country homestead that Nell had anticipated.

'Is it OK if I let Ambrose out of jail?' she asked Jacob.

He grinned. 'Sure.'

She released the catch on the cage and Ambrose approached his freedom cautiously, padding forward on soft paws with his tail high, like a feathery plume, as he explored the lounge room.

'Will the dogs be jealous if he's allowed inside?'

Jacob shook his head and was clearly very confident. 'Not at all. They're well-trained.'

Sharp-eyed Katrina was watching Nell closely. 'What do you think of the house?'

'It's beautiful,' Nell said diplomatically. She smiled warily at Jacob. 'Plenty of room for the three of us.'

'There are four bedrooms and a sleep-out on the veranda,' he said. 'Stacks of room for your quilting stuff.' He returned her smile and she fancied she caught a bright flash of warmth in his eyes, just for her.

Sam squirmed in Jacob's arms and let out a wail.

Nell recognised that cry. 'He needs changing.'

Katrina, smugly important, pointed to a room to their right. 'Hilda set up the cot and changing table in there.'

'Terrific.' Jacob headed in the direction she'd indicated. 'Let's get you comfortable, little mate.'

'Can't Nell take care of him?' Katrina interjected.

Jacob hesitated. Over the past few days he'd become almost as adept at nappy-changing as Nell. Now, he stood in the middle of the hallway, holding Sam while his frowning gaze flashed from one woman to the other.

'You didn't say what brings you out here, Katrina.'

'Oh, I was just passing this way and Hilda mentioned you were coming home today.'

He nodded cautiously. 'Thanks for dropping in.'

Katrina, hands on hips, watched him, watched Nell. Her mouth opened as if she planned to say something else, but then she seemed to change her mind and suddenly retrieved a tiny mobile phone from the pocket of her jeans. After flipping a few numbers and squinting at the phone's screen, she flashed them a triumphant grin. 'Something's come up,' she said. 'Sorry, I can't stay after all.'

Jacob's eyebrows lifted, but he said politely, 'That's a pity. Nell, can you take care of Sam? I'll see you out, Katrina.'

Nell decided that Sam needed a bath after the long and dusty journey. It would make him happy and would keep them both out of Jacob's way while he chatted with Katrina.

She had no trouble locating a bathroom and soon Sam was splashing happily in a few inches of water in the bottom of a big blue bath.

As Nell trickled warm water over his head and tummy, she could hear Katrina's voice coming from the side veranda and the low rumble of Jacob's responses. Fortunately, they were far enough away that she couldn't hear exactly what was being said.

Nell concentrated on Sam, telling him what a good boy he was as he splashed and cooed back at her and at last the voices stopped. Taking a soft, fluffy towel from the bathroom shelf, she scooped Sam up and bundled him in it. He looked impossibly cute and smelled wonderfully clean and soapy and so delicious that she couldn't resist showering him with kisses.

'I have to make the most of my opportunities while you're tiny,' she told him. 'There'll come a day when you won't relish being kissed by your grandma.'

A sound from the doorway startled her. Looking up, she saw Jacob standing there, one hand raised to grip the lintel, another propped on his hip, his expression closely shuttered.

'Oh, hello,' she said. 'I thought a bath would be refreshing for Sam.'

From outside came the sound of a car door closing and an engine revving. As the car moved away from the house, Nell felt a wave of sisterly concern for Katrina.

'I hope you were kind to her, Jacob.'

'I was exceedingly polite.'

Nell knew very well that politeness did not always equate with kindness, but she didn't think it was her place to say so now.

'And no, I haven't slept with her,' Jacob added, answering a question Nell hadn't asked but had certainly pondered. 'I'll start unpacking the car,' he said, turning abruptly, clearly upset or embarrassed. Or both.

Oh, boy. It wasn't the easiest of beginnings.

Nell looked down at Sam, who had found his thumb and had started to suck on it. Whatever the real story about Katrina was, her presence here had brought into sharp focus some home truths that Nell had diligently tried to overlook. No way had Jacob Tucker been celibate for the past twenty years.

And, while she and Jacob might be the same age, Nell knew that men, given half a chance, always went for younger women. Robert's new girlfriend was a perfect example. It was generally accepted that many men, like Jacob, got more interesting as they matured, while women...

Oh, heck, let's face it. Women simply...lose their looks.

Nell was pushing forty. There were stretch marks on her tummy and she was at least a whole dress size bigger than when she'd been nineteen. Perhaps she'd been totally, totally foolish to fantasise about Jacob falling in love with her again.

CHAPTER EIGHT

THE BEDROOMS AT Koomalong were large and cool with French windows opening on to the veranda. Nell was to sleep in a room next to Sam's, while Jacob's room was further down the hallway, closer to the kitchen.

She rather liked her room. It was old-fashioned and feminine with pale rose walls, a deeper rose carpet and soft white floor-length curtains. The double bed was covered in a white spread embroidered with sprigs of flowers and there was an English oak dressing table with a swing mirror and all manner of little drawers.

'This is lovely,' she told Jacob as he piled her suitcases neatly in front of the big silky oak wardrobe.

'Glad you like it. Come and take a look at the sleep-out on the side veranda. See if it will suit as a quilting room.'

It was, she soon discovered, perfect. A long section of veranda on the northern side had been closed in, with deep sash windows that looked out over a long, shady paddock. There was even a big old table there, perfect for laying out fabric and for fiddling with colours and patterns.

'Will this do?' Jacob asked, watching her face carefully.

'It's wonderful. So big. And it has lovely vibes. I'm sure this will be a very inspiring place to work in.' She beamed at him. 'And thank you for showing me this room before you showed me the kitchen.'

He looked surprised. 'I don't expect you to spend much time in the kitchen. I'm happy to do my share of the cooking.'

'Really?' Robert had never cooked so much as an egg.

Jacob was keen to show her more. 'Sam's still asleep, so why don't you come outside and I'll introduce you to the horses. I think you'll love Belladonna, my mare.'

'Oh, yes, your mare is Koomalong's star attraction.'

'She's the main reason you agreed to come here.'

'Exactly.'

Their voices were playful, but when their eyes met the playfulness vanished. A shiver trembled through Nell as she stood, trapped by Jacob's serious gaze.

If he'd looked at her that way when they'd been nineteen, she would have quickly closed the distance between them, thrown her arms around him and kissed him till he smiled at her. They would have ended up laughing in each other's arms, kissing some more, tumbling on to the grass together, making love.

At thirty-nine, Nell was much more careful. Walking towards the door, she said softly, 'Show me the way to these horses.'

At the back of the house there was the usual scattering of farm buildings—a machinery shed built from corrugated iron, garages, a laundry and, beyond these, the stables and a horse paddock.

As they walked, Jacob said, 'In case you were wondering, I'm not expecting any other women to turn up on my doorstep.'

'Oh, I wasn't wondering,' Nell lied. 'I know you can't have lived like a Trappist monk for the past twenty years.'

His mouth tilted in a crooked smile.

'I must say I'm surprised you've never married,' she continued, probing gently. 'I'm assuming you must have had serious relationships, though. There must have been women you've lived with.'

'Not for more than a few weeks. And there hasn't been anyone since I bought Koomalong.'

Nell stopped walking. 'A few weeks? Is that all? In twenty years?'

He gave an impatient shrug. 'My lifestyle hasn't suited settling down. I've been on the move a lot.'

'So if I stay here for a whole month, I'll be breaking some kind of record?'

'I suppose you will.' Jacob laughed gruffly. 'Of course I'm more settled here.'

She felt compelled to probe further. 'It's sad that you've had trouble committing.'

He shot her a hard look, thrust his hands into his pockets and squared his jaw. 'At least I didn't end up marrying someone simply because it might have been convenient.'

Nell blushed. 'Touché. Point taken.'

She was glad they'd reached the horse paddock and she could turn her attention to the four animals grazing there.

'Oh, they're lovely, Jacob. You've always had a good eye for horses.' She admired their lines and the healthy sheen on their coats. 'Who looked after them while you were away?'

'My neighbour's son was happy to keep an eye on them.'

'And ride them, I'll bet.'

'That was part of the arrangement.'

Nell pointed to the bay mare with a pretty white blaze on her forehead. 'Is this Belladonna?'

'Yes. What do you think of her?'

'Gorgeous lines. Fabulous legs.' Nell held out her hand and Belladonna, curious, came to the fence. Nell laughed as she gently stroked her nose and the horse nuzzled her palm, no doubt hoping for a treat. 'Sorry, Belladonna. I'll bring you something tomorrow.' She smiled into the horse's soft brown eyes. 'She looks sensitive, but rather gentle. I can't wait to ride her.'

'Exactly how long is it since you've ridden?'

It wasn't easy to admit the truth. Nell fiddled with a piece of wire wound around a fence post. 'I'm afraid I haven't ridden a horse since the day I last saw you.'

'That long?' Jacob sounded shocked. 'You'll get very stiff and sore, then.'

'I'll have to take it in gentle stages then, won't I?'

'You will. In very gentle stages.'

Nell looked up, caught the silvery shimmer in Jacob's eyes and her heart did a tumble turn. She was quite sure he was thinking about gentle stages that had nothing to do with riding horses.

Jacob set the wok of stir-fried beef and noodles at the back of the stove and went in search of Nell. She'd been feeding Sam and he wanted to tell her that dinner was ready when she was.

There was a lamp on in the lounge room and an empty feeding bottle on the coffee table, but no sign of Nell or Sam.

He headed down the hall to Sam's room, but was only halfway there when he heard Nell call, 'Jacob, is that you? Come here quickly.'

There was a sharp edge to her voice and he couldn't tell if it was excitement or panic. His heart leapt as he dashed to Sam's doorway. 'What's the matter?'

Sam was lying on the changing table, his bottom half bare, legs kicking. Nell had been laughing at him and she turned to Jacob, her face alight, glowing.

'Sam smiled at me,' she said.

'No kidding?'

'It was a genuine smile. Not an accidental, windy grin, but the real thing. A proper and deliberate smile. Look.'

Jacob stepped closer and Nell leaned over Sam, grinning at him madly. 'Who's a happy little man?' she asked in a high, animated voice.

Almost immediately, Sam's eyes lit up, his arms and legs pumped madly and his face broke into a smile, a broad, no-doubt-about-it, fully-fledged grin that mirrored Nell's.

Jacob let out a deep chuckle of delight. 'How about that? What a great little guy.'

'Doesn't it change him?' Nell said. 'The smile makes him look so grown up, like a real little human being.'

Jacob laughed, leaned forward and pulled an ultra-happy face at Sam and watched him smile back.

'This is his first important milestone—learning to smile, being happy. Doesn't he look gorgeous?' Nell's blue eyes shone with joy and excitement.

She looked luminous.

Jacob swallowed a sudden constriction in his throat. 'Have you any idea how gorgeous *you* look when you're glowing like that?'

Her eyes widened.

Unable to help himself, Jacob lifted a bright strand of her hair that had strayed from its clip and tucked it behind her ear. She stood very still as he traced the curve of her earlobe, caressed the pink warmth of her cheek. She gasped as his thumb brushed the soft underside of her lower lip.

'Nell,' he whispered.

'Jacob?' Her voice sounded faraway, dreamy.

'I told you that I had no romantic agenda for bringing you here.'

'Yes, you did.'

'I lied. I'm sorry.'

A rosy tide spread from her throat to her cheeks. 'You—you—'

'I want to kiss you.'

She smiled shakily. 'But—'

'No buts.' He touched a finger to her lips. 'I have never wanted anything more.' He'd wanted to kiss her for days, had been going crazy with wanting her. 'It's going to happen, Nell.'

She offered no resistance as he drew her in to him and, with gentle, devastating purpose, touched his lips to hers…

Ah, yes…she was so soft and sweet and tantalising.

Nothing mattered but this.

Nell.

He gathered her closer and kissed her less gently, teased her lips apart with his tongue and Nell was warm and pliant and melting into him. Her arms wound around his neck, her breasts pressed against him and her lips parted freely, welcoming him, urging him to deepen the kiss.

At last…

At long, long last…

Nell in his arms—his fiery, passionate Nell. A storm broke inside Jacob. He closed his eyes, let his senses drown in her.

This was how Nell tasted and how she kissed. These eager lips were her lips, this wonderful, womanly body hers.

How had he survived all these years without tasting and touching and loving Nell?

His fever was contagious. Nell threaded frantic fingers through his hair and wriggled closer, drawing him deeper and deeper into their private maelstrom. He cupped the fullness of her breasts through the soft cotton of her T-shirt, grazed his thumbs over their tips, and she moaned softly, destroying the last shreds of his control.

Beside them on the changing table, Sam let out a squawk of protest.

Nell stiffened as if she'd been shot. She pulled back. 'Oh, goodness.'

She pressed a hand to her throat, was panting a little as she looked down at Sam, who was bellowing now.

'Hush, Sam, what's the matter?' She lifted him up and soothed him. 'There, there. Were you getting cold? You're all right.' Over her shoulder she shot Jacob a gentle reproach. 'He might have fallen off the table.'

Too happy about their kiss, Jacob merely smiled. 'He was quite safe. He can't roll over yet.' With a hand at her waist, he said, 'Why don't we put him down and try that again?'

It was not the best joke he'd ever cracked and he realised that the spell, if that was what it had been, was already broken. Nell grabbed the chance to resume her former composure.

'Just behave,' she said, pushing him gently in the chest with both hands. 'And remember—'

'What? Remember what?'

She surprised him by kissing him quickly. 'We're all on probation here.'

Oh, yeah...

He supposed he'd spoil everything by rushing in foolishly, the way he had when they were young.

Sam had stopped crying and Nell laid him back on the changing table. Deftly she closed the tapes on his nappy and snapped the little studs on his sleeping suit.

'You're a dab hand at that now,' Jacob said. 'By the way, dinner's ready whenever you are.'

'Lovely. Thanks.' She gave him a grateful smile.

He knew he wasn't mistaken. There was an extra-happy light in her eyes that hadn't been there before.

'You're a good cook,' Nell said as they ate their evening meal at the scrubbed pine table in the kitchen. 'I suppose your mother taught you.'

'Yes, she seemed to enjoy passing on what she knew.'

'Maggie's a gifted teacher. Much better than the ones I had when I went to adult education classes.'

Jacob's eyebrows lifted. 'I've been meaning to ask. Why didn't you finish your university degree?'

She shook her head. 'I'm afraid I lost my enthusiasm for the arts.'

'But you loved your studies. You were mad about poetry.'

'I know, but... I took a job in a city bookshop.'

'OK.' He pulled a face as he accepted this. 'Is that when you started the adult education classes?'

'No, that came later. After I was married. I began with cooking classes because Robert wanted me to give dinner parties. And then I took classes in garden design and interior decorating so that our place in Toorak could look just right.' She rolled her eyes. 'It had to be *the very latest thing, darling.*'

'That doesn't sound like you.'

'I know. And then there was public speaking.'

Jacob looked shocked. 'Public speaking?'

She laughed nervously. 'I wasn't actually planning to speak in public, but I wanted to be more confident when I was talking to Robert's barrister friends.'

'For crying out loud. You were full of confidence when I knew you.'

'Was I?' She shrugged and said uneasily, 'That was different. Moving in Robert's circle, I felt I needed classes to help me to express opinions without sounding apologetic.'

This was greeted by silence.

Embarrassed that she'd revealed too much, Nell traced the willow pattern on her plate with her fork.

He said softly, 'I'm glad none of that really changed you, Nell.'

She looked up to find him smiling at her.

'Maybe you think that because I'm back in the bush.' She sent him a cheeky grin. 'I'm reverting to type.'

'Whatever the reason, I'm exceedingly grateful.'

It was one of those shining moments of connection, of *knowing*. Nell was on the brink of leaving her chair. Every instinct urged her to walk to the other end of the table, put her arms around Jacob and kiss him. But from beyond the kitchen came a wail from Sam.

And then there were more wails in quick succession.

She smiled ruefully. 'Sounds like he's going to have one of his restless nights.'

They spent the rest of the evening taking it in turns to pace with Sam while finishing their meal and tidying the kitchen. By the time they finally got Sam back to sleep, Nell was exhausted.

'You look dead on your feet,' Jacob told her. 'It's been a long journey today. Get to bed.'

The next day was set aside for settling in properly, finishing unpacking and taking a quick tour of the property and in the cool of the afternoon Jacob volunteered to mind Sam while Nell took Belladonna for a short ride.

'Are you sure you'll be OK with Sam?' she asked for the hundredth time.

'Of course. Anyway, you won't be gone long.'

'If he fusses, put him on the floor in the lounge room for a kick. I did that this morning and he loves it.'

'I'll remember. Now *you* remember to take it easy.' Jacob checked her saddle and girth straps and bridle as many times as Nell had quizzed him about Sam. 'It's a long, long time since you've ridden.'

She took Belladonna for a lap around the paddock to prove she still knew how to stay on a horse and Jacob was satisfied.

'I'll just take her down to the creek,' Nell said. 'I might sit there for a bit and enjoy the peace of the bush.'

'Why not? I guess it's a long time since you last sat on a creek bank.'

Nell nudged Belladonna forward.

'Keep out of tree branches,' Jacob called.

She smiled and waved and Belladonna broke into a canter and then a gallop.

Now *this* was living—the sense of gathering speed and the powerful rhythm of a beautiful animal beneath her. There was nothing Nell loved more than the rush of wind in her face, the smell of dust stirred by the horse's hooves, the hint of eucalyptus.

She reached the creek quite quickly. Too quickly. She

would have loved to continue, but she knew she would pay sorely if she went too far. Reining Belladonna to a walk, she continued along the high bank until she reached a point where the creek widened into a quiet pool.

With the reins securely tied to a tree branch, she sat on a smooth, sun-warmed rock and stared down at the water. It was so still she could see the sky reflected in it. There was a tangle of gnarled tree roots sticking up in the middle of the pool, no doubt washed downstream by the heavy rains of a previous summer. On the far side a lone white heron fished the shallows.

There was nothing special about the scene. It could have been any ordinary old creek anywhere in the Outback. But sitting there, alone, on a shelf of pink granite rock, looking out at the tea-coloured water, at the endless stretch of dry red earth and the wide, clean skies, Nell heard the call of a warbling magpie and felt hot tears stinging her eyes.

She swiped at them with the backs of her hands and was able to laugh. What a nostalgic old granny she'd become.

It was close to dark by the time she got back. The light was fading and in the horse yard behind the stables she couldn't see properly to undo Belladonna's saddle. She had to feel for the buckles and the girth strap and she lifted the saddle high to avoid hitting the horse's back. Then she hung the saddle and blanket on a fence railing, before carefully testing Belladonna's hooves with her fingers to check for stones.

Satisfied that all was well, she turned the mare loose in the paddock and stowed the saddle in the tack room.

From the house, the warm glow of the kitchen lights spooled out into the twilight-shrouded backyard and, as she

crossed the lawn, she hoped Sam had been on his best behaviour for Jacob.

Suddenly a cat's screech and a cacophony of barking dis-
rupted the peaceful twilight. Ahead of her, a marmalade
streak shot up the back steps, with Jacob's dogs tearing after
it. The kitchen door must have been unlatched, for it swung
forward and all three animals burst inside, the dogs barking
so loudly they sounded demented.

What an uproar! The dogs weren't allowed inside the house
and, in this frenzy, they could wreck the place. Nell hurried
after them.

As she reached the back steps, she heard Sam's piercing
cries in addition to the frenzied barking and the ear-splitting
yowls of feline terror.

She dashed through the kitchen, dimly aware of appetis-
ing cooking smells and that the table had been set with a
bright seersucker cloth. She followed the noise through to
the lounge room, taking in the scene at a glance.

Jacob was standing in the middle of the room, holding a
red-faced, screaming Sam and Ambrose was halfway up the
wall, clinging to the curtain. The cat's teeth were bared and
his tail bristled fiercely as he gripped the silky fabric for dear
life while the dogs leapt and barked up at him.

Then Jacob lent his voice to the general mêlée.

'Blue! Dander!' he roared at the dogs. 'Get out of here.
Now!'

Unfortunately, the normally obedient animals were
whipped into too great a passion and took absolutely no notice of their master.

Nell stepped into the fray, arms outstretched. 'Give me
Sam,' she called.

Jacob spun around. His eyes widened when he saw her,

but she couldn't tell if he was relieved or dismayed that she'd caught him in the middle of this dilemma.

She hurried forward. 'Here, I'll take Sam.'

He thrust the wailing baby at her. 'Thanks.' Then he dashed across the room and grabbed the Labrador by the collar. 'Sit!' he ordered.

The dog immediately stopped barking. He gave Jacob one brief look of outrage at being deprived of such fantastic fun, then sat.

'You, too,' Jacob ordered the blue cattle dog. 'Sit!'

And suddenly the only sounds in the room were Sam's terrified screams.

'There, there,' Nell soothed him and cuddled him close. 'You're OK now, sweetheart. Shh.'

'Out!' Jacob addressed the dogs and pointed to the doorway and, to everyone's relief, they obediently trotted forward. But they kept looking back, like children sent to their rooms for misbehaving, hoping Jacob's hard heart would soften and set them free to torment Ambrose again.

When the dogs were safely outside at last, Jacob turned to Nell. Sam was still snuffling and sobbing against her neck, but she had managed to reduce his terror.

'What happened?' she asked, patting his little back.

Jacob's eyebrows rose as he scratched his head. 'Blowed if I know. The dogs have been so good about the cat.' He looked up at Ambrose, still clinging to the curtain. 'Better get you down, mate.' Reaching high, he clasped Ambrose around the middle with one hand while he prised his claws from the fabric.

And then Jacob stood facing Nell, looking embarrassed and cradling the cat in his arms in much the same way that she was holding Sam.

'Is Ambrose OK?'

'Seems fine.' Jacob checked one fluffy orange flank and then the other. 'No sign of blood or missing fur.'

'That's good. Poor fellow. I think the fight started near the back steps. Maybe Ambrose tried to eat out of one of the dog's bowls.'

'You could be right.' Jacob gave the cat a thoughtful scratch between the ears. 'My fault. I forgot to feed him.'

Nell gave him a small smile. 'You've been busy dealing with Sam and dinner.'

'Yeah.' Ambrose twisted in his hands and Jacob was forced to release him on to the floor. As the cat began to wash himself, Jacob straightened and looked at Nell. 'Did you have a good ride?'

'It was wonderful, thanks.'

'Not too stiff?'

'Not so far.'

He had never looked more gorgeous as he stood there in battered old jeans and an equally old T-shirt with a hole near the neck. If she hadn't been holding Sam she might have dashed across the room and hurled herself into his arms, told him how very much she'd wished he'd been with her down at the creek.

But Sam began to fret. 'Did he behave for you?' she remembered to ask.

'He was just starting to grizzle before the cat and the dogs arrived.'

'I guess he's due for his evening bottle.'

'I'll take care of that.'

'But you've already done your share.'

'You need to soak in a warm bath. If you don't relax your muscles after the ride, you'll be sorry.' Jacob was wearing his masterful look now. 'After, with luck, we might be able to enjoy a drink before dinner.'

With meek thanks, Nell headed for the bathroom and, half an hour later, feeling wonderfully warm and clean and relaxed, she found the lounge room restored and Jacob pouring two glasses of chilled wine.

'Is Sam asleep?'

'Out like a light.' He handed her a glass. 'Take the weight off your feet.'

She sank gratefully into an armchair. 'This is very civilised.' She sipped her wine and wondered why she wasn't calm. She'd just had a beautifully relaxing bath and surely, by now, she should be able to sit in a room with Jacob Tucker without feeling as if she might swoon at any moment.

Jacob, on the other hand, seemed excessively calm, with his mind on other things entirely. 'Be honest,' he said with a sweeping gesture that took in their surroundings. 'Tell me what you think of this room.'

Nell followed his gaze. 'It's lovely and big.'

'What about the furniture?'

'It's very—' She hesitated.

'It feels like office furniture?' he finished for her.

'Perhaps,' she said carefully.

'It doesn't really feel like a home?' he prompted.

Nell nodded thoughtfully.

He angled a wry grin. 'If you'd decorated it, would you have used all this leather and chrome?'

'I tend to go for a more traditional look,' she admitted. 'This is such a lovely old timber home. I'd probably fill it with comfy chintz lounges and deckle-edged mirrors, lots more timber and antique furniture.' She smiled at him. 'I have something that might help to warm this room up a little.'

'Yeah?' He was intrigued.

'I'll be back in a minute.'

She hurried into her new sewing room and came back with her arms full of quilts.

'You could think about hanging one of these on the wall,' she said. 'Or even, if you draped one over the sofa, it would help to soften the starkness of the dark leather.'

With a flick of her arm, she opened a quilt and tossed it over the sofa. It was one of her favourites, a carefully pieced, dramatic blend of ochre, cream, aqua and green.

'Wow! That's beautiful!' Setting his glass aside, Jacob stood and examined the quilt more closely. He picked up a corner and fingered a fine seam. 'You're so talented, Nell. And it's the perfect colour combination for here. The colours of the Outback.'

'I made it once when I was feeling homesick for the bush.' She held it up against a blank wall. 'It goes well with this room, doesn't it? You could hang it here, or above the sideboard.'

'It would look stunning.'

'I have some leftover fabric. I could make throw cushions to match.'

'I wouldn't want to put you to too much trouble.'

'It's no trouble. Quilting's my thing. Honestly, I love it. I find it very comforting to be able to plan a whole quilt and have it turn out exactly the way I wanted it to.' She laughed. 'See? I'm a control freak.'

'You're a genius.'

Before she realised quite what was happening, Jacob was swinging her off her feet and the quilt dropped from her hands.

A laugh bubbled from her. 'I'm glad you like my quilts.'

'I like a damn sight more than your quilts, my girl.'

Their faces were inches apart. Nell was instantly ablaze as she looked into Jacob's eyes and saw his unguarded desire.

'I'm very taken with everything about you, Nell,' he said softly as he lowered her to the floor. 'Your quilts, your smile, the way you look when you hold Sam, the way you look right now.'

'How do I look right now?'

He squinted and pretended to study her. 'I'd say you look… like an incredibly sexy grandmother.'

She laughed again. 'Don't I look like a happy grandmother?'

His eyes shimmered. 'That, too.'

'I'm remarkably happy, Jacob.'

He framed her face with his hands. 'Any idea about the cause of all this happiness?'

'Oh, I think I like being here.'

'Here?' He dropped a tiny kiss on her brow.

'Right here,' she breathed, lifting her lips to kiss the roughness of his jaw.

'Anything special about here?' Jacob asked as he pressed his lips to her eyelids.

Nell was burning up. Any minute now, she would be a pile of cinders on the floor.

'Tell me,' he insisted as his lips roamed close to her ear.

She whispered, 'I'm rather partial to the way you kiss.'

'Great answer, Nell.'

Jacob's arms wrapped around her and he covered her open lips with his.

As soon as their mouths met, they both knew that tonight kisses would not be enough. Greedily, their hands sought to touch and explore and their bodies strained together, pressing in with an urgent and greedy precision.

'Come with me,' Jacob murmured, kissing her mouth, her jaw, her throat.

Anywhere, anywhere...she answered silently. And in a haze of heat she went with him down the hallway, through a doorway and into his bedroom.

CHAPTER NINE

IT WAS ONLY then, when Nell saw Jacob's lamp-lit room, his enormous bed with its solid timber headboard, its scattering of silver and grey pillows and huge black duvet, that she felt a splash of cold dismay. This was the first time she'd been with a man since her divorce.

Jacob sensed her hesitation. 'What's the matter, Nell?'

'I'm—' she swallowed the nervous blockage in her throat '—I'm so old now.'

He threw back his head and laughed. 'You're no older than I am.'

'It's different for a woman. Age matters more, makes more of a change.'

'Rubbish,' he muttered thickly and he pulled her towards him. 'Come here and tell me you're old.'

Against his shoulder, she protested, 'I'm certainly not the nubile girl you seduced.'

'Of course you're not. You're even lovelier, Nell.'

'I'm nearly forty.'

'So what?' Jacob kissed her jaw, her earlobe, buried his face in her neck. 'You smell nineteen.'

She couldn't help laughing. Jacob had always made her laugh. 'That's because I used Sam's baby soap.'

'I'll buy a truckload of Sam's baby soap.' He kissed her mouth, nibbled at her lower lip and stilled her laughter, sending fresh flames of longing coursing through her. 'You taste like my Nell.'

Oh, Jacob, you darling man.

His hands gripped her bottom and he held her against his hardness. 'You feel like my Nell.'

A soft groan came from him, a small whimper from her. He dipped his mouth lower.

Nell was grateful for the subdued lamplight as his hands slipped under her T shirt, guided it up and over her head.

Oh, gosh. Why hadn't she thought to wear a sexy bra, something lacy and pretty, instead of this plain white cotton? But apparently it didn't matter. Jacob was too busy hauling his T-shirt off. How magnificent his chest was. Such shoulders.

Then he was kissing her again, steering her backwards till her trembling legs met his bed. He eased her down to the mattress, joined her there, helped her out of her bra. And he was so enraptured by what he found that Nell forgot to worry about how round and pale her body was, forgot to worry about anything.

Her eyes drifted closed, her mouth fell open in a soundless exclamation as Jacob paid flattering homage to her femininity. She was nineteen again, head over heels in love with this man, wanting only this man.

And *how* she wanted him.

In a fever of haste they shed the rest of their clothing. A happy little cry escaped her as they came together once more, rolling into each other's embrace, desperate to savour the electrifying thrill of skin against skin, of Jacob's rigid nakedness against her soft contours.

He hugged her to him. 'You're beautiful, Nell. You're gorgeous. You haven't changed a bit.' Easing back a little, he traced the curve of her hip. 'All woman,' he murmured. And then, 'Ah, there it is.'

'What is?'

'The little butterfly-shaped birthmark on your hip.'

Bending forward, he kissed the spot on her hip, making a warm circle with his lips and his tongue. Longing and happy memories swept over Nell as he trailed kisses from the dip of her waist to the swell of her breast.

She fleetingly marvelled that everything was happening so easily. There was nothing awkward or jarring to hinder them and they found ways to please each other with surprising ease. Every touch, every kiss was fuel to the fire of their longing.

When Jacob paused to reach into a drawer in his bedside table, Nell almost protested. She felt so gloriously reckless she wanted to throw caution to the wind. But then sanity returned. After all, she was almost forty. They had a grandson.

And all she wanted now was Jacob.

She watched his eyes as he joined her, saw deep emotion married to dark hunger. Then she closed her eyes and cried his name once before she was submerged in a spiralling whirlpool of need.

She lay with her head on his shoulder. 'That was amazing.'

Jacob dropped a kiss on her forehead. 'I felt so close to you.'

Nell pressed her lips into his neck, tasted the salt on his skin. 'I didn't expect to be so uninhibited.'

He smiled at her. 'That's because this is where we're meant to be.' He let his hand trail down her arm, then drew a circle over her stomach. 'And this is where our little baby grew.'

'Yes.' The monosyllable caught in her throat.

He pressed his splayed hand gently against her stomach and she watched the darkness of his skin against the paleness of hers. She felt the warmth of him there, awakening memories of her pregnancy, of the weight of the baby inside her, the strong little limbs kicking.

The awful loss…

'Oh, Jacob.'

She wanted to tell him about Tegan, about her pregnancy and how she'd felt while carrying their child, but, without warning, tears spilled.

'What is it, Nell? What's the matter?'

'I loved Tegan.'

'I know, sweetheart. I know.'

'Even before she was born, I loved her so much.'

Suddenly, she was weeping—weeping for the loss of her baby and for the loss of this man whom she'd loved more than anything in the world. In one fell sweep she'd lost everyone who had mattered. And now Tegan was gone forever.

Jacob held her tightly and buried his face in her hair. She wasn't sure if he was weeping too, but they clung to each other, rocking gently, sharing the pain they'd borne for too long, offering the comfort that only they could give.

It was quite a long while before the flow of Nell's tears stopped, but she felt awed by a sweet sense of release, as if the crying had cleansed her.

She looked at Jacob in the faint lamplight, gave him a shaky smile.

He smiled back at her, kissed her nose, her damp cheeks and eyelids. 'Everything's going to be OK now, Nell.'

'Yes, I know.'

This was a new beginning.

'Roll over,' he said. 'I'll give you a massage.'

'There's no need. I'm OK now.'

'Roll over.'

Shooting him a shy smile, Nell obeyed. And very soon she was inexpressibly grateful as his warm hands rubbed and kneaded her back, soothing and freeing muscles that she hadn't realised had become tense, dropping warm kisses wherever he rubbed. She could feel her body relaxing and letting go, felt happiness spreading through her again like warmed honey.

Until gradually the tempo and rhythm of the massage changed. Jacob's hands slowed and his fingers began to trace gentle, dreamy circles on her back. He trailed feather-soft caresses down her spine to her buttocks and thighs and a new thrilling tension blossomed in Nell.

Rolling on to her side, she whispered, 'My turn.'

'You want to give me a massage?'

'More or less,' she replied, running seeking fingers over his magnificent chest, venturing lower. 'On your back, man.'

Jacob did as he was told.

He felt *so-o-o* good. Nell gloried in him, reawakening suppressed memories as her hands explored eagerly, rediscovering the wonder of his satiny skin stretched smooth and taut over masculine muscles, adding bold kisses wherever she touched him.

Soon it grew too much for Jacob and he took control again, moving over her, lavishing her with kisses as he took her, once more, to the moon.

When Sam woke it was still dark. His wails penetrated Nell's sleep and she sat up quickly, her heart racing. She didn't think she'd been asleep for very long, but it had been long enough for her to feel confused by her surroundings. She took a moment or two to remember she was in Jacob's room. In his bed.

He stirred beside her. 'Is that Sam?' he asked sleepily.

'Yes. He'll be hungry.' Nell yawned and her stomach rumbled. 'Actually, I'm hungry too.'

'That's because we forgot to eat dinner.'

'Oh, heavens, you were cooking something. What happened to it?'

'I turned the heat off while you were in the bath. I'm afraid the casserole's still in the oven.'

She giggled. 'It might still be OK. I'll check while I'm warming Sam's bottle. If it's burned, I might fix a snack. Do you fancy cheese on toast?'

'Sure. I'll help you make it.'

Nell was so used to the 'wifely' role she'd played during her marriage that she almost ordered Jacob to stay where he was, but he was already rolling out of his side of the bed. She wondered where her T-shirt was, switched on the lamp and saw it lying on the floor near the door. Actually, there were articles of clothing scattered all over the floor.

'Look at this room,' she cried, smacking her hand to her forehead in mock dismay. 'What shocking behaviour. You'd think grandparents would set a better example.'

'Some old folk have no sense of decorum,' Jacob agreed solemnly.

It became a pattern.

In the nights that followed, if Sam woke around two a.m.,

Jacob would grumble, but then good-naturedly head for the kitchen to heat his bottle while Nell changed the baby and brought him back to their bed. They would talk softly, weave dreams for Sam while he drank, brought up wind and fell back to sleep again, making soft baby sounds as he snuggled between them.

During the day, Jacob had work to attend to around the property but, as he still had cattle scattered on agistments around the state, his holding at Koomalong was relatively small and manageable and he made time to be with his new little family.

One day they had a picnic. Jacob and Nell took Sam in his basket and cooked sausages over a fire beside the creek. On another day they went for a long walk through the bush with Sam in a baby sling and the dogs hard at their heels. They even went riding together and Jacob carried Sam in the sling.

Many evenings, they spent on the western veranda, Ambrose purring, Sam in Nell's lap, or being walked up and down if he was restless. Jacob's dogs sprawled at their feet while they watched the sun drip molten gold as it sank into the distant hills and they listened to corellas and cockatiels calling to each other as they winged their way homewards through the purple light.

In the evenings, they cooked together in the homestead kitchen, experimenting with new pasta dishes, a fancy stir-fry or risotto.

Nell wrote a long letter to Jean to keep her abreast of Sam's latest antics. He was piling on weight and he smiled all the time now. He could hold his rattle and he was very close to rolling over from his back to his tummy. She spoke to Jacob's mother, who rang one night from the Kimberley and they had a long and cosy chat, just like the old times when they'd talked in the kitchen at Half Moon.

When Hilda Knowles, Jacob's cleaning woman, came to do the ironing and to give the house its weekly 'once-over', she made it quite clear that she very much approved of Nell.

'I've never seen Mr Tucker looking so well,' she confided.

Nell looked up from folding Sam's freshly laundered clothes. 'Has Jacob been ill?'

'Not ill, no. He's always been as fit as a fiddle. Perhaps *well* isn't quite the right word.'

Hilda set the iron to rest and her brow puckered while she gave Jacob's condition careful thought. 'There's always been something in his eyes that troubled me. A sadness. A kind of shadow. And it's gone now. When he smiles, his eyes light up as if there's a constant happy glow inside him. I reckon you must have put that there, love.'

Nell fervently hoped so, but neither she nor Jacob talked aloud about their Koomalong experiment. No doubt they were both frightened that talking about it might break the magic spell. But secretly she was confident that things were working out just fine.

The parcel from Jean arrived in the third week.

Sam was awake after his morning nap and he was kicking on a blanket on the lounge room floor when the mail truck's horn sounded. Most of the envelopes were addressed to Jacob, but there was a large rectangular parcel for Nell and she brought it into the lounge room to sit on the floor beside Sam as she unwrapped layers of brown paper.

Inside was a box covered with a collage of pictures cut from magazines—the kind of collage a child might create with pictures of rock stars, sporting heroes and film stars mixed in with whales, dolphins and baby seals.

Mystified, Nell opened the box and found a pile of Christmas and birthday cards—all the cards she had ever sent to Tegan.

Jean had written:

I was cleaning out Tegan's room when I found these and I thought you should have them. There is one we need to talk about.

'She kept them all,' Nell whispered, her throat tightening as the truth of this sank in.

Tegan had kept every single card that Nell had ever sent, all of them, right back to the card covered in mischievous tabby kittens, sent for her daughter's fifth birthday.

Nell had completely forgotten that card, but now, seeing those cheeky kittens playing with a ball of red wool, she could remember exactly how she'd felt when she'd bought it. She could recall the ages she'd spent in the newsagent's before making that selection, the agonies she'd gone through trying to decide what to write inside.

Finally, she'd settled on a very simple message: *Happy Birthday, dear Tegan. Love, Nell.* She'd only ever signed her name as Nell.

Now, as she sifted through the cards she'd sent, she felt renewed gratitude to Jean who'd allowed this precious contact.

How carefully she'd selected these cards. When Tegan had been small there'd been cute cards with fairies and flowers, kittens, puppies and ducklings. As her daughter had grown older Nell had chosen funny cards, or ones she'd hoped were funny, then something 'cool' during the teenage years.

At Christmas Nell had always sent Tegan an 'Australiana' card—beautiful scenes from the Outback, a gentle nudge to acquaint her daughter with her natural roots—creamy paperbarks beside a quiet billabong, a dog on a tucker box, gumtrees, blue hills at the edge of a flat, red plain.

Nell frowned as she reached the last Christmas card she'd sent Tegan. There was something tucked inside it—folded sheets of writing paper.

Puzzled, she unfolded the pages, then realised they were nothing to do with her. This was a letter for Tegan, written closely in a spiky, masculine hand. Goosebumps broke out on Nell's skin as she recognised Jacob's handwriting.

She shouldn't read this. But it was already too late. Her eyes had skimmed the opening paragraph, the first page.

Dear Tegan,

I can never thank you enough for writing to me. You have no idea what it meant to hear from you and I'm so happy to know you're alive and well. I have a daughter!!!! How fabulous is that?

At last I know what became of my child.

I understand that you must wonder why you were given up for adoption. Believe me, Tegan, I did not want to lose you. I wanted you. You are the result of my love for a very special woman. I planned to provide for you, to care for you and your mother, but circumstances beyond my control intervened.

Nell's vision blurred.

She couldn't bear this. Jacob's letter was so sweet, but she shouldn't go on to read the next page. Tears fell as she folded it and slipped it back inside the envelope.

Had Jean Browne known Jacob's letter was there? Had she read it?

Wiping her eyes with the backs of her hands, Nell looked down at Sam, kicking on the rug, batting his hands in the air as he tried to reach the bright, stuffed Humpty Dumpty that Jacob had bought him. The baby saw her looking at him and his little face broke into a grin.

Oh, the sweetheart.

The dear little man. Nell scooped him up and cuddled him close. How warm and alive and delightfully chubby he was.

Tegan's bonny little boy.

With the baby in her lap, she tidied the cards and picked up the box to return them but, as she lifted the lid, she saw something that she'd missed earlier.

A white envelope with a note attached by a paper-clip.

I only found this today, when I finally cleaned out Tegan's desk. I thought it would be best if you and Jacob read it first and then we need to talk, to work out what to do.

The envelope was addressed in round, girlish handwriting in purple ink and it was addressed to Mr Mitch Bradley who lived, apparently, in a suburb of Sydney. Tegan's address was on the back and the letter was stamped, but there was no postmark.

Mitch Bradley.

Nell had never heard of him, but she felt a ghostly premonition as she stared at the envelope. Why did Jean think this letter was so important?

Could he be Sam's father?

She was suddenly afraid. Sam's father.

Sam's father could threaten their happy little family.

Not again. Please, no, not Sam. I can't lose him, too.

The seal on the envelope had been broken and Nell could feel the sheets of stationery inside, but she couldn't bring herself to open it.

As she sat there, her hands shaking with her indecision, she was saved by the growl of an engine outside. Jacob had been checking fences and feeding supplements to his heifers in the breeder paddock and now he was back. Quickly, Nell stuffed the cards and letters into the box and closed the lid firmly.

With Sam in her arms, she straightened her shoulders, determined to be cheerful. She'd prepared a salad for their lunch, cold chicken and avocado. She would let Jacob enjoy his meal before she told him about the unsettling puzzle that had arrived in the mail.

Her heart gave a tiny, love-sick lurch as she watched him swing out of his truck and take the back stairs two at a time.

'And how are my two favourite people?' he asked, dropping a kiss on Nell's cheek and another on the top of Sam's head.

'We're as happy as fleas.' Nell dredged up a show of gaiety.

But perhaps she wasn't very convincing. Jacob's eyes narrowed. 'Fleas?' He smiled carefully, and asked cautiously, 'And how happy are they?'

Nell offered a smile in reply and gave a little shrug. 'How were your heifers and fences?' she asked, hoping to deflect him.

'The heifers are fine. But a few sections of fence needed mending.' He frowned, looked directly into her eyes. 'Are you sure you're OK? You seem tense somehow.'

'I'm fine. Go and get cleaned up. Lunch is almost ready.'

Nell put Sam in the baby swing they'd set up at one end of the kitchen and she set the table and took the salad from the fridge, added dressing and tossed it. Wished she felt calmer.

Having grown up at Half Moon, she knew the right questions to ask Jacob about the property, so while they ate she quizzed him about the bores and the pasture and the condition of the heifers. Unfortunately, Jacob wasn't easily deceived.

When the meal was almost finished and they were drinking tea, he challenged her again. 'There's something bothering you, Nell.'

Perhaps it was best to get this over with. 'Something came in the mail from Jean. Bring your tea into the lounge room. It's all in there.'

Her stomach tied itself in knots as Jacob followed her. 'Jean Browne sent me this box,' she explained, taking the lid off and showing Jacob the contents. 'These are all the cards I sent Tegan, and there's a letter.' Quickly she located the card in the pile with Jacob's letter inside it.

She handed it to him and watched his face as he unfolded the notepaper and recognised his writing. She saw his strong features tighten and the muscles in his throat work. When he looked up, his eyes were extra bright.

'You read this?' he asked quietly.

'Only the beginning. I'm sorry. I'd started reading before I realised what it was.'

He shook his head. 'I don't mind. It's only the truth about how I felt.' Carefully, he refolded the letter and slipped it into his shirt pocket, then looked at her with a worried frown. 'Is that what you're upset about?'

'No, not that. I thought what you wrote was beautiful.' Nell showed him the envelope. 'There was another letter.'

She held her breath as Jacob read Jean's note and then the address, turned the envelope over and read Tegan's sender details.

'You haven't read this one?'

'No. I was getting up the nerve when you arrived back.'

He tapped a brown finger against the front of the envelope. 'You know who this Mitch Bradley probably is, don't you?'

She swallowed a prickle of fear. 'I suppose he might be Sam's father.'

'I'd say there's a fair chance.'

For a long moment they stared at each other and Nell knew Jacob's thoughts echoed hers. These thin sheets of paper could reveal the one person in the world who could take Sam away from them.

'We'd better have a look at it,' Jacob said with the carefully composed expression of a doctor discussing his patient's need for open heart surgery.

'I wish we didn't have to.' Nell's voice vibrated querulously.

'We don't have any choice, Nell.'

She knew Jacob was right, but she felt ill. How could she bear to lose Sam?

From the kitchen came the sound of his whimpers.

She said, 'You read the letter while I get the baby.' It was cowardly to be scared, but she couldn't help it. She was glad to escape.

Sam needed changing and she took her time attending to him, gave him an extra cuddle and fetched a bottle of boiled water for him to drink.

When she returned to the lounge room, Jacob was sitting

in a deep leather armchair, his expression sombre. 'You'd better read it,' he said.

A disturbing light in his eyes made her heart leap. 'Is Mitch Bradley the father?'

Jacob nodded.

Nell groaned as she pictured an angry young man storming Koomalong, sweeping Sam out of her arms and out of their lives.

'I'll take Sam while you read it,' Jacob said, holding the letter out to her.

It was not a fair exchange, Nell thought. Her arms felt empty as she gave Sam up and she fumbled trying to prise the pages out of the envelope. Her heart hammered as she sank on to the sofa and began to read.

Dear Mitch,

This letter has been a long time coming, so long that you might have forgotten what happened when we picked peaches together in Beechworth last summer. I went to that raging Christmas party with you. Remember?

I've written so many letters and torn them up. I hope this time I'll get the words down without panicking. The thing is, I've had a baby, Mitch. He's almost six weeks old, so if you do your maths you'll see that I fell pregnant at the end of November.

OK, I'm sweating telling you this, but you're the father. I know this will be a shock because we took precautions, but something must have gone wrong. I swear I didn't sleep with anyone else the whole summer.

I very nearly didn't tell you, because I understand this will not be good news for you. I know you were only picking fruit for a few weeks and then heading back to

*Sydney to join your rock band and the whole father bit
will totally wreck your life.*

*But I'm adopted, you see. I don't think I mentioned
that before. And just recently I had a letter from my father—my real father. It blew me away. He's so cool. All
this time I never knew him and he sounds like the greatest guy. A cattleman. I can't wait to meet him.*

*Then I started thinking about Sam, my little baby, and
how he will never know his father and how sad that's
going to be for him.*

*Don't panic. I don't expect you to marry me or any-
thing insane like that. But you do have a right to know
about your son.*

After that, it's up to you.

*I might be too busy to write again because Sam keeps
me really busy, but at least now you have my address.*

Hope you're not too bummed by this.

Luv,

Tegan.

Nell looked up from the letter.

Jacob's face was solemn as he watched her. 'It's dated the
day before the accident.'

'Is it?' She hadn't taken any notice of the date and now
she turned back to the first page and saw that he was right.
'Poor Tegan.'

'Poor Mitch.'

'He's in for a shock.'

But she was shocked, too. Her gaze flew to Sam, who
looked so adorably cute and comfortable in Jacob's strong
arms. So at home, so right.

She tossed the letter on to the coffee table. 'It's so unfair to learn about this now.' She snatched up a cushion and hugged it to her chest. 'I've fallen completely in love with Sam.'

'I know. I know...' Jacob sighed heavily. 'But we'll have to talk to this Mitch Bradley. He's obviously Sam's father.'

'What if he wants to contest Sam's custody? I couldn't stand it.' Nell knew she sounded petulant, but she couldn't help it. 'It sounds as if he's in a rock band. He's probably as irresponsible as they come.'

'We don't know that, do we? You're prejudging the bloke.'

Was she? Was she really? How could Tegan's footloose young boyfriend have the same longing to care for Sam that she had?

'Jacob, don't you care that this Mitch guy might try to take Sam away from us?'

'Of course I do.'

He looked sad and too impossibly gorgeous, sitting there with Sam in his arms. Nell closed her eyes and struggled to think clearly, without bias. But she couldn't get past the mind-numbing thought that she and Jacob were facing the possibility of losing Sam, that the fragile dynamics of their relationship were completely threatened.

They'd only had a few short weeks, had just started to get to know each other after twenty years.

And the reality was that Jacob had only invited her to Koomalong because of Sam. She and Jacob were only back together because of Sam.

If Sam was taken out of the equation...

She couldn't bear to think about it.

Sam squirmed in Jacob's arms and she jumped at the chance to escape before she blurted out her fears and Jacob confirmed them. 'I'd better take him now. It's time for his feed, and then his naptime.'

* * *

Jacob felt as if he'd been slammed by a ten ton truck as he watched Nell leave the room.

In theory, he'd applauded the idea of finding Sam's father. He'd spent twenty years in the dark before discovering he had a daughter and he didn't want to see another guy suffer that pain.

This was not something that could be quietly swept under the rug. It was about honouring a man's rights, about giving him the knowledge, the very fact that he had a child.

But now…

Now, Jacob had to ask himself what this honesty might cost. Heaven help him. He had so much at stake.

Nell.

Sam.

His best chance at happiness.

And he was terribly afraid that Sam's young father had the potential to take all that away from him.

Anxiety propelled him out of his chair. He marched through the house to the back veranda and glared at the familiar view of sweeping paddocks dotted with gum trees and grazing cattle.

He knew he wouldn't be able to ignore this letter to Mitch Bradley. But right at this moment he wished that it had never arrived. Very soon, he would have to go inside to track down a phone number and ring this young man. And there was every chance that he and Nell would have to make a trip to Sydney to meet him.

Mitch Bradley might be smitten by little Sam—in fact, it was more than likely. And where would that leave Nell?

Deprived of her daughter, she'd given her whole heart to Sam. She adored him and to lose him now would be too, too cruel a blow. And to battle for him in court would be a horrendous business. Soul-destroying.

And the worst of it was that Jacob knew that he was ultimately responsible. For everything. That one unprotected act of lust all those years ago that had messed up so many lives.

What a fool he'd been then—too crazy about Nell to think straight. Problem was, he was just as big a fool now—he was still crazy about her. And he'd placed an extra burden on her by dragging her here to Koomalong.

His most foolish mistake had been thinking that if he got back together with Nell, the rest of their lives would fall into place. Happy every after. The whole damn fairy tale. As if life could be that simple, as if happiness could ever be free from the debts of the past.

With a groan of despair, he thought of the rings he'd bought on impulse when he was in Roma last week. They were in a jewellery box that he'd stowed away in the back of his wardrobe. What an idiot he'd been to think that just because Nell was spending a few weeks under his roof, she would be his forever.

He'd dragged her away from her lovely cottage, from her neighbours and friends, from the life she'd led for the past twenty years. He'd seduced her almost as soon as he'd got her under his roof and if she stopped to think about it, she would probably decide that he'd lured her to Koomalong with Sam as the bait.

Sighing heavily, burdened by the weight of his guilt, he went back into the house. He dreaded the way this might turn out, but he had no choice. He would have to find Mitch Bradley's number on the Internet…

* * *

Nell tucked a light blanket over Sam, then kissed two fingers and pressed them against his warm cheek. She tiptoed out of the room and found Jacob waiting in the hall outside. He looked dreadful. Pale despite his tan. Thinner, as if he'd lost masses of weight in the past thirty minutes.

'Have you rung Sam's father yet?' she asked.

He shook his head and she felt an instantaneous leap of hope.

'Do we really have to go through with this, Jacob?'

He smiled wearily. 'I know how you feel and I'm as worried as you are. But then I remembered something I couldn't ignore.'

'What?'

'We can't hide the truth. We'd be as bad as your parents, Nell.'

Oh, heavens. He was right. She had never been able to forgive her parents for their deception. This wasn't quite the same, but it was deception nonetheless, carrying the sins of her father into the next generation.

'How could I forget?' She gave a helpless little shake of her head. 'We can't ignore Tegan's wishes. She obviously meant Mitch to know about his son.'

'I've looked up his number,' Jacob said. 'But I was waiting for you before I called.'

She wished that he hadn't waited, but it would have sounded cowardly to say so. 'Right. I guess we'd better get it over and done with. We'll have to let Jean know what we plan to do as well.'

Heavy-hearted, she followed Jacob through to the study and sat on the deep window seat with her arms wrapped around her knees while he dialled. She watched his long fingers keying in the numbers and thought, irrelevantly, how lovely his hands were.

'Mitch?' Jacob said. 'My name's Jacob Tucker. I believe you knew my daughter, Tegan Browne. You were fruit picking with her at Beechworth last year.'

Nell had to admire how well Jacob handled his end of the conversation. It was a delicate situation, but he explained everything very smoothly and sensitively. From what she could tell, Mitch Bradley seemed to be taking the shocking news rather well.

Eventually Jacob paused. With his hand over the receiver, he looked directly at Nell. 'Mitch was shocked to hear about Tegan, but he's very excited to hear that he's a dad. He'd love to meet Sam.'

'When?' Nell asked dully.

'It's up to us. As soon as we're free.'

She felt strangely numb, as if all her emotions had been set in ice. Dropping her hands to her sides, she shrugged. 'I guess we'll have to check with the airlines and call him back.'

CHAPTER TEN

SECRETLY, NELL HOPED they wouldn't be able to get flights at such short notice, but she knew that was just delaying the inevitable.

Unable to sit still and simply listen while Jacob dealt with the airlines, she went to the kitchen and made coffee for them both. When she returned to the study, her hand shook as she handed Jacob his mug.

His eyes were watchful, his jaw tight as he accepted it with terse thanks.

'Any joy with the airlines?' she asked, trying to sound a hundred times more casual than she felt.

'Actually, yes, we're in luck. There are two seats available on tomorrow's early flight out of Roma. We can be in Sydney by tomorrow afternoon.'

So soon?

How could Jacob call that luck?

Nell's stomach churned and drinking coffee was suddenly impossible. Quickly, she set the mug on his desk. 'Tomorrow's a bit soon, isn't it?'

'We don't want this hanging over our heads, Nell. We need it settled.'

The determined light in his eyes dismayed her. Was he simply being a typical male—stoic and hiding his feelings? Or was he truly unconcerned that within twenty-four hours they could lose Sam and have their lives once again turned upside down?

'There's no point in putting this off,' he said again.

Of course, he was right. But his certainty annoyed Nell. And it frightened her. Was Jacob distancing himself now, because he thought it would all be over between them if Mitch decided to take Sam?

Worried beyond bearing, she whirled away from him, staring miserably out of the window, and saw darkness creeping through the bush, casting cold, grey shadows. The sunset was totally obscured by clouds this evening and the dusk was menacing, without any of the beauty she'd sensed on other nights. She was terribly afraid that she would burst into tears.

'I suppose you're right to be worried,' Jacob said quietly. 'If we—I mean, if you do lose Sam, it would probably make good sense for you to continue on to Melbourne after Sydney.'

Startled, she whirled back to face him. 'Are you sending me away?'

His face turned a deep red and he dropped his gaze to his coffee mug, fiddled with its handle. 'I'm just trying to be practical.'

After a moment or two, he seemed to regain his composure. Lifting his gaze once more, he looked at her with grey eyes that were carefully devoid of emotion. 'Whatever happens when we meet with Mitch tomorrow, there'll be legal issues to sort out, so it would make sense for you to continue on to Melbourne.' His gaze was sharp.

'Don't you agree, Nell?'

No, she wanted to cry. She knew that, of course, it was sensible, but right now her emotions were roiling and she had no desire whatsoever to be sensible.

She was falling apart inside. Jacob was doing everything he could to hasten her departure and that was killing her. Surely, if he loved her with the deep and overwhelming passion that she loved him, he couldn't possibly bear to be parted from her again.

Perhaps she'd been fooling herself when she'd believed that he'd wanted her at Koomalong because he loved her. It was more than likely that he'd only wanted her here as part of a package deal with Sam.

She wished she had the courage to ask those questions, but something about Jacob's frightening stillness silenced her.

Instead she agreed dully, 'I'm sure you're right. I suppose I'd better start packing.'

She held her breath and waited for him to say something—*anything*—that might offer her a tiny glimmer of reassurance. Heaven help her, a day ago he might have pulled her into his arms and murmured smiling endearments, but now he simply stood there on the other side of his desk, with his hands sunk into the pockets of his jeans, and he looked as solid and stern and stubborn as the old Brahman bull in the bottom paddock.

Giving a helpless shake of her head, Nell turned and left the room.

Nell spent the rest of the evening busily packing while Jacob remained in his study. She went between rooms, gathering up her things and Sam's. How on earth had they managed to spread so many of their belongings throughout Jacob's house? And, as she went, she could hear Jacob's deep voice as he talked on the phone, making endless arrangements with truck drivers about cattle shipments, with graziers about agistments, with stock and station agents about sales. There was even a call to Hilda Knowles asking her to care for Blue and Dander while he was away.

In fact, Jacob was so busy that he took a plate of heated leftovers back to his study and ate in snatches as he worked. Stunned and more upset than ever, Nell ate a sandwich perched on a stool at the kitchen window, staring out into the black night. Then she hurried back to her suitcases.

In his study, Jacob set down the telephone receiver and let out a weary sigh, picked up a pen and began to make tense cross-hatches on the writing pad in front of him. What a bloody awful night it had been. All evening he'd been fighting his emotions, keeping busy in a futile attempt to stop himself from thinking too hard about tomorrow. Crunch time.

By this time tomorrow night he would know the worst. The pen tore a hole in the paper. Angrily, Jacob stared at the mess he'd made on the page, quickly ripped it from the pad, balled it and binned it.

The damned thing was, the wonderful family life that he'd taken pleasure in over the past few weeks was as fragile as that paper. He and Nell had enjoyed such a short time together. They'd been the best days of his life, but now he was in danger of losing everything.

And, as far as he could see, there was not a damn thing he could do about it.

Curled in a tense ball on her side of the bed, Nell listened to the sounds of taps being turned off in the bathroom, then Jacob's soft footfall as he came across the bedroom carpet.

She felt the slight dip of the mattress as he got into bed, held her breath as he rolled towards her.

'You asleep?' he whispered.

'No.'

Her throat was tight with burning tears as she turned to him. A faint glimmer of moonlight outlined the bulk of his shoulder. His skin smelled clean and familiar and she longed to reach out, to touch him, to bury her face against his hard chest, to feel his warm embrace. But the prolonged tension of the evening had stifled the last embers of her confidence.

His hand reached through the darkness to touch her cheek.

She lay very still, hardly daring to breathe, willing him to keep touching her, to close the gap between them.

'Don't worry too much,' he said, stroking her jaw-line so gently she could barely feel it. 'I'll be with you tomorrow.'

A pitiful sob broke from her.

And, before she knew quite what was happening, he was leaning over her, lifting her hair away from her face.

'Nell,' he said once, and then he lowered his head, blocking out the moonlight, and suddenly her arms were about his neck and they were kissing and caressing and making love, swiftly overtaken by a passion so powerful she had no choice but to give in to it.

Even in their youth, they had never been this ardent, this intense. It was as if their bodies were trying to say what they hadn't managed in words.

And afterwards, when they lay in the pale shimmer of moonlight, disentangled and spent, like exhausted swimmers on the shore, Nell hoped they might talk. At last.

'I've almost broken your record,' she said lightly.

Jacob looked puzzled. 'What record is that?'

'I've stayed here for almost a month.'

'Ah…yes.' He smiled sadly.

She waited. Surely now, they could share their fears. Their hopes.

But Jacob closed his eyes and said, 'You'd better go to sleep now, Nell. We have a very early start in the morning.'

They stood on the front steps of a dilapidated flat in a suburb of Western Sydney. Nell was so nervous she thought she might be sick. Beside her, Jacob was grim-faced as he rang the doorbell.

They waited, listening while the ringing died away, for the sound of Mitch Bradley's footsteps. Nell's heart thumped. Jacob gave her back a comforting pat, but he couldn't quite manage a smile.

Hitching her bag of baby things higher on her shoulder, she held Sam more tightly. The baby grinned and cooed at her, caught a strand of her hair in his fist and pulled it towards his mouth.

'You little charmer,' she whispered, disentangling her hair gently.

Today she wished Sam wasn't quite so cute and appealing. There was a very distinct danger that Mitch would fall for him the way people so often fell for kittens and puppies in pet shops, only to find out too late they weren't able to care for them properly.

She couldn't help casting a dubious eye over the untidy flower bed beside the front steps. Apart from weeds, which were plentiful, the garden was littered with two empty soft drink cans and a screwed-up paper bag. No wonder the dusty rubber plants were struggling.

'Maybe Mitch isn't home,' she muttered hopefully when no one came to the door.

'He said he'd be here.' Jacob glanced at his watch. 'He might still be asleep.'

'At one o'clock in the afternoon?'

'He works at night in a rock band, don't forget.'

'How could I forget that?' Nell felt another nervous twist in her stomach.

Last night and today had been hideous. To her utter despair, Jacob had remained unbearably silent and withdrawn and she *still* hadn't found the courage to challenge him. Now it was too late.

'I'll try this again,' he said, lifting his hand to push the doorbell again.

'No, Jacob, wait.'

Finger poised, he frowned at her. 'We have to go through with this, Nell.'

'I know,' she said hurriedly. 'But there's something I need to ask you.'

He lowered his hand. 'What is it? What's the matter?'

She tried to moisten her parched lips. 'What will happen if we lose Sam?'

'What will happen?'

She was almost too scared to speak, but she'd been trying to get this out all day and she mustn't back down now. 'To us. We haven't talked about it and that's crazy. I can't stand it, Jacob. I have to know.'

'I—I—' His eyes glistened suddenly and his throat worked overtime. 'I thought it was settled. You'll go back to Melbourne.'

'Is that what you want?'

With an abrupt movement of his head, he looked away down the street. 'Of course it's not what I want, but I can't let what I want get in the way of your happiness. You have your friends in Melbourne. You have the theatres and book shops. Your cottage. If you lose Sam, you'll need those things. They—they'll comfort you.'

Nell swallowed the painful blockage in her throat. Her voice was shaking as she asked, 'But what about you? What if I need you more than any of those things? Where will you be?'

Slowly, Jacob turned back to her. He studied her face for five torturous long seconds and she saw realisation dawn at last, saw the beginnings of his gorgeous smile. 'Where would you like me to be?'

Before she could answer, the front door opened.

'G'day,' said a young man.

He was almost as tall as Jacob and dressed in a holey black T-shirt and ripped and faded jeans. His eyes were a sleepy blue, his hair tousled, long and blond. Blond stubble covered his jaw. He definitely looked as if he'd just rolled out of bed.

'Ah—' With obvious difficulty, Jacob dragged his eyes from Nell and offered the young man his hand. 'You must be Mitch.'

'Sure, man.' Mitch's gaze swept over them and landed on Sam and his face lit up as if someone had turned on a switch.

Nell's heart, already shaken, began a drum roll. She wanted to run away from here. She wanted to answer Jacob's question, to tell him that she wanted him to be with her, at Koomalong, anywhere, as long as they were together. And she needed to know his response.

'I'm Jacob Tucker,' Jacob said. 'And this is Nell and, of course, this is Sam.'

Mitch shook hands with them. 'Have you been waiting here long? I'm sorry, I didn't hear my alarm.'

'Not long,' Jacob assured him.

Mitch turned his attention to Sam. He took a step closer and his face softened as he stared at the baby. His Adam's apple rode up and down in his throat. 'Hey, isn't he a little dude?'

Nell smiled carefully and lifted Sam higher to give his father a better view and she wondered if they were going to be invited inside.

'Do you mind if we come in?' Jacob asked, as if reading her mind.

'Oh, sure,' Mitch replied after only the slightest hesitation. 'Come on in.' He sent a hasty glance over his shoulder and gave them a shamefaced smile. 'But the flat's pretty festy.'

As they went inside Jacob turned to Nell and smiled and she wished with all her heart she could interpret that smile. Was it saying, *Don't worry, Nell, I love you?* Or simply, *Chin up?*

At least the flat wasn't quite as bad as she'd feared. There was no lingering smell of cigarettes, which was a distinct bonus. There were dirty dishes in the sink and empty beer bottles and coffee mugs lying around, but she had to admit that it wasn't much different from the flats many of her friends had lived in when she'd been Mitch's age.

'You might like to sit over there.' Mitch pointed in the direction of an ancient vinyl settee.

Before Nell sat, she said bravely, 'Would you like to hold Sam?'

The young man gaped at her, clearly taken aback, but to his credit, he quickly recovered. 'I—I don't know.' He looked and sounded nervous. 'I've never held a baby. I'm scared I might drop him.' Then he flashed them a smile as charming as Sam's.

'That's how every guy feels when he first holds a baby,' Jacob assured him. 'Sam won't break. You'll be fine.'

'Perhaps if you sit down first,' Nell suggested. 'And then I'll hand him to you.'

'Right.' Mitch sat on the edge of an armchair that seemed to have lost its springs, his arms stiffly bent at the elbows. 'He's so little. I don't want to stuff this up.'

'You just need to have one arm under his back and make sure you support his head,' Nell explained as she gently lowered Sam into his father's arms. 'He's pretty strong now, but his head can still wobble at times.'

Mitch grinned at Sam. 'Hey, you're so tiny.' And then, 'It's me, your old man.' The baby looked up at him and smiled and Mitch laughed. 'Wow, does this kid have a cute factor off the scale, or what?'

Jacob and Nell took their seats on the settee and sat in tight-lipped silence while Mitch admired his son. His face betrayed a kaleidoscope of emotions—everything from joy, through hilarity to fear.

'He definitely looks like you,' Nell said.

'I know,' Mitch agreed. 'It's amazing, isn't it? I knew he was mine as soon as I saw him on the doorstep. It blows me away just thinking about it.' His smile vanished. 'I can't stop thinking about Tegan, though. It makes you wonder, doesn't it?' He shook his head. 'You just never know.'

She caught a distinctly misty dampness in Mitch's eyes and he quickly dropped his gaze and stared at the rust-coloured carpet at his feet.

Looking down at her hands, tightly gripped in her lap, she could hear the echo of her heartbeats drumming in her ears. Mitch Bradley was a nice guy and she felt comforted by that. For Sam's sake. And for Tegan's.

But Mitch was falling for Sam, just as she'd feared he would. She tried to squash her feelings of dismay and told herself that his interest in Sam was a good sign. Every little boy deserved his father's love and affection.

Beside her, Jacob drew a deep breath. He sat forward with his elbows propped on his knees and fixed Mitch with a steady gaze. 'I'm sorry you didn't know about Sam earlier.'

'Well, maybe that's my fault,' Mitch admitted. 'I didn't write to Tegan either. We didn't plan to hook up again, you see. It was just a—a summer thing.'

'Yes.' Jacob sent Nell a private look that told her he was remembering their own 'summer thing'.

She was so tense that she almost burst into tears.

'I'm very grateful to you both,' Mitch said. 'I needed to know about this. About Sam.'

And now it's the moment of truth, thought Nell. Any minute, Mitch was going to tell them that he and his family would take care of Sam from now on. She reached for Jacob's hand and was grateful when he enclosed her shaking fingers with his warmth and strength.

'Have you told your parents about Sam?' she asked.

Mitch shook his head. 'My parents are dead. My grandparents raised me and my sister.'

'Oh.'

A kind of awkward silence fell over them.

'So—' Nell moistened her lips. 'So, what are your plans, Mitch?'

He looked blank. 'Plans?'

'For Sam?'

'I—I don't know. What sort of plans do you mean?'

Beside her, Jacob cleared his throat. 'Let's not jump the

gun, Nell. Mitch has only just met Sam. He hasn't had a chance to think about the future.'

'Yes, I know but—' Nell saw the warning light in Jacob's eyes and stopped.

'I thought you guys were the ones with the plans,' Mitch said, clearly confused. 'You're Tegan's mum and dad. You'll be the ones raising Sam, won't you?'

Nell choked back an exclamation.

'Is that what you want?' Jacob asked quietly. 'You'd like us to continue to care for him?'

A look of panic crossed Mitch's face as his eyes flicked from Nell to Jacob. 'I didn't even think to ask you about that. I just—' He ran his tongue over his lips. 'Is there a problem? Can't you manage him any more?'

Somehow, Nell managed to stay calm. 'There's no problem, Mitch. We're quite prepared—actually, we'd be more than happy to continue to look after Sam.'

Mitch's shoulders slumped as he relaxed. 'Phew. That's a relief. You had me worried for a minute there.'

He looked down at Sam and gave a helpless shrug. 'Grand-parents are so great with little kids and I wouldn't know where to start if I had to look after him. I'm only just scrap-ing a living. And I don't know anything about nappies or feeding babies. I work crazy hours.'

'It's OK, Mitch. Stay cool.' Jacob smiled warmly at the young man, then at Nell.

'I'm not even sure how often I'll be able to see Sam,' Mitch said.

Jacob squeezed Nell's hand. 'I'm sure Nell and I will fig-ure a way to help you to see Sam on a regular basis.'

Mitch grinned, then held Sam out to Nell. 'Can you take

him while I get my camera? I'd like a shot of Sammy and me. And you two, of course. We should start a family album for the little bloke, don't you think?'

'I'll admit it now,' Nell whispered as Mitch left the room. 'I did prejudge him.'

'Forget Mitch,' Jacob said, surprising her. 'I'm more interested in the conversation we were having just before he interrupted us on the doorstep. You were going to tell me something important.'

'Oh, yes.' She cuddled Sam to her for courage. 'I was going to tell you what would have made me happy, if we weren't looking after Sam any more.'

'And I need to know the answer, Nell.'

The poor man. He couldn't have looked more serious if he were facing a firing-squad. Nell edged closer and lifted her lips close to his ear. 'I was hoping you'd let me stay with you.'

'At Koomalong?'

'Where else? Actually, I don't really care, as long as we're together.'

Jacob's face broke into a wide and radiant smile and then, in a heartbeat, he was hugging her and kissing her and squashing Sam.

'Of course I want us to be together.' He hugged her again. 'That's all I've ever wanted. I love you, Nell. And I swear I'll never let you go again.'

'Now that's a great shot,' called Mitch from the doorway.

They broke apart and Nell couldn't stop grinning. 'Jacob and I just had something to sort out.'

Mitch's cheeky smile reached from ear to ear. 'That's fine by me. I think it's absolutely cool. You old folks want to try that again? It would make a great shot for the album.'

* * *

They walked back to their car and Jacob took Nell's hand. 'Did you really mean that, Nell? That you want to stay at Koomalong?'

'You impossible man. Of course I meant it.'

'Even if we'd lost Sam?'

'Especially if we'd lost Sam.' She turned to him, her eyes huge. 'But I've been so scared that you wouldn't want me without Sam.'

'How could you think that?' Almost as soon as the question was out he knew the answer. She'd been gripped by the same uncertainties that had haunted him. He had to tell her again. 'I love you, Nell.'

'I know.' Tears sparkled in her eyes. 'I'm so happy.' The tears trembled on her eyelashes and spilled down her cheeks. 'I love you too, Jacob. So, so much.'

'But you're crying.'

'Because I'm so happy.'

They reached the car. Nell put Sam in the back and Jacob found a handkerchief and dabbed at her eyes and her cheeks. She took the handkerchief from him and blew her nose, gave him a wobbly smile.

'Let's get back to the hotel,' he said.

'Lovely.' She smiled at him. 'Actually, I'm so happy right now I would have said *lovely* if you'd suggested we swim to Africa.'

As they got into the front seats Jacob suddenly realised that *this* was the moment. There could never be a better moment. He couldn't—shouldn't—delay it a second longer.

'I have something important to ask you, Nell.'

He watched the surprise in her eyes, the swift colour in her cheeks, the soft O of her mouth.

'Here? Right now?'

'It's probably the wrong place and the wrong time. We should be down by the beautiful harbour, not stuck here on a busy road with traffic whizzing past, but I've waited too long.' Taking both her hands in his, he said, 'It's a question I asked once before. A long, long time ago.'

'Oh, Jacob. Oh, darling.'

'I haven't asked the question yet.'

'I know, but the answer is yes!' Nell slipped out of her seat belt and opened her arms to him. 'I love you,' she cried as she covered his face with kisses.

A horn blasted close by and a huge lorry rushed past them.

Looking out at the speeding traffic, Nell laughed and hugged him again. 'This is the perfect time and the perfect place. We've both waited too long for this.'

EPILOGUE

NELL LOOKED WITH wonder at the tiny bundle in her arms. Her daughter was gorgeous, with a cap of dark hair and bright grey eyes.

'My tiny, shiny girl,' she whispered.

There had never been a more beautiful baby.

Nell's obstetrician had expressed concern when he'd discovered that his forty-year-old patient wanted to give birth in his country hospital. He'd tried to persuade her to go to Brisbane for her confinement, but she had insisted that she would be fine. She wasn't being sent away to the city to have *this* baby.

Her faith had been justified and Caitlin had arrived in the early hours of this morning with a minimum of fuss. Jacob had been present for the birth, holding Nell's hand, rubbing her back, giving her ice chips to suck and generally cheering her on as their perfect daughter had slipped into the world.

'Does she look like anyone we know?' he had asked as their baby girl's hand gripped his finger.

'She looks very much like Tegan,' Nell had told him. 'Which means she's going to look like you, Jacob.'

'I hope she doesn't have my ears.'

'Or your big feet.'

They had laughed together and Nell's heart had been full to overflowing—with gratitude, with happiness, with love.

Now she heard footsteps in the hospital corridor and looked eagerly towards the door, seeing Jacob's long legs and his grin stretching from ear to ear above an enormous bouquet of pink roses.

'What gorgeous roses!' She smiled up at him and thought he was still the best-looking man she'd ever seen.

'These are for both of you.' He leaned down to kiss her. 'The two loveliest girls in town.'

Setting the flowers on a bedside table, he looked down at Caitlin.

'She's beautiful, isn't she?' Nell asked for the thousandth time.

'Utterly gorgeous,' Jacob assured her.

'But you must have bought every rose in town.'

'Only every pink one,' he admitted with another happy grin.

'Thank heavens Mitch was able to come and babysit Sam,' Nell said. 'Did you get through to Koomalong? How are he and Sam?'

'I did get through and Mitch was over the moon when I told him the good news. Would you believe he stayed awake all night? Said he had no idea waiting for a baby could be so nerve-racking.'

'Poor fellow.' Nell smiled down at Caitlin. 'You were worth the wait, weren't you, sweetheart?' Quickly, she asked, 'But how's Sam?'

'He's fine. He's been a perfect lamb, according to Mitch.

He's eaten an enormous breakfast and now Mitch is entertaining him with his guitar.'

'Oh, that's sweet.'

'Very sweet,' said Jacob dryly. 'I could hear Sam in the background, trying to play heavy metal on a saucepan.'

Nell groaned and smiled simultaneously.

Jacob chuckled. 'I told Mitch that was fine, as long as he doesn't get Sam started on drums.'

'Not till Caitlin's a little older,' Nell agreed. 'When's he bringing Sam in to see his little sister?'

'This afternoon.'

'I can't wait to see them together.'

Strictly speaking, Caitlin was Sam's aunt, but for the time being, as far as Nell and Jacob and the rest of the family was concerned, Sam and Caitlin were brother and sister.

'I rang everyone else,' Jacob said. 'They're all ecstatic, of course. Mum and Jean send their love and congratulations. They all want to be here for the christening.'

'It'll be just like the wedding. The whole clan at Koomalong.'

'I'll get Hilda to organise some extra household help. I don't want you overdoing things.'

'Oh, I'll be fine.'

Yes, she would be fine.

With a lump in his throat, Jacob touched his little finger to the palm of Caitlin's outstretched hand and again her fingers gripped him tightly.

He knew he was a lucky man.

'Where's my camera?' He smiled down at Nell as she relaxed against the pillows with Caitlin in her arms. 'You. Are. Glowing,' he said.

'Don't worry about the camera for now.' She patted the bed beside her. 'Come here.'

As he obeyed, she snuggled against him and lifted her lips to the underside of his jaw. 'Just remember, my darling man—for me, nothing is perfect without you.'

With her husband beside her and her daughter in her arms, Nell breathed a sigh of utter contentment. Their dreams might have been trampled and broken when they were young, but now they had been resurrected. Bright. Shining. Coming true.

* * * * *

Outback Wife
And Mother

For John Dow,
who was my father and my first hero

PROLOGUE

MUMMY WAS CRYING again.

Lying in his bed, the boy could hear her muffled sobs and his father's pleading voice in the next room. 'But, Vivienne, you mustn't go. You can't leave us.'

He could see the friendly silhouette of his teddy bear on the pillow beside him, but not even his favourite toy could help him feel safe or happy. Not when he could hear the desperate sadness in his mother's voice.

'I feel so—so stifled here in the outback,' she sobbed. 'I think I'll go mad.'

Eventually, he pulled the pillow over his head to shut out the frightening voices...

Then with the first creamy fingers of dawn, his mother crept into the room, smelling as fresh as flowers. She sat on the edge of his bed and he buried his head in her lap.

'Mon petit,' she whispered, stroking his hair. 'I will miss you so much.'

Something started to thump loudly in his chest. 'You don't have to miss me, Mummy,' he cried. 'I'm going to stay on Wallaroo with you and Daddy for always.'

With a choked moan, she hugged him close, cradling him with her soft, warm arms. 'Oh, cheri,' she whispered and, looking up, he saw her beautiful eyes fill with bright tears. 'Always remember, I love you very, very much. But you belong here.'

There was a crunch of tyres on gravel in the yard outside, and then heavy footsteps on the wooden floorboards of the veranda. Ned, the stockman, stood in the doorway. He cleared his throat as he fiddled with his wide-brimmed hat.

'Yes, Ned. I'm coming,' she said softly.

The boy felt her warm lips on his cheek and she held him so tightly he couldn't breathe. Then she stood up and drifted away from him, out of the room, as soft and pretty as the morning mist on the river.

His feet hit the cold floor as he hurried after her.

Outside, the bush was already waking. A huge flock of pink and grey galahs rose from the gum trees along the creek, filling the reddening sky with their raucous chorus. Ned opened the door to the truck and she slipped inside. The little boy could just make out her pale face through the window glass.

He ran faster, but as he reached the top of the steps, two strong arms caught him and lifted him up and he felt his father's bristly morning cheek pressed against his. 'We've got to let her go, Fletcher,' he said, his voice sounding gruff and strange. 'She doesn't belong in the bush. She needs the city lights.'

What was Daddy talking about? Of course Mummy belonged here. The truck's engine spluttered to life and the station dogs barked and yapped at its tyres.

'It's just you and me now, little mate. At least she let me have you...'

The truck rolled forward.

Thoroughly bewildered now, the boy struggled in his father's arms and cried out to her, 'Mummy, don't go!'

But the truck gathered speed. And she looked back at him one last time, raised a graceful hand to her lips and blew him a kiss.

CHAPTER ONE

FLETCHER HARDY RAN an irritated finger around the inside of his uncomfortably stiff collar and glared at the marbled floors and mirrored walls of the enormous ballroom. He had rushed straight to the hotel from a press conference about the drought in North Queensland and he had to postpone a dinner meeting with the Minister for Primary Industries— simply to watch half-starved girls sashaying around in outrageous costumes!

He prided himself on never doing anything against his will, but in a rare moment of weakness he had allowed his cousin, Lucette, to talk him into coming to a fashion show.

Grimacing as his shoulders met the unfamiliar constraints of his tux, he strode impatiently towards the rows of seats arranged around the catwalk. He ignored the swing of expensively coiffed female heads trailing after him like sunflowers following the sun.

And he scowled as he found his seat and lowered his long body into it.

Fashion! Ridiculous female obsession, he'd always claimed, happily overlooking the minor detail that he had, on odd occasions in the past, been known to admire an elegantly designed garment gracing a beautiful woman.

As soon as Lucette had heard Fletcher was travelling south to Melbourne, she'd begged him to come and watch the show so he could admire the set she designed especially for this exhibition. He'd found his kid cousin's enormous pride in her first real assignment quite touching and so, to humour her, he had come. But where was she now? The live band was blasting out its opening number and the lights were going down and still no Lucette! She'd left him to brave this torment on his own!

Typical. With any luck there would be an interval and he could leave.

Wrapped in these angry thoughts, he refused to join in the applause as the grinning compere, dressed in a gold tuxedo, approached the microphone, welcomed the audience and delivered a totally incomprehensible joke about fashion. The audience roared. Fletcher growled.

'This evening, the Quintessential Collection brings us a preview of the new season highlights from five of Australia's top young designers. We begin with the delightful Alexandra Fraser. I'm sure most of the menfolk here would agree with me, that Ally is herself rather beautifully designed...' Here the compere paused for a brief titter from the audience, while Fletcher almost groaned aloud. 'Today we see fine examples of her ultra-urban, minimalist designs in pale cashmeres and silks,' the compere continued with a wide, plastic smile. 'And you should note the clever addition of silk cummerbunds to her slinky pants and long evening skirts.'

Fletcher raked a hand distractedly through his thick, dark hair as, for the sake of his sanity, he turned his attention to Lucette's set. OK, it was good. Against an ethereal back-

drop resembling the sky at dawn—all pinks and golds—
there were delicate, gilded arches encrusted with winking
bud lights and a runway edged with more tiny lights and
misty clumps of tulle. It all seemed appropriate, he decided,
suggesting a show, which would present the quintessence
of earthly beauty. And as far as he could see the decor provided a suitable accompaniment for the palely elegant fash-
ions, which soon emerged.

But as for the deportment and grace of the models slink-
ing and strutting along the runway—he barely noticed them.
His eyes were squinted with his efforts to read his watch in
the darkened room. But his attempts were futile so instead
he began scanning the audience, searching for Lucette. After
several fruitless minutes, he tried the watch again. No use.
When could he safely slip away?

Restlessly, he squirmed in his seat. His elbow bumped the
thin woman sitting beside him and she glowered at him from
beneath her wide-brimmed hat.

About to scowl back at her, his attention was suddenly
captured by a woman emerging down the runway. Dressed
in the simplest of short gowns in deep purple, the colour of
crushed violets, she stood out in stark contrast to the whites,
creams and beiges worn by the models surrounding her.

'Ladies and gentleman, our very own Alexandra Fraser.'

So this was the designer of the first collection. She was
bowing as the crowd applauded her. Cries of 'Bravo' could
even be heard, so obviously she was being well received.

She smiled out into the audience and at that precise moment, the simple, two syllable word *woman* took on an entirely new level of meaning for Fletcher Hardy.

This woman was like no other he'd ever seen before. An
unnerving tension seized his body. His hands gripped the

upholstered arms of his seat and incredibly, this hardened man of the land's throat tightened over a huge lump of unexpected emotion as his gaze remained transfixed by the figure on the catwalk.

She was surrounded by tall, willowy models, but his eyes were drawn from their almost asexual leanness to her startling femininity. Her gleaming dark hair and pale skin were a perfect foil for the rich colour of her one-shoulder dress and the delectable curves it barely concealed. Her slender legs and the graceful movement of her dainty hands as she acknowledged the models were utterly fascinating. Spellbound, he watched this dark-haired, enchanting designer.

She was the most exquisite female he had ever seen.

Her features were delicate yet determined and her thickly lashed grey eyes sparkled with intelligence and spunk. Surrounded as she was by models looking as vacant as dolls in a shop window, this woman looked vibrant, incredibly alive, undeniably sexy.

And then she was gone, tossing a final smile over her one bared shoulder before disappearing with the models back through Lucette's golden arches.

Another group of models bounced onto the runway accompanied by wild heavy metal music. Fletcher had a vague impression of a kaleidoscopic mix of lace and satin teamed with psychedelic stockings and electric blue lips, but his mind was still totally absorbed by Alexandra Fraser. If only he had bothered to pick up a catalogue on his way in, he might have discovered more about her.

Restlessly he sat through the gyrations and outlandish creations of the second collection but as soon as its designer, a young man whose bald head was wildly tattooed, appeared to receive his applause, Fletcher rose from his seat and made his way quickly to the back of the ballroom.

He found a stack of catalogues on a small side table and hurriedly snatched one up, leafing through it impatiently. Reading by the light of a dimmed wall lamp, he found little to satisfy him. There was a brief description of Alexandra Fraser's collection and a list of several awards she had won and then a quoted comment.

'Alexandra says of fashion design, "I keep to simple lines, neat silhouettes, no frills or fluffiness, but this doesn't mean my clothes cannot be soft or reveal the body. For me design is a passionate experience. It fulfils me totally—mind, body and soul."'

To his annoyance Fletcher Hardy did not find the scraps of information at all comforting and he skulked around the back of the ballroom as the show continued, feeling startled and miserable. How could fashion fulfil such a beautiful woman?

And he knew then that, after the show, his next move would be to dismiss the waiting limousine, courtesy of the Cattlemen's Union.

And then he would be heading backstage.

Ally Fraser made her excited way through the backstage confusion. Around her, models were changing, some removing wigs or false eyelashes, while assistants gathered up costumes and shoes. As she passed, nearly everyone looked up to smile or to openly congratulate her. She was trying not to grin too widely, but her collection had clearly drawn the most enthusiastic audience response of the entire Quintessential show and she was over the moon. More importantly, she'd noticed at least two fashion journalists nodding and smiling at her when she'd taken her bow.

She stopped to check that several of her garments were being stored away properly and thought fleetingly of how wonderful it would be to be able to head straight for home and an early night. But although she was dead tired after the hectic pace of the past few weeks, she steeled herself to go outside to join in the cocktails and to be particularly pleasant to the fashion editors.

Quickly she glanced around the crowded room, making sure everything was under control before she left.

However there was a rather uncontrolled and excited babble erupting from the models in the far corner as a strange man walked into their midst. Ally stared, intrigued. These girls were so used to having all kinds of people wander in and out of their changing areas that they usually took no notice. But they were paying a great deal of attention to this good-looking stranger.

To her surprise, Ally saw that he was ignoring the girls' varied stages of undress as he advanced purposefully across the room. Most newcomers, especially males, couldn't keep their eyes from straying frantically. To her even greater surprise, she realised that the tall, dark intruder appeared to be heading straight for her. In his sleek, black tux, marching head and shoulders above the models, he advanced, staring at her so intently she felt her pulses begin to race.

'I'm looking for Lucette Hardy,' he said, as soon as he reached her.

His voice was deep and resonant and his claim sounded quite plausible and yet Ally found that she couldn't believe him. She had never considered herself to have telepathic insight, but this man's eyes were so fiercely fixed on hers that she knew straight away that he was seeking her out. And the knowledge held her, standing before him, mesmerised by his height, his strong, handsome face and his piercing blue eyes which looked exactly as if they had been made from summer skies.

As those eyes continued to explore every detail of her face, she struggled to speak. 'Poor Lucette's come down with flu,' she said. 'She's devastated to miss the show.'

'So that's what happened.' He looked away briefly and then his eyes found hers once again. 'You are—' he began and then cleared his throat as he corrected himself. 'Your designs are absolutely exquisite.' With a sweeping gesture, he indicated the racks of her clothes. 'The simple lines...' He paused, apparently lost for words.

'And neat silhouettes?' she supplied, her lips curled in sudden amusement.

He grinned then, a cheeky grin that totally transformed his face. 'OK, I read your comments in the catalogue. But honestly, I like the dress you're wearing best of all.'

'Thank you,' she replied. It was certainly not the first time she had received a compliment, but most of the praise that came her way was delivered with such a practised smoothness that it smacked of insincerity and slipped over her like an old, warm blanket that she took for granted. This evening her heart pounded erratically in response to his clumsy admission and she stared back at the sun-tanned, ruggedly handsome face knowing that she had never met a man like him. In contrast to her world of image-makers and haute couture, his masculinity seemed to be stripped of all pretension.

He frowned and she was surprised at the way his gaze dropped to his work-toughened hands as if he were suddenly shy. With a totally unexpected jolt of disappointment, she thought, soon he'll say it was a pleasure to meet me and then he'll be gone.

In the awkward silence, she looked back at him, taking in his broad shoulders, thick, black hair, rugged features and vivid blue eyes and wondered how someone who embodied the fantasies of half the women on the planet could make such a hash of what was clearly meant to be a simple pick-up.

'We haven't really met you know,' she heard herself saying a little too eagerly. 'You haven't even told me your name.'

He grinned again and visibly relaxed, his strong features turning so sunny that for a moment Ally thought the technical crew were playing tricks with the lighting.

'I'm Fletcher Hardy, Lucette's cousin. In Melbourne on business. I actually came to admire Lucette's work.' She half expected him to trot out something trite about ending up admiring the designer instead, but to her relief he didn't. Instead he asked, 'When do you finish here?'

'I'm afraid I've got to do my duty out there first.' She grimaced, pointing to the ballroom. 'Meet the press, that sort of thing.'

He pulled a face. 'You have my sympathy. I've had a day of that sort of thing myself.'

'Really?' She looked at Fletcher Hardy contemplatively. 'Now let me guess. You do something in the outdoors. A ski instructor? No, the press wouldn't bother you about that. Perhaps a mountaineer? Are you about to conquer something generally considered unconquerable?'

Fletcher laughed, throwing back his head and drawing sharp glances from others in the room, then he looked her over slowly and said softly and with wicked audacity, 'I'd say I might be in with a chance.'

The ripple of excitement that raced up her spine shocked Ally. This cousin of Lucette's was losing his shyness with breathtaking speed.

'I never was much good at guessing games,' she said quickly to cover her sudden self-consciousness. But she didn't mind his cheek. She'd never before felt such an immediate connection with another person, especially a man. No one else, on first meeting, had accelerated her heartbeat to such a heady, scampering pace. 'You'll have to remain a mystery for now,' she added. 'I really must go to this party. Why don't you join us?'

'Sure. Lead the way.'

Ally was aware of many eyes watching as Fletcher followed her into the cocktail party. As they helped themselves to champagne cocktails, Derek Squires, the bald-headed, much-tattooed designer rushed over to them.

'Darlings,' he crooned.

'Hello, Derek. I'd like you to meet Fletcher Hardy.'

'And hello-o, darling,' smiled Derek, eyeing Fletcher with open interest. Fletcher nodded politely.

'How's it all going?' Ally asked.

'Just keep me away from that dreadful woman,' shuddered Derek.

'Who's that?'

'Phoebe Hardcastle. She had the cheek to criticise my lovely blue lipstick. Said my girls looked half drowned.' He trembled in horror. 'She has the creative imagination of a fruit fly.'

'She certainly can be very cutting,' agreed Ally, flashing a quick glance at Fletcher to see how he was reacting to the conversation. His eyes were wide with interest.

'She has no understanding of fashion flair. Stupid cow.'

'Now let's not get too critical of cows,' cut in Fletcher. 'They're my stock-in-trade.' Both Derek and Ally looked at him curiously, waiting for more explanation. 'I raise cattle,' he said with a shrug.

'Oh, how awful for you,' murmured Derek, backing off hurriedly.

Ally smiled, her grey eyes dancing as she looked up at Fletcher from under her thick, dark lashes. 'I knew you did something in the outdoors.'

'Ally Fraser,' boomed a commanding voice from behind them. 'Spare me a minute or two if you please.'

An alarming-looking woman with bright red hair, thick spectacles and a heavy jaw pushed her way next to Ally.

'Oh, Phoebe. How are you this evening?'

'Tolerable, dear. But I've deadlines to meet. Can you answer a couple of quick questions?'

Ally shot Fletcher a swift, mildly apologetic glance and nodded. 'Fire away.'

'What I want, darling,' the redhead began, shoving a small tape recorder under Ally's nose, 'is for you to sum up in a nutshell...who you're trying to appeal to...who you expect to wear your clothes...who is going to connect with them.'

'But I've told you all that many times,' Ally protested.

'New show, new comments,' the journalist shot back, her eyes hard and unsympathetic.'

'Very well,' replied Ally after only a moment's hesitation. 'I think my clients are people who are looking for value... for something contemporary, but with classical elegance as well...'

She felt a strong hand pat her heartily on the back and looked up to catch Fletcher winking at her.

There were more questions which Ally answered as best she could, but the whole time she was terribly conscious of the way Fletcher's hand stayed there, resting on her bare shoulder. Her skin beneath the warm hand tingled deliciously in response.

'And are you planning to launch a range of perfumes, like some of the other more successful designers?' Phoebe was asking.

Ally wavered. This was something she had been considering, but it was too soon to talk about it.

'Good question,' cut in Fletcher. 'And when we have the answer to that, you'll be the first to know. We'll give you an exclusive, but for now we have another engagement.'

'Who are you?' spluttered Phoebe, looking up at Fletcher, her red-painted mouth agape.

'I'm Ms. Fraser's public relations consultant. It was very nice of you to give us your attention, but I'm afraid that's all we have time for.'

Ally gave a startled gasp, but the hand on her shoulder remained firmly in place as she felt herself gently but purposefully led away.

'What do you think you're doing?' she cried, twisting around to face him.

'Ssh. I'll explain in a minute.'

Frowning, and with lips pursed, Ally walked quietly beside Fletcher until they made their way through the throng and reached the main door of the ballroom.

'OK, now tell me what you're doing,' she demanded, still frowning and with her arms crossed over her chest.

'I'm abducting you,' he said quietly.

Then as she opened her mouth to retaliate, Fletcher placed a finger over her lips. 'I'm taking you away, because you're the most intriguing woman I've ever seen and I don't have much time in Melbourne and...we don't have time for all the social niceties.'

They stood staring at one another, his finger still warm on her lips. Ally was stunned.

'But my career hangs on these interviews,' she stammered.

'Do you really think so?'

She hesitated. It was a question she'd asked herself many times. She had always tried to 'do the right thing.' It was the way she'd been brought up, but she knew that little of what she'd actually said to a journalist ever appeared in print and usually when it did, she was furious at being misquoted.

Fletcher continued. 'These journos have already made their notes and taken their photographs. And they've already made up their minds about your clothes. Now all they want is free food and grog, to be seen with celebrities and to catch up on the hot gossip.'

Ally suspected that he was right. And, she reflected, she'd placed work before pleasure for so long now that she could hardly remember the last time she'd given in to capricious self-indulgence. If she hadn't been so certain this man was going to be incredibly important to her, she might have wavered. But her mind was too distracted by the thrill of intense excitement and heady anticipation she'd felt from the moment she first saw him. And that simple touch of his hand on her shoulder had seduced her body more surely than the most concerted efforts of any of her previous admirers. She could have been making the biggest mistake of her life, but suddenly she didn't care. Being with Fletcher Hardy became the only possible option.

'Where would you like to go?' she asked with a smile.

'Do you like Thai food?'

'Love it.'

They took a taxi to the best Thai restaurant in the city.

'You know Melbourne well?' Ally asked as their taxi wove through the traffic.

'Only the inner city area. I usually only come down for conferences once or twice a year.'

'And these cows of yours. Beef or dairy?'

'Beef. I own a cattle property on the Burdekin River. Wallaroo Downs.'

'The Burdekin? That's in North Queensland, isn't it?'

'Sure is.'

'A long way from here.' Ally tried not to sound too bothered by this news.

'About three thousand kilometres.'

'And you like living up there?'

'Yes. I do.' He slanted her a slow smile and stretched his arm along the back of the seat. 'And I like visiting down here.'

The restaurant was fairly crowded, but there were still some tables to spare. The gleaming timber furniture, soft cream wool carpeting and enormous ceramic urns of beautiful fresh flowers provided a formal enough atmosphere for them to feel at ease in their elegant evening wear.

'It's been too long since I dined out,' Fletcher commented after they were seated.

'Well, at least you have an excuse,' said Ally. 'I don't suppose there are too many restaurants on your block, but I'm surrounded by them and I still don't indulge much.'

'So, tonight is a treat for both of us,' smiled Fletcher, and Ally wondered if she had ever seen quite such a sexy smile.

It was ridiculous to feel so excited, so expectant, as if she were a child on her birthday surrounded by beautifully tempting, as-yet-unopened presents, or a skydiver on the brink of a thrilling leap into the unknown.

She willed her stomach to stop fluttering as they chatted

about the menu, discussed the food and wine, their likes and dislikes. When the waiter came, Fletcher pronounced the Thai dishes with surprising fluency.

'You've been to Thailand?' she asked.

'Not as a tourist. Strictly business.'

'But you took time out for the important business of eating.'

Fletcher grinned and reached out to take her hand. 'I'm rather glad Lucette harangued me into coming to your show.' He looked down at her hand, which seemed so small and white in his sun-tanned grasp. 'No rings,' he said and then added with a lift of one dark eyebrow, 'Does that also mean no strings?'

'My work pulls me in all kinds of directions,' Ally admitted. 'But no strings of the personal variety. I've been rather single-minded about focusing on my career.'

'I can't believe there haven't been numerous attempts to sidetrack you.'

She tasted the crisp, white wine Fletcher had chosen while she considered his comment.

'A girl has to be careful.' She looked straight into his bright blue eyes. 'There have been plenty of wolves in the forest, but I always thought Little Red Riding Hood was far too easily led. I've mostly ignored them and just kept on going, heading straight for Granny's house.'

'In this case, Granny's house being the Quintessential label?'

'Yes.' She smiled.

'So, after the resounding success of this evening's show, perhaps you've earned yourself a little diversion,' he said.

'Per-perhaps.'

But, just remember, a warning voice sounded in her head,

that is all this man who lives three states away can possibly be—a temporary diversion. A pleasant—an extremely pleasant—dinner companion.

The meal was superb. A delicious soup of seafood simmered in coconut milk, ginger and coriander was followed by special Thai curries—a green beef curry for Fletcher and a red chicken version for Ally. Both dishes were accompanied by aromatic spoonfuls of fluffy, jasmine rice.

For Ally, the meal, the wine and the accompanying conversation were highly charged. While no one else had ever made her feel so comfortable, her bubbling emotions continually kept her on edge—incredibly excited and happier than she could ever remember, but nervous, too, wondering what on earth she would do when this meal was over and it was time for them to go their separate ways.

They talked and laughed together and she found herself telling Fletcher more about her love for fashion and her ambitions, and he listened intently, making her feel that she was a fascinating conversationalist. He talked a little about the conference that had brought him to Melbourne and very briefly about Wallaroo Downs.

Throughout the meal, his eyes were watching her. They seemed to travel restlessly from her face and throat to her arms and back again and she knew he was as sensitive as she was to something intensely strong and powerful filling the space between them. It was a heady, almost suffocating tension. This must be what they call sexual chemistry, Ally thought with bewildered fascination. Until now men had only ever induced in her a kind of bemused, gentle stirring of her senses. But Fletcher's compelling masculinity triggered an elemental need that startled her.

So that when they left the restaurant and stepped out onto

the street, Ally found herself turning to Fletcher and saying a trifle nervously, 'My apartment's only two blocks away. We could walk there if you like—for coffee.'

'Great idea,' he said with an easy smile and took her hand as they set off.

You've only just met the man, Ally kept reminding herself as they passed late-night coffee shops and silent, darkened office buildings. So, your hormones have come out of hibernation, but just remember you never, ever sleep with anyone on a first date.

'How long are you in town for?' she surprised herself by asking. It was a question she'd avoided all evening.

'Three days.'

Only three days! 'Oh.' Ally bit down hard on her lip, but it was too late to stifle the cry of disappointment.

Perhaps Fletcher shared her reaction, for he paused and, drawing her into the shadows of a shopfront, gathered her closer to him.

'And that reminds me...' he murmured.

'Reminds you?' Ally's voice trembled, her breath snatched away by his proximity. Up so close, she could feel his warm breath on her cheek, sense the strong muscles beneath his suit jacket and smell the spicy tang of his aftershave. In the scant light thrown by a street lamp some distance away, she could see his delicious smile. His eyes held hers and as she looked into the blue depths, she knew she had never wanted to be kissed more than she did now.

If only he needed to kiss her as much as she needed to taste his beautiful, sensuous mouth. Her ears buzzed, her heart had surely stopped beating. Was she breathing? Everything seemed to have stopped.

'I'm reminded,' he whispered, 'that it's time to start kissing you now. We really don't have time to waste, do we?' His hand cradled her cheek. 'I've been wanting to kiss you all evening,' he said. Then he lowered his lips to hers, to take her mouth gently in a kiss so tender, so tempting, that it only served to fire a desperate longing for more. Her lips parted eagerly as his mouth met hers again, to kiss her more deeply, more urgently, his arms binding her hard against him.

Ally hardly knew how to cope with the jolt of wild sensations that surged through her.

'O-oh,' she moaned softly, wondering if her feet still touched the ground, knowing at once that she belonged in this man's arms. Not wanting his mouth to ever leave hers. Nothing had ever felt so right.

He broke away as footsteps approached.

'We need somewhere private where I can kiss you very thoroughly.'

'We've nearly reached my place. It's just around the corner,' Ally replied, ignoring with reckless ease the alarm bells rung by her well-exercised conscience.

They walked quickly. The lift shot up to her apartment, and once inside, Ally switched on the low table lamps. In the warm pool of light, Fletcher looked at her, holding out his arms with a smile that banished any lingering inhibitions. And she walked into them, as eagerly and gladly as if it were what she was born to do. He threaded his fingers through her dark hair.

'You know, Ally, I don't consider myself a wolf. It's not usually my policy to rush these things.'

She felt a ridiculous stab of dismay at the note of caution in his voice.

'Well, to be honest, I like to get to know a man before I let him…kiss me,' she forced herself to admit.

'It's a bit reckless, can be dangerous in fact.'

'It certainly can be,' she muttered, burying her head into his chest and breathing in the mixture of cotton and silk of his clothes combined with the cleanly masculine scent of his skin. Hearing the pounding of his heart.

'So perhaps I should leave now?' he breathed against her cheek, as his fingers gently stroked the nape of her neck.

'Do you really want to know what I think?' she asked, closing her eyes and arching her curves closer into his strength.

'Uh-huh,' he murmured, while his lips trailed dizzying circles over her jaw in a manner that could elicit only one possible answer.

'I think we're wasting valuable time standing here talking.'

CHAPTER TWO

ALLY LOOKED UP sleepily as Fletcher emerged from the bathroom, a huge white towel looped around his lean hips. Her breath caught in her throat. All this dark-haired, broad-shouldered, lean-and-muscled masculine perfection was about to walk out of her life just as abruptly as it had appeared. How could the time have flown so quickly?

Monday morning had never felt so bad.

Over the weekend, she and Fletcher had been together for every moment their work commitments spared them, and Ally was delighted to discover that there were so many other wonderful qualities about this man apart from his superb body. She and Fletcher had meshed on so many levels—emotional, physical and intellectual. It had been like meeting a soul mate.

But it had been all too short.

'Did we really only meet two night's ago?' she asked, while her thoughts echoed silently—I feel as if I've known you all my life.

Her knees tucked under her chin, Ally watched from the

bed as Fletcher slowly buttoned his shirt, looking down at her with a regretful, thoughtful smile.

He crossed the room to sit on the edge of her mattress. 'I think there's a New Age term for the way we met,' he said. 'We experienced a defining moment.' He lifted his hand as if he were going to reach for her, but stopped, the hand hovering in midair. He sighed and stood up again, reaching instead for the lavender lace nightdress which was crumpled at the bottom of her bed. Tossing it to her, he flashed a cheeky smile. 'And I'd say you've been redefined as a purple passionfruit.'

Ally plucked at the garment. Her fondness for all shades of purple had amused and enchanted Fletcher. Until now it had simply been a colour she often chose to wear because it complemented her dark hair, pale skin and clear, grey eyes. But Fletcher had insisted her favourite colour was symbolic of the newly discovered passionate side to her nature she had never known existed.

She tried desperately to smile back at him. But it was difficult to hide the despair she felt at the reality of Fletcher's leaving. Any minute now the taxi would be pulling up in the street below and he would be walking out of her life, catching the early flight back to North Queensland and his cattle and his outback. He might as well be heading for Mars.

'I suppose you could call our meeting a defining moment,' she said, but then in the next breath, she blurted out, 'But what about the old-fashioned description—love at first sight across a crowded room?'

'Love?' Fletcher looked down at her, startled. 'When I'm about to catch a plane to the back of beyond...' He paused in the act of threading a plaited leather belt through the loops of his jeans and his eyes darkened to a worried navy blue. 'We can't afford to get overly romantic, Ally.'

She felt her face flood with scarlet and a cold hand clamp tightly round her heart. She'd been caught out making the oldest mistake of all. Confusing passionate sex with love and respect and compatibility. Fletcher had never promised her anything more than three nights.

And now their time was up. And she was grown up. This was the real world.

But how could she bear it?

Then it happened just as Ally knew it would. The taxi arrived, with a screech of tyres and a blast of its horn. Fletcher clasped her to him, kissed her, held her, whispered soothing nothings, kissed her again. And then he was gone. The door closed behind him with a soft sigh and she heard his footsteps on the pavement below, the slam of a car door. And it was all over. Just like that.

She couldn't move. She should have been eating breakfast, dressing for work, but she lay there in the bed wondering how something so wonderful could leave her feeling so lonely and desolate. The usual expectant tingle she felt at the start of the working week had vanished. Her mind, her heart, her body—all of her was numb—a huge gaping vacuum.

Well, she thought with chagrin, Fletcher Hardy had taught her one thing—actually, several if the truth be told. She had never known that lovemaking could be so imaginative, beautiful and exciting all at once. But the end result was her very sure knowledge that she was not the type to enjoy casual sex. It had never happened that way before. Never before had she simply met a man she wanted and thought that alone was an excuse for intimacy. And now she was paying the price for giving away her heart and her body so easily.

She had fallen in love. Hopeless, unreturned love.

She rolled over and buried her head in the pillow, giving in to the luxury of tears—of huge, gasping, noisy sobs.

She wasn't sure how long she had lain there deep in her misery before the phone on her bedside table rang loudly, startling her. Automatically, she lifted the receiver without stopping to consider that she was in no fit state to take a call.

'Hello, Ally. Ally, are you there?'

'Yes,' she blubbered, shoving the bunched-up corner of the sheet into her mouth to stifle more sobs.

'Ally, it's Lucette.'

'Oh, hi. How—how are you?'

'Much better thanks. But I was knocked out by this flu. I can't believe my rotten luck missing the show.'

'Oh, Lucette, you poor thing. I meant to ring you, but—I got caught up. I know that sounds a rather lame excuse. Your set was wonderful! It really was marvellous.'

'I'm glad everything was OK. Do you have the flu now, Ally? You sound awful.'

'My nose is a bit stuffed up,' admitted Ally, reaching for a tissue. 'By the way, I met your cousin,' she added, regretting, even as the words left her lips, her feeble, weak will.

'Fletcher? Really? I hadn't heard from him so I assumed he didn't make it to the show. Poor fellow, I bet he hated it. It's not really his scene at all.'

'Oh, he seemed fairly interested in some aspects of it.'

'What did you think of him?' asked Lucette, a subtle lilt in her voice implying past experience of Fletcher's effect on women. 'Most of my friends think he's pretty cute.'

I'll bet they do, thought Ally with a stab of foolish jealousy. How many other friends of Lucette's had Fletcher dallied with? 'He—he seemed very presentable,' she mumbled.

'Anyhow you'd be wasting your time looking twice at Fletcher,' continued Lucette.

'Oh?' Ally tried for nonchalance, but the word emerged as more of a desperate honk.

'Oh, he has too much bush in his blood. I mean, I grew up in the bush, too—on a property not far from his, but I was glad to leave the outback. But Fletcher will never leave. He's totally committed to his property. Passionate about the land. So there's not much future for a city girl with a man like him.'

'Fair enough,' replied Ally, trying to sound bored, wishing she'd had more common sense than to allow this conversation to turn to Fletcher. 'Did you read the coverage of our show in the newspapers?' she asked, trying to steer Lucette back to safer ground.

But she didn't hear Lucette's reply. As she sat there on her bed, the phone clutched in one hand and a bunch of tissues in the other, she heard a familiar, authoritative knock at her front door. Her heart stilled.

Ally dropped the phone, then picked it up and spluttered. 'I—I'm sorry, Lucette. I've got to go.'

Then, her heart thundering in her chest, she bounded out of bed and snatched up a towelling bathrobe, tying it around her as she hurried across the room. It couldn't be! Surely not.

At the front door, she paused and took a deep breath. Don't be ridiculous, she warned herself. He's on the plane. This will be someone from work. Get a grip! But it was a shaking hand she raised to the latch.

She inched the door open. At first, all she could see was an enormous bunch of Cooktown orchids with lilac petals and purple throats. But then, from behind them, came Fletcher's uncertain smile.

'Oh!'

'These were the only purple flowers I could find,' he said with an apologetic grin and a slight shrug of one broad shoulder. 'I know it's your favourite colour and—'

'Fletcher, you're still here.'

'I couldn't do it, Ally,' he whispered into her hair as she flung her arms around him. 'I don't know what this means, but I couldn't get on that plane. I...'

The rest of his words were lost as she linked her hands behind his neck and, with a gesture that felt as right and natural as breathing, pulled his face and his beautiful, sensuous mouth to meet hers.

She managed to wangle a week's special leave. The following days and nights were perfect. They drove into the country and wandered hand in hand through fields of springtime wild flowers. They dined out, cooked for each other, brought home take-away meals and watched movies together. Sensational days and nights. Ally had never had so much fun, had never felt so happy. It was a happiness she knew could not last, but she refused to think about the future, and had absolutely no inclination to think about her work.

And the Cooktown orchids were the first of many purple presents. Fletcher showered her with gifts; chocolate hearts with violet cream centres, a purple velvet evening bag, a box of crystallised violets and finally a beautiful pendant with amethysts set in filigree silver.

Two nights before she was due back at work they lay together on her wide bed, their bodies gleaming in the silvery light of the moon that shone through a high arched window, listening to one of Ally's favourite Brahms sonatas. Rolling onto his side so that, propped on one elbow, he could look into her eyes, Fletcher smiled tenderly. 'I shall never, ever forget you, Ally.' With a long finger, he traced the silvery outline of her body. 'This neat silhouette will be my most precious memory,' he told her, his voice husky.

'I've never been so happy.' She laughed, kissing him. 'I've quite shocked myself.'

Fletcher's blue eyes widened. 'Shocked as in horrified, or shocked as in surprised?'

'Oh, surprised. Very pleasantly surprised.' She bent over him, enjoying the hungry glint in his eyes as her breasts grazed his chest. She nibbled gently at the stubble on his chin. 'I've never been like this before. Wanting to make love over and over. Never having enough.'

'Some people might find that shocking,' Fletcher agreed with a happy chuckle, 'but I don't have a problem with it.'

'So, you're not sleepy yet?' she asked, her voice sultry with desire.

'How could I sleep with your tempting little body draped all over me. Watch out, Ally, you're about to be shocked some more, but I promise you'll love it.' And Fletcher was as good as his word.

The happy bubble burst with a phone call at breakfast.

Ally was making fruit salad, scooping out the fleshy pulp of a passionfruit and laughingly claiming that she bore absolutely no resemblance to the round purple fruit Fletcher had coined as her nickname.

The shrill summons of the telephone came from the lounge room.

'I'll get it,' said Fletcher, helping himself to a cube of mango before he swung his long legs off the pine kitchen stool.

With a contented smile, Ally watched him stride across the

room, then she continued to chop banana and squeeze lemon juice over it before adding it to the bowl. She was stirring all the fruits together, delighting in the fresh colour combinations of the different melons—the pale green of honeydew, combined with the deep pink of watermelon and the delicate orange of rockmelon—when she sensed Fletcher standing very still and quiet in the kitchen doorway. She looked up and was startled by his stunned, sad expression.

'Fletcher, what's the matter?'

'There's been an accident,' he said quietly.

Ally felt her stomach lurch with a sudden horrible fear. She watched him walk towards her slowly, awkwardly, his mouth twisted with the effort to hold his emotions in check. 'My best friend, Jock Lawrence and his wife, Lisa—killed in a car accident in Sydney.'

'Oh, I'm so sorry.'

'Yeah.' Fletcher let out a weary sigh and sank back onto the kitchen stool, his shoulders slumped. Ally quickly moved to the other side of the bench and slipped her arms around him. She rested her cheek gently against his and he turned and kissed her in a brief acknowledgment of her offer of comfort. 'I just can't believe it. He was such a great guy. We went to school, to university…'

There was nothing she could say or do except stay there, holding him, letting him talk slowly, haltingly.

'I'll have to go, Ally. I mean I'd go to the fune-funeral anyway. But there's his son—little Connor. He was the only—only survivor, strapped in one of those little seats in the back. I'm his godfather and, according to old Mr. Lawrence, I've also been named as his guardian.'

'Guardian? Does that mean he'll live with you?'

'Perhaps. I'm not sure yet. He's with his grandparents in

Sydney at the moment, but they're pretty old and frail. Jock's father sounded very shaken.' He stood up quickly, so quickly that her hands, as they fell away from his shoulders, slapped against her sides. 'I'll have to ring the airlines and make a booking. Oh, God, I can't believe it.'

Ally followed him into her lounge room and sat some distance away watching as he dialled and waited for a connection, before speaking to the airline. She felt cold and lonely, knowing with a sudden certainty that this time when Fletcher left Melbourne he would be walking out of her life. Going back to his own people—where he belonged.

Eventually he hung up and told her softly. 'I got a cancellation on the 9:00 a.m. flight.'

'This morning?' cried Ally in panic. 'That's only two hours away.'

'I'm sorry, Ally, but Jock's parents—I don't know that they have anyone to help them deal with this.'

'Of course, I understand,' replied Ally, ashamed of her selfish outburst. 'I'll make us a pot of coffee.'

Fletcher was still sitting in the lounge chair, staring thoughtfully at a spot on the rug when she returned. He looked up.

'Smells good.' He smiled, his blue eyes warming as they linked with hers.

She handed him a steaming cup and then sat opposite him, curling her legs beneath her and hugging the mug of coffee to her chest as if for comfort.

'I guess this brings back bad memories for you,' he said gently.

Ally felt her eyebrows lift in surprise. She had told Fletcher just about everything there was to know about her and she guessed that he was referring to her own parents' death in an aeroplane crash when she was seventeen. But that was not on her mind now. Sad as this accident was, all she could think about was what it meant to her relationship with Fletcher. There was so much she wanted to say, had needed to say all week.

In all the talk and all the passion and happiness they shared, they learned a lot about each other, but they skirted round the truth. They had never discussed their future because the horrible truth was that there was no possible future for them. Fletcher's biannual visits to Melbourne were hardly the grounds for an ongoing relationship.

Fletcher put down his cup of coffee and stood up. He looked at her so sadly Ally felt tears spring to her eyes.

'Ally, I'm sorry about this...'

'Don't be, Fletcher. You have to go.'

'No, I mean I'm sorry about us, about coming back and making things worse. If I'd left on Monday...' He reached down and scooped her into his arms. 'I should have been stronger. Should have been able to resist your spell. You're so damn beautiful, Ally.'

How perfectly her body nestled into his. How much she wanted him to go on telling her she was beautiful.

'But what you're trying to say is...we come from two different, totally incompatible worlds,' she said, her voice shaking with the effort to sound calm.

'Too right,' he sighed. 'You do understand, sweetheart, don't you?'

She nodded her head against his chest. Her throat was burning with hot tears. Fletcher's long fingers played with her hair.

'They warn us so much these days about the need for

physical protection in a relationship, but that's easy to look after. But protecting our emotions, that's a different story.'

'Perhaps there's a solution,' she couldn't help adding.

'No, I've thought and thought about it. There's no way ahead for us, Ally. You have your career and I have my cattle.'

'City girls have been happy in the country before today,' she offered timidly. 'Perhaps I should come and live with you on Wallaroo Downs.'

He broke away from her then, staring at her, his sky blue eyes puzzled, clearly shocked by her words. He shook his head slowly.

'That's a pretty fairy tale, and if it could come true I'd be the happiest man alive, but it wouldn't—it couldn't end in happily ever after.'

Ally felt a painful lump form in her throat, preventing a reply.

'You see,' he continued, the tone in his voice a daunting mixture of tenderness and regret, 'there are more differences between us than my paddocks and your tar and cement. You'd hate the life I lead, Ally. You live in a world you've worked so hard to reach—and it's so elegant and artistic.'

'It's not glamorous all the time,' Ally managed to protest.

'Sewing machine oil is the closest you'd come to grease and dirt,' he said with a lopsided smile that wrenched at her heart. 'I'm just sorry I've messed you up. I've never done anything so damned stupid in my life before.'

Ally's chin came up defiantly. 'I don't think it was at all stupid. I've never had anything so wonderful happen to me— ever.'

Fletcher groaned and pulled her to him. 'Listen, passion-fruit,' he whispered, 'I have to pack and then I'm going to Sydney. And after that I'll almost certainly have to get back to Wallaroo. There's a muster coming up and I have to be back for that. Then, with a bit of luck, there'll be a wet season. I can't see us getting together again in a long while. You're a beautiful, clever woman and this is where you belong. You have to get on with your brilliant career. There's no other way of looking at this.'

She knew that as a woman of the nineties she should be able to handle this. People had relationships and then they moved on. It was as simple as that. It happened all around her all the time.

But not to her.

Ally glanced at the clock on the wall behind Fletcher. If he were to make it to his flight, he would have to get moving.

'I'll check out the laundry basket. See if you've left anything there,' she said grimly with a small, dismissive shrug of her shoulders.

Fletcher packed in silence while Ally tidied the kitchen. They had never been so quick and efficient together. She insisted on driving him to the airport.

As her small sedan zipped along the freeway, she tried to forget about her own sadness and think of the poor little boy left without parents.

'This little boy, Connor. Do you know him very well?' she asked.

'No. I have to admit, I haven't seen all that much of him,' admitted Fletcher. 'I went to his christening when he was just a tiny tadpole—hadn't even reached the ankle-biter stage. He must be three or four now. Last time I saw him he'd just started toddling around. As far as I remember, he looks like Jock.' His voice broke a little. 'Brown hair and eyes—going to be tall.'

Once they reached the busy, bustling airport, and Fletcher

had queued then checked in, there was little time for conversation. And there was certainly no privacy for the kinds of things Ally would have liked to discuss. All too soon the flight to Sydney was boarding and for the last time she felt Fletcher's strong arms around her, and his warm, delicious lips on hers.

'Be beautiful, Ally,' he whispered, his eyes glistening with a betraying dampness. Then he swung away quickly and strode through the doors of the departure lounge, leaving her without looking back.

She was prepared for his silence; she hadn't expected him to ring her from Sydney. And she was prepared for the sense of desolation that swamped her. But what she hadn't expected was the lassitude with which she returned to her work. She'd hoped that once back in the swing of things, the old enthusiasm for dealing with designs, textiles and market trends and the fascinating array of individuals associated with that world would rescue her from her misery.

It was with a growing sense of alarm that she faced each day at the office. She took her designs home to work on at night, hoping the soothing atmosphere of her own apartment would help inspiration to flow. With the spring and summer collection behind her, Ally had to plan for next year's winter season and a juicy contract with the wool board was on offer. Normally she would have been thrilled. But she couldn't concentrate and what was worse, much, much worse, she couldn't bring herself to care.

Her mind and her emotions were totally absorbed with Fletcher. Where was he now? Had he gone back to North Queensland? Had he taken little Connor with him? Did he think about her the way she thought endlessly of him?

After three weeks of silence and despair, she could stand it no longer. She had to make some kind of contact with him. Her first step was to ring Lucette.

'Have I heard from Fletcher, Ally?' Lucette repeated, her voice squeaking with surprise at Ally's first question once the greetings were over. 'Why, yes, I have actually. He rang from North Queensland just yesterday.'

'You see,' Ally offered with a silly little laugh, 'I ended up seeing quite a bit of him while he was down here, but then he was called away for the funeral...' Her voice trailed away as her tightly strung nerves clenched a notch tighter.

The stunned silence on the other end of the line didn't help her feel any more relaxed.

'Really?' Lucette managed at last.

'Does he have the little boy with him?'

'No, not yet. Connor's still in Sydney with his grand-parents. But as a matter of fact that's why Fletcher rang me. He's guardian for Connor and he wants me to find a nanny to travel up to Wallaroo Downs and help take care of him there.'

Ally closed her eyes against the frightening wave of dizzi-ness that swamped her as a host of different pictures crowded her mind: pictures of Fletcher, sun-tanned, astride a horse somewhere in North Queensland; of Fletcher and a little brown-haired, brown-eyed boy walking hand in hand along a shady creek bank; of a young attractive nanny living with them both day in, day out.

'Ally, are you still there?'

'Yes, Lucette. I'm here. Listen, would you mind terribly much if I came and visited you? I need to talk.'

'That's fine,' replied Lucette, unable to disguise her sur-prise. 'I'll be home all evening. You have my address?'

* * *

'But, Ally, this is impossible!' Lucette exclaimed an hour later as the two women sat opposite each other at the kitchen table in her tiny bed-sit apartment. 'For starters you underestimate the stubbornness of the Hardy male. There's no way Fletcher would have someone like you as a nanny on Wallaroo Downs.'

Ally's chest tightened painfully at Lucette's words.

'I think Fletcher came to care for me. In fact I know he did.'

Something in her expression seemed to capture Lucette's attention. She stared at Ally for several silent moments and then she reached over and took Ally's hand.

'I'm sure he does feel very strongly about you,' she said gently. 'Fletcher's usually very wary about getting entangled with women, because of where he lives. He believes only women who grow up in the bush can take the harsh life of the outback. So if he allowed you to understand he cared…' Lucette paused and smiled ruefully. 'Then I'd say chances are he was totally smitten.'

'I'm prepared to take a gamble on it.'

'But your career!' Lucette cried. 'How could you possibly turn your back on everything you've achieved?'

'I don't know,' admitted Ally. 'A month ago I would have said it was totally impossible, but…' She paused, taking in a deep shuddering breath. 'Have you ever been in love, Lucette?'

'Of course,' the girl laughed, 'hundreds of times.'

'No. I'm talking the real thing. I can't go on without him. I can't work. I can't eat or sleep.' She paused and shook her head at Lucette's wide-eyed response. 'I can't believe I'm saying all this. I used to be the first person to condemn girls who went all drippy over males. I mean, I used to think that all it took to resist falling into that kind of trap was a modicum of intelligence. But honestly, Lucette, I've no choice. I've got to go to him.'

Lucette sighed and refilled Ally's coffee cup. 'Ally, I really feel for you, believe me. But I don't think Fletcher would have a bar of it. And it wouldn't be because he doesn't care for you. It's simply that he couldn't imagine how you could possibly be happy out there. He'd worry about taking you away from everything you've achieved.' Lucette eyed her crestfallen friend with concern. 'This is all my fault!'

'What do you mean?'

'Well, if I hadn't been so jolly eager to show off my set designs when he was in Melbourne for that conference, he would never have come to the show and fallen for the lovely Alexandra Fraser.'

Ally closed her stinging, tear-filled eyes as she remembered that moment when a tall, dark grazier marched into the models' dressing room! She stared into her coffee cup. 'I think I've got to do it, Lucette. I'm prepared for everyone telling me I'm mad. I'm prepared for Fletcher to be a little angry at first, but I think he'll get over it. It's just that I've found someone I love more than my career and I think I can convince him of that, too. I've fallen in love and I can't just sit here and do absolutely zilch about it!'

'Well, apart from anything else we've covered, there might still be one major hitch,' said Lucette tentatively.

'Which is?' asked Ally, lifting her chin in a brave effort at defiance.

'What experience have you had as a nanny?'

'Aha! I can answer that,' cried Ally triumphantly. 'All the time I was at college, I worked as a nanny for the Johnstons.

You know Dr. James Johnston and his wife Helen—the pae-diatricians? Nights, weekends, holidays. I looked after their four children on and off for three and a half years.'

Lucette raised her fair eyebrows and looked back at Ally with eyes the same sky blue as Fletcher's. She took a long, deep swig of her coffee. 'Then perhaps we'd better take a closer look at this,' she said with a solemnity which was to-tally spoiled when her face broke into a cheeky grin, again alarmingly like her cousin's. 'But we're going to have to plan it all very carefully.'

CHAPTER THREE

THE BEST LAID plans of mice and men... The unwelcome quotation flashed through Ally's mind again as it had on repeated occasions over recent weeks. But now, with Connor's little hand clinging to hers as she crossed the steamy car park at Townsville airport, she refused to think of defeat. Together with Lucette, she had schemed and plotted so that this risky enterprise would run like clockwork and the journey was almost complete.

She'd been nervous about going to Sydney to meet Connor, but the few days she'd spent there getting to know the little boy had been delightful. They had enjoyed a trip to the beach and to Taronga Park Zoo, as well as some quiet times at his grandparents' house. Then, to her relief, he had come with her and Lucette on the plane flight to Townsville without objection. All that was left was the final leg—driving out to Wallaroo Downs.

And to Fletcher.

Ally shifted the weight of her large carry bag higher onto her shoulder and smiled at Connor, who looked back at her with trusting, big brown eyes.

'This should be our vehicle,' said Lucette, indicating a sturdy-looking station wagon in the line-up of hire cars. She pushed their heavily loaded luggage carrier the last few metres and clicked the central locking button on her key. 'Hey, presto! Look, Connor,' Lucette cried as she swung the car door open. 'Magic doors!'

But Ally could feel Connor backing away, his hand in hers struggling to be freed.

'No!' he cried. 'No! I don't like that car!' His little face contorted in fear as he tried to pull away.

Ally dropped to her knees and threw her arms around him.

'No!' he sobbed. 'I don't like that car!' His voice rose in alarm, but he clung to Ally. She could feel his little body trembling and her heart nearly broke for him.

'Oh, you poor darling,' Ally murmured as she hugged him to her. She realised at once that his parents must have been driving a similar car when they were taken from him so horrifically.

Lucette hovered uncertainly near the luggage.

'Sweetheart, look. I've got something to show you,' Ally said as she dipped her hand into the large carry bag and drew out a soft toy she'd been keeping for such a moment.

The sobs subsided slightly. 'What—what is it?' Connor hiccupped, staring through his tears at the furry brown creature Ally held.

'It's a platypus, Connor. I had him made just for you.' A plump little hand reached tentatively towards the ball of fur.

'Plat-pus?' he whispered.

'That's right,' said Ally. 'See, he has a fluffy tummy and a lovely black bill and four little black feet.'

Connor fingered one webbed foot, beautifully crafted from the finest black leather.

'That's amazing,' exclaimed Lucette from behind them. 'It's so lifelike. Did you have it made at work?'

Ally nodded. 'A few people owed me favours.' She spoke to Connor. 'Real platypuses live in creeks out in the bush. And that's where we're going. Uncle Fletcher lives there, too.'

'Can I hold the plat-pus?'

'Of course you can, darling. He's yours to keep.' Aware that Lucette was quietly loading their luggage into the back of the station wagon, Ally continued talking as Connor cuddled his new toy. 'When I was a little girl, my favourite story was about a platypus called Shy. Would you like me to tell it to you?'

The little boy nodded solemnly, blinking away his tears.

'Well let's you, me and your platypus make ourselves comfortable in the back of the car here and I'll tell you about Shy.' Ally held her breath as she gently guided Connor towards the car door. He hesitated and turned to her.

'Can I call my plat-pus Shy?'

'Of course you can. It's a lovely name, isn't it,' Ally reassured him, and he allowed himself to be buckled into his car seat without another murmur.

And as Ally began her story of the platypus family who lived in the riverbank, Lucette slipped into the driver's seat and the car slowly edged out into the traffic.

Shy had been a big hit with Connor, Ally reflected hours later, as she sedately guided a gentle mare down a quiet bush track at Wallaroo Downs. One hurdle had been cleared, but a still higher one faced her. She had yet to discover how Fletcher would react when he returned from a day's branding to find her already settled into his home.

Grateful for the shady protection of whispering casuarinas, she tried to shrug off her nervousness by focusing on the soothing sounds of the quiet bush; the steady clip, clop of Juno's careful steps and the peaceful hum of cicadas in the trees around her.

No wonder Fletcher loved his outback. It was so remote, so alien in its stark, dry beauty—another world. Separated from Melbourne by thousands of kilometres, it was hard to believe she was still in the same country. On the drive inland from Townsville airport they'd travelled through heat and dust and past endless paddocks of brown, lifeless-looking stubble, but here, by the creek, it was cool and shady and perfectly serene.

Until...the afternoon peace was split by the sudden roar of a motorbike.

To Ally's horror, her startled horse whinnied and reared, hooves striking at the air. Then, within breathless seconds, she felt the reins snatched from her trembling hands and a furious voice roared at her.

'Alexandra? What the hell are you doing here?'

Panic flared!

Common sense should have told her the danger was over. The dreadful motorbike's engine had cut off, the mare was calming down and the bush was quickly returning to its former languid stillness. So she knew the wild thumping of her heart was an overreaction. There was no longer any excuse for her to crouch low against Juno's neck with her eyes squeezed tightly shut.

Except that she knew that voice.

She knew exactly who was bellowing at her and it was the very last person she wanted to meet until all her plans were in place.

He wasn't supposed to be down here!

With trepidation, she lifted her head, blinked, and her stomach clenched. A fiercely scowling Fletcher stood within arm's reach, Juno's reins gripped tightly in one strong brown hand.

She found herself fighting a nervous urge to look away, yet she forced her eyes to hold Fletcher's scalding gaze. Agitated as she was, she couldn't stifle a swift glow of admiration. He was as rugged and tall, as wide-shouldered and lean-limbed as the memory she had treasured these past weeks. And his eyes, piercing blue as ever, were a perfect match for the flashes of brilliant sky she glimpsed between the swamp bloodwoods behind him. But the smile, the special, heart-flipping grin, was missing. She had never known Fletcher not to smile at her!

This was nothing like the reception she had hoped for and pictured hundreds of times during the last few weeks. She manoeuvred her strained features into something resembling a smile.

'Er…hello, Fletcher… I'm, um, I'm practising riding.'

'I see.' His clipped reply dropped unhelpfully into the space between them.

Ally shivered. It was then she noticed the trail bike he'd abandoned when she and Juno blundered onto his path, now slewed against an old tree stump a metre or so behind him. The realisation of her guilt sent her heart sinking further.

'I'm sorry I nearly ran into you.'

The apology was clearly not accepted. Fletcher merely continued to glare at her in silent anger while her wretched eyes took in more details. His crow-black hair, his bare chest and shoulders all glistened with water and his jeans clung to his hips and thighs in dark, damp patches that blatantly outlined his flagrant masculinity.

'You've been swimming?' she stammered.

'Yes,' he replied. The briefest flicker of a smile twitched the corners of his mouth. 'If you'd been a few minutes earlier, you would have found me in the creek.'

Heat stole into her cheeks. He would have been swimming naked. She had no doubt about that.

She whipped her eyes away from his damp lower region as he growled at her, without smiling. 'I suppose it's too much to ask for an explanation as to why you've suddenly appeared here, and just happen to be riding one of my horses without any invitation?'

'I was planning to give you a very good explanation.'

'Planning, Ally? Hell! You practically caused a serious accident.'

His hostility was enough to wither her tiny stock of courage even before she began to defend herself.

'I said I'm sorry.' Ally's grey eyes blazed briefly, then her lashes lowered over them as she mumbled her excuse. 'Your stockman said I could use this horse—that you were out branding somewhere. I didn't know—'

'You came over three thousand kilometres just to take in a little horse riding practice?'

She nearly lost her nerve there and then. Clearly he regarded her as an intruder—uninvited and unwanted. Tears gathered swiftly, burning the backs of her lids.

How could this happen? This was the man she loved! This was her Fletcher! He had come to the city and made exquisite love to her and changed her life forever. But now he had the audacity to glare at her with outright rejection clearly stamped in the firm set of his jaw, the frowning black stripe of his eyebrows and the white-knuckled clench of his fists.

She took an agonising breath hoping to calm her frantic,

self-defeating thoughts. 'You're surprised to see me,' she whispered, and her wide eyes anxiously darted away from his unyielding gaze.

'Surprise is one word I could choose, I guess,' Fletcher drawled, his deep voice rumbling with sarcasm. But now he was staring back at her, hard. His eyes travelled—very deliberately—over her slim frame, her jeans and soft, white shirt buttoned low over a pale lavender crop top. They rested for the longest time on her pale face. 'What are you doing here?' he repeated, his voice less harsh this time, as if he had run out of breath suddenly.

'I—I've— Your cousin and I have brought your little godson— Connor.' The words tumbled out of control like beads spilling from a broken necklace.

Fletcher scowled. 'You came with Lucette?'

'Yes. You're his guardian now...'

'I know damn well I'm his guardian, but what I still don't understand is what you've got to do with it?'

'Well, Lucette was looking for a nanny for Connor so that you...'

'You're sidetracking,' Fletcher snapped. 'Get to the point.'

'Well, the point is,' resumed Ally, running her tongue nervously over parched lips. 'I'm his nanny.'

'What?'

Startled, Ally watched as the colour in Fletcher's face deepened and then leached away while, with the worst sense of timing, a kookaburra broke into raucous laughter in a gum tree overhanging the track.

'Hell, Ally! You can't be!'

'I've had some training as a nanny,' she offered tentatively, then began to chew the inside of her cheek while her fingers nervously played with the horse's mane.

'Damn it to hell! Of all the crazy…!' He studied her through narrowed eyes. 'How much?'

'How much what?' she repeated lamely.

'How much training have you done to be a nanny for heaven's sake?'

'That's how I put myself through Art College—working as a nanny for…'

Interrupting her with a fierce curse, Fletcher tossed the reins back over Juno's neck before striding across the track away from her, shaking his head, clearly unimpressed, quite obviously more angry than ever.

'I know it might look as if I'm trying to profit from a little boy's tragedy,' Ally called after him.

But he ignored her.

Snatching a faded blue cotton shirt from the seat of his trail bike, he shrugged his broad brown back into it and Ally half expected to see the thin cotton split beneath the savagery of his movements. He prowled slowly back to her and when he spoke again, his voice was weary—as if he had fought a long battle.

'You've spent years of training and hard work to become a leading bloody fashion designer, so stop spinning me this yarn about nannies and tell me what you're really doing here, Alexandra Fraser?'

Ally gulped. This was all so dreadfully different from how their meeting was meant to be. She could see her careful plans collapsing as helplessly as a child's sandcastle beneath the tide. Of course, she had expected Fletcher to be surprised, even shocked when she arrived on his property out of the blue, but she had never dreamed that their meeting would be so…so vitriolic.

This was certainly not the time to confess that she had

given up everything just to be here with him. She felt another blush mount embarrassingly into her cheeks as she mentally dumped her real reason, that she wanted to spend the rest of her life at his side. If he had caught her red-handed, duffing his precious cattle, he couldn't have scowled at her with any more venom.

But, she acknowledged wretchedly, she'd come a long way and, while now, face-to-face with Fletcher and his outback, nothing seemed clear and logical like it had in Melbourne, she really had no choice but to hang on to her pride and continue. She straightened her shoulders.

'I have told you,' she began frostily. 'I want to stay here and be Connor's nanny. As you know I lost my own parents in a plane crash when I was seventeen.... I was much older than Connor, of course, but I do understand something of what he's going through.... Besides,' she offered a tiny white lie, 'Lucette had all sorts of trouble trying to find someone suitable.'

'Someone suitable?' He laughed bitterly and the blue eyes glittered coldly. 'I thought Lucette would have known better. She grew up on a cattle property and knows what it's like here. She couldn't have found anyone less suitable than you.'

'No-o!'

He might just as well have slapped her hard. As if in sympathy, the mare stepped sideways with a swaying lurch. Ally reached for the pommel to steady herself and if possible, her cheeks burned even hotter.

Surely she was the biggest love-struck fool in all history! Somehow she forced herself to stare back at Fletcher's glowering face, but as she did so, Ally was compelled to ask herself the dreadful, but oh so obvious question—how in heaven's name had she ever been so certain that this man loved her?

'Let's go back to the homestead to sort this out.' Fletcher's businesslike voice broke into her wretched thoughts. 'I take it you didn't just dump my godson on the doorstep. Lucette stayed behind with Connor?'

'Yes,' Ally managed, blinking back tears. 'But she can't stay for long. She's going on to Richmond this evening.'

'And then she'll leave you holding the baby?'

'But I don't mind at all. And he's hardly a baby. He's four and he's an absolute darling—a bright, good little boy.'

'Of course he is. Jock, his dad, was the finest mate a man could ever want. But for Pete's sake, Ally, you could have warned me that he was coming...' Fletcher paused and Ally looked away guiltily, unable to meet his accusatory gaze.

'I should apologise,' she said softly. 'The secrecy was deliberate—a kind of surprise.' It seemed absurd now, but she had hoped the element of surprise would give her an advantage. In her career, she'd always had to plan ahead, anticipating breaks, then snatching opportunities whenever they presented themselves. And she certainly hadn't wanted to allow Fletcher the opportunity to reject her out of hand before she at least had the chance to see him again.

But clearly seeing him had been no help at all.

'It shouldn't be too hard to get a quick replacement nanny,' he said grimly. She opened her mouth to try to reply, but this time could find no words at all.

How could Fletcher be so unfeeling when they had been so close? Close? she thought ruefully. They had been inseparable! Now, he could at the very least be kind; he must have realised that she wouldn't have come so far unless she cared for him very much. Tears stung her eyes and she blinked them away quickly.

'Move back behind the saddle,' he commanded, his tone underlined by a new note of challenge.

Shock waves jolted through Ally so that her voice emerged as a pitiful squeak.

'You're getting onto my horse?'

'My horse,' he reminded her with scalding accuracy.

How could she possibly have him so alarmingly close when her nerves were already stretched unbearably? Surely her heart rate would go through the roof! Her anxiety must have amused him, for the faintest glimmer of a smile dusted his features.

'What about your motorbike?' she asked, her voice faltering.

'It'll be quite safe here for now. Now make room.' He fitted a boot to the stirrup. 'You look like you're going to fall off Juno any minute.' With his face now only inches from hers, her heart beat a frantic tattoo. Up close, his mouth, even when it was grim and disapproving, was gorgeous—surely designed for passion rather than barking orders?

'Get back,' he muttered abruptly, and indicated with a jerk of his head that she should move quickly. Ally scrambled to obey and Fletcher swung a long leg over Juno's back and slid into the saddle. 'Hang on!'

His order was accompanied by a flick of the reins and Juno took off at a brisk canter. Ally's arms instinctively flew around him and as she clung to his hard, muscled back, the electricity of the contact nearly stopped her heart altogether. But any thrill soon short-circuited as Fletcher yelled over his shoulder, his voice just reaching her over Juno's pounding hooves, 'This is a bloody mess, Ally. You know I told you not to come out here.'

* * *

'Don't say it!' Ally pleaded with Lucette hours later as they sat on the wide front veranda of the magnificent Wallaroo Downs homestead. 'I underestimated the stubbornness of the Hardy male.'

They had finally settled a rather puzzled Connor to sleep in the strange, old-fashioned, brass and iron bed with its voluminous mosquito net. Fletcher was closeted in his study at the end of the hall, presumably attacking some important paperwork.

'Even I was shocked at just how keen he was to get rid of you,' commented Lucette.

Ally's chest tightened painfully at the accuracy of her friend's words. Fletcher had insisted that she leave as soon as possible. 'You tried to warn me,' she sighed. 'I thought you made up all that stuff about the kind of woman needed in the bush. But Fletcher believes it!'

'He also believes,' added Lucette, 'something he read once about fashion design being your passion, fulfilling you totally...'

'Well...' responded Ally, 'people change. I've...metamorphosed.'

She thumped the flat wooden arm of the squatter's chair with a force that made her wince, as she slumped in its comfortable canvas seat, her mind full of choking unhappiness. Then she rallied, her anger surfacing again. 'What right has Fletcher to suggest that I'm likely to leave a job half-done just because I get sick of the scenery?'

'If anyone can stick at something in spite of difficulties, it's you, Ally,' Lucette agreed as she dumped her overnight bag at the top of the veranda steps, ready for her departure. Part of their 'perfect' scheme had included Lucette's leaving as soon as possible after she had escorted Ally and Connor onto the property.

Ally stared out into the black night beyond the glow cast by the homestead lights. The two friends sat in miserable silence.

'I'd better go.' Lucette's voice interrupted Ally's misery. 'It's a good four hours to Richmond and Mum and Dad will worry.'

At Lucette's words, Ally realised that this was her chance to acknowledge her mistake and get out before this ridiculous venture turned into a full-scale disaster. She could go with Lucette to their property at Richmond, and from there she could catch a bus to the coast. She could be back in Melbourne in a day or two.

'I guess I may as well leave now, too. Fletcher will soon find another woman to look after Connor. And he and Mrs. Harrison can cope between them in the meantime,' she said with an exhausted sigh.

'No,' came a deep voice from the darkness of the unlit hallway behind them. 'That's not convenient.'

Fletcher stepped onto the veranda. Ally's heart stilled and she attempted a smile, but the evening's argument repeated on her. Her face felt painfully stiff from holding back unshed tears of disappointment.

'I certainly will find a suitable nanny as soon as possible, but as you have arrived without warning, Ally, I will need your help tomorrow. Ned tells me stock are getting out of the five mile paddock. We've got to mend the fence there in the morning. And Mary Harrison will shortly have her hands full feeding the mustering crew. She won't have time to keep an eye on a youngster, as well.'

'That's fine,' answered Ally in a flat monotone, but contradicting the voice, her spirits lifted ridiculously at the knowledge that she was needed on Wallaroo Downs, at least for a short time. She was smiling as Lucette's Land Cruiser took off into the dark night.

Ally watched the twin red eyes of the vehicle's rear lights winking as the car wound its way along the bush track. She was excruciatingly aware that, apart from the old stockman and his wife, and a few stable hands and ringers, who had retired to their own cottages for the night, she was now alone, kilometres from anywhere, with Fletcher.

He stood beside her on the veranda, also watching the retreating vehicle, his hand resting near hers on the timber railing. She stole a quick glimpse at his profile as he continued staring into the inky depths of the bush. For a moment she had to shut her eyes. What was it about this man that so totally wrecked her equilibrium?

But she knew the answer. His rugged masculinity and natural earthiness tugged savagely at her senses. She carefully glanced his way again. There seemed to be nothing to talk about now that their favourite topic—how they felt about each other—was taboo.

'We just might be lucky and get some rain.'

His words brought a weak smile to her lips. She should have guessed he would choose something innocuous like the weather.

'How can you tell?' Ally asked, trying to make her voice sound calm. He smelled delicious and she was swamped by memories of his arms around her, the heat of his hard body meshed with hers and the heady taste of his lips.

Sensations she would never experience again.

She forced herself to follow his gaze up into the sky, looking for indications of rain. And she wondered vaguely where the moon was. The world beyond the veranda was pitch black, but then that was to be expected at night, wasn't it?

'No stars,' he said. 'Out here, away from city lights, we usually have hundreds, thousands of stars. They're all covered by cloud, now. It doesn't always mean rain, but you never know. There's a low up in the Gulf.'

'I guess you need rain badly.'

'That's a bit of an understatement,' he said harshly. 'It hasn't rained here for three years.'

'Of course, I did know about the drought.' She tried to cover for herself quickly. Hadn't she driven through endless kilometres of dusty, drought-stricken country?

'Drought, floods, bushfires. It all happens here,' he said. 'It's not an easy life.'

'I never thought it was,' whispered Ally, looking away, her heart thumping wildly as she realised how quickly their conversation had come dangerously close to the heart of their disagreement—the question of her suitability to life in the bush.

The same thought must have occurred to Fletcher because he thrust his hands deep in the pockets of his jeans and quickly steered the conversation back to safer ground.

'Of course, it probably won't rain. The weather forecasters have said it will and they never get it right.' He laughed raggedly. 'If we really are going to get a wet this year, the rivers will come up and cut us off. It could happen anytime from now on. So we'll have to get you out of here, soon.'

Ally felt her lower lip droop forward. With a supreme effort of will she drew it in, sucking in a deep breath at the same time. She had to try again, to really get to the bottom of the reason he wanted her to go.

In spite of all the words that had been flung back and forth earlier in the evening, she could not bring herself to believe that Fletcher didn't feel the same need for her now as he had in Melbourne. There was a tension, a guarded wariness about him, that signalled to her he was afraid of releasing telltale emotions. To become a good designer she'd also had to be a sensitive artist. She'd learned to look beneath people's exteriors, to really study them, watching their reactions, learning to read their real moods. It seemed to Ally that Fletcher was displaying an awful lot of tension just to tell her she was unsuitable for the job.

'You think if I lived here, I'd let you down, don't you?' she began.

If it was possible he stiffened even further at her words.

'You would soon get sick of it.'

'Not—' She was glad that he was still facing away from her, his profile in deep shadow. At least she couldn't see his reaction as the pride she had so tenaciously clung to fell into tatters. 'Not with you here. I'd never tire of you, Fletcher.'

Fletcher's blue eyes seared into Ally's upturned, pleading face.

'You don't think it could happen, but you would soon grow tired of the life out here, hundreds of miles from anywhere. No city, no friends, no fashion except jeans and riding boots.'

'I hear they have some pretty glamorous outback balls,' Ally said with an effort to smile.

But ignoring her comment, he stepped towards her, his face dark and intense. 'There's no way I would take you away from your career. I know how much you love it. I understand what you've sacrificed to get to the top.'

From somewhere deep inside, Ally dredged a final morsel of courage. 'But,' she began, as confidently as she could, 'you haven't taken me away. I've left of my own accord. I was happy to resign.'

'What?' Fletcher looked as if he had been slugged by an unexpected sniper's bullet. There was a visible slump in his broad shoulders and his mouth hung open. 'You're mad,' he whispered. 'Resigned? This is insanity!'

'You see,' Ally whispered back, her voice trembling along with her entire body. 'I want you more than all that, Fletcher.'

He thumped his fist onto the veranda railing with such force she was sure he must have hurt himself. Then he stared once more out into the night and his voice when he spoke again was gravelly, as if he had swallowed stones.

'No, Ally. I won't let you give it all up. You're too damned good. I sat in the audience in that show down south and saw all those people watching you, cheering you, saw the journalists flocking round you. They love you. They'd never forgive me for taking you away.'

Her vision was suddenly blurry.

'Poor Fletcher,' she whispered. 'How can I make you understand? They would let me go if they knew how happy I was.'

Ally reached out shaking fingers and lightly touched Fletcher's hand as he continued to grasp the veranda railing. Holding her breath, she traced with her forefinger the veins standing out against the sun-tanned skin. Her own body was so tight with tension that Fletcher's trembling response to her fingertips startled her.

Slowly, agonisingly slowly, he turned her small white hand over in his and then lifted it to his cheek and Ally's breath caught in her throat when the familiar, masculine roughness of his day-old beard grazed her palm.

I've lost all my self-respect, she thought dazedly, as, standing on tiptoe, she ran the tip of her pink tongue over her lips, then licked at his earlobe. 'Fletcher, aren't you even a little bit glad to see me?' she whispered.

He didn't flinch, but out of the corner of her eye, Ally glimpsed a muscle twitch in his cheek, twice, and then his eyes fixed on the curve of her mouth. She stifled a sob as she watched a brief but unmistakable tremor pass across his strong features.

'Oh, for heaven's sake, Ally,' he murmured huskily, and released her hand only to reach out and almost, but not quite, touch her dusky pink cheek.

They stood in awkward silence, his lean, brown hand hovering inches away from her and his blue eyes glittering while he stared at her in the soft moonlight. Nervously she returned his gaze as he lingered over each separate detail. Holding her breath, she watched as he allowed his eyes to travel slowly over the silky, dark frame of her hair and the outline of her face. His gaze rested on her eyes as if he were committing their colour and texture to memory. Finally he focused, as if mesmerised, on her lips, and she could sense just how ripe and rosy they were, ready for kissing. His breath expelled wearily on a long sigh. With a groan, Fletcher dipped his hands into the silky dark tresses of her hair and drew her to him.

How wonderful he smelled. She buried her face into the soft cotton of his shirt, relishing the warm, musky strength of the chest beneath and allowing the comforting tenderness of his embrace to seep into her. This was where she belonged. He could protest all he liked about their incompatibility, but with Fletcher's strong arms holding her close, she knew differently.

Her ears caught the erratic racing of his heartbeat and she looked up in alarm, only to meet his mouth reaching for hers.

Hungrily, desperately, his lips drank at hers and his arms crushed her to him. He tasted divine. His invasion of her mouth was so intimate, so right! This mouth, these hands, this lean, powerful body linked to hers felt so perfect it was almost frightening. She began to shake.

'Ally,' he groaned, his voice raspy with longing. 'I want you so much.'

'Well, my darling,' she stammered, 'I—I'm here and—and I'm yours.'

Then she was winding her arms around his neck and threading her urgent fingers into the rough curls that lay against his collar. She clung to him, moulding her slender curves temptingly against the solid muscles of his chest and thighs, knowing full well she was exploiting his weakness.

'No!'

The single syllable had never sounded so terrible. As it tore from Fletcher's lips, he wrenched himself away with a force that spun Ally against the veranda rail. He stood some distance away, staring at her, his breathing ragged. 'I made enough mistakes in Melbourne,' he gasped. 'This has got to stop, Ally.'

Why? she wanted to cry. Why, when it was so obvious that they belonged in each other's embrace as surely as birds belonged to the skies? But she couldn't bear to hear all over again his litany of reasons for rejecting her. Although she remained silent, her body protested loudly. Her hands fluttered in frustrated gestures of helplessness and she shook her head desperately.

Gently, his hands, reaching to cup either side of her face, stilled the motion, and with his thumbs, Fletcher wiped the tears on her cheeks. 'It's time to face reality, Ally. There's no future for us, so we shouldn't even begin to pretend that

there is.' Then he stepped away, gesturing along the veranda.
'Now let me show you to your room.'

Sleepless hours later, a dreadful noise erupted above Ally. It
was still pitch-black as she sat up in bed, startled by a roaring clamour pelting on the corrugated iron roof above where
she'd been trying to sleep.

'Rain!' she heard Fletcher shout from the veranda outside her door.

Leaping from her bed, Ally ran to her doorway.

'Doesn't it smell wonderful? Don't you just love that
sound?' Fletcher called to her.

Ally's nose twitched as her nostrils caught the musty,
metallic odour of dampening earth. Fletcher was dancing
wildly along the veranda. His powerful naked body gleamed
in the flashes of white lightning and, as if to match the wild
elements outside, a ripple of uncontrollable, useless longing
like a roll of thunder, ignited low within her.

But before she could submit to more self-pity, a little wail
reached her ears through the roar of the driving rain.

Connor! Of course! He would be terrified by the racketing
noise. She swung back into her room to gather up the clothes
she'd left beside her bed and dragged them on quickly, as the
poor little boy's cries grew more frightened.

'Can't you hear him?' she called at Fletcher as she charged
past him, along the veranda to Connor's room.

'What's that?' he cried, obviously deafened by rain and
the excited barking of the station dogs.

'Put some clothes on,' she yelled back.

Connor was such a tiny, trembling heap, lost in the big bed,
that she could only just see him even when she switched on
the lamp. She quickly gathered him to her.

'Hush, sweetheart,' she murmured into his warm cheek. 'It's okay. I'm here now. You know it's only rain.'

'Rain?' Connor looked up at her with huge, disbelieving brown eyes. She could guess what he was thinking. How could this dreadful hammering be rain? Rain in the city never sounded like this.

'I thought it was the accident,' he whispered, and buried his head against her chest and began to sob. Ally held him tight and rocked him back and forth.

'No, no, no,' she crooned, remembering how the nightmares had continued for many months after her own parents' accident. 'It's all right. It's all right. You're safe.'

A shadow fell across them. She looked up. Fletcher was beside her, dressed in jeans but bare-chested. 'He's frightened,' she said quietly. 'He remembers the car crash of course.' Even though she spoke softly, Connor heard her and his sobs broke out afresh. 'Hush, baby, hush,' she whispered. 'Perhaps some warm milk?' she asked Fletcher, and he was gone in an instant.

When he returned, it was to find Connor much calmer, still curled in Ally's arms. She took the china mug of milk from him.

'I put some honey in it, too,' he said.

'Wonderful, thanks.' Ally smiled at him and thought how gorgeous he looked with his hair all tousled and dark stubble lining his jaw. 'I'll stay the rest of the night with him.'

He reached down and stroked the little boy's soft damp curls, his blue eyes dark and brooding. 'Thanks for looking after him. His dad was a special guy. I really want him to be happy here.' Then he squeezed Ally's shoulder and with a regretful smile, he turned to leave. 'Catch you later,' he whispered, and she smiled back, silent but unaccountably happy.

Then she settled down beside Connor and cuddled the

warm, sleepy child gently in her arms. Perhaps things would turn out all right, after all, she thought with a contented sigh. If she just had enough time to show Fletcher that she could fit into the outback way of life, perhaps he would change his mind. Perhaps he would admit that he really did love her.

Perhaps they could have a future.

It seemed only minutes later that she heard a footstep on the floorboards nearby. She forced leaden eyes open to see Fletcher standing over her. Her first reaction was to smile, but in the dim, grey light she watched the initial softness in his eyes vanish and the hardening of his jaw told her something was wrong.

The rain was falling as forcefully as ever.

'What time is it?'

'Half past eight. You've been asleep for hours. Listen. The river's rising already. We're going to have to get you out of here.'

'What's that? Why?' Ally struggled to make sense of his words. Connor stirred beside her.

'I've got your bags. You'll have to stay in the clothes you have on. Here's a cup of tea to wake you up.'

Bags? Tea?

'What are you talking about?' Instantly awake, Ally sat up.

'I told you,' Fletcher muttered harshly. 'The river's rising. If we don't get you out of here today, we might be cut off and then you'd be stuck here. We mightn't be able to get you out for weeks. You've got to leave now!'

CHAPTER FOUR

'I CAN'T,' ALLY pleaded desperately, her mind in sudden turmoil. 'Fletcher, I can't go now. You want me to look after Connor. You said last night…'

'Obviously,' cut in Fletcher, cocking his head towards the thundering rain outside, 'the situation has changed since last night. Now, please get up. We can't discuss this in here. No need to upset the little guy more than necessary.'

What about upsetting me? Ally fumed as she stumbled out of bed and pulled on her jeans, shivering in the damp morning air. Her turmoil was rapidly consolidating into righteous anger. She glared at Fletcher's stiffened shoulders as she followed him out into the hall. Surely he must know how hurt she felt—to be evacuated without delay or warning! She wasn't a highly contagious patient whose presence threatened the lives of everyone in the vicinity—she was simply in love with him.

Fear twisted to frantic life in her stomach. That was why he had to get rid of her. She was too emotionally threatening.

Ally's heart sank miserably as, looking down the hallway to the scene outside, beyond the huge baskets of ferns hanging from the edge of the veranda, she saw nothing but a wall of thick, grey rain. The drumming on the iron roof continued relentlessly. She shuddered and forced her eyes to return to Fletcher's grim face. But he spun around quickly and his riding boots struck the floorboards loudly as he led her down the polished hall and into his study.

As she followed him into the room, Ally considered with a sharp pang of regret, how very little of Fletcher's home she had actually seen. This was clearly his refuge—a pleasantly shabby room with softly glowing timber floors scattered with very old Oriental rugs and timber walls lined with books. There were several low tables piled with his journals, books and newspapers. In the far corner, in front of a red and gold stained-glass window stood his enormous silky oak desk, beside it a narrower table held a computer and fax machine. In the centre of the room clustered a circle of deep, cane lounge chairs lined for comfort with plump, claret-coloured cushions. He gestured for her to sit in one and then drew another closer for himself, chasing a fat ginger tomcat out of it with a distracted shove.

'It's not going to be a pleasant drive,' he said abruptly, and handed her the mug of tea he'd been carrying.

Her mind frozen with despair, she took the mug and noticed how he assiduously avoided any contact with her. She sipped at the tea mechanically, her eyes staring vacantly at the paintings on the opposite wall as she shrugged off the last shreds of sleep and tried to fully take in the grim reality of his news.

'Why not at least wait till it stops raining?' she asked at last. 'Surely unpleasant is an understatement. It's got to be downright dangerous to drive on those narrow dirt tracks through the bush in this weather.'

'We can't wait. It'll be too late. The floodwaters up in the Gulf will link up to the rivers just north of here.'

He hadn't turned on any lamps and in the dim, grey light his eyes were a startling aqua. His gaze locked into hers as he spoke slowly and with exaggerated patience. 'The Fanning River can come up in a matter of hours. And when that happens this property is cut off—caught between the Fanning and the Burdekin rivers—then no one can get out. Sometimes it takes weeks.'

'I'm not a dimwit,' she flashed at him. 'I understood that the first time you told me but, I—I don't mind, Fletch. I'd look after Connor for you. I'd help around...'

'You're going,' Fletcher interrupted gruffly. 'You can't stay. Now don't argue. You don't understand anything about living in the wilderness.'

Wilderness? Ally's eyes wandered around the room, taking in its books and comfortable furniture. Her gaze swung from the vast collection of jazz and classical CDs to the tastefully framed Drysdales and Blackmans hanging around the high-ceilinged, tongue-and-groove walls.

'You have an interesting definition of wilderness,' she responded at last.

He shrugged dismissively. 'Surely after the thousands of kilometres you've travelled—especially the track in from the highway—you must understand how isolated this homestead is. OK, it is a beautiful home. I love it, but it's the only homestead for at least fifty kilometres.'

His sermon was somewhat spoiled by the ginger tom, indignant at being de-throned, jumping onto Ally's lap. She started a little as its tiny claws reached her skin through her denim jeans, but the cat soon settled into a purring, glowing, orange ball beneath her stroking hand.

'What's his name?' she asked, glad of any diversion.

Fletcher stared at her slim fingers as they played with the cat's ears.

'Lightbulb,' he offered, his voice sounding distracted and impatient. 'He's so damn bright, he practically glows in the dark.'

She smiled, but the smile faded as the irony of the situation suddenly struck her. Everyone else was pleased to have her here. Ned Harrison, who saddled the horse for her yesterday, had said as much.

'Sure, you're very welcome' he'd repeated over and over. 'It does a man good to have someone young and pretty about the place. Boss doesn't have…well, anyway, good to see you.'

And Connor certainly needed her. Heaven knows Fletcher didn't know a thing about little children…and Mary and Ned had never been blessed with youngsters. And now even the cat seemed to have taken a fancy to her…

But not Fletcher. Everyone was megahappy for her to stay on Wallaroo Downs except the very man she most wanted to be with in the world. The only man she had ever wanted to be with.

She had sensed from the moment she'd been so roughly woken, that opposition would be pointless, but she couldn't help herself. Last night she'd been silent, but this morning, faced with instant dismissal, she had to keep trying.

'Connor's only just arrived. He doesn't know anybody here. He needs me.'

His face stiffened into hard lines and his eyes were once more fixed on hers with a fierce determination.

'He only got to know you a few days ago. Better that he doesn't get too attached to you, only to lose you again.'

'Lose me? But I wouldn't…'

'Ally, we went over this last night. Of course you won't stay here forever. Please, be sensible about this.' There was a tightness in his face and voice as if he were willing her not to argue—to go quietly.

Well, he could think again! Ally decided as she took another deep swig at the cooling tea. 'Fletcher, I do know what I'm in for here. I told you I haven't lived in Melbourne all my life. I have spent quite a bit of time on cattle properties before. Perhaps you don't realise how well I understand the life. When I was at school, I spent weeks of my holidays every Christmas on Mt. Freedom station with my friend, Roberta Savage and—and I loved it all. I much prefer the bush and the excitement of the cattle yards to the hectic parties and surfing that all my city friends were so crazy about. My parents got quite upset because I'd rather go up to Mt. Freedom in the summer than go to the Gold Coast with them.'

Fletcher listened with narrowed eyes that appeared to be concentrating on the scrolled leaf pattern edging the carpet. 'What you're saying is you've visited properties. There's a big difference between spending a few days in a place and lasting a lifetime.' He paused and Ally felt tiny hairs stand up on the back of her neck. His voice dropped. 'A lifetime. That is what you're talking about, Ally, isn't it?'

'W-what do you m-mean?' The knot in her stomach pulled tighter and her heart pounded as if she'd run a marathon.

Fletcher reached over and ran a gentle hand down her cheek. She felt her skin reddening under its path. His fingers cupped her chin and tilted her face back, but she kept her eyes lowered. She couldn't bear to look into his eyes, to read the truth there.

'Alexandra Fraser,' he said so softly, her name sounded like the title of a love sonnet, 'you've given up your career and you've come with your bags packed. You didn't come all that way just because you wanted a change of scenery.'

She felt a desperate, panicking surge of helplessness, as if she were drowning with no hope of rescue.

'You came because you want to stay here and—' his hand trailed down her neck to her trembling shoulders '—and that's just not going to work.'

A sudden tremor in his voice betrayed his apparent calm and in the brief moment that their eyes met, Ally read in them sadness and a kind of consternation. Then he turned away, but Ally couldn't accept his words.

A small choking sound erupted in her throat, a mixture of embarrassment and fear. Surely there had been more to their lovemaking in Melbourne than mere sex?

Fletcher had been so passionate and their fiery encounters had been interspersed with long, lingering and sensuous lovemaking, so beautiful she would have been willing to bet everything she possessed that it was real love. And their minds had met, as well. The music, the movies, the food and laughter they'd shared... Even last night, she knew he had been fighting a fundamental longing for her based on something much stronger than the mere urging of hormones.

She jumped to her feet, needing to put some distance between them, and began to pace the floor before him, no longer able to pretend they were having a civilized conversation. There was nothing civilized about the angry hurt that was tearing at her chest.

With both hands, she clutched the mug against her breast.

'You mean you were happy to make love to me in my home in Melbourne, but you don't want me hanging around your place?' she asked, her voice querulous even though her chin jutted forward challengingly.

'That's what I mean.'

He spoke quietly, his eyes fixed, hard, blue stones as he also stood up, towering above her now, regaining all the advantage of height.

Ally's knees almost buckled beneath her, but somehow she managed to hang on to a shred of her rapidly diminishing strength.

'I don't believe you,' she retaliated, her voice matching his quiet tone, her own smoky eyes staring with unflinching directness up into his, even though her heart quailed with fear. 'I'm sorry, Fletcher, but I don't.'

He stood stock-still before her, but his face was very white and a tremor shook his tall frame as if something deep inside fractured.

'What you believe is not really relevant anymore,' he muttered swiftly. 'The fact is we are facing the prospect of a flood which might cut us off from the coast and you have to get off here before that happens—even if I have to pick you up and carry you kicking and squealing.'

A fearful, desperate battle light glinted in Ally's eyes.

'So,' she said softly and evenly, her heart pounding several beats to every carefully delivered syllable, 'you're telling me I can't stay on Wallaroo because you don't love me.'

She ducked her head to hide the quick tears that accompanied those terrible words—words that could bring about the total destruction of everything she believed they had between them. Surely she had pushed things too far, now.

A long, chilling silence was accompanied by the incessant thrumming of the rain.

'That's right.' He sighed as if suddenly very bored with the whole subject. 'I'm so relieved you've finally got the message.'

The mug of tea slipped from her nerveless fingers and crashed on the floorboards between them as Ally reached at the chair's arm for support. Vaguely she was aware of his arms flying around her, holding her steady as her knees collapsed beneath her. His lips were in her hair.

'Ally,' he whispered, 'don't fight me on this, please, please.'

White-faced, trembling, she stared with aversion at the dark hairs springing from the tanned skin of his arm as it tightened around her waist.

'I'm such a fool,' she gasped. 'I had it all wrong.'

His silence offered her no comfort as she stood there sick with horror, but nevertheless leaning against him because she had no strength of her own. She wanted to die. If only she could die now—it would be much easier than facing this awful, awful truth.

'Ally, don't look like that. Ally, you'll be all right. Oh, God, Ally, don't you understand?'

'I don't think I understand anything anymore,' she whispered, tears starting again from beneath reddened eyelids. She gulped back a sob, which clearly almost broke through her self-control, and shook her head. 'I certainly don't understand how you were able to use me the way you did and just cast me aside,' she sniffed, determined not to let the tears fall.

'For God's sake, Ally. I'm sorry about that.'

'Sorry? A-about making love to me?' She wanted to cry so badly. How could she possibly stop herself from bursting into loud, embarrassing sobs?

'Yes. I told you in Melbourne we had no future. I shouldn't have stayed and you shouldn't have come here, Ally. You know I can't resist you. But what you just don't understand is the loneliness, the isolation of this place, the heat, the flies… no concerts, movies, theatres. No fashion worth bothering about out here, for God's sake… You'd miss all that glamour and fame.'

She could not speak to defend herself. The huge swelling in her throat prevented it.

'I can't ask you to put up with it all, Ally. I'm not going to. That's why you have to go.' And he swung away from her, storming for the door. 'I've already put your bags in the back of the Range Rover. In five minutes I'll be back to pick you up. Be ready.'

He disappeared.

Ally ran to the hallway, a lone cry bursting from her, as she watched his retreating back. She felt she was watching her lifeblood slip away. How tall, broad and unrelenting that back looked as he grabbed an oilskin coat from a hall stand and, raising it to cover his head, disappeared onto the veranda.

Alone. Ally gave in to tears now. He didn't love her. Fletcher didn't love her. Now there was no escaping this shocking reality. She loved Fletcher, wanted him, craved him. He could live on a coral cay in the middle of the Pacific, in Antarctica or on the top of the Himalayas, for all she cared. As long as she could be there, too. She couldn't stop loving him any more than she could will herself to stop breathing.

But he was only interested in her body and even then he could take it or leave it. Right now his only concern was to get rid of her. A loud, agonised sob tore itself from her throat and Ally shoved her hand into her mouth to stop more.

How had it all gone so hopelessly wrong? How could she have been such a lovesick fool clinging to a useless dream?

She stumbled down the hall towards the veranda, but came to a hasty, frozen stop in the doorway. Fletcher hadn't left; he was still leaning on the railing near the top of the steps, his face buried in his hands, his shoulders slumped in exhaustion.

As Ally stared, bewildered, Fletcher gave a groan and she quickly stepped back out of sight, her heart thudding painfully in her chest.

But, as if he sensed her there, he suddenly straightened quickly and jumped the few steps from the low veranda before striding off into the rain.

She closed her eyes in confusion. Clearly he didn't feel quite as offhand about all this as he pretended. But, in a few short minutes she would be leaving, never to see Fletcher again. If only she could hate him!

She forced her stiff legs back to Connor's bedroom to take one last look at him. Amazingly, he was still asleep. Obviously, the long journey from Sydney had exhausted him more than she realised and the continuous beat of the rain had definite lullaby qualities. His little body looked smaller than ever in the middle of the big white bed, his eyelashes lying softly against cheeks that were warm and pink with sleep. Damp, dark curls of hair lay flattened against the side of his head.

He was such a sweet little boy.

Although she had only just started to get to know him, already he tugged at her emotionally in a way that her nephew and nieces, her sister's children, didn't. He seemed so vulnerable, so innocent and alone, so needing of love.

She wanted to kiss him goodbye, but was afraid he would wake and she couldn't bear to have to explain why she was going.

'I hope they look after you,' she whispered. 'I'll miss you, sweetheart.'

There was a step in the doorway behind her. Fletcher was there, standing dark and stern in his dripping coat. He indicated with a jerk of his head that she should leave. Kissing her fingers, she dropped them to the pillow beside the little head, turned and stepped quietly away.

'Put this on,' he said, handing her a coat as she joined him outside the room.

'Who's going to look after him now?' she asked.

'Mary Harrison. I've spoken to her.'

'I thought she was too busy.'

'Don't start that again, Ally. As I said, things have changed. She's an adaptable woman. She'll cope. There's no mustering now with all this rain, so she'll have time.'

'She's a good bush woman, I take it,' Ally replied through gritted teeth as she shrugged her arms into the coat he held for her.

'Exactly,' Fletcher replied, and his lips closed over the word with a definite air of finality.

'But I need to tell her about Connor, about his needs...'

'Why?' Fletcher asked, looking at her with widened, wary eyes. 'He's not ill, is he? Not on medication?'

'No, nothing like that. But he's still very frightened of loud noises and he has one favourite story he must hear every night before he goes to sleep...'

'Did you bring it with you?'

'Yes, of course. It's on his bedside table.'

'And it's called?'

Where is my mother?

The shock was clearly evident on Fletcher's face. 'That's a bit morbid, isn't it? Considering what happened to his own mother?'

'I know,' Ally replied. 'That's what I thought at first, but he insisted. It was the only story that would settle him. But...' She looked away from him, twisting her hands nervously.

'You see, whenever I read it to him I change the ending. He can't read and he seems quite satisfied…'

'What do you mean?'

'Well, I…I thought Connor should be helped to accept the truth…that sometimes we can't find our mothers anymore… so, in the story, when I get to the part where the little bird finally finds his mother, I change it so that he doesn't find her, but instead he finds a—a godfather.'

From under her thick, dark lashes, she shot him a quick glance. He was staring back silent and still as a statue. She continued. 'Connor was very pleased with the idea. And he is so happy now that he has found his own godfather.' She forced herself to smile at him.

White-lipped, Fletcher continued to stare at her for another long, difficult moment and then he spun on his heel and marched towards the waiting car.

'Let's go.'

Once she was in the vehicle, there was no chance for backward farewell glances at the homestead. With an angry firing of the motor, the Range Rover leapt into the grey wall of rain, its windscreen wipers valiantly trying to clear a small glimpse of the muddy, slippery-looking track ahead.

'Is having to delay the muster a problem?' Ally asked tentatively, straining her voice to reach Fletcher over the roar of the engine, the clatter of the wipers and the drumming of the rain all around them. Her attempt at conversation was met by a grunt. Fletcher's concentration was focused on the steering wheel and the road ahead. After only a night's rain, the track was already starting to wash away in places and it was littered with fallen branches. As the car swerved to avoid one of these, Ally was thrown sideways onto Fletcher's arm. Her head ended up resting on his shoulder—a hard and unyielding shoulder from which she flinched back quickly.

'Put your seat belt on,' he barked. 'It's going to be a rough ride. Can't be helped.'

It didn't feel as if she could actually be leaving Walla-roo Downs. Firstly, she'd hardly seen anything of the place and secondly, the journey was too hazardous, too much like some wild adventure, to be concluded by simply dumping her at a bus station, but that was what she assumed Fletcher had planned.

As if reading her thoughts, he spoke. 'With a bit of luck we'll get to Townsville before dark. You can fly to Melbourne direct from there.'

'You're taking me all that way to the coast?'

'Only a few hours once we get on the highway.'

'You want to make sure I get completely out of the district, don't you?'

This was met by a silence, which unnerved Ally and sent her voice shooting several decibels higher. 'You're scared I'll come sneaking back and make a nuisance of myself.'

'Don't get hysterical.'

'Hysterical?' *Hysterical?* This time Ally couldn't help herself. After the remarkable restraint she'd exercised all morning, there was no way she was going to be accused of hysteria! How dare the man! Maybe she *could* hate him! 'I think I'm behaving with admirable calm and decorum. One thing you don't have to be afraid of is that I'll come scurrying back halfway across the nation to throw myself at you again.'

'Hell.'

'What's the matter?' It only took a split second for Ally to realise that Fletcher hadn't been listening to her pathetic little tirade. The vehicle had come to a sudden stop and his eyes were fixed on the road ahead where it dipped steeply away from the ridge on which they were poised. Ally peered through the rain to see what had caused them to stop.

It was difficult to see more than a few metres of the gravel road ahead, but the track looked more like a creek, as streams of swirling brown water rushed down to meet more water below. It was then she realised what had happened. The road disappeared into the river.

'The blasted Fanning's up already,' muttered Fletcher, jamming on the hand brake and cutting the engine.

'Is that the river washing across the road?' asked Ally lamely.

'Across the bridge, damn it. It's only a low concrete bridge, no sides or anything, but it serves us through most wets. This water must have come already from the headwaters up in the Gulf. It's been raining up there all week.' Ally stared at the frothing, muddy flood rushing below them. The current was obviously very strong, but she had no idea how deep the water was. Surely Fletcher would not attempt to drive through it, even in a four-wheel-drive vehicle?

He opened his car door.

'Where are you going?'

'Having a closer look. Stay in the car,' he ordered with maddening abruptness.

With gritted teeth Ally watched as his dark-cloaked figure strode down the incline towards the water. It was impossible to see through the windscreen, so she wound down the window beside her and stuck her head into the rain. A metre or so away from the water's swirling edge Fletcher paused, hands on hips, staring ahead of him. Then slowly he began to take off his coat and roll it up before placing it next to a nearby boulder.

'What are you doing?' she screamed through the rain as he began to walk towards the swirling torrent.

'Testing the water. Stay there!'

Not likely, Ally muttered to herself as she shoved open the door on her side.

'Fletcher, don't be ridiculous!' she called as she raced down the slope towards him. Her coat flapped open and her head and shirtfront were quickly drenched, but it hardly mattered if Fletcher had taken leave of his senses. The creek seethed, the mud-brown torrent hurling itself forward at suicidal speed. 'You're not going in there?' she panted as she reached him. He scowled back at her.

'Calm down, Ally. I know what I'm doing. It's not wise to drive through floodwaters till you've tested them out first on foot.'

'Oh, and that's really wise, isn't it? Fletcher, please, don't go in there. It looks dreadfully dangerous.'

'I doubt it's more than knee deep.'

Ally bit back another retort. Fletcher glared at her, his eyes dark blue slits and his heavy overnight stubble outlined a determined jaw. It wasn't difficult to read his thoughts. He knew this environment, this land. She was only a city slicker and a female to boot. With an exasperated sigh she shrugged and gestured for him to go about his manly business.

Fletcher stepped forward purposefully, his elastic-sided riding boots disappearing somewhere below the brown, swiftly flowing stream. One step, two, three. Ally supposed she should be pleased that he'd been right. The water wasn't deep. A good few centimetres of jeans below his knees were still dry. He turned and winked, flashing her a cheeky grin that made her insides melt. But she couldn't force a return smile. Each dangerous step he took dealt a humiliating blow to her battered self-esteem. His desperation to get rid of her meant he would risk his life rather than have her stay with him indefinitely!

He was nearing the middle of the wide stretch of water and now it was above his knees, but only just. A sudden swift surge in the current buffeted him a little, making him side-step to retain his balance and Ally gasped, hardly aware of her hands clasped tightly together as if in prayer. She couldn't stop herself caring for him, fearing for his safety...loving him, even in the face of his outright rejection. This useless love was a burden she would have to carry to her grave. She bit her lip painfully as she watched him stand still and feel the ground below him carefully with one foot. Then slowly he edged forward again.

Something dark snaked its way into the corner of her vision. A tree branch was hurtling along in the whipping water.

'Look out!' she screamed.

Fletcher turned and she caught the quick flicker of concern, which tightened his features as he tried to step backwards, out of the way. Too late!

'Fletcher!' Horrified, Ally watched the tree branch ram into him. Then in dread she saw his knees buckle as he was swept away by its force. 'Oh, no! Oh, God!' She ran towards the water, but already Fletcher's dark head was all she could see and a split second later it was disappearing around a bend as he was dragged off by the savage current.

Sobbing, Ally stumbled through the still streaming rain along the slippery bank. Where was he? All she could see was disgusting, ugly brown water rushing headlong as if possessed. Surely it was faster now than when they first stopped.

'Fletch! Oh, Fletcher!' She ran on, oblivious to scratches and stumbles, her eyes riveted to the swirling mass, desperate for that dear, dark shape of his head. Just when she thought she could see it, it would disappear again. It was so difficult to see anything through all the dratted rain. Suddenly she let out a yelp as she lurched into something sharp. It was barbed wire. A fence line was running down the slope and across the river, disappearing underwater at the centre.

Her eyes scanned its length. There he was! Caught against the barbed wire! Thank heavens. He was moving, trying it seemed, to untangle himself. The water would be pinning him unmercifully against the sharp barbs. But maybe he'd be able to pull himself along the fence and back to safety.

'Can you follow the fence?' she yelled.

'I'm stuck!' There were more words but the wind whipped them away. Stuck! His clothes must be wound around the wire somehow, imprisoning him. Ally closed her eyes as a sickening wave of fear engulfed her. There was nothing else for her to do but to go in after him.

CHAPTER FIVE

IT WAS JUST as well Ally hadn't tried to sound heroic when she called back to Fletcher above the thunder of the water, for her words trailed off in the wind. But Fletcher must have heard, because as she raised a tentative boot to step into the flood, she heard him roar back.

'Stop!'

Feeling guiltily relieved, she paused. With luck she might not have to go in the flooded river. Perhaps he'd already freed himself and was about to make his way back along the fence. Standing on tiptoes, she peered at the spot midstream where she had last seen him, and her heart leapt to her throat. He had disappeared! And when she checked the fence line, he wasn't making his way along that, either. All she could see was the wide stretch of racing, evil water.

Sheer panic clutched her chest in a vicelike grip. Fletcher drowned?

Drowned while attempting to escort her off his property? Drowned because she had forced her love onto him when he had not asked for or wanted it. Because she'd chased after him with the same pig-headed determination that had been her lifelong trademark—to achieve whatever goal she'd set before herself.

Mesmerised by the swirling, coffee-coloured flood, Ally was unable to think past her guilt, and she felt the weight of it pour over her and flood into her veins, as if she, too, were drowning.

Then at last, right where he had been before, she caught sight of Fletcher's dark head as it popped to the surface and she understood that he'd been trying to free something caught down low. It was only when a loud sob broke from her lips she realised she'd been holding her breath.

She waited to see if he was now free to move, but it looked unlikely. In fact he looked as if he hardly had the strength to cling to the fence and hold himself above the water. Dragging off her coat, which she knew would be a hindrance in the current, Ally took a deep breath.

'Hold on, Fletcher,' she called. And this time there was no protest.

I don't know if I'm strong enough for this, she thought as she plunged into the swirling current. The first few steps were easy enough except that every time she grabbed a fresh hold on the barbed wire, she felt its stinging jab. But as she moved into knee-deep water, the force of the current kept slamming her slender frame against the fence, which ripped and tore her clothes and flesh. There was also the added danger that she, too, would become trapped and tangled up in the hideous wire but she kept on, each step more difficult.

Her arms ached from holding her body out from the wire as the swiftly eroding riverbed kept shifting beneath her feet. She was very tired. At any moment she would be out of her depth and there was no way she could hold herself upright then. I'm no use to Fletcher at all, she thought wretchedly.

'Ally, hold it! I'm OK. Go back.'

As his beautiful, authoritative command reached her, every terrified nerve in her body sang with relief. She would give anything to go back. But when she looked towards the bank, the return journey looked as bad as that still ahead. The thought of dragging one foot behind the other in either direction was almost too much.

'Ally, stop. I'm free.'

Although she couldn't see much past the wet hair plastered on her face and the swirling waters all around her, she could make out Fletcher's dark shape working his way along the wire. 'My boot was caught, but I got it off,' he called. 'Hold on, I'm coming.'

Eagerly she tugged sodden lumps of hair away from her eyes to see better. With his strong arms, Fletcher was holding himself off the barbs as he edged towards her. And he actually had the audacity to be grinning at her, his brilliant blue eyes the only spots of colour in the murky river.

At the sight of him free again, no longer depending on her to rescue him, Ally's courage and strength seemed to falter. The force of the chest-high water became almost impossible to withstand and the horrid brown tide pinned her relentlessly to the barbed wire.

She struggled to lift herself away from the wire and move back to the bank. She couldn't fail now and force Fletcher to rescue her on top of his own exhaustion. It became of the utmost importance to stop thinking about how every part of her body was bruised or cut or exhausted.

The distance to the bank looked impossible now. How had she crossed it before? She willed her hands and feet to continue moving in spite of the cruel pressure of the current.

It didn't work.

'Ally.' Fletcher's voice was much closer. She would have answered back if she had sufficient leftover energy. Another step. And another. Her ankle wobbled dangerously beneath her. She couldn't, mustn't slip.

But she did.

Rushing muddy water filled her mouth and she spluttered and coughed as she was raised briefly by the force of the water and thrown again onto the barbed wire. Her head grazed the timber fence post. But before she could grab it, once more she slipped down into the filthy rushing stream. She couldn't find the strength to fight. It was too much. She tried vainly to struggle to the surface, but in the black, murky depths she could hardly tell where it was. Grabbing frantically for the wire, she no longer felt the stinging, ripped skin. Surely she could pull herself up? If only she could breathe!

Something grabbed her shirt collar. She was being lifted. Bursting above the surface of the water, she gulped and coughed and gasped and spluttered.

'Woo-a, Ally, you'll be all right, now. Just breathe, slowly and deeply.'

Fletcher was holding her. God, she wasn't going to die after all. She sank against him. Lovely Fletcher. She would thank him if she didn't need all her precious energy just to keep breathing.

Her head resting against his chest, she felt for a moment that she could stay there forever, sleep perhaps. In the safety of Fletcher's arms, she hardly noticed the murky water rushing around her.

'Come on, let's get moving,' Fletcher said close to her ear. Move? Did she have to? She tried to reach out to the wire, ready to haul herself forward, but two strong hands tightened around her hips and raised her up. 'Just as well you're only little—as light as a feather,' he grunted as he lifted her above the water level. Instinctively she tucked her legs up, realising that it would be much easier for him to carry her above rather than through the current. He slowly made his way to the bank holding her high. Ally felt her lips curl into a smile. Wonderful Fletcher.

Almost near the edge, he stumbled a little and lowered her quickly into the ankle-deep water.

'Sorry.' He smiled crookedly. 'A little woozy. I think I gave my head a pretty hard whack on that fence post.'

'You've a nasty red gash on your temple.' Ally reached up to gently touch the side of his forehead.

'It'll keep,' he sighed. Then he smiled down at her. 'Thanks for coming to my rescue.'

Ally shook her head. 'Fat lot of good it did. I was about as much help as…as a fashion designer in a flood.'

Fletcher threw back his head and laughed at her weak joke and then he winced, his hand flying swiftly to his temple. Ally frowned. Clearly he'd had a very nasty blow. They should get out of the water.

'Hey, I was so wet I hadn't noticed. The rain's stopped. Let's get out of here.' She took Fletcher's hand and stepped towards the bank, but he drew her gently back to him, enclosing her in his arms, both of them dripping wet.

'I meant it, passionfruit.'

'What's that?' she murmured huskily.

'Thank you for coming to my rescue.' His kisses were surprisingly warm on her cold cheek. 'It was madness, of course, but very brave.'

'I was so frightened. I thought you were going to drown,' she whispered, noticing how weary he looked and how much the escapade had taken out of him. His normally tanned face was pale and his eyes were underlined by deep shadows, emphasising his exhaustion.

'But you still came after me, even though you were frightened. You're such a gutsy little thing.' He grinned, his lips grazing hers teasingly.

She didn't dare ask the questions that whirled desperately in her head about what would happen now that they couldn't cross the river. Instead she smiled.

'Perhaps I earned my first points as a bush woman?'

His thumb outlined her jaw and trailed up to circle an earlobe. 'You know,' he said gently, 'even when you look like a drowned rat, you're ravishing.'

Ally knew then that she would not get the answer she wanted. She consoled herself by leaning into Fletcher's strength, parting her lips to meet his.

His stubble grazed her chin, but its scratchiness didn't bother her, just as her stinging cut skin and the floodwater still swirling round her ankles hardly registered. She didn't notice anything but Fletcher's kiss, which deepened as his hands slid down to her buttocks and held her tightly against him. She could no longer remember that she had thought it unwise for them to stay there in the water rather than get dry and warm again.

With his tongue seeking out the velvet softness of her mouth, she surrendered completely to the heady sensations he always aroused in her. She shifted her body even closer to his, wanting to feel all of him. She could hear herself moaning softly, melting as she always did under Fletcher's overwhelming, seductive power. Reaching her hands to the sides of his head to hold his face against her own, she felt something warm and sticky. She gasped. It was blood. And it was streaming out of the wound on Fletcher's forehead.

'Fletch, we've got to do something about this. It looks bad.' He released her reluctantly. They both stepped the few short paces to the bank. And then Fletcher collapsed. Swaying briefly beside her like a weakened tree in a storm, he lurched forward to become a crumpled heap in the mud.

'Fletch!!' Ally dropped frantically to her knees. He looked so deathly pale, so still and—lifeless. Panic seized her. She kissed his cold cheek, his lips—no, surely, surely not? She looked at his chest, appalled. Was it rising and falling? Was he breathing? At first, in panic she could see no movement. But, no, there it was. Thank God he was alive.

So, she told herself, he had fainted. It was important to stay calm—simply a matter of getting him to the truck and back to Wallaroo homestead, to help.

Simply? Ally swallowed the dryness in her throat.

'Fletch, why are you so damned big!' she sighed as she tried to lift him up the bank. Even as she was making laborious progress away from the water's edge, his feet, one without a boot, dragging behind, Ally's mind raced ahead to her next task. She knew it would be almost impossible. There was no way she could lift an unconscious Fletcher up into the elevated cabin of the Range Rover, built for high clearance on rough bush terrain.

'I'll have to leave you here and go for help,' she whispered. 'Sorry, Fletch. I'll get your coat and mine and wrap you up. At least it's not raining anymore.' With a flash of inspiration from a distant first aid class, she rolled him onto his side into the recovery position. Then she dropped another flurry of kisses on his unresponsive cheek and dashed to find the coats.

As she tucked them around him, her determination almost failed her. She couldn't just leave him alone out here. Big, strong, mountainous Fletcher looked so vulnerable, lying in-active on the muddy bank. His face was white and the con-trasting harsh red wound on his forehead alarmed her so that she almost gave in to tears.

But she had to go.

She kissed him again, felt his pulse, which was steady and then, with a supreme effort of will, forced herself to head off.

To her surprise, the Range Rover was no more difficult to drive than her own small city sedan. Now that the rain had stopped, she could see the track quite clearly and the power steering enabled her to dodge fallen branches quite expertly, while the huge tyres gripped the slippery surface safely. By the time she reached Wallaroo Downs, Mary and Ned were already at the front steps, clearly puzzled that the vehicle should be returning so soon.

'Fletcher's had an accident down at the creek,' she sobbed as soon as the engine died. 'He's too heavy for me to lift, but we should get back quickly in case he wakes and tries to walk somewhere.'

'I'll take the tray-backed utility,' shouted Ned. 'It'll be eas-ier to put him in the back. Mary, you ring the Flying Doc-tor and find out how far away he is. Come with me, Miss.'

In no time at all they were skidding back down the track.

'I left Fletcher on the bank to the right, just near where the fence runs down across the creek.'

'You should have used the CB radio. There's one in the Range Rover. Then you could have stayed with him.'

Ally felt very foolish. She hadn't even thought of a radio, let alone looked for one. And anyway, she wouldn't have had the first idea how to use it. Perhaps Fletcher was right. It seemed that in the bush she was only a nuisance.

'Oh, heavens, he's got to still be there,' she prayed.

He was. In fact, to Ally, who leapt out of the vehicle before it had completely stopped, and dropped to her knees beside the dark shape on the ground, it looked as if he hadn't moved at all since she left. He was still pale and unconscious, but breathing.

'Fletch,' she cried, lifting his cold hand in both hers. She kissed it, rubbing her face against his palm in an effort to warm it. 'Ned, what do you think?' she called as the stockman hobbled stiffly towards them.

'Well, he's out to it all right. Colour's not too bad. You think anything could be broken?'

'No, no limbs or anything,' she replied, remembering how easily Fletcher had carried her through the swift current. 'But I think he's been knocked out by a blow on the head. Look here.' Gently she turned Fletcher's head to reveal the deep, red wound. A soft moan drifted from his lips.

Ned nodded. 'Right. Then we just have to get him back and let the doc have a look at him.'

Ned had lowered the tailgate on the utility, and between the two of them, using Fletcher's strong, oiled canvas coat as a stretcher, they were able to lift him into the back and settle him on some old sugar bags on the floor.

'I'll stay with Fletcher,' she said, sitting cross-legged beside him on the floor of the ute's tray back and tucking a coat under his head.

'Good idea,' Ned remarked. 'Hang on tight, won't you?'

She was grateful that he had warned her, because as the truck took off, Ally only just had time to grab the sides for support. She found it easiest to kneel and hold Fletcher's head steady between her knees, as she needed both hands to brace herself against all the bumps, even though Ned was taking it quite slowly.

Around and above them, tall eucalypts, wattles and paperbarks dripped quietly, but beyond the treetops, the sky still loomed dark, burdened with heavy, black clouds. There would soon be more rain.

The trip back was slower than the other journeys and Ally was sick with anxiety by the time the low, iron roof and bull-nosed front veranda could be glimpsed between the huge tamarind trees in front of the Wallaroo homestead.

She looked down at Fletcher and longed for the life to spring back into his features. He still looked quite superb, but it was distressing to see that strong, powerful face lying still and slack. Even if he opened his eyes and told her to get lost, she would at least know he was all right.

'Here we are. Home safe and sound,' she murmured to his inert, quiet body. His eyelids fluttered and she bent low, eagerly kissing his cheek, his brow, his lips. 'Oh, Fletch, wake up, wake up,' she urged. She fancied his lips curved into a smile and she kissed them again.

'Beautiful,' she thought she heard him whisper.

Above, she heard the put-put-put sound of a motor in the air.

'Chopper's coming,' called Ned as he jumped from the truck's cabin. 'Probably been roped in to take him to hospital in the Towers. Flying Doctor's plane wouldn't be able to land in this weather. It's wet enough to bog a duck. He'll be right now, love,' he added as he patted Ally's shoulder. She was still crouched low beside Fletcher. 'No sweat. They'll have him back on deck quick as a flash. Not the first time this bloke's copped a dong on the head. You wait and see, he'll bounce back cheekier than ever.'

Ned kept up the comforting patter all the time the helicopter circled above the homestead and then slowly settled to land in the home paddock about a hundred metres away.

'I'll drive 'im over nice and slow, now,' Ned said gently as he swung back into the cabin. 'We'll look after him, love. Perhaps you could go and tell my missus to put a cuppa on for us.'

Ally knew she was being dismissed. There was no more she could do. And as she had no claim on Fletcher she could hardly insist on flying to Charters Towers with him. It wasn't as if she was next of kin or anything. She was merely the girl who'd brought Fletcher's godson up from the city. With tear-filled eyes she watched the utility drive carefully and slowly away and she could see the dark bulky outline of Fletcher lying in the back. All alone.

It was over a week before the helicopter brought Fletcher back. A long, frightening time during which those waiting at the homestead received patchy telephone messages from the hospital. He regained consciousness the day after the accident, but there were complications. X-rays and tests took up the next few days while Ally nervously paced the verandas at Wallaroo and the rain returned fiercer and more monotonous than ever. She kept herself as busy as possible with Connor, reading to him, drawing and singing with him; playing with the many toys they had brought from Sydney.

She helped Mary about the huge house and, with Connor, took over some of the chores such as feeding the chickens and weeding the kitchen garden which, though waterlogged at present, would thrive once the rainwater drained away. But always, dominating everything else, was Fletcher. Her fear for his condition consumed her so that she couldn't eat or sleep, and during the day a restless energy kept her continually on the move, never able to rest.

Finally, more news came through one afternoon when Ally had joined Mary and Ned for afternoon tea in the cheery, old-fashioned kitchen. Mary came hurrying away from the phone to tell Ally and Ned the news as they sat at the old scrubbed pine table. Fletcher was going to be all right, but he had amnesia.

'Amnesia?' queried Ned. 'Like last time?'

Panic ripped through Ally like a flaming arrow. She stared at Ned in horror.

'Yes,' nodded his wife, her shiny sunburnt face looking solemn. 'Apparently this accident shook up his old wound again.' She noticed Ally's white, puzzled face and added for her benefit, 'Fletcher had a bad fall from a horse a few years back when he was riding at the Mingela Rodeo—lost his memory for about a month until it all healed up.'

'He forgot everything?' asked Ally, her mind reeling, her heart racketing around wildly at the news. Somehow, the thought of big, handsome Fletcher losing his grip on the past frightened her terribly.

'No, not everything. It was funny really. It was only things that had happened recent like that he forgot—for about six months back—but he could remember who he was and who we were and how to run a cattle property and everything important like that.' Mary grinned as she lifted the enormous blue teapot and poured her husband another cup of tea. 'Of course he couldn't remember the accident or which bills were owing…but in time it all came back right as rain.'

'And that's what he's got again, is it?' Ned asked as he took his big mug of tea between two huge hands.

'Seems so,' said Mary. She looked at Ally quizzically. 'I suppose he mightn't remember you, love.'

'Perhaps not,' whispered Ally, and fresh panic leapt into her chest so that she could hardly breathe. If Fletcher did not know her, what could that mean? If he'd forgotten meeting her, their time together in Melbourne...?

'Does he know about Connor?' she heard herself ask.

'Plenty of time to explain to him about that,' interrupted Ned. 'One shock at a time will be enough for now.'

But by the time Fletcher returned, there had been several long telephone conversations with Ned and he'd been brought pretty much up to date. He knew about the floods and that the mustering had to be delayed and he also knew that he was now legal guardian of his godson and that the boy had arrived with his nanny and was well settled in.

But that was all he knew.

The days were agony for Ally. It seemed terrible that she couldn't talk to Fletcher, couldn't hear his voice for herself, but the Harrisons never invited her to the phone and she could hardly insist. One night, when they had retired to their own little cottage several hundred metres away, she walked to the telephone standing on the front hall table and very nearly rang the hospital and asked to speak to him. But, as she stood there, her trembling hand poised above the receiver, practising what she would say, the futility of it all sank in.

She could picture Fletcher sitting in his starched, white hospital bed, holding the phone to his ear, listening to her patchwork explanation, his features clouded by a look of total disbelief. What was she going to say if he didn't remember her? If he had no idea who she was, how could she begin to explain why she had rung? She could hardly tell him, 'I'm your lover. We are one very hot item together. I thought you might like to know.'

She walked away from the phone; her shoulders slumped with disappointment and her hands hanging limply by her sides.

Perhaps when he saw her again, he would know as soon as he looked at her that they had a very special relationship. But what if he didn't? How could she bear it if Fletcher treated her with the complete indifference of a stranger?

Now, her real torment began. During the day she could usually occupy herself to a degree by entertaining Connor, but the nights were agony. For hours she would lie, twisting her thoughts into tortuous knots as she tried to imagine meeting Fletcher all over again.

Would he know her? If he did, would he send her packing straight away? If…if… What if…? Could she bring herself to leave now, when she had begun to feel so at home here? She had spent the days familiarising herself with every nook and cranny of the homestead where Fletcher had spent his whole life. It was a huge and beautiful old home and she was beginning to love it almost as much as its master.

'Stop fretting. He'll be all right, love,' Ned would reassure her when she appeared, her eyes ringed by dark circles in the morning. 'He's the strongest man I know and I've met lots of tough men in the bush. And he's the best,' he muttered with a sincere smile. 'They surely got the recipe right when they made that man. But then again, it's high time he had someone pretty to worry about him,' he added with a knowing smirk.

By the afternoon Fletcher was due to return, the rain had stopped and Ally had hung some washing for herself and Connor on the clothesline, which stretched from the ancient mango tree in the yard behind the homestead. Mary had been quite agitated, insisting that washing wasn't a part of a nanny's duties, but Ally needed to keep busy. She was far too nervous to sit still. Even washing wasn't really enough activity to calm her tense, fluttering stomach.

She put Connor to rest with Shy, his platypus, and a few favourite books on a daybed on the screened back veranda where he could enjoy a sleep in the fresh air.

Apart from her frantic nervousness, she was feeling happy at the thought of seeing Fletcher again. The day was clear and fresh after the rain and she took time during Connor's nap to shower and change into clean jeans and a simple white linen shirt—one of her own designs. She tied her dark shiny hair back from her face with a deep violet satin ribbon, so that without make-up her clear, fresh complexion was displayed in stark contrast to her dark hair.

It was as she was unpegging a row of Connor's striped socks that the helicopter engine erupted once again in the sky above her. She looked up and saw the metallic monster glinting in the sun as it circled above, dropping closer. Ally felt her already high anxiety levels increase dramatically. As the helicopter swooped across the clothesline, sending the clothes dancing from the blades' down draught, she could see Fletcher sitting in the front seat, dark and handsome as ever, staring down at her. In an instant he was gone, over the homestead roof to land on the broad run of lawn out the front, but that brief glimpse had been enough.

He had stared at her with a puzzled frown creasing his broad forehead. There had been no sign of recognition.

She suddenly felt sick, her body chilled, almost numb. Hastily she dragged the rest of the washing from the line, her heart racing frantically. By the time she'd thrust the last of the clothes in the wicker basket, she was trembling violently. It had been bad enough when Fletcher had wanted to send her away, but at least then, there had always been Melbourne, and their special week could somehow remain a tenuous bond, a fragile link she would always have with him whatever else happened. But now, if their past had been wiped out, erased from his mind as surely as if they had never met, he would treat her like a complete stranger and she wondered if she could bear it.

She rushed across the lawn, dumped the washing basket on the veranda, and swept up Connor. She had no idea where she would take him, but one thing was certain; she had to get out of the house. She couldn't line up with Mary and Ned as part of the reception committee welcoming back the master.

'Let's go for a walk,' she said, forcing herself to sound bright and enthusiastic. 'There's a nice track going down to the creek.'

'OK,' responded Connor happily. Fortunately he was a child who wakened easily and he was always ready for an adventure. Ally tied up his sneakers quickly and was soon rapidly making her way away from the house and towards the line of trees at the far end of the paddock.

They were halfway across the sweep of paddock when the helicopter took off again and Connor looked up waving excitedly. The pilot saw him and waved back and even leaned forward to take a closer look at them both.

Of course they couldn't get down to the creek. It was still in flood and the track was washed out in several places. Ally realised guiltily that Fletcher had probably never retrieved his trail bike from where he'd abandoned it the day she arrived and by now it would probably be swept away. Fletcher wouldn't even be able to remember what had

happened to it unless she told him, she thought with a painful stab of remorse.

'Perhaps we'd better go back after all,' she said, eyeing the
muddied track. 'It's about afternoon teatime,' she added in
case Connor protested. And the promise of milk and Mary's
Anzac biscuits was enough to turn him around without once
questioning Ally's contrariness.

I guess I'll just have to face the music, she thought nervously as they retraced their steps across the paddock. But
when they reached the homestead, her courage failed her and
she pushed Connor forward towards the kitchen.

'You go on in and find Mary and she'll give you your afternoon tea and you'll be able to see Uncle Fletcher, too,'
she said, giving him a gentle shove towards the passage,
which led to the kitchen. Connor looked at her with wide-
eyed curiosity.

'What about you?' he asked.

'I'll…I'll be along later,' she said. 'I've got a few things
to do. I need to fold the washing.'

'OK.' Connor smiled at her and obediently trotted off.

Flustered, desperately anxious in case she saw Fletcher
at any moment, Ally snatched up the basket of clothes and
headed to the far end of the long veranda. She almost stopped
to work there at the little table where she and Connor often
occupied themselves, but then she decided it was still too
visible, so she continued on to her own room and began to
fold the clothes frantically, setting them out on little piles
on her bed.

The folding was almost finished when she heard firm, deliberate footsteps marching along the veranda. They had to
be Fletcher's. Ned's arthritis caused him to walk with a limp

and Mary shuffled around quietly in slippers that were kind to her bunions. Was he coming to find her?

Ally stiffened, fear prickling her spine while Lightbulb curled comfortably in the middle of the bed and swished his tail lazily. Her palms grew sweaty and she pressed them together as she stood rigid with tension, her back to the door. She caught her reflection in the oval mirror on the opposite wall. Her pale, wide-eyed face framed by a bell of dark hair looked so vulnerable. If only she could look more sophisticated and sexy—or at least more in control. The steps grew closer and Ally saw an embarrassing tide of blushing pink sweep up her neck and into her cheeks.

Then a shadow fell across the bed as she sensed a tall form block the doorway and a familiar, deep voice drawled, 'So this is the nanny's hide-out.'

CHAPTER SIX

STAY CALM! Ally warned herself as she turned around slowly. Fletcher stood in the doorway with a piece of sticking plaster high on his temple, the only evidence that he'd had an accident.

He was smiling at her with a devastating twinkle in his blue eyes. Her heart seemed to stop beating and a painful jolt tightened her chest so that she had difficulty breathing. He looked for all the world as if he were waiting for her to run into his arms and welcome him back.

But of course he wasn't and she couldn't. He didn't know her. His smile was simply the same charming grin he used to dazzle any mere mortal who crossed his path. There was no underlying message, no hidden flash of understanding, no shared memories.

He had absolutely no idea who she was.

'How do you do?' he said, extending a strong, brown hand. 'I believe we have met, but I'm afraid I need to start over again.' He grinned once more, his eyes sparkling at her and his smile warm enough to melt her bones.

'Hello.'

It was an inadequate response, but it was the best she could muster. She stood almost shivering under his curious gaze, while in contrast, her cheeks continued to blaze relentlessly.

He leant a broad shoulder casually against the doorframe and folded his arms across his chest, so that Ally's attention was drawn to his powerful, tanned forearms. She found herself taking in every detail—the black, finely knit polo shirt tucked into tailored grey slacks, his damp and neatly combed hair and smooth, clean-shaven jaw. He looked wonderful. Just as sexy as he did in his everyday jeans, cotton shirts and riding boots or, in a tux, as he'd been when she had first met him at the show.

Doing her best not to be overawed by his physical presence, Ally carefully composed her features to seem unimpressed and calm, but of course she was neither. Fletcher had been gone for ages and her whole face felt as if it was beaming ridiculously with the sheer joy of having him so near again. It was as if now that he was back, the world was spinning safely on its axis once more. She could look forward to each day following the next.

It was a foolish reaction really, for she knew that as soon as Fletcher's memory returned he would be just as angry as he'd been before and he would send her packing. He was only being charming because he didn't know who she was.

His eyes slid politely over her and then narrowed as he quickly scanned the room and her belongings. 'I see you've settled in. That's good. Are you comfortable?'

'Oh, yes. I'm very comfortable, thank you. You have a very lovely home.'

He shrugged. 'Yes, it's not bad, is it? It's been in the family for over a century. My great-grandfather was one of the first settlers in the district.'

I know! Ally wanted to reply. You told me all about this home, about your life, when we were in Melbourne.

She turned away awkwardly to hide her hurt and bent to stack Connor's folded clothes. As she straightened, her eyes met his, reflected in the mirror. She could have sworn he'd been staring at her behind. An unbidden pulse began to race. Their eyes met in the mirror and he grinned again, sheepishly.

'Er...I was wondering,' he said, actually having the grace to sound uncomfortable. 'Did I hire you?'

A surge of guilt prickled in Ally's chest. For a woman who had spent weeks planning and scheming her arrival on Wallaroo Downs, her preparation for Fletcher's return from hospital lacked foresight. She really should have spent more time considering how she was going to handle all his unanswerable questions. Instead, she'd wasted all her emotion on missing him and hadn't even begun to consider the complications she would now have to deal with on a day-to-day basis.

There was no option really. If she tried to be anything except the hired help, she would face probing questions that would only lead to another argument and her dismissal. And now that she had another chance to stay at Wallaroo, she wasn't about to cut the ground from under her own feet.

She took a deep breath and looked at him directly. 'No. Your cousin Lucette hired me in Melbourne. We travelled up here together.'

'Really?' He allowed his sapphire gaze to linger on her approvingly. She could feel beads of perspiration forming on her skin as if the sun was reaching right into her room. 'My little cousin shows great taste. I hope I've thanked her appropriately.'

Ally almost choked, remembering how before the accident, he had jeered, *She couldn't have found anyone less suitable than you!*

She drew in a sharp breath, then bit down quickly on her lip. 'You probably didn't have time,' she muttered, hoping against hope that Ned had kept his word and provided a plausible explanation for how Fletcher came to be crossing the Fanning River with her so quickly after she arrived.

Easing his wide shoulder away from the doorframe, he took a step into her room and Ally almost jumped out of her skin. If she just reached out she could touch his brown forearm. Another step and she would be able to smell his familiar, tangy aftershave and the subtle, muskiness of his skin.

The cat stood up in the middle of the bed, stretched and miaowed, then jumped down and padded towards Fletcher to rub his golden head against his master's legs. If only I belonged here like you do, Lightbulb, Ally thought.

'I hear you've taken on quite a few chores, perhaps more than necessary,' Fletcher commented.

Shrugging, Ally spread her damp palms down her thighs to dry them. He seemed intrigued by the movement and she quickly closed her fists.

'I like to keep busy,' she said quietly.

'And you like purple,' he responded with yet another sizzling smile while her mind whirled crazily and her body froze.

'How do you know? How could you possibly know about that unless...'

'Unless?'

Unless he remembered intimate details of their relationship! She had to clutch the carved post at the end of the bed for support as she remembered Fletcher smiling at her shyly from behind an enormous bunch of orchids.

Fletcher let his gaze rest on her for a thoughtful moment and her nerve endings jangled. His eyes gleamed with gentle mockery as he observed the confusion in her blushing cheeks and her obvious need for support.

'I'm sorry if I've embarrassed you, Miss Fraser,' he murmured, turning her skin to goose bumps of apprehension.

She tried to pretend nonchalance. 'Not at all. I was just surprised that…that you…' It didn't work. She couldn't talk her way out of this one. The lazy amusement in his eyes sparked her anger and she retaliated without thinking. 'Well, how did you know?'

'That you have a fetish for purple underwear?'

'It's hardly a fetish…a fondness perhaps… But?'

She couldn't continue. It felt distinctly absurd to be discussing such intimate details with a man she hardly knew and yet, at the same time, knew as closely and completely as she knew herself. It was desperately confusing. She felt ill.

Then she caught his amused gaze. He was almost winking at her before switching his gaze to the piles of clothes on her bed. She looked and blushed again. There, next to neat piles of T-shirts, socks and undies for Connor, were piles of her clothes. A couple of blouses were set aside waiting to be ironed, but next to them were her bras—white lace, coffee satin, wispy and dainty and then a pile of her panties. They were clearly on display—purple stripes, purple hearts, purple spots and flowers, lilac lace and violet satin—some of which Fletcher himself had purchased.

His comment had been based entirely on his observation of her folded washing and it didn't take a Sherlock Holmes to come to the same conclusion he had.

Such clear evidence of his loss of memory brought a huge

wave of cold sadness, as if an ocean of Antarctic water had been dumped on her.

She swept her eyes up to his and tried to shrug casually.

'You've caught me out already, Mr. Hardy.'

'I guess I shouldn't come barging into a young lady's boudoir,' he replied gallantly. He gestured towards the doorway. 'Come and take a little walk with me. I need to have a bit of a look at the old place. I feel as if I've been away six months instead of just a week.' Then he frowned and once more grinned endearingly. This time, though, the smile was a little lopsided. 'I guess in one sense I have been away that long.' His hand ran swiftly across his brow and took a deep breath.

The amnesia bothered him, but he was pretending it wasn't a problem, Ally decided. For a brief moment, he looked lost, all alone. As if he needed someone. If only she could offer him some comfort—even a little squeeze of the hand.

'You should have seen this place from the air—water everywhere—just what this country needed,' he said, shooting her a swift glance as if warning her that he wanted no sympathy.

She hunted around for something practical to discuss and suddenly remembered, with a surge of guilt, her responsibilities.

'Should I collect Connor? He must have finished his afternoon tea by now,' she offered hurriedly.

'He's onto seconds.' He took her arm to guide her out of the room and Ally almost flinched at his touch. 'Let Mary spoil him,' he said with a chuckle. 'She looked after me when I was a nipper and I loved it. Now, enough of these formalities. Can we get straight to first names, Alexandra?'

The terrible tension which had seized her as soon as he

arrived tightened another notch. She struggled to make her
voice sound normal.

'Oh, please, call me Ally. Everybody does. I only use Alexandra for...' Gulping, sucking in a quick breath, she thanked
her lucky stars that she'd stopped herself in time. She'd been
about to mention her career, but a sixth sense warned her to
avoid talking about fashion to this new Fletcher. 'I mean,
Alexandra sounds so formal, doesn't it?'

'Not as bad as Mr. Hardy. I won't hear that again, will I,
Ally?'

She shook her head slowly, unable to speak. The pleasant camaraderie he was so quickly establishing caught her
completely off guard. It was so very different from the afternoon she had arrived. And it was nothing at all like the
evening they first met. His fascination with her then had left
him quite tongue-tied. There was none of that tension now.

Fletcher led her to a timber garden seat under one of the
huge tamarind trees flanking the front lawn. From there they
had a view of the whole of the front of the homestead. Ally
sat rather primly beside him, fearfully conscious of his relaxed sprawl. His long legs stretched interminably in front of
him, while a casual arm rested lightly along the back of the
seat. He showed absolutely none of her unease. There was
definitely no sign that he was experiencing any of the vibrat-
ing physical awareness that was causing her such discomfort.

'Ah, it's good to be home and such a pleasant surprise to
find the company has expanded so delightfully,' he said with
another of his heart-stopping grins.

Wallaroo Downs, the home that Fletcher had so clearly
missed, had what real estate agents might have termed 'street
appeal' if it had been anywhere near a city. It was a long, low
house set back behind a wide expanse of lawn. One end of

the long, deep front veranda was enclosed with lattice over which sprawled a rioting cascade of crimson bougainvillea.

Enormous tubs of tropical palms and hanging baskets of ferns were dotted along the veranda. And, in gardens stretching on either side of the front steps, were masses of vividly coloured shrubs—poinsettia, hibiscus, crotons and acalyphas kept alive through the drought by Ned who'd linked up an ingenious irrigation system from the creek. The reds, pinks and oranges of these shrubs provided a lively contrast to the deep shady trees whose trunks were home to enormous staghorns and bush orchids and beneath which sheltered more ferns. Already, in a week, Ally had become very fond of the house and garden.

Mary, bearing a large wicker tray, ambled towards them, her round cheery face flushed and beaming.

'Ah, Mary. Thanks so much.' Fletcher sprang to his feet and helped the housekeeper to settle the tray onto the low garden table beside where they sat.

Ally knew she looked surprised. 'Mary, how lovely.'

The tray held afternoon tea things—a coffeepot, two mugs, a milk jug and sugar basin—all made of beautiful earthenware pottery. There was also a plate of Mary's delicious pumpkin scones with little tubs of butter, jam and cream. Ally felt embarrassed. She was, after all, only supposed to be the hired help and now here she was being treated more like a special guest. Mary gave her a shy grin and quickly made to depart.

'How's Connor behaving?' Ally felt compelled to call after her.

'Like a little lamb,' Mary reassured her almost too heartily and as quickly as her bulky shape would allow, she scuttled away across the lawn and into the house.

'How do you like your coffee?' Fletcher asked, as if he noticed nothing at all strange about Mary's manner. He lifted the pot and the aroma drifted towards her. 'They don't make coffee like this in the hospital,' he said with an appreciative sniff.

'Oh, white, no sugar,' she responded automatically.

Fletcher handed her a cup of coffee and poured one for himself. Ally took a sip. It was very strong, brewed coffee—perhaps what she needed to give her stamina to face this strange situation. His eyes, as he looked at her over the rim of his coffee mug, had taken on a smoky haze that softened their brightness and she wondered, just for a moment, if perhaps he wasn't quite as confident and relaxed as he pretended.

But his next question showed her that she couldn't afford to let her mind wander. She needed to be as alert as a witness before a Royal Commission.

'Tell me about yourself,' he drawled softly. 'What experience have you had of life on a cattle property?'

The huge gulp of coffee scalded her throat and, while she desperately didn't want to cough and splutter, that was exactly what she did. Loudly and dramatically. She couldn't have reacted more guiltily if she had suddenly donned dark glasses and a raincoat. Her behaviour didn't go unnoticed.

Fletcher's eyes cooled and narrowed and he straightened to a more erect, alert seating position. 'Do you need water?' he asked politely, guardedly.

'No, no. I'm sorry. The coffee was hotter than I realised,' she stammered. She quickly replaced the coffee cup on its saucer and reached for a scone. Without butter or jam she bit into it, her mind racing, her heart hammering and her throat so tight she wondered how she would ever be able to swallow the small morsel.

And even more importantly, how on earth was she ever going to answer this question? In just thirty seconds she could tell this man enough to have him reject her out of hand. The truth would have him standing and towering over her, his beautiful mouth grim and disdaining, as he informed her that unfortunately there'd been a misunderstanding and she was not suitable for the position of nanny on Wallaroo Downs. Once again she would be packing her bags and being dismissed. A dreadful sense of futility and failure threatened to swamp her so completely that she almost sobbed.

But Ally had never given in. The tough dog-eat-dog world of high fashion had presented her with many knocks, scores of seemingly impossible challenges, and always, she'd hung in there, keeping her goal in sight. This, she decided quickly, was just one more challenge. This time her goal was even more important. Fletcher Hardy meant more to her than fashion design ever had.

'I…I grew up in…' she began. To her horror she heard her voice sounding uncertain…timorous. This wasn't good enough. She needed to lift her act.

Fletcher leaned forward, his attention fixed on her with total concentration. She sat beside him, rigid with fear, willing herself to continue. Her racing heart would not calm down and her breathing was out of control. In the trees behind her a flock of apostle birds began their noisy squabbling. Think of what it will mean if you have to go back to Melbourne, she told herself. Think of never seeing him again!

Summoning every ounce of strength she possessed, she lifted her head and looked straight into his beautiful blue eyes.

'I grew up on a cattle property down near Rockhampton,' she lied in a cool, controlled voice. 'Friendship Creek sta-

tion. You've heard of it?' she added with just the right shade
of curiosity, knowing that he couldn't have. The name had
popped into her head as she spoke.

His eyes narrowed and he gazed at her thoughtfully, his
glance running over her, sending quivers darting down her
back.

'No, I haven't,' he remarked, breaking his gaze to take
one of Mary's scones and spread it liberally with homemade
Burdekin plum jam.

'It's not far from Mt. Freedom station,' she supplied,
quickly throwing in the name of the place where she had
spent several school holidays.

'Ah, yes. I know that place. Quite a big property. Belongs
to the Savages.'

'Yes, that's right.' She took a quick breath to help gather
her composure.

He smiled at her again and as usual the charm worked.
She felt warm, glowing relief seep into her veins. It seemed
her deception, terrible as it was, would be worth it.

She should have known his charming smile was the result of a lucky mix of genes and was not an indication of a
sensitive, courteous nature. It was in fact as dangerous as a
crocodile's leer.

'Tell me,' he said, 'how Lucette came to choose you to be
Connor's nanny.'

For an awful moment, all she could think of was the truth.
How she had begged Lucette to allow her to come. How she
had plotted and schemed to arrive at Wallaroo Downs with
Connor and win back Fletcher's heart. How futile that scheme
had proved was so strongly impressed on her now, that for
the life of her she could not think past it.

'Lucette knew that when I was at Art College I'd been a nanny for the children of two doctors in Melbourne.'

Fletcher inclined his head. 'Art College?' He leaned back in the seat. 'Tell me what else you do.'

Hesitantly, she began, treading cautiously around the truth, using just enough to give her story substance. 'I've tried to make a living from art. I always wanted to be a fashion designer…but it's so hard to get into that field. So I've drifted a bit…I've done a little modelling, some freelance sketching for calendars and…and some work as a nanny.' It was amazing really, how once she started to lie, the rest came so easily. As she spoke, he watched her. He watched the way she talked and the movement of her hands as she developed her story.

He was watching so closely that she wondered if he could see through her artifice. Her skin was so very fair. She didn't really look like she'd spent much time out in the bush. Her hands were soft and white and carefully manicured, each finger tipped by a well-shaped nail and revealing a neat half moon; not like Mary's which were rough and red from years of hard housework, or Fletcher's, which were brown and callused. Her deception weighed on her like a heavy yoke.

She had fought hard for what she wanted before, but she'd always fought fairly. But now the stakes were higher. If she could somehow win Fletcher back, surely a few little lies would be worth it.

He didn't comment. His deeply blue eyes squinted thoughtfully as though he were trying to will his memory to return so that he could match up her story with what he already knew. What he used to know.

She drank the rest of her coffee hardly tasting it. If she blew her chances now, there would be no more. She looked at him steadily, trying to hide the yearning from her face.

If she wanted to prove her usefulness on a cattle property, she would have to concentrate on practicalities and forget romance completely.

Forget it as completely as Fletcher had.

She was distracted from her thoughts by Fletcher leaning forward to replace his coffee cup on the wicker tray. He sent another of his caressing smiles rippling over Ally before he spoke. 'As I said before, it's great to have you as part of our little team. Lucette has shown admirable judgment. Now I guess I'd better let you get back to your young charge.'

He stood up, towering above her and then bent towards her with the relaxed, unconscious confidence of well-bred manners, a hand at her elbow.

'I'd like to see Connor really experience a taste of life here. Let him play with the dogs. I have the perfect pony in mind for him, so you can teach him to ride. Take him fishing when the waters go down—that sort of thing... You do know how to fish, don't you?'

'Um...yes. I know the basics.' She knew that you needed a hook on the end of a line.

'And of course, you know the most important thing to teach him.'

Her grey eyes widened. 'I do?'

His serious expression made her suddenly nervous. 'To have absolute respect for his godfather.'

She almost punched him for that and she couldn't resist putting him in his place. 'Absolute respect cannot be demanded,' she replied archly. 'It must be earned. Connor's godfather has a responsibility to provide an impeccable role model.'

His blue eyes gleamed like expensively cut sapphires.

'Not a problem.'

Then as if in retaliation to her impudence, his hand moved towards her and she felt it brush her neck and sweep back a wing of hair from her face. The fleeting touch made her tremble helplessly and every instinct urged her to lean into the curve of his hand, but somehow Ally willed herself to pull away.

'Except that—I'll also be—' he murmured, as his fingers traced a path up the violet ribbon that tied back her hair.

'What are you doing?' she gasped.

Fletcher did not answer. He simply stood there, his warm hand against her cheek, his deep forget-me-not eyes studying her thoughtfully. Ally's heart began to jog and then to canter erratically.

'I'm remembering...' he said eventually.

'Re-remembering? Really?' She blanched, faint with alarm. If his memory had returned already, that heart-wrenching smile was about to turn to disgust as the full truth dawned on him.

'Yes,' he went on huskily. 'I'm remembering all those lovely purple garments of yours. If you want me to behave impeccably, don't leave anything like them lying around, Ally.'

Then, he smiled down at her slowly, seductively, so that she wanted to curl herself into his arms. She felt her lips part and her entire body fill with an overwhelming yearning for the warmth of his body against hers once more, to run her fingers through his thick glossy hair, to have his mouth hungrily devouring hers. The force of her feelings terrified her. At any minute she would give herself away.

But, totally unaware of her turmoil, Fletcher turned casually and strode off across the lawn and back towards the homestead.

CHAPTER SEVEN

ALLY MANAGED TO get through the next few days without a mishap and by the end of the week was beginning to feel more relaxed. For most of the day, Fletcher was gone, taking off to different parts of the property, and at night they dined with Ned, Mary and Connor.

She was grateful to be able to keep well out of Fletcher's way. Any time alone with him could spell disaster. What she needed was enough time before he regained his memory to prove to him that here on this property with him was where she belonged.

And she also needed to comply with some of his requests. There was no way she could teach a four-year-old boy to ride Fletcher's 'perfect pony,' so she decided to settle on fishing.

The floodwaters had almost completely receded and the creek below Wallaroo homestead, although a little more swollen than before the rain, was flowing once more at a sedate, leisurely pace. The muddiness had given way to fresh, clear water that sparkled in the afternoon sunlight.

It was quite fun to spend a lazy afternoon supervising Connor's first attempts with a fishing line. The grass on the creek bank had already sprung back fresh and lush after the recent rain, and the sun had dried and warmed it so that she found it was a perfect spot to sprawl in old denim shorts and a T-shirt.

Smiling to herself as she watched Connor staring eagerly into the water below, she realised that she wasn't really missing her work at all. She looked around at the gently whispering bush and at the distant hills warm and golden in the westerly sun and released a happy, satisfied sigh.

It was so beautiful here, so peaceful. A picture of Melbourne with hooting traffic and jammed streets, the smell of petrol fumes and jostling, busy, people-filled shopping malls flitted across her mind. For most of her life, she had enjoyed being a part of the rat race. Until now, she'd always lived in a metropolitan city, and she found the frenetic pace invigorating, but looking at the picture postcard scene before her, she wondered if she could ever enjoy it quite so much again.

Here, the air was clear and still and the corellas and budgerigars provided a delightful background chorus. If it weren't for the constant fear of her lies being revealed, she could certainly feel at peace. I could so easily be happy here, she thought. Why can't Fletcher understand that?

'Why won't the fishy bite my hook?' Connor asked Ally for the umpteenth time, as he plonked his muddy self at her feet. Ally shook her head in frustration. She had no idea and she was beginning to share the little boy's weariness with the sport of fishing. At least for her, there was an afternoon's enjoyment of the quiet, chuckling stream and the tranquil bush to delight in, but such pleasures were unlikely to impress a four-year-old.

'Would you like to stop fishing and make some boats?' she asked.

'Stop fishing? That's no way to teach him patience,' a familiar, masculine voice erupted behind them. Fletcher loomed above, walking his horse along the top of the bank.

Ally winced. His approach must have been silenced by the leafy bush track. If Fletcher was about to inspect her methods of teaching the noble art of fishing, she was in deep trouble. And as he dismounted and tethered his stallion to a nearby tree, she realised that was exactly what he had in mind.

'Any luck, mate?' he asked Connor in the man-to-man tone he had come to adopt with his godson and which the boy clearly relished. Connor looked up at his hero as he strode down the creek bank, his eyes shining with respect, but then he looked at Ally and pulled a face.

'No, fishing's boring.'

'Good grief, Ally.' Fletcher pointed to Connor's fishing rod then turned to her with a mixture of puzzlement and fury. 'What do you call that?'

'He's only a little boy playing at fishing,' she muttered defensively, then added, 'It's his fishing rod, of course,'

'It's a bloody log!'

She ducked her head. 'Well I made it from a tree branch. I thought it had to be reasonably thick so it wouldn't break when the fish pulled on the line.'

Fletcher stepped toward Connor and held out his hand for the boy to surrender his fishing tackle, shaking his head in amazement as he examined Ally's fearful construction. 'A tree branch, red string, a huge safety pin and no bait, Ally? What in hell's name were you expecting the boy to catch with that? A bunyip?'

'What's a bunyip?' asked Connor, but for once Fletcher ignored him. He was waiting for Ally's answer, his expression tyrannical.

'There *was* bait. I put a worm on. I've a whole bucketful of worms.' She'd dug the disgusting things up herself and been very proud of her willingness to get her hands so filthy.

'Good. Show me how you baited the hook.'

'Fine,' Ally replied with an air of hurt dignity, not liking at all the tone of his voice. 'I just pick one up, like this.' She tried particularly hard not to pull a face as she extracted a worm from the muddy bucket, and did her best to hold the squirming, slippery invertebrate casually, but firmly. 'And I stick it on the hook like this.'

'Is that all?'

'What do you mean, is that all? What else is there to do?'

'For Pete's sake, Ally, there's no way that worm will stay on that hook. You've simply jabbed it through once. It would probably slip off the minute it hits the water. You have to thread a hook—and I mean a proper hook, not this poor excuse for one—through the worm several times to make it stay on.'

'Not always,' she replied airily. His lecturing tone was irritating enough to make her defiantly toss the baited safety pin back into the water.

'There's no way you'll catch a fish with that. And just for the record, what's with the red string?' Fletcher shoved his thumbs into his belt loops and favoured Ally with a disparaging sneer.

'It's the only sort I had. I brought it with me for Connor. Children like bright colours and…well…I thought maybe it wouldn't matter. Didn't you know fish are colour blind?'

The blue eyes bored into hers. 'If that's the case,' he drawled, 'why is it, do you think, that fishermen go to so much expense to buy clear, monofilament lines?'

She stared at him, furious, wishing some clever answer

could spring to her lips, but no words would come. Instead she felt like slapping that beautiful, smug face. She was trying, damn him. She was trying so hard to be a good nanny. Since when did nannies have to be experts on all aspects of male sports? Next he would probably want Connor taught Rugby and cricket. Connor had no complaints. Why couldn't Fletcher just leave her to get on with her job?

The branch nearly jumped out of her hand.

'What was that?' she asked, and immediately blushed at her foolishness. There was no doubt what it was.

'I think you have a bite,' offered Fletcher dryly.

Ally held the shaking branch with both hands as she felt the powerful tug on the line. 'W-what do I do?'

A dark eyebrow rose questioningly. 'My dear Ally, it's quite simple. You pull it in.' He was mocking her, looking down with sardonic amusement at her dilemma. How could he do this to her?

But what he did next was worse.

Two strong arms came round her to take the rod and she felt Fletcher's breath fan the nape of her neck as he tugged at the string. Against her back she could feel the muscled breadth of his chest and his denim-clad thighs hard against her buttocks. She knew she shouldn't allow his entire body to mould so firmly against hers, but her own body ignored any feeble warnings her mind tried to transmit as the warmth of him, mingled with his heated, manly smell, enveloped her.

The fish came out of the water with a splash, gleaming silver, thrashing and struggling on the line. Somewhere nearby she could hear Connor's excited squeals. If she could have spoken, she would have begged Fletcher to return the fish to the creek, to leave it to swim free. But the closeness of him, the delicious pressure of his body against hers, robbed her of any hope of speech. She didn't take much notice of how he landed the fish, but she was very, very aware of the startling location of Fletcher's mouth.

It would only take the slightest sideways movement of her head to have her lips touching his. A surge of heat scorched through Ally's body. I should be backing off from this, one part of her brain urged her. But then as strong fingers gently lifted her chin, coaxing her round, tempting her to lean even more deeply into him, she remained silent.

Why was she allowing this to happen? she asked herself dazedly, as she recognized the fierce darkening of desire in his eyes. Surely this wasn't wise? She ought to struggle—to protest—push him away. If Fletcher knew her real identity, he would not be breathing so raggedly. His hands would not be sliding so sensuously down her back, sending shivers of pleasure rippling through her entire body. She shouldn't just stand there, quivering with desire, her tongue tip flickering over her lips, willing this man who didn't know her to take her mouth with his.

Which was exactly what he did.

She thought she knew all the secrets of Fletcher's lovemaking, but she was unprepared for the seductive gentleness of his kiss. It was as if he were drinking a delicate wine, tasting her slowly, exploring her mouth with mesmerising thoroughness and extracting from her the most flaring, uncontrolled desire. His heartbeat was pounding close to hers. She wanted to moan, to sink down onto the grassy bank and have that mouth continue its sensuous journey. Even though he did not know it, this was her man…her lover and she wanted his kisses to go on forever.

But he was drawing away, his blue eyes regretful, his hands still resting possessively on her slim hips. Then he looked down and she followed his gaze. Connor was standing tugging at the knees of Fletcher's jeans.

'Uncle Fletcher, Uncle Fletcher, what's a bunyip?'

Fletcher released her, smiling a long, slow sigh, which ended in a rueful chuckle. He allowed his eyes, sultry with desire to linger on Ally.

Her mouth was dry. Every nerve, every pulse in her body wanted him to continue what he had begun. If Connor had not been there, she knew she would have disgraced herself. She would have dragged Fletcher down onto the bank and torn off her clothes, begging him to take her eager breasts into that gorgeous mouth of his.

Her mind was filled with memories of Fletcher's beautiful body—all muscle and taut, sun-drenched skin, needing her, loving her, taking her.

His soft voice stirred her back to the present. 'I must apologise.'

She drew in a sharp breath at the unexpectedness of his words. The Fletcher she knew would certainly never have apologised for stealing a kiss. Trying unsuccessfully not to appear surprised, Ally stuttered, 'Yes, Mr.—um, Fletcher, that—that was uncalled for.'

Once more, a strong finger was beneath Ally's chin, tilting back her head so that she was forced to look up into his narrowed eyes. 'Nothing uncalled for has happened, Ally. Now, before you get those lovely purple knickers in a knot, I am not apologising for tasting your sweet mouth, little nanny… it's my criticism of your fishing line that was wrong. Obviously it's just what silver perch like,' he added with a sparkling grin.

Then, while she disintegrated into a jigsaw puzzle of conflicting emotions, wanting to simultaneously hug him and thump him, Fletcher calmly reached down and lifted a delighted Connor onto his shoulders as easily as if he were a silk necktie.

'How'd you like a ride on my horse, youngster?'

'Oh, yes please,' breathed Connor, his eyes round and shining.

'And,' added Fletcher as he placed the perch in a canvas bag hanging from a saddle strap, 'thanks to Ally, you can have fresh, fried fish for your dinner.'

'Yum! Can I have chips, too?'

'We'll have to talk to Mary about that. Now say goodbye to Ally.' The blue eyes flickered gently over her.

'Does Ally have to walk all by herself?'

'Oh, Connor, it's only across the paddock, you know that,' Ally said quickly.

Then she watched Fletcher lift Connor high up onto the big, black steed. She frowned as she noticed a moment of fear pucker his little face when he found himself alone on the stallion's back. But he was all smiles again as soon as Fletcher was mounted behind him.

'But tell me really and truly, what is a bunyip?' she heard the little boy's piping voice ask again as the horse set off and she watched them go, man and boy, the makings of a new family, while the alarming sensations aroused by his kiss remained surging through her.

Alone on the creek bank, Ally didn't move to follow them. She was lost in her memories of the taste of Fletcher, his smell, the feel of him, and of her own clamouring senses yearning for him. Wrapping her arms around herself, she frowned, feeling quite miserable again. She couldn't afford to let something like that kiss happen again, but did she have the strength to prevent it? And where could her venture to

Wallaroo Downs possibly be heading, except headlong into disaster?

If Fletcher became interested in her for a second time and then found out again who she really was, he would be doubly furious with her. He would hate her for deceiving him.

There was no doubt she was taking a foolish risk in staying on Fletcher's property under false pretences when there was almost no chance it could turn out well.

But there was no way she could bring herself to leave. Everything would be so much easier if she could. She almost wished that she didn't have to love him, but that was as impossible as changing the weather; it was something she couldn't alter or escape from. She was more certain of that now than ever before, but, given Fletcher's attitude to Alexandra Fraser, fashion designer, her feelings about him were never going to be satisfied.

She sighed heavily. Everything had seemed so easy before she set out for North Queensland. She was so sure that all she had to do was show Fletcher how happy she was to live in the bush and take care of Connor and he would ask her to marry him. But Fletcher the master of Wallaroo Downs obviously had a different set of priorities from the happy lover of Melbourne.

The day was turning to dusk, time to go back. Ally shrugged herself out of her mist of thoughts and climbed to the top of the bank. From the creek, frogs croaked, and Ally could hear cicadas humming in the trees. The sky over the hills was flushed with the blushing, late afternoon colour of ripened mangoes and already the evening star was blinking.

The transition from dusk to night was short and swift in the tropics.

By the time she returned from the creek bank, she found

Connor eagerly watching Mary preparing his fish for supper. He seemed fascinated by the shiny, sharp knife as it sliced the fillets from the backbone.

I guess that's another extremely useful skill that a good bush woman has, Ally thought with a grumpy sigh.

Mary looked across at her, her eyes shrewd, but sparkling as if they were lit by an inner excitement. 'So tonight's the big night. A proper dinner party for you and Fletcher—how lovely.'

'Really?' Ally asked, not sure how she felt about this news.

'Good idea,' chipped in Ned who had just come in from setting sprinklers around the homestead garden.

'I'd consider it a privilege to put the little fella to bed if he's still awake,' added Mary.

Why does this feel like a conspiracy? Ally asked herself as she looked at the grinning couple. Ned seated himself at one end of the roomy kitchen table and began to chop vegetables for Mary, who was looking remarkably satisfied with the state of affairs. Mary was giving the fish scraps to an ecstatic Lightbulb and Connor was watching with fascination. Then all three looked at Ally expectantly.

'I haven't been consulted about any dinner party,' she said stiffly, finding their curiosity stifling.

'Well, that's as may be,' mused Mary. 'But I've got my orders.'

'And Fletcher needs a little partyin',' added Ned. 'And so do you, lass. Young people need to—to—enjoy themselves a bit.'

Ally resisted telling them both that under the circumstances, parties—in this case, the dinner for two that Fletcher had obviously conned them into—would not bring enjoyment to either herself or to Fletcher. It would almost certainly end in her revealing something about her past that would incriminate her. It would be as dangerous as whitewater rafting without a paddle.

But if the dinner was risky, it was also beautiful. Mary's cooking was a surprise. The wholesome meals she had served until now had led Ally to assume that on a cattle property, one always ate beef—as steak, or roast, corned or casseroled. But tonight they dined on delicious seafood garnered from the huge cold room at the back of the kitchen. It was dressed in a delicate, creamy sauce and accompanied by fettuccini and a crisp garden salad. The table was set with antique silver on an immaculate, starched, white damask cloth.

And, what was even more pleasing, was that, rather than attacking her with personal questions, Fletcher seemed happy enough with the relatively harmless topics Ally neatly introduced herself—initially questions about Connor's parents and then about the families who lived on the surrounding properties.

She found herself beginning to relax a little—perhaps with the help of the classic, dry white wine, which she was drinking a little too quickly. As long as the conversation stayed general and kept well away from the personal, she was safe, she reassured herself. So she was caught out by the unexpected.

'You look beautiful this evening, Ally.'

Twin reactions of pleasure and alarm swamped her suddenly. She had dressed carefully in a simple but elegantly cut linen dress and had blown her hair dry to sit neatly just above her shoulders. She thought she had managed to look neat and ordinary, just as a nanny should.

'I can see why you wear that colour—the colour of violets. It makes your eyes go all smoky and mauve like distant hills at sunset.'

Fletcher waxing poetical! It was enough to make her put down her crystal wineglass very smartly and think seriously about eating. Even more than revealing her true identity, she was desperately afraid of letting down her guard and revealing her true feelings. If she wanted to stay on Wallaroo Downs, it was imperative that she continued to appear indifferent to Fletcher Hardy's charm—especially after the afternoon's little lapse.

Ally mumbled her acknowledgment of his praise and swiftly steered the conversation back to books and travel—subjects she knew were safe from their discussions in Melbourne. The candlelight, the good food and more of the beautiful Clare Valley Chardonnay combined with the formidable charm of Fletcher's company; all worked their magic so that she was lulled once more into a sensuous, relaxed mood. A surge of sheer, unalloyed desire streamed through her veins. Heavens above, she thought, lowering long lashes over her telltale eyes, how can I ever pretend I'm not madly in love with this man?

Their romance had started at the wrong end, of course—mad, passionate lovemaking, with only sketchy understandings of each other as a person. Now, the more she learned about Fletcher, the more certain she was that she was in the right place with the right man.

'I think you should come on a tour of the property with me.' Fletcher's words startled her out of her musings. 'I want to check out some of the outer areas before we start the muster—I can't for the life of me remember where all my cattle are,' he continued. 'And you can get to know a bit more about the place. Mary will mind the little chap for a day or two. She'd love it.'

He looked across at her, his blue eyes twinkling and his smile warm and charming.

'Would—would we be riding horses?' Ally asked cautiously, not allowing herself to think about how those blue eyes would chill and the smile vanish if he knew that at best she could only ride at a slow canter.

Fletcher's smile glowed in the subdued lighting. 'We'll do it in style and throw our swags and an esky in the back of the Range Rover.' His eyes slid over her slim frame. 'I figure that neat little behind of yours would be black, blue and purple after a day in the saddle.'

'Well, you're right,' Ally admitted carefully. 'It has been a while since I left the bush.'

'So you'd like to come with me?'

'Yes, I'd love to.' The eager words had left her lips before she considered just how enthusiastic they sounded. Too late, she realised that she had just volunteered for more time alone with Fletcher, more opportunities to stir his memory. She looked away quickly, but not before she caught a curious sparkle in Fletcher's eyes.

'Good, that's settled then,' he said quietly.

After breakfast the next day, Connor, with Mary at his side, waved them off from the front veranda quite happily. They left with the morning sky still streaked with pink and gold. Ally sat quietly, remembering the last time she had driven beside Fletcher when he'd been escorting her off his station. Now he was taking her on the grand tour and she should have been relaxed and thrilled that he wanted to share his home with her.

If only she didn't have to feel so guilty.

What bothered her was the knowledge that as each day passed, the moment when his memory returned drew nearer. Over and over again, Ally tried to convince herself that she wasn't being foolish. Given a little more time, surely she could convince him that her place was beside him here at Wallaroo Downs.

She thought of the two swags, rolled and buckled and lying side by side in the back of the vehicle. Tonight, she and Fletcher would no doubt be lying side by side. They would be camping under the stars, sleeping together in the bush. A heated coil of pleasure uncurled deep inside her. Did he plan to continue where the other day's kiss left off?

Would she make love to him, knowing that she was deceiving him?

Could she resist?

There were kilometres of plains, no longer dry and dusty but lush with bright, fresh grass stretching around them on all sides.

'Best sight a cattleman could ever hope to see,' said Fletcher nodding at the vast stretches of grassland.

As they bumped along the dirt track, Ally found herself drinking in the wide expanse—blue sky going on forever and the grey-green plains dotted with cattle and reaching to the distant, purple hills.

'That's where we're going to camp tonight,' Fletcher said, nodding his head towards the hills, 'on the river bank at the foot of that range.'

Ally concentrated on the scenery close by, unwilling to let her mind dwell any further on the night to come. But her eyes were continually drawn back to the man beside her. Silhouetted against the bright sunlight outside the Range Rover's cabin, every detail of the man she loved was clearly defined.

The little bump on the bridge of his nose, the unexpected symmetry of his mouth, the dark curls emerging from his open collar, and the power in his hands as they rested lightly on the steering wheel. He had looked wonderful in the city, but here in the bush where he belonged, with the wide, vast outback all around, he looked perfect.

They stopped for lunch on the edge of the Burdekin River. Enormous paperbarks curtained the banks, some still standing in water, a legacy of the recent rains. And as Ally and Fletcher munched on their sandwiches and downed cans of cold beer from the esky, he pointed out black ducks, pelicans, wood ducks and egrets flitting across the water, or swooping to catch fish. Behind them, huge basalt outcrops loomed majestically like castles on the Rhine.

Ally was overawed by the sheer drama of the setting with the wide river full of busy bird life, the imposing trees with their beautiful trunks of creamy, peeling bark and the towering cliffs of grey stone. Everything was bathed in clear, bright sunlight beneath a brilliant blue sky.

'Wallaroo Downs is a beautiful property,' she said. 'It must mean a lot to you.'

Fletcher stretched back and rested on his elbow. 'This spot always blows me away. Of course, everything always looks better after some rain. It's not always this pretty.'

'Oh, I know. I did arrive here before the rain, remember?'

'No, I don't,' Fletcher replied quietly, and Ally bit down hard on her lip. She saw a shadow of annoyance cross his features and he picked up a small stone and threw it fiercely into the river, causing some ducks to take off with loud, protesting honks. He looked away, down the river and then to the rocks behind them. 'Want to climb up there?' he asked, as if to change the subject.

'Sure,' she responded.

Ally was glad she had worn sturdy boots as she clambered up the rocks behind Fletcher. As they reached the top, a fresh breeze drifted up from the river.

'This is just amazing,' murmured Ally, looking with total awe at the wall of rock beneath her, the wide Burdekin River below and the rolling green country stretching away on the far side.

'It's pretty amazing to think it was all under the sea once,' Fletcher said, crouching on the blue-grey rock and tracing its surface with his hand.

'You're kidding?'

'Not at all. Look at this.' Fletcher reached up and took her hand, pulling her down beside him. He was pointing at a mark in the rocks. Ally looked more closely.

'It looks like a—a piece of coral,' she said.

'That's right,' he said. 'It's fossilised coral. And that's a mollusc and there's more coral over there. And what do you think this little curly thing could be?'

'Oh, I don't know. It's a kind of horn or something.'

'It's a form of ammonite. A little sea creature from the Mesozoic Era. They became extinct around the same time as the dinosaurs.'

'Really?' breathed Ally.

'Millions of years ago, before the ice age, this was all under the sea. Hard to believe, isn't it?'

'Thinking about the land and how long it's been around—it always makes our little lives seem rather insignificant, doesn't it?'

'Oh, I don't know,' mused Fletcher. 'Perhaps if we take ourselves too seriously it might. I rather like to think of myself as a part of it all. I want my bones to rest here one day—become part of the land again.'

'You really love this country, don't you?' Ally asked softly.

'It's in my blood.'

Ally felt her breath catch as he turned to look to the south so that his profile beneath its shady hat was silhouetted clearly against the bright sky.

I love it, too, she wanted to say, but she contented herself with, 'It's going to be a wonderful place for Connor to grow up.'

Fletcher grinned, then stood up beside her. 'Always the little nanny,' he chuckled. 'Come on, let's go or we won't make the hills before dark.'

Ally spent the afternoon relishing the cosy, companionable peace. Fletcher rattled the four-wheel-drive vehicle along the bumpy track, at times stopping to check on stock or on the condition of fences, or to show Ally a particularly interesting landmark. As the shadows lengthened, tawny kangaroos emerged from the bush to join the grazing cattle while overhead, squadrons of flying foxes winged silently across the reddening sky to feed on ti-tree blossoms. Ally felt so happy and peaceful. Everything would have been just perfect if she could have curled up on the seat beside Fletcher and rested her head on his broad shoulder.

The track wound back down to the river bank again. At the point where they set up camp, the grassy bank was high on their side and low and sandy on the far side of the river. Together they gathered some firewood and piled it at a perfect spot for a campfire where they would have a view up and down the river.

'Time for a swim,' said Fletcher, and immediately began to pull off his shirt. As the broad, brown back emerged, rippling and male in the red-gold light of dusk, Ally nervously wondered if he would be swimming naked.

'What—what about crocodiles?'

Fletcher shot her a reassuring smile. 'Not this far inland. There might be the odd freshwater croc, but they only eat fish.'

'Well—I brought my bathers,' she said quickly, disappearing behind the truck to change. By the time she re-emerged, wearing a demure black one-piece swimsuit, Fletcher was already in the water. He turned over, floating on his back and watching her as she self-consciously made her way down the steep bank. She knew he was having a long look at her slim figure and legs. To her own surprise, she found herself posing on a log at the water's edge. Have an eyeful, Fletch, she told him silently. You found me pretty irresistible once.

Then she slipped into the cool water and boldly swam towards him.

Fletcher remained, treading water, watching her as she drew nearer. Ally switched to breaststroke so that she could observe his face as she swam slowly up to him. His eyes were fixed intently on her.

A few metres away, her heart began to thump painfully in her chest. I'm going to seduce him, she realised. It hadn't been a conscious decision till then. She'd merely acted on instinct—an instinct which compelled her to forget about being Connor Lawrence's nanny. She was Ally Fraser, alone with the man she loved and, in spite of the wild alarm bells ringing in her head, she was going to teach him to love her again.

CHAPTER EIGHT

ALLY SWAM CLOSER to Fletcher.

Treading water, he watched her approach. His eyes remained locked with hers and there was an unreadable expression, a fierce concentration in his gaze, which brought colour to her cheeks, despite the temperature of the river. She could almost sense his driving need for her to close the final, short gap between them.

'The water's colder than I expected,' she said with a forced smile as she reached him.

'It doesn't take long to get used to it.' His voice was thick and even deeper than normal.

Self-consciously she added, 'It's the best way to cool off after a long, hot day.'

He grinned and his eyes sparkled expectantly, but he made no move.

The pink and orange lights of late afternoon danced across the rippling water, bathing his skin in a golden glow, enhancing his hard-muscled male beauty.

Oh, how she loved him. If only… But now was not the time for wishing. Action was required.

Without allowing herself time for second thoughts, she swam over to him and placed her hands boldly on his shoulders. With only a moment's hesitation, he crushed her to him, his lips closing on hers with a breathless hunger.

Cool water encircled them as his body told her the truth. There was absolutely no doubt that he wanted her. He lowered his head to kiss her throat and shoulders; his lips caressing while his hands moulded her tightly against his strength. Ally felt herself arch towards him provocatively in a fever pitch of need.

'Dear Ally. What a little temptress you are.'

Just to prove the statement, she kissed him back, deeply, daringly. Then she ducked out of his arms and began to swim back towards the bank. Her smile widened as he caught her easily and rolled her over in the water, playfully drawing her slim body against him and kissing her once more, his tongue exploring the inner softness of her mouth.

She heard a strange, animal sound rumble in her throat. And he echoed her need with a hungry growl, holding her head in both hands so that he could kiss her thoroughly, possessively.

A deep, primitive tremor shook through her body. At that moment she didn't care that he might soon remember who she was and once more evict her from his property. For now, in his arms, she could forget everything except that Fletcher wanted her and she wanted him.

Gently, he guided her back towards the bank. Glorious sensations were building up, driving her to cling to him, her body meshed with his, begging a closer intimacy. Her breasts pushed through the filmy swimsuit into the hairy wall of his chest. Fletcher lifted her out of the water to kiss each aching nipple through the thin, wet fabric and a loud moan burst from her lips. Then she felt the rough sand under her feet and realised they had reached the shallows. Urgently, Ally slipped the clinging bathers from her shoulders to reveal her breasts, wet and gleaming in the fading light and swollen with desire.

'Oh, sweet heaven, Ally. What are you doing to me?'

'I want you,' she answered, her voice pleading. She was a siren, a water nymph, heady with a desire that endured since time began. Her lover was a tall, bronzed god.

'You're divine,' he whispered back, drawing a line with his finger down her throat and across her quivering skin, to trace the outline of a nipple, taut with need for him.

Then he froze and a puzzled expression slipped over his features before he stepped back abruptly. For a long, tortuous moment, Fletcher stared at her. He was about to speak, to touch her again when he turned abruptly, and left her to gaze mutely at his back and buttocks as he strode up the bank.

Ally remained in the ankle-deep water, stunned and shivering, hardly aware of whether it was the evening air or his rejection that caused the sudden chill to invade her entire body. Dimly, she was conscious of Fletcher drying himself roughly with a towel he'd snatched from the back of the Rover and dragging jeans back over his long limbs.

And as he made his way back down the bank towards her, the towel slung around his bare shoulders, her first reaction was to become embarrassed, crossing her arms over her bared breasts, but her humiliation quickly turned to anger. How could he do this to her? The Fletcher she knew could never have been so cruel and he would never have had the strength of will to walk away from what she so generously offered.

Too soon, he reached the sandy ledge at the bottom of the

bank, and a stab of icy fear sliced through her when she saw the glazed shock in his eyes.

Had he remembered? Is that why he walked away?

He stepped towards her, his eyes dark, reflecting deep pain. 'Ally. I'm so sorry. Please, let me explain.'

His voice was so considerate, so tender, that she found herself calming in spite of her apprehension. He handed her the towel, with which she immediately covered herself, then she stepped back, her head haughtily high. If there was one thing she could resurrect from this disaster, it would be her dignity.

'It's so strange,' he began hesitantly. 'I wanted you so badly, and then, just as I was going almost out of mind with desire, I had this terrible feeling, a conviction if you like, that I—that before I lost my memory, I was already committed to someone.'

He stared down at her with a bewildered, shy smile. Her heart pounded with accelerated speed as she took in what he was saying.

'You mean you—you think there's somebody else?'

'Well, I can't bloody remember anybody else,' he exclaimed with a frustrated grimace, 'but there's this feeling that—well, I don't exactly know, but, until I get my damned memory back, I think I shouldn't get too involved. I guess it sounds pretty weird, but I kind of feel as if I may already be in love with someone.'

You are, you great galoot, she wanted to scream. You're madly, deeply in love with me!

'I'm sorry, Ally. I should have thought of this before. I shouldn't have started this.' Here he was again, just like in Melbourne, apologising for loving her, when it was all she wanted him to do. 'But if there is someone else—well, I've never believed in two-timing. Do you understand?'

His expression was so intense, pleading with her, that she felt a queer, quiet exhilaration spread through her. If only Fletcher could remember how much he loved her! Slowly her intense disappointment was overtaken by a tingling dawning of hope.

The hopeful feeling stayed with her all evening as they lit the camp fire, cooked crispy, homemade sausages stuffed with herbs, onions and tomatoes in an old, blackened frying pan and boiled the billy, throwing in a good handful of tea leaves to be stirred with a gum tree twig.

Above them, a sliver of moon painted the bush and the murmuring river with a thin, white light as, slowly, the stars emerged in the smooth, black sky. Even when the mournful cry of a curlew reached them from further downriver, Ally continued to nurse the little ball of hope deep within her.

She thought briefly of the glittering hotels and theatres and busy streets of Melbourne at night, lit by the headlights of thousands of cars and flashing neon signs. And she realised that her life in the south now seemed strangely distant, vague and not quite real—like something she had seen on television. This bush was her reality now. She was sure she understood Fletcher's feeling for the land. Her family might not have owned the land for generations, but she still loved it. She loved the slim, white trunks of the eucalypts as they gleamed in the moonlight, the moody river returning back to its usual sleepy languor, the glowing camp fire crackling contentedly. And, of course, she loved it because this was where Fletcher belonged.

They sat by the fire on their rolled-out swags and after they drank their tea, Fletcher leaned over and took Ally's mug. 'Let me get you some real bush tucker,' he said with a grin.

She watched in silence as he walked over to the vehicle

and pulled out a bottle from which he poured a small slug into each mug. Then he added some water from the canvas sheathed bottle and came back to crouch beside her.

'Rum and river water. Best nightcap for the bush.'

'Rum? Fletcher, I don't think I—'

'Just give it a go. Think of it as good medicine.'

Ally took a tentative sip. The rum was strong, fiery and sweet at the same time.

'I guess I could get used to it,' she said, smiling.

A blackened log cracked loudly and fell down into the glowing embers. Fletcher stretched out a leather-booted foot to kick it further into the middle of the fire.

In the firelight, his tanned skin took on a ruddy tinge and his thick, black hair, rumpled and unbrushed, gave him a wild, untamed look. It took all of Ally's willpower not to reach out and touch that hair or to place her hand against his bristly cheek, but somehow she stayed still, sipping the rum and trying to stare at the fire rather than the rugged, masculine form beside her. But if she couldn't reach him physically, the need to make emotional contact grew overpowering.

'This girl you might be in love with,' Ally began nervously, 'when do you think you will remember her?'

Fletcher took a deep swig from his mug, his eyes fixed determinedly on the bright flames. 'Can't say. Doctors said it could be a couple of weeks. It's so damn annoying,' he said with a frustrated sigh, 'like I've been put on ice for six months and the world's kept on going without me or—or like I'm missing some vital pieces in a jigsaw puzzle.'

'I wonder how it will happen,' Ally went on, a strange, masochistic force urging her to persist. 'It must be strange to get your memory back. I wonder if it will happen slowly with little snippets of memory popping into your mind here and there or whether it'll come all in a rush.' She curled her legs beneath her and leant towards Fletcher.

She had absolutely no idea how appealing she looked, her slim, lithe body bathed in dancing firelight, her dark hair falling softly to frame her pale face.

'I guess I'll wake up one morning and—hey presto! The missing pieces will fit back in the jigsaw.'

'But I wonder how you'll actually remember her...this girl you think you're in love with...'

'If she exists—' Fletcher interrupted.

'Well, okay, just assuming she does exist. I wonder what you'll remember first.'

Fletcher turned from the fire then to stare at Ally, his dark brows meeting over blue eyes.

'You mean, will I, for example, remember her voice first?'

'Yes, or—or perhaps the colour of her...hair.'

'Or her eyes,' he added slowly, gazing deep into Ally's eyes as if he were seeing them for the first time. She looked away quickly, afraid she might be tempting fate. If his memory were to return now, her gamble could lose out. And yet, morbid curiosity compelled her to press dangerously on.

'Maybe it'll be an event—something you did together,' she suggested to the flames.

There was a long pause while the only sound was the quiet crackle of the fire.

'Like a kiss, Ally, is that what you mean?'

Ally felt her blushing reaction rising swiftly.

'Perhaps, I will remember making love to her,' said Fletcher, his voice rumbling suggestively, causing a wave of impulsive desire to sweep through Ally so strongly she almost cried out. 'I might remember her soft, round breasts or her silky thighs...'

Looking quickly at Fletcher, she found his eyes challenging her as she sensed a similar need pulsing through him. He was swallowing rapidly and grasping the chipped enamelled mug so tightly that his knuckles were white.

Uncomfortably aware of the sudden blaze of pure chemistry sizzling between them, Ally bent forward and picked up a twig to throw into the fire.

Fletcher's gaze followed the sweep of her hand as it tossed the stick. 'Or it could be some little thing about the beautiful way she moves...' he said softly.

Startled, she looked at him.

'I think it's very noble of you to—to be faithful to her,' she said forcefully.

'Well I don't really think there's much nobility involved,' he replied with a rueful grin, 'it's just that I'd hate all the explanations if things got too complicated. That's the way I am. You see, I couldn't lie to anyone—not to her or to you.'

As Fletcher threw his head back to drain the last of the rum, Ally felt guilt prowl up her back and wrap its clammy hands around her throat.

You had to lie, she reassured herself. He left you no alternative. He'll understand when the time comes.

Miserably she watched as Fletcher put his mug down and said, 'Enough of this. Time to catch some shut-eye. I want to make an early start in the morning.'

He took both mugs over to the truck and returned carrying two thick jumpers. 'It can get really chilly, especially in the early morning just before dawn.'

'Thanks,' gulped Ally. She stood looking down at the swags—two big, khaki green canvas envelopes lined with checked woollen blankets. They were so glaringly self-sufficient. Not what she'd had in mind at all.

During the journey out, she had imagined that she would spend the night in the warmth and safety of Fletcher's arms, but there was a considerable gap of leaf-strewn dirt between the two swags.

And now, she felt just a little nervous of the great expanse of pitch-black bush which stretched all around them just outside the small circle of firelight.

'Is anything the matter, Ally?'

Of course there is. I want to be sleeping with you. Not all neatly tucked up and alone. I want you to pull me down beside you and wrap your gorgeous body up with mine. I want you to check out my breasts, my silky thighs. I want you, Fletcher. I love you. I need you. I need you now, tonight and every night.

'I was just hoping Connor got to sleep okay,' she said softly.

Fletcher banked up the fire. 'He'll be fine. Mary was tickled pink to have him to herself.'

Ally got into the swag and lay stiffly, staring at the night sky. The myriad of stars, pinned to a black satin background, stared back at her like thousands of blinking, uncaring eyes. Ally miserably acknowledged that it was going to be a long night. And in the vast, remote depths of the universe she, and her petty little needs, rated as insignificant. Tonight, even the moon, which sometimes looked so golden and friendly, had reduced itself to a thin, cold slice of silver and, in callous disregard of her loneliness, it trailed its meagre light across the river with a ghostly finger.

Fletcher lay with his back to her. It was difficult to tell if he was asleep, but he looked very relaxed and comfortable, without any sign of the tense, nerve-tingling anxiety she was experiencing. A mopoke called suddenly from a nearby tree, frightening her, and she thought of snakes and wondered if they would dare to crawl anywhere near her when she was so close to the fire.

She rolled onto her side so that she lay facing the fire instead of the night sky. She'd heard of the mesmerising effects of staring into the flames. If she watched them flicker and didn't let herself think about the man nearby, perhaps she would fall asleep.

It must have worked because the next thing she knew was the sound of an axe chopping wood and she woke to find the fire almost out and the bush filled with the pale, creamy light of dawn. On the river below, a fine, white mist was trailing along the surface of the water. Some distance beyond the camp, Fletcher, bare-chested, wielded his axe at a fallen log with astonishing ease, his muscles flexing rhythmically with each movement.

He stopped, bundled the chopped wood under one arm, swung the axe over his shoulder and walked back to their fireplace with long, effortless strides.

'Did you sleep well?' he asked as he dropped the logs and bent to remake the fire.

'Yes, I did actually,' she replied, not hiding her surprise.

'Must have been the rum,' he said with a grin. 'Now, you stay there and relax while I rustle up some breakfast. How about some nice unhealthy bacon and eggs?'

'Sounds great.' She smiled, enjoying the way he set to preparing breakfast with boyish enthusiasm.

After breakfast, they set off for what Fletcher called the back-country. This was rougher land and for hours they wound their way in and out of the foothills of range country where many cattle had virtually gone wild.

'A lot of cleanskins in here,' Fletcher told her. 'Cattle

that've never been branded. We'll bring in a helicopter to chase them out of these nooks and then later the men on the ground will take over.'

By late afternoon, they had reached very different country. They parked beside a swamp where huge, pink lotus flowers floated on the still surface and above which cruised black and white magpie geese. From the swamp they walked upstream and as they climbed, the water grew clearer and faster flowing.

'It's actually spring fed,' said Fletcher. 'This water comes bubbling out of the basalt further up.'

Ally noticed that the vegetation was changing as well and soon they reached a pocket of rainforest thick with lilly pilly trees and wild bananas.

'This is another favourite spot of mine,' he said. 'There's something here I want to show you,' he added, taking her hand and leading her along a faint wallaby track through the forest.

They reached the prettiest creek Ally had ever seen. The water was so clear she could see every round, smooth pebble on the bottom. Soft, green ferns and baby palms lined its banks while mossy logs or smooth stepping stones provided comfortable seats to rest and take in the tranquil beauty.

'Let's sit back a bit on the bank,' whispered Fletcher. 'If we're very patient, we might just see something pretty special.'

'Not a platypus?' squeaked Ally, incredulously. 'I've never seen one.'

'Ssh!' said Fletcher, and he crouched low, pulling Ally beside him till they were both sitting close together on a fallen log. Hardly daring to breathe, Ally sat perfectly still beside Fletcher and kept her eyes roving up and down the creek with intense concentration. All through the rainforest, the late afternoon shadows were lengthening. In the canopy above, birds were busy calling to each other, but there was no other sound except the quiet chuckle of the water as it bubbled over rocks.

Ally began to grow stiff from sitting so still and she wriggled a little. Fletcher stilled her with a strong hand on her arm. Slowly he pointed downstream. In the dim light, Ally could just make out a little brown form moving upstream towards them, close to the river bank. A thrill of excitement surged through her. As it drew closer, she could hear the little splashing sounds it made as it snuffled its bill through the soft mud on the creek bottom. Hardly bigger than Fletcher's hand, the platypus dived and resurfaced, busily hunting and feeding in the twilight creek.

Just in front of them, it stopped and looked at something on the bank. Still as a statue, Ally's thrilled eyes drank in every quaintly absurd detail—the little flat paddling tail, the round furry abdomen, ducklike bill and flippers and beady little brown eyes, ringed with gold. It only paused for a few moments and then it was off again, sifting the bottom of the creek, hunting for worms and beetles like a busy shopper, hurrying to get the ingredients for supper before the shops closed.

Eventually it disappeared around a bend in the creek and Ally turned to Fletcher, her face alight. 'That was just fabulous!' she cried and threw her arms around him in a spontaneous hug. 'A platypus! All my life I've wanted to see a live one in the wild. Oh, thank you so much, Fletcher, I feel so honoured. We'll have to bring Connor here and show him.'

He smiled as he gave her a return hug, but then he drew back and looked down into her face, his hands still resting on her shoulders and his happiness was replaced by a more serious, disturbing expression. 'It was an honour to share it with you,' he said softly and bent his head to touch his lips to the tip of her nose.

Ally caught her breath.

'Stop looking at me like that,' he whispered.

'How, Fletcher?' she asked lamely.

'Like you want to be in my bed.'

Ally gulped and felt a hot tide of colour sweep over her. 'I—I…' What could she say? He was right and he knew it.

His hand gently caressed her face, sliding beneath the curtain of her silky, dark hair to stroke the nape of her neck while he kissed her eyelids and her chin. His other hand slowly pressed into her spine, feeling her shudder with longing as he drew her closer.

'We shouldn't be doing this,' whispered Fletcher and he left a trail of feather-light kisses down her neck.

'No,' agreed Ally, wrapping her arms more tightly around him and murmuring against his cheek. 'That other girl mightn't like it.'

'Maybe she wouldn't mind just…' Fletcher tasted her lips, moving his mouth over hers in a soft caress, then drew back '…a little kiss,' he whispered.

'I'm sure she wouldn't,' replied Ally, and in case Fletcher had any further doubts, she clung to him, her mouth avidly seeking his.

It was a deep, hungry kiss, fed by the longing that had consumed her for days. Breathless, they broke apart at last, only to laugh shakily and seek each other again. And then Fletcher's kisses became even more urgent. He crushed her against him and took her mouth in fierce, starved passion. Ally felt happiness bubbling from deep inside her and surrendered completely to his male dominance, letting herself drown in the wonder of being back in his arms, of the glory of his mouth as she opened her lips wider to welcome him.

She moaned under his onslaught. 'Oh, Fletcher, oh yes, please.' Her pleas excited him further, urging him to kiss her again with feverish savagery, raining kisses on her eyes, her throat, his hands cupping and teasing her breasts, his breath coming in short, gasping moans.

Ally returned his kisses ardently, almost biting him in her desperate need to be a part of him. 'Oh, Fletcher,' she groaned. 'I love you so much.' Her eager words sounded suddenly loud in the quiet bush and to her mortification, she felt Fletcher draw back.

He was panting and his wild, darkened eyes revealed an intense yearning. But he sighed and, taking her hand, he kissed each of her fingers in turn.

'Unfortunately,' he murmured, 'if we don't get back to our vehicle before dark, we might get ourselves lost or at the very least break a leg among the basalt rocks. We've no food, torch or matches in here. It would be a long, cold night.'

Who cares? Ally wanted to cry, but she had to acknowledge that all around them, the bush was growing much darker. Long shadows were already making the track quite hard to see. Reluctantly, she drew away from Fletcher. 'If you insist on being practical, I guess we'd better go back,' she replied, pretending to grumble.

'Let's hurry,' he murmured breathlessly. 'I don't think I can stay practical for long.'

They sprang up and made their way quickly down the track, like excited children.

Ally knew her smile was as wide as the plains they'd travelled over. Her imagination danced with excited possibilities. She had never felt so quietly confident that all would be well, so deliciously expectant. As she walked lightly beside Fletcher, she felt utterly peaceful, and enveloped by a warm hopeful glow. Fletcher could surely not resist her again tonight. He was clearly very attracted to her. He seemed to like Ally the nanny as passionately as he'd liked Ally the fashion designer. She felt a growing confidence that when he discovered they were both the same person, he would be doubly pleased.

But it was more than a physical hunger they shared. On this journey, as they'd enjoyed the tranquil beauty of the bush, the plains and the rainforest, they had experienced a special closeness, a complete understanding that came from something much deeper than basic lust.

They made their way as quickly as possible, following the stream back down the hillside. As the track thinned, Ally walked ahead of him a little with eager, skipping steps, her heart light, thinking of the night ahead and the promise conveyed in his passionate kisses. They had almost reached the bottom, when the ground began to level out and the track widened once more into a small clearing bordered by wild bananas and a creeper covered in round yellow fruit.

'Are these edible?' she asked. 'Perhaps we could have some for dessert.'

She sensed Fletcher stop suddenly behind her and turned to see his body stiffen perceptibly.

'They're wild passionfruit,' he said quietly.

'Really?' she replied, trying to still the sudden savage beating in her chest. Why had Fletcher's answer felt like a physical blow?

'They taste the same as the cultivated variety except that they're not...'

He paused and Ally wished for all the world she could stop him from saying what had to come next.

'...Purple. These passionfruit aren't purple,' Fletcher repeated softly. It was even darker now, but Ally could see the bleak expression on his face and she could hear the subtle change in his voice.

He spoke again, very slowly and quite coldly. 'Passionfruit.' Then he stepped towards her in a stiff, broken manner, as if he'd been struck from behind. 'Ally,' he whispered. 'Ally, it's you, isn't it?'

'What—what are you talking about, Fletch?' she asked, her voice shaking with growing fear. But she knew.

He had remembered.

'Oh, hell! Damn you, Ally.' Fletcher ground out the words. Pushing her roughly aside, he strode past her.

Horrified, Ally stumbled after him, almost falling in her haste. She reached out to grab at his arm.

'Fletch, wait! What is it? What's the matter?'

He turned and scowled down at her, wild-eyed. 'How can you pretend you don't know, you scheming little liar.'

'Fletch, you've got it all wrong. I didn't really mean to trick you.'

But he strode away from her, his face twisted in anger and his shoulders hunched forward aggressively.

Running to catch up, Ally grabbed at his arm once more and sobbed at him to stop. She stood, panting, tears streaming down her face. 'I'm sorry, Fletcher,' she said. 'I really am. It was wrong of me to—to not tell you the whole truth. Please, please forgive me.'

For a fraction of a second she thought she saw a softening of his grim features. He looked down at her, breathing savagely. His eyes searched her face wildly and she put a tentative hand on his arm pleadingly, but then he shook her off.

'How could you do it, Ally? If it wasn't almost night, I'd be driving you straight back to the homestead now,' he roared hoarsely. 'Instead, we leave at first light. And this time, you are going home to Melbourne and there won't be any floods to stop you.'

CHAPTER NINE

A FEW MORE angry strides brought them out of the scrub and back to the parked truck. Fletcher grabbed the axe straight away, muttering something about firewood.

'Fletcher, we've got to talk about this. I've apologised. A few minutes ago we were kissing for heaven's sake. You didn't want me to leave then.' Even as Ally spoke, the memory of his urgent desire gave her courage.

'A few minutes ago I didn't know you were betraying my trust.'

She flinched, stepping back, as she felt the bitterness of his words hit her.

'You know,' she began, but her voice cracked. She took a deep breath and tried again, not at all sure where her pride had gone or why she persisted, but knowing there was only one way for her to survive now and that was to fight back with whatever weapon happened to be at her disposal. Unfortunately, all she had left was the truth. 'You know I love you. You must know why I came here.'

His eyes, sad and angry, met hers fleetingly and then he looked at the ground between them. 'You can't stay here,

Ally. There's no place here for you in the outback.' He lifted
the axe and shook it at her and then, with a bewildered expression, seemed to realise what he was doing and put the
axe down on the grass beside him.

'You made that pretty clear once before. But, Fletcher,
you're wrong. I can stay here. I have stayed here. I stayed on
and I fitted in,' Ally countered.

He stepped towards her and grabbed her shoulders with
both hands, shaking her angrily. 'Why are you so stubborn?
You must go back to the city. I don't want you here.'

'That's rubbish and you know it,' Ally fired back.

A wary gleam flickered in Fletcher's eyes but he insisted
fiercely, 'It's absolute common sense, Ally. It's totally im-
practical for you to consider living on Wallaroo Downs. It
just won't work.'

'Why not?'

'Why not? It's glaringly obvious.'

'Not to me it isn't.'

'Ally, what's happened to your vision, your ambition?'

'It's very clear,' she replied softly. 'It's just shifted focus,
that's all.'

Fletcher stared at her, his face pale and drawn. For a
moment she thought she'd connected, that he finally understood just how serious she was, but his next words dashed
her almost-extinguished hope.

'I've let you stay on here because you conned me into be-
lieving you were suitable, but there's no way I want you staying on now I know the truth.'

'You—you're not a very good actor, Fletcher.'

His blue eyes darkened formidably. 'Acting? Don't kid
yourself. I've never been more serious in my life.'

He reached for the axe again and heaved it onto his shoulder, turning to walk away. There was no way she was going to accept this without a fight. Not now when she was sure he really did love her. Desperate, Ally ran up to Fletcher and stopped him by planting both hands firmly in the middle of his huge chest.

'What went wrong? What changed after you left Melbourne? Why are you doing this to me?'

He shrugged her off as if she were a bothersome insect and headed for some fallen timber a few metres away. Ally followed.

'This is getting a touch monotonous. I have my own lifestyle here and you just don't fit in. As I said before, you should never have come chasing me out here, Ally. I tried to make a clean break, when I realised what a serious mistake we were making...' He swung the axe high above his head. 'Step back,' he warned. 'You should also never stand in front of a man with an axe, especially in this poor light.'

Ally stepped away quickly as the axe smashed down, splintering the timber and sending little pieces flying. Mistake...the word buzzed in her head. So she was a mistake?

'Why don't you come straight out and tell me what's wrong with me,' she yelled as he eased the axe out of the timber it had split. He paused and glared at her.

'You lied,' he said coolly.

'But, even before that, when I was being completely honest, you wanted to get rid of me then, too.'

He straightened and the blue eyes regarded her for ten seconds as if he were remembering and piecing together the details of the other time he tried to evict her. She capitalised on his hesitation.

'How much do you really remember, Fletcher? Perhaps you have forgotten how strong our feelings were. Even now, you say you don't want me, but, heavens above, your body tells me something else. You do want me, Fletcher—just as much as I want you. We can't just ignore what we had before. How can you just pretend that nothing happened?'

His jaw tightened. 'For your information, I do remember everything—unfortunately. You can have no doubt of that.' His shoulders stiffened as if he was gathering strength before he spoke again. 'It may have been special for you, but you've no idea how I felt.'

'Don't I?' she spat back. 'You showed me how you felt when you kissed me back there. And yesterday in the river,' she added with a sudden surge of confidence. 'You said then that you were already in love with somebody. Well, here I am.'

The simplicity of her logic took him aback. Fletcher stared at her for at least a minute, his hand clasping and unclasping the axe and he gave a little negative shake of his head as if she had almost convinced him, but when his eyes fixed on hers again, he spoke with biting calm. 'Ally, face the facts. What we share isn't love. Love and all that it involves—sharing a future together—requires a compatibility of many dimensions, not just an unfortunately strong sexual magnetism. I don't think I ever claimed to be in love, but remember I was suffering from amnesia. I obviously got it wrong.'

The battle was over.

Ally cringed, eyes closed, hands shaking, facing defeat. She had stubbornly refused to see the startlingly obvious. All this time she had continued to believe in romantic dreams of love and commitment, when, as far as Fletcher was concerned, all they had ever shared was straightforward lust. She had to admit he had never pretended otherwise.

She had failed.

He raised the axe again. 'Now, if you don't let me chop this firewood, we'll have no light and no warmth and no dinner. We're in for a wretched night anyhow, but let's at least make it a bit comfortable.'

She had failed completely. Ally backed away across the clearing, watching him begin to chop the wood with reckless energy. The sun had almost set and the sky behind Fletcher was navy blue streaked with blood red. The air was cooler than the night before so she gave no thought to another swim. He chopped the wood quickly and brought it over, nearer to the camp.

'This do for the fireplace?' he asked.

Ally shrugged, wishing she could just tell him to drop dead, but she had lost the will to fight. Walking around to the other side of the vehicle, she hauled out the swags and dumped them on the dusty ground.

Fletcher came over and checked the contents of the esky. 'What would you like for dinner?' he asked politely. 'How about a steak?'

'I'm not really hungry,' she muttered.

He chose to ignore her petulance and carried two large steaks over to the pan, which was already heating on the fire. He sliced some tomatoes and opened a tin of mushrooms to heat up for the steaks. Then he snapped the tops off two beers and offered her one. 'They're not very cold anymore,' he said. 'The ice has just about melted.'

Ally took the proffered can and when she flinched from the touch of his hand against hers, Fletcher froze briefly, his face a blank mask. Looking away, Ally leaned back against the truck's tyre and took a long gulp of beer. She'd never really enjoyed beer all that much, but her throat was dry and the liquid wet and cool. Her throat seemed to be the only part of her body with any feeling. The rest of her felt strangely numb, desolate.

Nothing had worked out as she had hoped. This whole venture had been a monumental failure. But her mind wouldn't let go of the puzzling fact that one minute, Fletcher could kiss her hungrily as if he needed her desperately, and then in virtually the next breath, he could claim that he never wanted to see her again. Love and lust. How many other poor fools had confused those two? She had been so ecstatic in his arms, revelling in his kisses, sure that he had never stopped loving her. But then he had so effortlessly stifled the last tiny shred of hope.

Maybe it hadn't been quite effortless, she conceded as she thought about the pain in his eyes as his memory relentlessly returned. Watching him glumly as he hunkered down over the fire, turning the steaks, Ally wondered again if there wasn't a more complicated reason for his rejection of her.

He was prepared to be very interested in her living here when he thought she was a nanny from central Queensland, but had absolutely no interest when he discovered she was a fashion designer from Victoria. She had never really accepted Lucette's warning that he had very fixed ideas about what kind of woman belonged in the bush, but obviously his cousin was spot-on.

The bottom line was that she had failed miserably. She had tried to win him by fair means and she'd tried deception. Neither had worked and now she had no alternative but to do as he asked—to leave Wallaroo Downs and return to the city where she would be greeted by raised eyebrows and knowing smirks and the news that her contracts had been passed on to other designers. Terrific!

Her mind churned furiously. Like a cat unable to leave a

mouse, her relentless mind toyed with every possible way to examine her plight. She tried to put herself in his position. If he had arrived on the doorstep of her Melbourne flat and announced that he'd sold Wallaroo Downs and was planning to find a job in the city, she would have been shocked and outraged, too. She would never have wanted him to make himself miserable, giving up the country and the work he loved for her. Definitely not. But she would have been touched by his willingness to sacrifice everything for her. Wouldn't she? Just what would she have done? The more she tried to unravel her thoughts, the more impossible the problem seemed to become.

The night was as long and as wretched as Fletcher had predicted. Ally ate very little of the juicy steak and later, although she stared into the flames once again, they had no more power to lull her to sleep than a pack of dingoes howling around their camp. The ground beneath her felt hard and rocky. Mosquitoes circled and dive-bombed repeatedly despite the smoke from the fire. Ally lay tense and miserable, watching the flames gradually die down until only the big logs and the ashes beneath them glowed red. With weary eyes, she traced the journey of the Southern Cross from the horizon as it climbed up the sky and her ears strained, listening to the silence of the wilderness which grew more menacing with every passing hour.

She suspected Fletcher was not sleeping too well, either. He tossed and turned several times and there was no regular, soft breathing to indicate sleep.

They were both up as soon as the first glimmer of dawn tinged the eastern sky, as if neither of them wanted to stay in the swags a moment longer. Fletcher's face looked strained and weary and Ally was sure hers must be worse. They both agreed that a mug of tea would be sufficient for breakfast and before the sun was completely up, they were packed. They took the most direct route heading straight for Wallaroo homestead. It was a difficult, tense journey, long and hot with virtually no stops.

Both were wrapped in their own thoughts. Ally's were desolate. She had no choice but to do as Fletcher asked—demanded. And she dreaded the thought of explaining to Connor why she had to go.

She was completely exhausted by the time the long, low roof of the homestead, surrounded by its circle of ancient trees, appeared on the horizon and she knew that, after driving for hours, Fletcher must be ready to drop.

When they reached the yard, Ned was already there. On hearing their vehicle approach, he'd hobbled out of one of the machinery sheds to open the last gate and he didn't attempt to hide a knowing grin when he saw their sleep-deprived faces.

'What's amusing you?' Fletcher snapped.

'Just pleased to see you back, boss,' Ned replied quickly, the smile disappearing fast. Then he added smartly, 'You've got visitors.'

'You're joking,' Fletcher groaned.

'No. It's Tom and Ruth Neville and their littl'uns. They came over to meet Ally and Connor.' After delivering his message, Ned hobbled away quickly, clearly uncertain of his boss's reaction to the news.

Ally stole a look at Fletcher's expression and was relieved to hear him chuckle in laughing disbelief. 'There's fate for you,' he sighed as he dragged a hand through his matted hair. 'They're my neighbours from Mungulla Station. Actually,' he added with a wry grimace, 'I told them to come over and meet you both anytime they liked. But they've got lousy timing.'

Ally regarded him for a long moment. 'I guess, even though they're neighbours, they spent most of the day getting here.'

'Exactly.'

'So you can't tell them sorry, come again another day.'

'Well, of course I could, but the Nevilles and I go back a long way. But for heaven's sake, tonight of all nights!'

They both sat staring ahead through the dust-spattered windscreen.

'Nevertheless you wouldn't want to spoil a good friendship.'

'Not if I can avoid it.'

'Then it's settled then.' Ally turned up her palms and twisted her features into something approaching a smile. 'I'll behave myself if that's what you're worried about. I won't turn on any tantrums.'

Fletcher nodded grimly. 'This doesn't change a thing, Ally. You'll still have to go.'

'Of course,' she sniffed and, reaching to the cabin floor, she picked up her carryall. 'I'll get the esky out of the back and take it in to Mary.' She opened the car door and got out, closing it forcefully behind her. 'See you later,' she called as he began to drive towards the garage. He turned to look at her, but said nothing and drove on.

When Ally reached the kitchen, she was grateful to find it empty. Mechanically, she unpacked the few perishables they had not used and stacked them in the refrigerator, disposing of the one or two items that were beyond salvage. Then she rinsed out the esky, left it upturned on the draining board, and hurried quickly to her room. Her number one priority was a long, hot shower.

She also longed to sleep, but at least the shower helped to soothe her exhausted body. After the dust and smoke of the camp and the sweat of the long journey, soap had never smelled so good. Showered and a little refreshed, she brushed her clean hair and changed into comfortable silk-knit slacks and top and wondered if Fletcher had been able to enjoy a clean up, as well.

Stop thinking about him! she admonished herself. He's not yours to care about and the sooner you accept that idea the better. But she knew it was no use. Learning to stop loving Fletcher was going to take her a long, long time. She didn't know if it was ever possible.

'Ally!'

A little bundle of four-year-old boy hurtled through her doorway and hugged her tight.

'Connor, darling. How's my big boy?'

'We've got visitors,' the child announced importantly.

'So I hear. Where are they?' At that moment, Ally heard a little giggle and then another. She looked over Connor's shoulder to see two little girls peering around the door. They had identical round faces covered in freckles, topped by bright red hair. Their brown eyes were enormous.

'They're twins,' whispered Connor.

'I see,' agreed Ally. 'Are you going to introduce me to your friends?'

'Katie and Lissa,' he said shyly, but his eyes were glowing.

'Melissa,' corrected one of the little girls boldly, entering the room and addressing Ally. 'That's my sister. Connor can't say her name properly yet, 'cause he's only four.'

'We're five,' contributed Melissa.

'Hello, Katie and Melissa. It's lovely to meet you.'

'We're going to start school of the air next year,' added Melissa, emboldened by Ally's warm smile.

'Connor, isn't this lovely to have some friends to play with? What have you been doing?'

'He's been showing us his pony,' interrupted Katie, her eyes widening even further. 'He's so lucky. We don't have our own ponies yet and we're bigger'n Connor.'

'But Daddy says we might buy two from Uncle Fletcher at Christmas time,' added her twin, not to be outdone. Then she turned to Connor excitedly. 'We usually come over here for Christmas and have a big party.'

The little boy smiled happily and squeezed Ally's hand.

'Won't that be nice,' whispered Ally, stifling the cold wave of despair that threatened when she thought of them all celebrating Christmas without her.

Where would she be by Christmas? Back in Melbourne, sitting in her apartment, alone. At the mere thought of her neat Melbourne home, surrounded by other city apartments with their pristine urban gardens, devoid of scraggy eucalyptus trees, wildlife, creeks or mountains, she felt an overwhelming sense of loss. For a while she had tasted a different life, been in a different world and, while the major draw card had been Fletcher Hardy, the unique beauty of the outback had won her heart as well. Now she would have to leave the bush and there was nothing she could do about it.

'Is this where you've got to?' A feminine voice broke into Ally's thoughts. She turned to see a smiling woman standing in the doorway. 'Hi, you must be Ally. Sorry they've barged in on you like this. What are you scallywags doing invading this poor woman's bedroom?'

'They're fine,' smiled Ally, liking instantly the other woman's laughing face, and her friendly manner. 'You must be Mrs. Neville.'

'Oh, please. You must call me Ruth.'

Ruth Neville, Ally guessed, was in her mid-thirties, around the same age as her sister, and, like Victoria, she had the calm, happy air of a wife and mother who loved her family and who was loved in return. Blond, sun-tanned and with minimal make-up, she looked smart yet comfortable in a slim-fitting blue linen shift and strappy sandals.

'Now, come on, you lot. We'll leave Ally a chance to catch her breath before dinner. We can talk to her as much as we like then.' She turned to Ally. 'Take your time,' she said. 'No need at all to rush.' She bundled the children, Connor included, out onto the veranda. 'Fletcher's only just hit the shower and I can give Mary a hand. See you for dinner at seven.'

Ally watched them leave with a sense of gratitude—an hour or so to rest was exactly what her aching body needed. If only her mind would let go, too.

Fletcher had dressed for dinner in an open-necked, white dress shirt and dark slacks which accentuated his dark, rangy masculinity to a painful degree, and Tom and Ruth had also changed for dinner, so Ally was glad she'd decided to dress up a little. She chose a quiet, pearl-grey crepe, cut in a simple style with thin shoulder straps, fitted bodice and a softly flared skirt. It always made her feel particularly feminine and she needed to feel good about something tonight. She knew the soft grey shade matched her eyes exactly. At the last minute, she added Fletcher's amethyst necklace. But as she entered the dining room and saw Fletcher's face grow pale and taut as his eyes rested on her, she wondered if she had gone too far.

Nevertheless, tired and drawn as he clearly was, Fletcher's innate good manners ensured that he was a charming host. Adults and children all shared the meal at the big table in the dining room. To her surprise, Ally found she was to sit opposite Fletcher at one end of the table, while the Nevilles and Connor were ranged on either side. It looked for all the world like she was the lady of the house and during the meal, her eyes inadvertently locked with Fletcher's so that, for frantic seconds, her mind lost the thread of a conversation.

But if Tom or Ruth Neville noticed, they very adeptly covered up with subtly introduced small talk or by allowing one of the children to distract them at just the right moment.

Tom Neville was a tall redhead who had clearly passed his distinctive colouring on to his daughters. He chatted to Ally about the floods and the property and about her job as a nanny.

'Ruth would never hear of a nanny for our pair,' he said, shaking his head at his wife with an affectionate smile. 'And next year she's planning to teach the twins school, as well.'

'But tell Ally the rest,' interrupted Ruth. 'I used to be a schoolteacher before Tom sailed into Charters Towers and swept me off my feet,' she explained for Ally's benefit.

'I rescued you from a fate worse than death,' argued Tom. 'Admit it, you'd never go back to living in town now, would you?'

'Well, not until I'm old and grey,' smiled Ruth, her eyes resting lovingly on her husband. Then she turned to Ally. 'Are you enjoying your taste of the outback enough to want to stay?'

Ally felt her face burn. She stared at her food, not daring

to look at Fletcher, while the words to answer Ruth's question kept sliding out of her mind before she had time to voice them. The silence was so protracted she began to feel quite faint with apprehension.

Twice Fletcher looked like he was going to say something, but no words emerged. Katie, who had not been listening to the conversation because she was too busy polishing off her ice cream, saved the awkward tension at last.

'Uncle Fletcher, are you going to play the piano for us tonight?'

Ally nearly choked. What next? Fletcher, grazier and bushman extraordinaire, could play the piano? It was a concept that had her reaching for her wineglass. She took a deep swig, and glanced quickly at Fletcher, but he was studiously examining his dessert fork.

'Katie,' interjected Ruth, her warning tone implying she was treading carefully through what she found to be a minefield. 'We agreed not to bother Fletcher tonight.'

'Sorry,' murmured the little girl with a heavy sigh.

'I'll practise up ready for the carols at Christmas,' promised Fletcher, clearly relieved to be let off.

Connor, who had been sitting quietly through the meal, obviously a little overawed by the constant teatime chatter, suddenly spoke up.

'My mummy had a piano.'

'Did she, dear?' asked Ruth, instantly all motherly concern for the poor little orphaned boy.

Ally observed Connor thoughtfully. This was the first occasion she had actually heard her little charge speak of his mother. She caught Fletcher's eye and a silent message there confirmed that his thoughts echoed her own.

'That's right, Connor,' Fletcher said gently. 'Your mother played the piano beautifully.'

'Can you play "Twinkle Twinkle Little Star"?' Connor looked at his godfather with such a bright, eager expression, Ally could see Fletcher weakening.

'I think I can manage that,' he said with a wry smile.

That settled it. Dessert was finished in an excited flurry, children's hands and faces were washed and everyone except Ally adjourned to the huge room commonly referred to as the ballroom. She stayed behind in the dining room, despite protestations, to help Mary clear the dishes. Somehow, the sight of Fletcher seated at a piano, his huge brown hands moving over the keys, was more than she could bear tonight.

But her ears were riveted to the next room, where she could hear laughter and the first tinkling notes of Connor's request. She loaded a tray with the glassware. Although it was good quality crystal, the care she took was rather more meticulous than necessary, because she found she didn't want to miss one note of Fletcher's playing. Within a few minutes, the simple notes of 'Twinkle, Twinkle' were elaborated and expanded into trills and runs, flourishes and variations, that revealed an astonishing virtuosity.

Stunned, Ally headed for the kitchen with the glass-laden tray, her heart suddenly catapulting. Why, she asked herself, did the thought of Fletcher displaying such prowess at the piano disturb her so much? But she knew the answer. It was so unexpected and yet so right that someone as sensual as he was would have an artistic streak. But why had he hidden it from her? He knew she loved classical music. Together, they had listened to many of her favourite CDs.

Mary, who was at the sink, up to her elbows in dishwater

and detergent bubbles turned to her. 'It's lovely to hear him tinkle the old ivories again, isn't it?'

Ally nodded dully. She was saved from having to contribute further to the conversation when the music stopped and Ruth Neville came into the kitchen with the children trailing behind her.

'The girls were wondering if Connor could sleep on the veranda with them tonight,' she said. 'Whenever we come here in the summer, they always sleep outside our room on put-up stretchers. They think it's wonderful fun.'

'Would you like that?' Ally asked the little boy quietly.

His shining eyes were answer enough even before he added a fervent, 'Yes, please.'

'Then off with you three to clean your teeth while we make up your beds,' Ruth ordered the delighted trio.

Ruth showed Ally where the folding canvas stretchers were stored and then they raided the linen closet for sheets and pillows. As Ally sorted through the piles to find three pillowslips, Ruth spoke in quiet conspiratorial tones.

'Forgive me for blurting this out, but I've realised who you are,' she said. 'It's been puzzling me all night where I've seen you before, but it's just hit me.'

'Really?' Ally replied. She wasn't alarmed. There had been too many surprises and adjustments to cope with for her to react with anything but resignation.

'You're Alexandra Fraser, the fashion designer, aren't you?'

Ally nodded.

'I'd been admiring your dress all evening. It's so classically simple yet soft,' smiled Ruth. 'Then I remembered reading an article about you and seeing photos of you and your designs in a magazine!'

'That would be right,' sighed Ally.

Ruth stood in the hallway, her arms full of bed linen and her knowing expression lit by an unshaded bulb dangling in front of the still-opened closet.

'I won't pry,' Ruth said, even though she was clearly bursting with curiosity. 'Just let me say I'm absolutely thrilled.'

'You are?' asked Ally weakly, her mind whirling.

'I certainly am. I've known Fletcher for about seven years now and he and Tom grew up together. We both really care about him.'

Ally hugged the bed linen to her chest. She wasn't sure what Ruth was leading to. 'That's great!' she said lamely, her voice shaking.

'You must love Fletcher very, very much.'

'How did you—I mean, um, what makes you think that?' Ally asked, keeping her head lowered.

Ruth laid a gentle hand on Ally's arm. 'Do I really need to explain? It's pretty clear to me. A. You're here. That says heaps. B. I've seen the way you look at him. That tells me more. C. I've seen the way he looks at you. That tells me everything. And that's why I'm so happy. I'm right, am I not?'

'Almost.' Ally hadn't the strength to tell Ruth just how wrong she was.

'That's splendid,' smiled Ruth. 'I have a selfish motive, too, of course. Even though we've just met, I like you, Ally. I'd love to have you as my permanent neighbour. And just think what you could do for the morale of women in the bush if you helped us all to dress as elegantly as you do.'

Ally sighed. The cloak of sadness that had been hovering over her all day seemed to settle solidly on her shoulders and when she spoke, her words were little more than a whisper. 'Well I'm very sorry to disappoint you, Ruth. But I'm not staying. Tomorrow I start packing. I'm going back to Melbourne. For good.'

CHAPTER TEN

'OH, ALLY, WHY? Why on earth do you have to go?' Ruth looked genuinely disappointed and puzzled. 'I don't know how you came to be here in the first place. I guess it's really none of my business, but I do realise what a sacrifice it must have been.'

'There was a time when I thought coming here was more important than a career,' Ally said softly, aware of the wide-eyed concern in the other woman's eyes.

'Then perhaps it still is. Already you're indispensable.'

Ally wished she could believe that, but she knew that in fact she was easily dispensed with. Whatever niche she'd imagined she could fit into on Wallaroo Downs, had been obliterated with the return of Fletcher's memory.

'Fletcher has no use for me here,' she murmured. Speaking about this was painful; there was a catch in her voice.

'Nonsense,' Ruth insisted. 'If he believes that, he's deluding himself.'

Ally wished she could accept her new friend's reassurance, but Ruth hadn't seen the look on Fletcher's face when he told her she meant nothing to him. She hadn't heard the cold, biting dislike in his voice.

He wanted to be rid of her and the sooner the better.

'One little bit of advice from a former city girl,' Ruth urged. 'If you really want him, and I suspect you do, don't give up, until you're absolutely convinced it will never work.'

It was well-meant advice, but Ally knew she had already reached that conviction. She tried to smile, but it felt twisted and weak. Squaring her shoulders instead, she resolutely suggested that they had better get the children's beds made up.

Gaiety abounded on the veranda as three stretcher beds were lined up and made comfortable for three very excited children. Once they were settled into the beds, a huge mosquito net was hung from a hook high on the veranda wall and then spread to cover them all.

Three little faces were kissed goodnight by both women and then Ruth retired to her bedroom nearby so she could monitor the children's settling down, while Ally went thoughtfully back along the veranda towards her own room. She had almost reached her doorway when a familiar tall, male figure stepped out of the shadows. His eyes, dark as storm-tossed seas, were watching her with a fierce wariness.

'Oh, hello, Fletcher,' she said awkwardly.

'You were talking a long time with Ruth,' he growled.

'Yes, she's a very friendly woman. I like her a lot.'

He looked even more displeased as if he didn't want to hear this. 'Wonderful. I guess you're already the best of mates. I hope this isn't some new tactic you're trying so that you can stay.'

The remark was so unfair, Ally couldn't respond.

'As it happens,' Fletcher said, speaking more calmly. 'It will be difficult for us to leave tomorrow before the

Nevilles go, so it will have to be the day after. It means you will have more time to pack. And time to explain to Connor why you must leave.'

How kind and thoughtful, she mused sarcastically before tossing back her reply. 'Thanks for being so considerate.'

Then she pushed past him into her room and pulled the French doors behind her forcefully, sending the bolt home with a hefty shove.

It was a relief to be able to hate him at last.

Ally stomped around her room, pulling off her clothes, hurling open drawers and kicking off her shoes to remain lying wherever they fell. All she needed was more time to explain to Connor why she was abandoning him!

With an almighty tug she reefed back her bedclothes and flung herself onto the bed. She had no idea how to explain to the little boy that she would be leaving Wallaroo forever. Perhaps, she should only say she was going away for a little while—and gradually he would forget about her.

For hours she tossed and turned and fumed until eventually pure physical exhaustion began to wear her down and finally her anger collapsed into utter misery.

She cried herself to sleep.

It was very late when she woke. She emerged midmorning with a headache from her tears and she was grateful to have escaped breakfast. She was even more pleased that the Neville children were still around to occupy Connor while she set about the dreadful task of packing. And she was thankful that Fletcher, Tom and Ruth appeared to be closeted in the study for most of the morning, busy discussing station business.

Keeping herself as busy as possible, she washed and ironed a huge pile of clothes, vacuumed, dusted and polished her room to within an inch of its life, and packed with great care. It was ridiculous really. She couldn't have cared less what state her clothes were in, but she had to keep busy. The activity couldn't stop her from thinking and feeling utterly miserable, but it used up some of her nervous energy.

She didn't tell Connor she was leaving. She couldn't.

The Nevilles drove off straight after lunch so that they could get back to Mungulla before dark. The children made so much noise calling countless goodbye messages to each other that there was little chance for the adults to do more than exchange polite farewells, but Ruth managed to give Ally a hug and whisper, 'I wouldn't give up yet, if I were you.'

If you knew what I do, I'm sure you would, thought Ally as she waved the chattering family farewell.

Luckily, Connor was happy to have an afternoon nap after the excitement of the past two days and when Ally had finished attending to her things, she started on his, telling herself that it was important that she left his clothes, toys and room spotless for his new nanny.

When he woke, they went for a quiet walk along the creek, and visited the stables to check once again on the pony Fletcher had presented to Connor. Ally kicked fiercely at a tuft of grass as she and the boy walked back across the home paddock, but the action brought no comfort as a light breeze drifted across the summer grass and the afternoon sun tinged the tips of the distant hills with gold.

Her eyes lingered over the scenery surrounding her. The hills, the paddocks, the creek made up this land and it had been lying here, supporting life, for millions of years and would go on doing so for countless more. And she would not be a part of it. She wouldn't be here next time the rains came. She would never take Connor to the platypus creek or swim again in the river at dusk. Fletcher, Connor and the Nevilles would all be here. But she would be gone.

She wouldn't see Connor grow up or Fletcher grow old. Her children would never ride Wallaroo's horses or chase each other along the homestead veranda.

And Fletcher would never again take her in his arms and hold her tight, needing her passionately. He would never again whisper her name as he kissed her, tasted her, loved her.

'Ally, are you crying?' Connor's high-pitched question startled her. She put a hand to her cheek and was shocked by its wetness. Quickly she wiped her sleeve across her face and sniffed hard.

'No, darling,' she said, trying hard to keep the tremble out of her voice. 'I must have had some dust in my eye.'

But all through dinner, she knew she still looked awful. She could not disguise the dark circles under her eyes, and her nose, despite lashings of face powder, remained pink and shiny. She was unnerved to see that Fletcher didn't look much better. His blue eyes were definitely bloodshot and it appeared he had forgotten to shave or comb his hair. As he sat, quietly munching on his chops, his general demeanour suggested the superhero had been downgraded to something more like the vulnerable Clark Kent.

After the morose meal, Ally took Connor to his bedroom and read him several stories interspersed with frequent cuddles, but eventually, although Ally would have liked to go on reading to him for longer, the boy's eyelids became heavy and drooped over his big brown eyes. She kissed his warm cheek, whispered goodnight and tiptoed out of his room for the last time.

Fletcher was leaning against the veranda rail, his arms crossed over his chest.

'We need to talk.'

'We do?'

There was no answer. Fletcher simply turned on his heel and expected her to follow. Ally knew this was not going to be reconciliation. He was going to lecture her about staying right away from Wallaroo forever. The only hope she could cling to now, was that she would be able to leave in the morning with dignity.

She didn't enjoy feeling like one of the station dogs as she followed at his heels. He led her into his study and, in a gesture disturbingly reminiscent of another occasion, indicated she was to sit in one of the deep cane lounge chairs. Then he inched his length into a chair beside her and began to speak quickly, as if driven by an inner tension.

'In the morning, I will drive you to Townsville and see you safely on a plane south. Once you are back in Melbourne, you will see that I am right. It is for the best.'

'If it's for the best,' she couldn't stop herself from asking, 'why do you look so sad?'

It was true, his face and shoulders sagged and his eyes looked washed out like faded denim, desolate.

She dropped her gaze, aware that he could read too much sympathy in her face.

'Sad?' he barked. 'After all your deception you expect me to be happy?' He swore. 'My God, Ally, how much longer did you intend to keep me in the dark? What if my memory had taken weeks or months to return? Were you ever going to honour me with the truth or did you plan to marry me and then reveal that the bride had duped her husband?'

'No! No, Fletcher!' Ally shouted her defence so loudly she frightened herself. She dropped her voice to a milder tone. 'No, Fletcher, you've got it wrong. I certainly didn't ever plan to trick you into marriage.' She reached out to touch his arm in a gesture of apology—the first time she had voluntarily touched him since they'd returned.

'Then what exactly was the plan?' He sat very still, not moving the arm she touched.

'I just wanted to prove to you that even though I'm a city girl, I can live in the bush and, I'd like to think that, given some time, I could have actually been of some use.' Ally was unable to keep the deep emotion out of her voice. But she saw Fletcher's face harden and she quickly withdrew her hand. He sat staring at the place on his thick forearm where her hand had rested as if she had left a brand.

At the sight of his pensive stare, a tiny quiver of hope tweaked her mouth into a tight smile. 'You see, I used to think you loved me—and, um—that you were just worried about me giving up my career.'

Fletcher stood up then, shaking his head, towering over her. Even now, when there was no sense to it, she couldn't stop her eyes from drinking in the full measure of his physical attractiveness. He had no right to look so sexy when he wasn't even trying. He raked his hand through his hair and gave a bitter laugh. 'That's exactly where you're so mistaken. Even if I—even if I was madly in love with you, love is just not enough for a marriage to work in the outback.'

Ally sat, staring up at him, totally stunned. For several moments she sat completely still and silent, digesting this new information. 'How can you be so sure that love isn't enough?'

He gave her a strange look. 'I've had the very best of evidence—personal experience.'

Her brow wrinkled. 'You—you've been married before?' She worried her bottom lip with her teeth.

'No, no, nothing like that. But my mother—oh, hell!'

His mother! Ally realised then that Fletcher had never elaborated on why his mother lived overseas. She knew his father had died some years ago and she had always assumed that his mother had left after that.

He thrust his hands deep into the pockets of his jeans so that they were stretched tight across his muscular thighs. 'My parents' marriage didn't work for exactly the same reasons that we wouldn't make a go of it.' He paused and took a deep breath, which escaped again as a loud sigh. He sat down again and leaned forward, resting his elbows on his knees, his hands hanging loosely in front of him. His voice, when he spoke again, came out rough and ragged as the confession was torn from his throat. 'My mother left us when I was four.'

'Oh.' Her mouth stayed poised in the shape of an O. Fletcher had only been a little boy like Connor when he lost his mother, too. 'I'm sorry,' she whispered.

'She couldn't take it anymore. Said the bush was stifling her.' The edge of bitterness in his tone was very clear. 'She went back to the city where she had grown up, where she lived an exciting, glittering life. She was a brilliant artist. Just like you, Ally, only she was a musician—a concert pianist. At first she was willing to give up her career, but...'

He paused and Ally didn't interrupt, although protests were rising readily to her lips.

'She really loved my father,' he said softly. 'I'm sure from what people tell me that she was quite besotted with him when they were first married, but...' He swept a hand to the far windows and the moonlit paddocks beyond and shook his head. 'Eventually the bush life took its toll, wore her down...' His tired blue eyes rested on her sadly. 'I've come to realise that the only kind of woman who can take it—this life—is one who's grown up in the bush. One who knows what to expect. I'm sure far too many marriages fall apart because people think they can change—either themselves or their partners.'

Ally couldn't contain herself any longer. Her fighting spirit was simmering fit to boil. 'For goodness' sake, Fletcher, I'm sorry about your mother. Truly sorry. But you can't use that as your sole reason for sending me away. How on earth do you think all the pioneer women who first settled these places coped? They all came from towns and cities. And they put up with conditions a lot worse than this.' She threw her arms wide to take in the comfortably furnished room, the beautiful paintings and the latest technology.

'They were obviously built very tough,' Fletcher tossed back, his eyes raking over Ally's slender frame, inferring that it would never stand the test. 'And they weren't artists, Ally, like my mother and you. They were battlers. Don't forget, my own personal experience has taught me a much more meaningful lesson than some outback folklore. I was a very lonely little boy, without my mother. But my father! Even at my young age, I sensed the change in him. He was a broken man. Oh, he carried on here, but he was alone, very hard and very bitter. He died when I was still at university… I believe his heart had been broken for all those years.'

He picked up the pastoral management textbook lying open on the desk beside him, shut it and placed it back on a shelf. The room was totally silent except for the slow swirl of an overhead fan. 'Mine wasn't a happy childhood. If it hadn't been for my uncle, Lucette's father, and Ned and Mary Harrison…if I hadn't loved the land, the mustering, the life with the stockmen, the peace of the bush…. You see, Ally, you have to love the life, not just the man. There's more to marriage than lovemaking, unfortunately.'

Desperately, she shook her head at him, the dark curtain of her hair falling across her face. 'Of course there is,' she said, pushing the hair back to tuck it behind one ear in a manner that held his complete attention. 'I understand that marriage requires a great deal of commitment...'

He leant forward and grabbed her hand, gripping it fiercely.

She tried to ignore the effect of his fingers closing round her wrist and kept talking. 'I do love the bush life. I'm going to really miss it! I'm sorry your mother didn't like it here, Fletch, but I do happen to like it very much. I really do.'

His thumb was caressing the back of her hand as he gazed at the floor thoughtfully. She couldn't be sure that he was listening.

'Who was your mother, Fletcher? What was—or should I say—is her name?'

'Oh, she's very well known,' Fletcher replied. 'She is Vivienne Reynaud.'

Ally gasped. 'The French pianist who brought out that wonderful Ravel CD last year?' Suddenly the conflicting images of Fletcher, outback cattleman, and Fletcher, classical musician, slotted into place.

Fletcher's eyebrows rose in surprise then he frowned again. 'Exactly. After she left us her career was more glittering and successful than ever before.'

'How—how did your parents meet?'

'In Paris. My father was over there on a holiday. He went to a concert and fell in love with the beautiful young woman on stage.' His grim facade broke down then and he fixed Ally with a rueful grin. 'Sound familiar?'

It did and perhaps from his perspective there was a weird kind of logic to his thinking.

'You're worried about history repeating itself?'

'It's a pattern as old as time itself.'

'But when Vivienne Reynaud, your mother, came to Wallaroo Downs, she had only ever lived in Europe before?'

'Yes,' Fletcher agreed.

'She grew up in…Paris, perhaps?'

'Yes, she did.'

She glanced quickly at Fletcher's face, but read no sudden understanding there, so she pressed on. 'Paris is very different from Melbourne…'

'Of course, Ally, but…'

This time there was going to be no buts. Ally allowed herself the luxury of giving full vent to her feelings. She snatched her hand away from his and jumped up, confronting him with as much physical advantage as her small frame would allow.

'Do you mean to tell me that you're comparing me—an Australian girl who's spent heaps of time in the outback—who knew exactly what she was coming to—with a woman from *Paris?*'

She flounced away across the room, too upset for words. This was what had been at the heart of all her sorrow and disappointment. How dense was this man she'd once credited with intelligence as well as a body to die for?

Fletcher was clearly angry, too. She could read the signs—the dangerously hooded eyes, the colour spreading along his cheekbones, the compression of his lips.

'Of course, I didn't make direct comparisons,' he ground out. 'But just because you know a little bit more about the bush than a Parisian, doesn't mean that you won't eventually get bored. The novelty will wear off, Ally. And when the spell fades, Alexandra Fraser will want to return to the glamour of fashion again.'

Ally shrugged. 'And if she does, she will do it from here, designing clothes for women in North Queensland to wear to balls and parties, or sending designs south via your computer.'

Fletcher shook his head, his eyes belying his words by roving hungrily over her as she stood before him. 'It's a pretty little fantasy, Ally, but that's all it is. A totally unrealistic dream.'

Ally bent forward and took his stubbled face in her hands. Her heart beating wildly, she forced her voice to stay calm as she said, huskily, 'How about a little dose of reality therapy, Fletcher? Why don't you say all this again after you kiss me?'

'Ally.' Fletcher said her name pleadingly, his own voice shaking.

She kissed his lips, lightly but lingeringly. He sat there stiffly as if hypnotised. Her hands slipped under his denim shirt, and she caressed his hair-matted chest, all the while kissing him, not giving him a chance to speak, only to feel.

He gave a deep, shuddering groan and she began to undo the buttons on his shirt. Burying her face in his chest, she tasted the salty tang of his skin.

'Ally, we mustn't, Ally—'

But she went on kissing and caressing him and then she leant closer to whisper against his cheek. 'Say goodbye to me properly, Fletcher. One last time.'

'No. You don't understand.'

'I do. I promise I won't beg you to keep me, or anything like that. Make love to me, please, Fletcher.'

But he held her hands still in his and forced her to listen.

'Don't you see, Ally. I would be the one begging you to stay.'

'You would? Well that's all right then, isn't it?' Ally wriggled provocatively on his lap, guiltily aware of his arousal.

'Damn you, no, Ally, it's not.' Fletcher stood up abruptly, forcing Ally to slide to a crumpled heap on the floor. He bent to help her up, but she slapped his hand away in frustration. Humiliated, she struggled to her feet, her knees almost buckling beneath her.

'This is ridiculous,' she fumed. 'You know what's the matter with you? You're a coward! You're scared of admitting that you're in love with me. And you're terrified of risking failure. How do you think the settlers made a go of the outback in the first place if they didn't take risks? They squared up to face failure year in, year out, and they faced it courageously.'

She paused to take a great, gulping breath and then rushed on. 'I love you, Fletcher Hardy, for better and for worse, unfortunately! But I sure as eggs don't admire you!' And she rushed blindly out of the room.

CHAPTER ELEVEN

As she left the Lygon Street coffee shop, Ally pulled up her collar to keep out the chill Melbourne air. Gusts of wind were blowing scraps of paper about her legs as she walked. Only a very few people were hardy enough to sit at tables on the pavement on this dull, depressing afternoon.

She had been dreading having to tell Lucette about the monumental failure of their plans. But Fletcher's cousin had been an empathetic listener. It had been Lucette's idea to meet in her favourite coffee shop, where they could enjoy delicious coffee and cakes as well as the cosily elegant decor.

'It's all so transparent now,' Ally had confessed. 'As far as Fletcher was concerned, our romance was simply a fling. A careless fling! Fun while it lasted—nothing more. I'm a sophisticated city girl. I'm supposed to understand that. Instead I went running after him like some annoying little lovesick schoolgirl.'

Lucette had made appropriate noises as Ally poured out her misery.

'And then I made it ten times worse by brazenly throwing myself at him, and when he lost his memory, I started tell-

ing him barefaced lies. No wonder he was so furious with
me. No wonder he insisted I leave!'

'The accident certainly complicated things,' agreed Lucette.

'Oh, it only delayed the inevitable.' Ally was sure of that
now. That final dumping from Fletcher's lap to the hard floor,
followed by the embittered, tense journey to Townsville airport the next morning, had at last brought her to her senses.
'Lucette, you have every right to tell me "I told you so,"' she
admitted as she toyed with her cake fork, pushing cherry rum
torte around on her plate.

Her friend shook her head. 'Men can be so dumb sometimes, can't they? I think they're born with this in-built conviction that they are right. Have you ever noticed how often
they listen to the opinions of another man before they'd listen to a woman?'

Ally nodded. 'But the experience of Fletcher's mother
leaving him when he was still so little had a drastic impact,
didn't it?'

'It certainly did,' agreed Lucette, 'but you know, Ally, a
couple of years ago I visited Aunt Vivienne in Paris and she
told me that if Fletcher's dad had tried to get her back she
would have come. But she was too proud to come uninvited
and Uncle Andrew was too stubborn and too jolly proud to
go begging. So they both stayed alone and miserable.'

'That's terrible,' cried Ally. 'Does Fletcher know that?'

Lucette's blue eyes had darted to her coffee cup before she
offered an evasive, 'I—I'm not sure.'

'It wouldn't make any difference,' Ally sighed. 'He's obviously inherited stubborn genes from both his parents. So
he's doubly pig-headed.'

'Perhaps,' replied Lucette gently. 'Oh, Ally, you poor thing, you're not even enjoying your coffee and cake. Can't you drown your sorrows in a few hundred calories?'

Ally smiled. 'I do appreciate your invitation,' she said. 'This is the first time I've been out of the apartment in the three days since I got back. I wouldn't even admit to my sister just how silly I've been. You're the only person I can talk to about this.'

As she headed for home, Ally was miserably conscious of just how cold and grey and dreary Melbourne could be even in December after the bright sunshine of the tropical outback. Men and women, dressed alike in sombre, dark business suits hurried on and off trams, their pale faces tense and strained. There were no smiles, no one strolling along looking relaxed.

She wondered how many of them had ever seen a platypus in the wild.

They wouldn't care—wouldn't give it a thought, she decided. Until recently, she was like them. Focused on the hectic world of business. Too busy, too ambitious and too self-centred to imagine there was any other satisfying way to live. Now she doubted this city life could satisfy her anymore. Her misery hurt so badly. A deep, heavy pain was lodged permanently in her chest.

She called in at the mini-mart on the corner of her block. She should force herself to make a proper meal this evening. Spicy vegetarian pasta was what she felt like, she decided. She would most definitely avoid beef. She would probably never eat beef again.

It would only remind her of what a fool she had been.

She carried her purchases the last half block to her apartment, trying to psych herself into feeling enthusiastic about preparing a tasty meal. Perhaps she should open a bottle of wine, as a kind of celebration of her entry back into the real world.

Except of course, that she didn't feel celebratory at all.

At least she had kept up the rental on her apartment. A home was something to be grateful for. As she neared her building, a delivery van pulled out of the driveway. We Deliver Anything Anywhere the painted advertisement on its doors claimed. She wondered which of her lucky neighbours had received the delivery. A purchase? A surprise gift?

A final, sudden gust of wind sent her hurrying into the foyer, glad of shelter again.

'Ally, thank heavens you're back.' Mr. and Mrs. Rilke, who shared her floor, were waiting together by the lift. They'd always reminded Ally of a pair of garden gnomes—small, round-faced, with rimless spectacles, they were the most physically alike couple she'd ever encountered.

'What's the problem?' Ally asked.

'Well, dear,' Mrs. Rilke began, 'we're having a bit of trouble getting into our apartment.'

'Have you lost your key?' Ally asked.

'No, dear. It's just that there are all these things blocking the hallway.'

'Purple things,' added Mr. Rilke impatiently. 'We were about to call the caretaker.'

'Purple things?' Ally managed to ask above the sudden violent fluttering of her heart. 'How, how strange.'

'They're for you,' continued Mrs. Rilke. 'I hope you don't mind, dear, but we read some of the cards.'

'So if you'll come on up, we'll help you get them into your apartment, so that we can find our way to our front door,' Mr. Rilke demanded.

'Of course,' whispered Ally, feeling dizzy as her body surged with a dozen different emotions at once.

What could this mean? She leant against the cool metal wall of the lift as they shot to the sixth floor. All she could think was this had something to do with Fletcher, but what or why or how was beyond her. She felt sick.

The lift doors lurched open to reveal a purple spectacle. 'Oh, my!'

The narrow hallway was packed with purple. Pots of purple petunias, vases of purple irises, hydrangeas, pansies and orchids—huge balloons shaped like purple fish floated near the ceiling, while enormous bunches of balloons were tied to an arch suspiciously like one of Lucette's designs. There were purple chocolate boxes, a purple teddy bear and on a small round table in the middle of it all, an enormous heart-shaped bowl of purple passionfruit.

Stupefied, breathless, Ally stared around her, her heart-beat roaring in her ears.

She was dimly aware of the lift doors closing behind her.

'I—I'll just find my key. I'm sorry about this,' she stammered.

'It's mighty weird,' commented Mr. Rilke, shaking his grey head. 'Some people have more money than sense.'

'George,' admonished his wife. 'You keep your opinions to yourself. I think it's romantic.'

'Humph,' muttered her husband.

'OK. I've got the door open,' called Ally. 'Now that archway's the main problem. We'll need to take the balloons off before we can get it through the door.' She had no idea how she managed to think of practical solutions to their dilemma while her heart was pounding fit to burst. With shaking hands she began to untie a cluster of balloons.

Then together with Mr. Rilke, she began to manoeuvre the arch through her doorway.

The lift doors opened with a faint ping.

'Looks like you need a hand,' a familiar deep voice sounded. Ally spun round to see Fletcher stepping through the lift doors, his tall frame almost filling the little remaining space. The Rilkes looked up at him with round, curious eyes. Fletcher scratched his head as he looked at the confusion in the hallway.

'This place is a little smaller than I remembered,' he offered with a smile and a shrug. 'But hold on, I'll get it cleared in a jiffy.

'What—what are you doing here?' Ally gasped.

'Shopping,' he said with a grin as he took the arch from her and guided it through the doorway with infuriating ease.

'No, I mean it. What are you really doing here?' Ally followed him, a pot plant in each hand. Why was she having so much trouble breathing, speaking and moving?

'Now...' He paused and flashed her one of his trademark grins. 'I think you've stolen my lines. If I remember rightly, a whole lot of trouble started when I asked you those exact questions when you came to Wallaroo.'

Ally noticed the Rilkes standing wide-eyed in the middle of her lounge room with armfuls of purple objects.

'Oh, thank you so much.' She managed to smile at them both. 'Just put those things anywhere you can find a place. The floor will be fine. Is the hallway clear yet?'

'Enough for us to get to our door,' said Mr. Rilke sternly. 'My dear,' he added, eyeing Fletcher up and down with cold suspicion, 'just remember we are right next door if you need help.'

'Oh, yes. Thank you so much. I'm sorry about the—the clutter,' she said as she walked with them to her door.

After Fletcher gathered up the final items and brought them into her lounge room, Ally closed her door and then leant against it, grateful to have something to hold her up.

'What's going on, Fletcher?'

He stood in the middle of her room looking wonderful. His thick, black hair needed cutting and was curling over the top of his cream cable-knit sweater and his cheekbones seemed to stand out more than she remembered.

And he looked tired.

A purple fish floated between them. 'I—I've got something to tell you.'

The bottom suddenly dropped out of her stomach. What on earth could he mean? He looked as nervous and uncertain as he had on the night they first met.

She felt all the colour drain from her face. 'Connor, is he all right?'

'Yes, Ally. Connor's fine. Mary and Ned are spoiling him rotten. But he's missing you.'

That news at least brought a welcoming flood of relief, but the odd tone in his voice bothered her—something edgy and defensive that she couldn't quite put her finger on. And his eyes—what was it about his eyes? Why was he looking at her like that? Something about his expression made her stomach tighten alarmingly.

His throat worked. 'Connor's not the only one who's missed you, Ally. I've come to take you back.'

'What?' she asked after a long moment.

'I know this sounds crazy...'

Ally just stared at him, blinking rapidly, hating the ridiculous tears that stung her eyes. 'You want me to come back to Wallaroo?'

He squared his shoulders. 'I'm asking you to forgive me. No, damn it. Well, yes, I am, but, Ally, I want more than that. I want you to marry me.' He spoke quickly, nervously.

Ally felt dizzy.

Fletcher walked towards where she stood stiffly against the door. 'I've been a fool,' he whispered, and lifted a gentle finger to trail down one tear-stained cheek.

'But you never meant to get involved,' she protested. 'I—I forced myself on you. You were right. I'm...'

'Ally.' He placed the finger firmly over her babbling mouth. 'Be quiet.'

She looked up at him as he leant closer; so close she could see each individual eyelash around his deep blue eyes. She stood there ramrod-stiff while her eyes searched his face wildly for a clue to this behaviour. Her mind seemed to have turned to cotton wool. Nothing made sense.

'Sweetheart, listen to me carefully, please. Admitting even once that I've been a total idiot doesn't come easily.'

Her eyes widened further and her heart began to pick up pace again. Behind him all she could see were splashes of purple.

'I know I had a bang on the head, but that's not really enough of an excuse for the way I treated you.' He held her shoulders in both hands, his thumbs outlining her collar-bone. 'Everything you said the other night is true, Ally. I have been an absolute coward. I've let one little childhood fear about my parents hold me back from reaching for—for the ultimate happiness.'

Perhaps she was dreaming. Had she suffered a caffeine overdose from her afternoon with Lucette?

Fletcher dipped his head towards her and his lips brushed hers, a feather-light touch, sweet and tender. She shivered.

He smiled wryly. 'My poor, brave little Ally. You've taken so many risks for me. You put absolutely everything on the line. You gave up your career, sacrificed your pride. How can I ever thank you?'

She was beginning to think of some pretty audacious ways, but for the moment, she stayed quiet and still, not daring to prick the fragile bubble of hope that was forming somewhere deep inside.

'As soon as I put you on that plane I knew I'd made the most terrible, terrible mistake.'

Was she really hearing this?

'I should have known that we can never be certain about the future. Somehow, I'd convinced myself that saying no to what I really wanted was the courageous option. You, you sweet, gutsy little angel, showed me just how off-track I was. I was fooling myself and I was trying to fool you.'

He grinned then, a shy, uncertain offering. 'Can you forgive me?'

She felt her mouth begin to split into a wide answering grin. 'I might be able to,' she whispered, looking at him, her eyes bright.

Suddenly his arms were around her, lifting her up, pulling her tightly against him. His mouth closed over hers, sealing her to him and his hands ran over her desperately, as if wanting to feel all of her at once. His touch made her feel weak and shivery and melting inside.

He drew back to gaze at her, his eyes glinting with something remarkably moist. 'Thank God, you bullied me,' he sighed at last. One hand stroked her hair as she looked up at him smiling broadly. 'Thank God, you wouldn't give up,' he said, his eyes gleaming as they took in every detail. It was as if he were examining a very, very precious gift.

'Fletcher,' she murmured, her voice low and husky, treasuring the name as it left her lips. With a happy sigh, she brought his head down to hers for another longer kiss.

'Marry me, Ally. Please marry me. If you hate the bush, we'll leave together. We'll make a new life somewhere else, but I've got to have you. I can't bear to let you go.'

'Idiot,' Ally laughed as she kissed him gently on the nose. 'I'm not going to want to go anywhere else. You're there. That's all I want.' She nibbled his chin playfully with her neat white teeth, relishing the masculine texture, then ran happy kisses over his neck. 'You're all I've ever wanted. I happen to love you.'

He crushed her to him, as if afraid she would suddenly disappear.

'Let's go somewhere more comfortable,' she murmured, leading the way out of the lounge room.

In her bedroom, they lay together for a moment, lost in each other's arms, savouring the moment, wanting to make it a lasting memory. He raised his head and smiled down at her. 'I really didn't want you to have to give everything up. You are such a clever designer.'

Ally pushed him gently away and fixed him with a stern glare. 'Fletcher, let me get this into your thick head for the last time. I want you. Nothing else. I love you more than catwalks and luxury fabrics. I love you more than magazine coverage. I'm not giving anything up. I'm getting what I want.' She touched his cheek and saw him tremble. 'You're all I've wanted ever since I met you. Hey, I'm getting the most gorgeous guy in Australia. And, as a bonus—I—I think he loves me.'

'Think? Ally, rest assured. I don't deserve you, but I love you.' He kissed her. 'I love you.' Then he kissed her again.

Ally kissed him back and it was the longest time before they drew apart.

'How did we end up on my bed?' she murmured seductively as she began to unbutton his shirt.

He kissed her again, a long, slow, sensuous kiss this time and it was dreadful when he finally broke away to ask huskily, 'Hold on a minute, little minx, you haven't answered my question yet.'

'I haven't? What question was that?' Her eyes twinkled wickedly as her hands reached his belt buckle.

'I've asked you to make an honest man of me. You haven't said you'll marry me.'

'I haven't said?' Ally cried. 'Fletcher, my darling, that's why I came to Wallaroo Downs. You couldn't doubt that I want to marry you. I've practically begged. You just want to hear me say yes?'

With a growl of pleasure, Fletcher rolled her across the bed, so that his entire weight was pinning her with delicious strength to the mattress. 'Yes, Alexandra Fraser. I want—I need to hear you say yes.'

She eyed him. 'Yes, Fletcher Hardy, my dearest man. Of course I'll marry you.' She offered him her lips, which he took in another deep, lingering kiss and from which she only just dragged herself away. 'But I have a special request.'

'Anything, my sweet.'

'I want the wedding to be at Wallaroo. I want all my friends to come and see my man and his land.'

'It's a deal,' he whispered.

EPILOGUE

AS HIS HORSE slowed to a trot, Fletcher Hardy lowered his hat so that it shaded his eyes from the glaring afternoon sun. That was better. Now as his mount carried him up from the creek, he could have an uninterrupted view across the home paddock towards the homestead.

It always gave him great satisfaction to see his home come into view at the end of a long, hot day in the saddle. Circled by the huge shade trees, its long rambling roofline fringed by the deep verandas always induced a welcome sense of calm. He squinted, trying to make out the shapes on the veranda. There was little Sarah, hopping and skipping in time to a definite rhythm. Last week, Ally had taught her how to work the tape recorder, so that she could play her favourite music and dance to her heart's delight whenever she chose.

At three, their dark-haired, blue-eyed daughter was already showing a noticeably artistic bent, but she was far too bossy. He felt sorry for the new baby when it arrived in two months' time. With Sarah for a big sister, it would have to come out fighting.

He could see Ally now, walking along the veranda—to call

Sarah in for her bath, most likely. He felt his smile widen as he watched his wife's blossoming figure trundle along. He loved her more than ever when she was pregnant. She positively glowed with good health and happiness as if the baby she nurtured was a health tonic.

He had been so worried the first time, when their son Fraser was born. But Ally had never been more serene. A week before the due date, she asked him to drive her into Charters Towers and two days later, produced a fat, bouncing boy—a wonderful companion for Connor.

By the time he reached the stables, his boys, Connor and Fraser, were already there, mucking out their horses' stalls. It was their favourite haunt. At ten, Connor was a tall, strong boy who was as easygoing and good-natured as ever. Fletcher had always felt his godson was a great role model for his own son and they would all miss him badly when he left after Christmas for the boarding school Fletcher and Jock Lawrence had attended.

He stabled the horse and, with a nod to the boys, moved off to hang the saddle away in the tack room.

'I thought I might find you in here.' Ally's lilting voice reached him as she crossed the old brick floor to greet her husband. Standing on tiptoe to kiss him, she wound her cool arms around his neck.

'Mmm,' murmured Fletcher, nibbling her neck. 'You smell wonderful, delicious.'

Ally laughed. 'You smell—well like a man who's been in the saddle since dawn. Dusty but nice.'

Fletcher growled. 'Be careful, wife, there are no children in sight and I haven't yet made love to you in here.'

'Well, there aren't many places left we haven't tried,' rejoined Ally with a wicked gleam in her eye. 'But,' she added, punching him playfully, 'Mary has dinner almost ready and your tribe will be ravenous as always.'

'And their mother is ravishing.' Fletcher smiled, holding her at arm's length to take a good look at his wife. Her dark hair was twisted into a fetching knot at the nape of her neck and she was dressed in a soft smock that leant violet tints to her clear eyes, now shining with love. Her cheeks were lightly flushed and she was breathtakingly beautiful.

'Thank goodness you bullied me into marriage,' he said softly as he had a hundred other times, lifting a fine strand of hair and tucking it behind her ear. 'I love you, Ally Hardy.'

Ally sighed happily, drawing close to her husband again, clearly revelling in the joy of his strong arms around her. He saw her beautiful smile drawing up the corners of her mouth. 'I love you back,' she murmured.

'Now, no more talk. I'm going to kiss you before these children…'

He didn't finish the sentence. Ally lifted her face to his and whatever he was going to say seemed a precious waste of time.

* * * * *

Rancher's Twins:
Mum Needed

I'd like to thank Anne Gracie
for her wonderful insights into adult literacy,
and Elliot, my live-in bush poet.

CHAPTER ONE

THEY WERE ASLEEP.

At last.

Holly held her breath as she closed the storybook, then backed out of the children's room with the stealth of a special ops soldier.

The caution was necessary. Really. These kids could sleep soundly through the familiar blast of car horns and sirens from the busy New York street below, but the tiniest squeak from within the apartment could rouse them to instant panicking wakefulness.

This evening, to Holly's relief, neither child stirred. They lay perfectly still in their matching bunk beds. In striped pyjamas, one dark head and one fair, they clutched their favourite fluffy toys—a kangaroo for Josh, a koala for Anna—and their eyes remained blessedly closed.

Holly reached the doorway without a mishap and quickly flicked the light switch, plunging the room into darkness. For once there were no responding squawks or protests. Just sweet, blissful silence.

She tiptoed down the hall…and the silence continued.

Fannnntastic. With a little luck, tonight would be a good night. No wet beds. No nightmares. In the past month there'd only been a handful of good nights. But, before Holly could even think about letting out a sigh of relief, her cellphone rang.

No-o-o!

With the speed of a baseball short stop, she dived across the room, snatched the phone from the coffee table and darted into her bedroom, closing the door quickly but softly behind her.

The phone's screen identified the caller. Her boyfriend, Brandon. *Wonderful.*

'Hi, Brand,' she whispered.

No squeaks emanated from the bedroom down the hall and she sank gratefully onto the bed.

'Holly, why are you whispering?'

'I've just got the twins to sleep.'

'Oh, right.' Brandon gave an audible sigh. 'How are they coping this week?'

'A little better.'

'That's great.'

Great wasn't quite the word Holly would have chosen to describe the small improvement in the children's progress, but of course she wouldn't correct Brandon. He'd given her fabulous support during the funeral and its aftermath.

'I got your message,' he said.

'Right. Thanks for calling back.' Holly took a moment to relax into the pillows and she deliberately lightened her tone. 'So, what do you think? Can you wangle a leave pass for this weekend?'

She crossed her fingers as she waited for his answer. *Please come, Brand. I need you.*

Brandon's family owned a dairy farm in Vermont and his dad's health wasn't the best, so the responsibility of running the enterprise had fallen squarely on Brandon's shoulders.

So, yes—it was asking a lot to expect him to get away to New York again so soon. Last month, after Holly's cousin Chelsea's sudden and tragic death, he'd taken almost a whole week off to be with her and to help with the children.

That was pretty amazing, actually. Holly had been touched and surprised. Since she'd moved away from Vermont to study in New York, she'd come to accept that if she wanted to see her boyfriend it was up to her to make the effort. She'd grown up on a dairy farm, too, so she understood the demands and she'd been prepared to be the one who did all the travelling. Even so, she'd only been able to see Brandon a handful of times in this past year.

If he came this weekend, she would make sure they had time alone together. She and Brandon had been an item since high school, almost six years. Very soon now, she would be finished with her studies, Anna and Josh would be settled in Australia with their father, and she was looking forward to going home to Vermont to settle down with Brand.

She could so easily picture their lives together—Brandon with his dairy herd, while she worked in the local school, the two of them balancing their day jobs with their life at home, and eventually, with a family of their own—copper-haired children like their dad.

Holly was very happy with that picture, and thinking about her boyfriend always made her feel cosy and safe.

Admittedly, most girls might not place cosiness and safety high on their wish list when it came to boyfriends, but Holly wasn't looking for a guy who spelled excitement and passion.

Her cousin Chelsea, the twins' mother, had taken that risk and the result had been divorce and heartbreak.

'I don't know if I can get away this weekend,' Brandon said suddenly.

Holly suppressed a sigh. 'I do understand, honey, but—'

'Do you?' His voice bristled with unexpected impatience. 'Because I *don't* understand why you're complicating this, Holly. The children's father is on his way at last, so why do you need me? Why do you need my help if he's going to be there, too?'

'It would just be good to have your support. I've looked after the twins for a month and now I have to say goodbye.'

Holly suppressed a sigh. She needed to be calm and composed when she talked with Gray about his children, and she would have liked a little backup from Brandon. She needed to explain to Gray about Anna and Josh's schooling needs, their eating habits, their fears…

The twins had been at home on the day Chelsea had collapsed, and it was six-year-old Josh who'd courageously dialled 911. They hadn't only lost their mommy; they'd suffered a terrible trauma. Anna's nightmares were truly terrifying.

Holly needed to explain all this to their estranged father, but it would be so much easier if her steady and reliable boyfriend was there as well. As a buffer. An anchor. A safety net.

'Actually, Holly, I can't come this weekend.'

The sudden nervousness in Brandon's voice penetrated the whirl of Holly's thoughts.

Why was he nervous? Brandon was never nervous. Was something wrong?

'There's…um…there's something I should tell you,' he said.

'What is it?'

'It's really hard to explain. I…I don't know how to say this, but…'

Holly's insides froze and she was gripped by a terrible deer-in-the-headlights fear.

Brandon cleared his throat.

She forced herself to ask, 'Brandon, what's the matter?'

'I didn't want to tell you before—because of Chelsea and everything…'

'Tell me what?' she almost screamed. He was scaring her.

Brandon cleared his throat again.

Holly gripped the phone tighter, squeezing her eyes to hold back threatening tears.

Was Brandon trying to break-up with her?

No. No. Surely not.

Like someone drowning, her mind flashed back through precious memories. The school dance when they'd first met. Brandon helping her with algebra homework at the big scrubbed table in her mother's cosy kitchen. The familiar, comfortable texture of his lips. The ruby heart locket he'd given her on Valentine's Day three years ago. The way she liked to bury her nose against the warm freckles on his neck when he held her. The cosy sense of safety that she'd always felt with him…

Now, suffocating panic filled her throat.

She couldn't bear to think about losing him, especially not when she'd just lost Chelsea. Fear pulled tight knots in her stomach.

Brandon said, 'You have to agree it's not really working for us.'

'What do you mean?' she bleated.

'We only see each other a few times a year.'

'But I've almost finished my studies.' Her voice was shrill now. Pleading. 'I'll soon be home for good and we can—'

'I'm so sorry, Holly. You see, the thing is…I…I've met someone else.'

CHAPTER TWO

As THE TAXI pulled into the kerb on West 69th Street Gray Kidman was thinking about the first time he'd arrived at this red-brick apartment block. He'd been a bridegroom then, fired with love and certainty and hope, with no premonition of the heartache that lay ahead of him.

This time he knew what he was in for, knew the challenges and the very real chances for failure. Right now, as he stepped onto the pavement and looked up to the level where his children were waiting, his stomach felt like a jar full of jumping grasshoppers.

His hand was actually shaking as he pressed the security buzzer.

The children answered immediately.

'Daddy!'

'Hi, Dad.'

Gray closed his eyes, momentarily stunned by the emotion his children's voices aroused. For three long months he'd been waiting for this. First, the wet season floods had held him up, then a broken ankle after a desperate attempt to cross a raging creek. Now, at last, he dipped his head to the speaker phone. 'G'day, scallywags.'

Anna squealed, 'I'll press the button to let you in.'

'I've already pressed it,' shouted Josh, full of self-importance and equally excited.

A wry smile tilted Gray's mouth and the glass doors slid open, allowing him access to the apartment block's foyer. He hefted his duffel bag over one shoulder and strode with only the slightest hint of a limp across the blue-tiled floor. As he pressed the lift button, he reminded himself that he must remember to call this an elevator now. His kids would be quick to correct him.

His kids…

His stomach jumped like crazy.

Taking sole charge of Anna and Josh was a huge task, probably the toughest challenge he'd ever faced. He wanted the very best for them. If it was in his power, he'd give his children the perfect foundation for their lives—a safe and comfortable home, a loving family network, and the best possible education.

The irony was that they had all of the above right here in New York City. This apartment block was secure and modern. His ex-wife's teacher cousin was a first-rate nanny, and the children's doting grandparents were nearby. The school they attended had won all kinds of awards for educational excellence.

Although it had nearly killed Gray to let his wife walk away from his Outback cattle property, taking their children with her, he'd been forced to accept that Anna and Josh were better off here in New York than in his home in one of the remotest corners of Australia.

He hadn't given in without a fight but, despite his heart-break, he'd eventually let his family go.

Yet, tragically, here he was, reclaiming his children and taking them halfway across the world to the very situation their mother had fled from.

Gray had no other option. Running a cattle station was his only income-earning skill. Jabiru Creek Station was the best he had to offer. It was all he had to offer.

He was very afraid it wasn't enough.

The elevator arrived and shot him quickly to the third floor, and when the doors slid open his children were waiting for him.

'Daddy!' Anna launched herself, like a small torpedo, straight into Gray's arms.

He let his duffel bag slip to the floor and lifted her high and she clasped him tightly around his neck.

'Daddy! My daddy!' She buried her face into his shoulder and her silky fair hair smelled wonderfully of flowers.

'Hey, Dad.' Josh was standing close, looking up expectantly.

Crouching, Gray juggled Anna onto one knee and hugged his son. What a fine little fellow Josh was. Gray had been moved to tears when he'd heard that his small son had been brave and quick-thinking when his mother collapsed at home, rushing to dial Emergency.

Now…how good it was to embrace them both. At last.

They seemed fine. Gray had been worried he'd find them pale and pining, but they looked happy and healthy and bursting with energy. It was such a relief.

'That's some welcome,' a voice said and he looked up to see a young woman with dark hair and dark shiny eyes standing in the apartment's open doorway.

Holly O'Mara, Chelsea's young cousin. Gray sent her a smile that felt crooked with emotion. He winced at the twinge in his ankle when he stood once more.

'Holly,' he said, holding out his hand.

'It's good to see you, Gray.'

He didn't know this young woman very well. On the rare occasions they'd met at family gatherings, Holly had always been shy, keeping well in the background, as if she preferred her own company, so he'd never gone out of his way to chat with her. Besides, she was training to be an English teacher, which meant she was as well educated and cultured as his former wife, another woman destined to remind him of his inadequacies.

But he couldn't deny he owed her a great deal. She'd been sole carer of his children for three long, difficult months.

With the twins skipping at his heels, he followed Holly inside the apartment. It was then, without warning, that he was sideswiped by a new emotion—the realisation that his beautiful bride was gone for ever.

It was crazy to feel like this now. Truth was, Gray had already lost Chelsea three years ago when she left him. He'd done his grieving then, and in time he'd moved on, eventually finding comfort in a healthy cynicism for the married state.

Now, suddenly, the finality of her passing hit him like a physical blow. A sense of loss descended like black, suffocating cloud.

Don't break down. Not now. Not in front of the children.

He heard Holly say gently, 'You've had a long journey. Why don't you go through to the living room? Take the weight off. I have coffee brewing.'

Gray was grateful for the normality and everyday ease

of her welcome. 'Thanks,' he said. 'Thanks for everything, Holly.'

Their gazes met in an unexpected moment of connection. Holly was smiling, but Gray thought he saw tears glistening in her dark eyes and he felt a painful tightening in his throat.

He spoke more gruffly than he meant to. 'Come on, kids, show me the way.'

Holly told herself to keep smiling as she watched Gray and his children head down the hall. Alone in the kitchen, however, she was fighting tears as she filled the coffee-maker.

It was two months now since her break-up with Brandon, but Gray's arrival *at last* brought it all back—memories of the horrible phone call, the heartbreak in the following weeks of anxiety, of hoping against all hope for another call. *It was all a mistake, Holly. I really do love you.*

But on top of that pain…she felt so tense, so conflicted about this reunion.

Oh, she was very happy for Anna and Josh. She knew how much they needed their father, and it was wonderful to see how thrilled they were. But she wasn't sure she could bear to let them go all the way back to Australia.

Of course, Gray had every right to take his children home, and there was no denying that he loved them.

Just now, when he'd hunkered down in the corridor to hug them, Holly had seen the way he closed his eyes and held them close against his heart. She'd watched the concentrated emotion in his face, and she'd been so moved she'd almost spoiled the moment by weeping.

Until then, she hadn't realised how fragile she was after the emotional pressure cooker of the last three months.

She and the children had been through so much together,

and they'd grown incredibly close. When Chelsea had died so suddenly, the very foundations of their world had been shaken and Holly had needed to dig deep, discovering a sensitivity and wisdom she hadn't known she possessed.

Even though Chelsea's parents lived close by in a luxury Westside apartment, they'd been too shocked and grieving to be of much help. They'd gladly handed over their grandchildren into Holly's full-time care until Gray Kidman arrived to claim them.

Looking back, Holly wasn't quite sure how she'd managed. In a cruelly short space of time she'd lost Chelsea, her cousin and her best friend, and then Brandon. Filled with despair, she'd wanted to crawl away and hide for a decade or two, and she might have done exactly that if Anna and Josh's needs hadn't been even greater than hers.

To give them the love and attention they'd needed, she'd been forced to put her own heartbreak aside.

So…in a way the children had saved her. But right now, she was finding it hard to accept that her role as an integral player in this little team was almost over. She couldn't imagine living without them.

'Look, Daddy.' Anna lifted her top lip.

'Wow. You've lost a tooth.'

The little girl grinned proudly, revealing the gap. 'I left it under my pillow and the Tooth Fairy came.'

'Lucky you.'

'Josh hasn't lost any teeth yet.'

His son's lips were tightly pressed together, and Gray caught a flicker of embarrassment in the boy's eyes. Clearly, sibling rivalry was alive and well, and no doubt Josh felt left behind in the race to shed baby teeth.

'Josh must have extra tough teeth,' Gray suggested.

The boy sent him a grateful smile.

To change the subject, Gray unzipped a pocket on the outside of his duffel bag and drew out a small packet.

'Is that a present?' asked Anna, eager-eyed.

'It's a game to share with your brother. A card game. Snap. With pictures of the Outback on the back.'

'Your Outback?'

He smiled uncertainly. 'Yes. My Outback.'

The twins had been three when they'd left his home—he doubted they'd remember it.

They knelt at the coffee table as Gray fanned the cards onto its smooth glass surface, showing bright photos of kangaroos, pink-flowering gum trees and wide red plains shimmering beneath sunburned skies.

'Is that where you're going to take us?' asked Josh.

Gray nodded.

'Is your house like this one?' Anna picked up a card that showed a faded, shabby homestead with a broad iron roof standing alone in the middle of a sparse red desert.

'More or less,' Gray admitted with some reluctance.

The little girl stared with large worried eyes at the rather ugly house and stark forbidding landscape.

'We have more trees than that and quite a decent garden,' Gray amended, feeling rather like a real estate agent trying to sell inadequate property. 'My homestead is painted white, and there are lots of extra buildings.'

'What kind of buildings?'

He realised now that he should have brought proper photos of Jabiru Creek Station, instead of these generic tourist images. 'We have machinery sheds and storage sheds and houses for the ringers.'

'What are ringers?'

'They're stockmen.'

'Cowboys,' added Holly cheerfully as she came into the room with a coffee pot and two black and white mugs.

'Except that in Australia we don't call them cowboys,' Gray amended with a smile.

'Can we ride horses?'

The animated excitement in Josh's face was a stark contrast to the sudden fear in Anna's dark brown eyes. Gray's chest tightened. His daughter looked so much like her mother. So beautiful, like a delicate flower, and right now, so worried and sad.

'I have a nice little horse that you can learn to ride,' he told Josh. For Anna's sake he added, 'But you don't have to ride if you don't want to.'

He tried to cheer Anna with a smiling wink. She wouldn't remember how she used to love to ride in the saddle in front of him, while he kept one arm around her and one hand holding the reins. To his dismay, her lower lip trembled. Damn. He had so little experience in handling kids. The simplest thing could suddenly become a huge problem.

Holly, who'd made herself comfortable in an armchair, leaned forward and picked up another card—a picture of blue sky reflected in a large pool of water at the bottom of a steep red-walled gorge.

'Look, Anna,' Holly said. 'Isn't this beautiful?'

Over the children's heads, her expressive dark eyes sent Gray a silent message. They needed to change the subject.

'Do you have beautiful places like this on your ranch?' she asked him.

'Sure. We have a fabulous deep gorge and a sizeable river.'

'Can you swim there?' Holly asked with an encouraging smile.

Not unless you're willing to risk being eaten by a crocodile.

Sidestepping that question, Gray said instead, 'There's a dam near the homestead where you can swim.' *When it's not too hot or muddy.*

He tentatively touched his daughter's arm. Her skin was soft and smooth and perfect and his heart lurched. He hated to think of her being muddy or sunburned or in any kind of danger from the harsh environment that was his home.

Would he be able to take proper care of her? He hunted for something positive to tell her.

'Do you like puppies, Anna?'

She nodded solemnly.

'I have a nice kelpie and she's going to have babies very soon. By the time we get home there might be puppies.'

'How many puppies?'

'Maybe three or four.'

Anna's eyes widened. 'Are they all in their mommy's tummy?'

'Yes. They're growing fat and wriggly and they're almost ready to be born.'

'Like Josh and me? We were together in our mommy's tummy.'

Gray tensed, expecting his daughter to burst into tears now that she'd inadvertently mentioned her mother. His skin grew clammy. His heart picked up pace. Hell. What should he do and say now?

Holly spoke for him. 'That's right, Anna. The puppies are just like you and Josh, all together in their mommy's tummy.' She said this smoothly and calmly, as if nothing awkward or dangerous had happened. 'If there are three puppies, they'll be triplets. If there are four they'll be quads.'

To Gray's surprise, Anna grinned, clearly pleased with Holly's answer.

'Why don't you two have a game of Snap while your dad drinks his coffee?' Holly suggested next. 'Take the cards through to your room. I'll call you as soon as lunch is ready.'

'Is Dad having lunch with us?' Josh asked.

'Of course. He'll be staying here with us for a few days.'

Satisfied, the boy began to gather up the cards and the two trotted happily off to their room.

As they left, Gray sent Holly a surprised smile, shaking his head. 'They did exactly what you asked. Are they always so obedient?'

She laughed. 'Heavens, no. Although they're getting better all the time.' She poured coffee into two mugs. 'Here's your coffee. Drink it while it's hot.'

'Thanks.' He relaxed into the sofa and took a deep sip. The coffee was indeed hot and strong and of very good quality.

Over the rim of his mug he stole a closer look at Holly O'Mara. Although he'd only met her a few times, he was sure there was something different about her. He tried to decide what it was. Was her face thinner? Was that why her dark eyes now looked larger, her mouth more curving and lush, her cheekbones more defined?

Or was there something different about her expression?

The change was hard to pin down, but he sensed a depth in Chelsea's young cousin that he'd never been aware of before. He knew these past three months must have been very hard on her. No doubt she'd had to grow up fast.

Whatever it was about Holly that was different, the change

seemed to suit her. *And* she'd clearly done a very good job of looking after his children.

'I hope you realise how very grateful I am,' he said. 'Honestly, the way you've taken care of the twins has been amazing. Fantastic. It can't have been easy—being dumped with everything after...after Chelsea...'

Holly nodded. 'There have been some grim moments, but each day gets better.'

Gray wondered, somewhat anxiously, about the 'grim moments'. He sat for a bit in silence, wrapped in worried thoughts as they drank their coffee.

'How's your ankle?' Holly asked politely.

'Oh, it's fine.' He pulled a face, remembering the exasperation of the floods, and then the further frustration of his accident. 'You have no idea how maddening it was not being able to get here any sooner.'

She let out a soft huff. 'I'll admit it wasn't easy at this end, either, trying to convince Anna and Josh that you were held up all that time by floods.'

'I'm sorry.'

She shook her head. 'No, you couldn't help it, and you did the right thing when you asked me not to tell them about the accident. They'd just lost their mom. They would have been devastated if they'd heard their dad was hurt, too.'

'I wouldn't have been much use to them on crutches.'

'Imagine your journey home,' Holly agreed, smiling. 'Twenty-something hours on a plane and trying to manage six-year-old twins while you're hobbling on a cast.'

'Exactly.' Gray sat forward, eager to voice the question that had been plaguing him. 'So—how do you think Anna and Josh will cope with going back to Australia with me?'

He hoped she would answer with an easygoing shrug and a quick reassurance.

They'll be fine. They're over the worst now.

To his dismay, she dropped her gaze to her coffee cup and twisted it in her hands.

His throat tightened uncomfortably. 'I thought my place—somewhere completely different—might help them. Might be a...a distraction.'

Holly looked up again and, when her dark eyes met his, she was frowning. He saw no hint of reassurance.

He spoke again quickly, needing to strengthen his case. 'This apartment must hold so many sad memories for the children. Won't it help them to get away?'

Her mouth opened again as if she was going to reply, but then she hesitated.

Gray's entire body tensed. 'You agree, don't you?' He forced an awkward shrug. 'I admit you know my children better than I do. I'd value your opinion.'

She responded with a faint smile. 'I certainly hope they'll be fine, but I can't promise it's going to be easy, Gray. I'm no expert, but from everything I've read—'

'Everything you've *read*?' He felt himself tense. As a cattleman who'd always relied on purely practical skills, he was sceptical about the glorified merits of the written word.

Perhaps Holly sensed his doubt. Her cheeks flushed deep pink but, when she spoke, she lifted her chin and her dark eyes narrowed. 'I've never had any first-hand experience of grief, certainly not with helping children who've lost a parent. So I consulted a GP who referred me to a psychologist, and I've done some reading, too. After all, the books are written by experts.'

The skin on the back of Gray's neck grew hot. Not quite

meeting her gaze, he said, 'So what did the experts have to say?'

Holly set her coffee mug on the table with exquisite care, as if it were a rare antique. 'It seems that children who've suffered a loss can benefit from a predictable routine and structure. The familiarity of a routine helps them to feel secure.'

A predictable routine.

Structure.

Security.

Gray's heart sank. Predictability and security were scarce commodities in the Outback. Cattlemen and their families lived at the mercy of the elements, or at the whim of fluctuating markets. Daily, they dealt with the problems caused by isolation and vast distances.

He recalled all the things his ex-wife had hated about his lifestyle, and he thought about his experience over the past three months—being cut off by the floods, almost running out of supplies, busting his leg in a flooded river.

Doubts crowded in. What was he doing here? How could he take his kids away from this safe and secure world that they knew and loved?

Abruptly, he stood and strode to the window where he dipped a slat in the blinds with one finger and stared down at the crowded pavements and busy traffic below.

Without looking at Holly, he said grimly, 'If the experts in your books are right, the last thing my children need is another big change.'

Unhappily, he folded his arms over his chest and his jaw jutted belligerently. 'I'm planning to drag Anna and Josh halfway across the world to a place that's completely different from here, and your book-writing experts are telling me it's the worst thing I can do.'

CHAPTER THREE

FOR A MOMENT, Holly was seriously tempted to tell Gray that yes, his children would be much better off if they stayed right here in Manhattan. Of course they'd be happier if they were allowed to continue in this familiar environment—living in this apartment, going to their highly acclaimed school, playing with their select circle of appropriate friends.

For three months she'd been trying to follow the psychologists' advice. She'd built little rituals into the children's days so they always had something to look forward to.

She'd carefully planned mealtimes around their favourite nutritious foods, and she'd scheduled regular after school treats. Of course, she'd made sure that bedtime was special with their favourite stories. And plenty of hugs.

But she couldn't suggest that Gray would not be able to meet his children's needs. She'd witnessed his deep emotion when he'd first greeted his children, and she could see the incredible tension in his face right now as he waited for her answer.

Gray wasn't just a proud, possessive male reclaiming his rights. He was a man who loved his children very deeply.

Chelsea's parents had told her that over the past three years he'd made the arduous journey from Australia to America several times a year, just to see them.

Holly knew that her possibly selfish opinions about the benefits of staying in America had no place in this conversation.

She drew a deep breath. 'Anna and Josh want to be with you, Gray. You're their father.' After a beat, she added gently, 'They've missed you very much.'

His face softened a fraction. 'But it's still going to be hard for them to leave here and to make the change, isn't it?'

She couldn't deny this. 'You should probably be prepared for one or two tricky moments.'

'I was hoping that if I stayed in New York for a few days, and gave them a chance to get used to me again—'

'I'm sure that will help. And, while you're here, we can both talk to them about what to expect on the journey and when they arrive in Australia.'

Gray nodded, and let his thoughtful gaze fix on the row of windows on the opposite wall, as if he was seeing far into the distance. Then he sent Holly a slow smile.

Despite the fact that Holly was thinking about Gray's children and not his looks, something very odd happened to her insides. She dropped her gaze from the sudden flare in his light blue eyes and found safety in the tan leather duffel bag, dumped on the floor by the sofa.

It was the sort of bag that would look at home on a dusty homestead veranda, or in the back of a battered pickup. Here, in this city apartment, however, the scuffed leather holdall looked out of place, almost like a symbol of everything that had been wrong about Gray's marriage to her cousin.

Chelsea had rarely talked about the problems that had

sent her scurrying home from Jabiru Creek to New York. It was clear to everyone that her decision had been painful—that she hadn't stopped loving Gray, but that she'd loved her ballet and choreography more. There'd been no jobs for a choreographer of Chelsea's calibre in Outback Australia and, in the end, she'd found it too difficult to relinquish her city life and her career.

She'd told Holly once, 'It was a fatal attraction. Gray and I were wrong for each other and in almost every way. I think we both sensed from the start that our marriage was doomed, but our feelings were so intense we still had to give it a try.'

Now, sitting mere metres from Gray Kidman's intensely masculine presence, Holly was all too aware of the force that had urged Chelsea to take that risk. He was still disturbingly attractive. Looking at him, the word *manly* seemed to take on new meaning.

Abruptly, she jumped to her feet. 'If you've finished your coffee, I'll show you to your room and you can stow your things away.'

She charged across the room, feeling a need to put a sudden distance between them.

'Holly, before you go—'

Slowly…she turned.

Gray offered a dangerously shy smile. 'I know I'm probably old-fashioned and you're a contemporary New Yorker, but I just wanted to make sure you're completely okay with having me stay here in your apartment.'

'Of course. It's perfectly fine.' Holly tried to sound off-hand. 'It makes sense.'

'And your boyfriend? Is he cool with it, too?'

A horrible knife-in-the-heart pain pierced Holly, the pain she always felt whenever Brandon was mentioned. After two months, the shock was still very raw—especially the painful discovery that Brandon had been seeing Maria Swain for six whole months before he'd found the courage to tell her.

Somehow she forced a breezy smile. 'That's not a problem. I'm between boyfriends right now.'

Not wanting to see Gray's reaction, she hurried on to the spare room. 'It's important for you to stay here, Gray.' She tossed the words over her shoulder. 'You need to maximise your time with the children before you set off.'

'Thanks. I appreciate that.'

At the doorway, she stepped aside to let him into the room. 'It's nothing special, but I guess it's adequate.'

'It's terrific.' Gray dropped his bag onto the rug at the foot of the single bed. Holly was about to leave when he said, 'What about you, Holly?'

'Me? Oh…my room's…um…just down the hall.'

Gray looked a tad embarrassed and scratched at the side of his jaw. 'I wasn't asking where you sleep. I meant—what are your plans now—once the children are off your hands.'

'My plans? Oh…' Holly gulped. Talking to this attractive man about bedrooms must have scrambled her powers of thinking. 'I've just finished my final exams, so I've started sending out job applications. Who knows where I'll end up?'

With luck, anywhere except Vermont.

Taking three quick steps backwards, she added, 'Right now, I need to fix lunch.'

'Anything I can help with?'

'No, thanks. It's only chicken salad. You go and see the children. Join in their game.'

Gray suggested a trip to Central Park after lunch. He always felt more at ease entertaining his children in wide open spaces with grass and trees and blue sky overhead, instead of pavement and department stores and hurrying crowds.

This time, Holly came with them.

Initially Gray hadn't invited her. He'd assumed she'd be keen to grab a few hours of freedom to paint her toenails, or go shopping, or whatever city girls liked to do when they had time to themselves.

Just as the children and he were about to leave the apartment, however, Holly had handed him a pamphlet.

'This shows you everything that's going on in Central Park,' she'd said.

Gray had dismissed this with a quick, 'We'll be fine.'

Even though he was only familiar with a tiny section of Central Park, he could find the zoo, and the carousel. Anna and Josh had never complained. 'We'll play it by ear, won't we, kids?'

Holly looked surprised and she tapped a brightly coloured centre page. 'But this pamphlet lists all the children's activities. And there's a puppet theatre.'

'Puppets!' Anna and Josh both squealed in chorus. 'We want to see the puppets. Please, Daddy, please!'

Holly was still pointing to the printed page and Gray felt the first squeeze of panic. The words on the pamphlet danced and jumbled before his eyes and his chest tightened as frustration and inadequacy—two foes he'd been fighting all his life—surfaced.

'Why don't you come along with us?' he asked her then. 'And bring your pamphlet.'

Her cheeks turned pink—a very pretty pink, a perfect foil for her dark eyes and her shiny dark hair. The blush surprised Gray. Perhaps she was shyer than he'd realised.

'Yes, Holly, come with us,' Anna was pleading and grabbing her hand. 'Please, come. Please!'

Holly shook her head. 'But this is your special time to be with your daddy.'

However, she didn't need much convincing.

'Would you like me to try for last minute tickets for the puppets?' she said next and already she was pulling her cellphone from her pocket.

They were in luck. There were four tickets available for the last performance that afternoon and when they set off for Central Park Gray noticed that Holly's shyness was quickly evaporating.

It was soon clear that she genuinely *liked* to spend time outdoors with his children. She laughed a lot and her eyes shone, and she looked somehow just right in slim blue jeans and a simple grey T-shirt, with her dark hair tied back in a ponytail and her face free of make-up.

He thought, uneasily, that his children were really going to miss Holly when it was time to leave. He couldn't help noticing how totally relaxed they were with her. Affectionate, too. Josh was perfectly happy to hold her hand when they crossed the busy streets, and Anna, all excited after a super-fast slippery slide, exchanged ecstatic high fives with Holly. The gesture was so automatic and natural Gray knew they'd done this many times.

And Holly's pamphlet proved to be a great asset. It showed where the really cool playgrounds were, like the Ancient Playground based on the Egyptian Temple of Dendor, with model pyramids for climbing. And after the children had climbed and run and explored the zoo and thrown Frisbees and eaten ice creams, they all headed off to the puppet theatre in an old Swedish cottage.

The show turned out to be lively and hilarious, full of drama and excitement and silly pranks that were impossible not to enjoy.

All the children in the audience were encouraged to call out advice and warnings, so they practically lifted the roof off the ancient cottage. So very different from the serious, respectful hush of the audiences at the ballets Chelsea had dragged him to.

At one point, Gray glanced over Anna and Josh's heads and caught Holly watching him. Her dark eyes sparkled with amusement and he realised he'd been laughing out loud.

Strewth. When was the last time that had happened?

They emerged from the theatre in the late afternoon, and together they strolled through the park in the softening light of the late spring evening. The children skipped ahead, wide smiles on their faces as they imitated the Big Bad Wolf, playing hide-and-seek behind tree trunks.

His kids were okay. They were happy. And Gray discovered that he was completely and totally relaxed. He hadn't realised how tense he'd been, but now, for the first time since he'd received the shocking news about Chelsea, he was conscious of having truly unwound.

'You shouldn't have to cook again tonight,' he told Holly. 'Why don't we eat out? My shout.'

She laughed. 'I was going to suggest grabbing a meal on the way home. We have a tradition of eating out at our favourite diner on Saturday nights.'

A tradition? Gray wondered uneasily if Anna and Josh would miss these traditions. Would they be willing to help him create new traditions? He couldn't take them to a diner near his Outback home. The nearest café was a hundred kilometres from Jabiru Creek. Could a campfire on a river-bank be a reasonable substitute?

As they pushed through the swing doors of the diner on 81st Street they were greeted by laughter and happy chatter and the appetizing smells of frying bacon and coffee. The waiters recognised Holly and the children and welcomed them warmly.

Gray was introduced.

'My dad from Australia,' Josh said proudly.

They slipped into a booth with Gray and Anna on one side, Holly and Josh on the other. The waiter handed out menus.

Gray barely looked at his. 'I'll have a hamburger.'

Holly shot him a surprised glance. 'What kind of hamburger? There are at least six varieties.'

He shrugged, cracked a careless smile. 'I've worked up an appetite. Whatever's the biggest.'

'That would be the Mighty Mo,' the waiter told him with a grin.

'Thanks. Sounds perfect.' Gray turned to his daughter. 'What about you, princess? What would you like?'

He watched Anna study the menu, following down the lists with her finger.

'A grilled American cheese sandwich,' she decided.

'And I wanna hot dog,' said Josh.

'I'd like a hot dog, please, Daddy,' Holly reminded him.

'I'd like a hot dog, please, Dad.' His son sent him a cheeky grin.

'You're both excellent readers,' Gray said.

His children smiled politely, as if they were thinking—*Of course. It's only a simple old menu.*

He asked quickly, 'What are you having, Holly? Let me

guess. A Greek salad?' This had always been Chelsea's choice and, judging by Holly's slim build, Gray assumed she was equally diet-conscious.

'Actually,' she replied with a raised-eyebrow smile, 'I rather fancy nachos with cheese, guacamole *and* sour cream.'

It was hours later, close to midnight, when Holly woke to the sound of high-pitched screaming. Her heart pounded as she leapt out of bed. Anna was having another nightmare.

She hurried through the apartment, not bothering to turn on a light. She was so familiar with the route from her bedroom to the children's room that she could easily dodge furniture and find her way in the dark.

But tonight, halfway down the hall, she ran into a solid object. Six feet three inches of near-naked male. Gray's warm bare chest and arms. His shoulders, bulky and smooth. His sculpted, cow-wrangling muscles. And he was only wearing boxer shorts.

'Gray.' She was suddenly breathless and flushed and—

'What's the matter with Anna?' he demanded, stepping past her.

Holly came rapidly to her senses. 'She's having a nightmare.'

As they hurried into the children's room, she gave herself a mental slap. Okay, so having a close encounter with this man's partly naked body was likely to send almost any female into a tizzy, but what had happened to her priorities? What about poor Anna?

In the children's bedroom she switched on a lamp and the room was illuminated by a soft pink glow. Anna was huddled in a tight ball in the middle of her bed, sobbing, 'Mommy! Mommy!'

Gray looked appalled and helpless, but Holly was sadly used to this scene. Kneeling on the bed, she drew the little girl into her arms. 'There, there. It's okay.' She stroked Anna's silky hair. 'It's okay, honey. You can wake up. You're all right.'

She felt the mattress dip beneath an extra weight. Gray was sitting on the other side of the bed, his eyes fierce and filled with concern. Lifting a shaking hand, he touched his daughter's tear-stained cheek.

'Anna,' he whispered. 'Anna, baby.'

'Daddy!' The little girl lifted her head from Holly's shoulder, then turned and hurled herself into her father's arms. Within minutes her shuddering sobs calmed and she buried her face into his chest.

Holly couldn't blame her. What little girl wouldn't want to be held safe in those big, strong, manly arms?

Just the same, she couldn't help feeling rejected. After weeks of comforting Anna during these middle of the night crises, Holly had suddenly become redundant.

She looked across to Josh's bed. In the early weeks he'd been the first to jump up, trying to calm his sister. Lately, he'd been more inclined to lie quietly, wide awake, knowing that Holly would come, that Holly knew what to do and that the storm would eventually pass.

'Hey there, champ,' Holly whispered.

'Hey,' the boy returned softly and then he yawned.

'You go back to sleep.' She leaned over to drop a kiss on his warm, still baby-soft cheek. He really was the greatest little guy. She adored him.

Adored them both.

When she turned back to see how Anna was now, she found Gray watching her, and it was then, in the warmth of his gaze, that she remembered that he wasn't the only adult in this room who was half undressed. She was in her thin cotton nightie—little more than a long, baggy T-shirt with a trail of dog's paw-prints stamped across her chest.

She tried to shrug off the intimacy of this situation, of being here with Gray, both in their pyjamas, tending to his children in the middle of the night. But the intimacy seemed even greater now after their afternoon in the park and their shared meal. Almost as if the four of them were a little family.

Good grief, what am I thinking?

How could she betray Chelsea with such thoughts? Very soon she would be waving goodbye to this father and his kids. In the fall, she would embark on an exciting new career.

Enough already.

Determined to be sensible, Holly said softly, 'I think Anna will be okay now.'

In the early weeks, she'd taken the little girl back to sleep in her bed, but lately she'd been weaning Anna out of that habit.

'Perhaps she'd like a drink of water.' Holly handed Gray a glass from the nightstand and watched as Anna took a few sips. 'We can leave the lamp on for five minutes,' she said.

'Okay, princess?' Gray gently eased his daughter back into bed.

Holly pulled up the covers and tucked her in. 'Night, night.'

The little girl looked peaceful again, curled on her side, eyes closed, golden curls gleaming softly in the lamplight as she clutched her favourite fluffy koala.

Gray gave his daughter a kiss and his son a gentle shoulder thump.

''Night, Dad.'

When Gray and Holly were safely down the hallway once more, Gray let out his breath with a whoosh.

'My God,' he said quietly. 'That scared the living daylights out of me. I'd rather hear a crocodile growling at my elbow than my own daughter screaming.'

'Anna's screams are heart-rending,' Holly agreed.

'Has this been happening all along? Ever since Chelsea—?'

Holly nodded. 'It was worse at first. She's getting better. This is the first nightmare in a while.'

'Maybe she's had too much excitement for one day.'

'Perhaps that's it.'

Gray let out a heavy sigh. 'I'm sure I'm not going to be able to get back to sleep.' He ran stiff fingers through his thick dark hair. 'It's two o'clock in the afternoon where I come from. Would I disturb you too much if I made a cuppa?'

'No, not at all. Go right ahead.'

'If I make tea, would you like a cup?'

'Tea?' She laughed. 'English tea?'

He shrugged. 'English, American…I'm not fussy.'

'I'm afraid I only have green tea or camomile.'

He pulled a face. 'How about wine, then? I bought a couple of Australian reds in the duty-free.'

No, thank you.

Holly was sure she should get straight back to her room. Right now. She should not sit around in the middle of the night in her jammies having cosy chats and glasses of vino with her charges' scarily handsome father.

'I…I'd love a glass. I'll…um…just grab a wrap.'

Okay, I'm a bird-brain, but I do have a good excuse, Holly consoled herself as she hurried away. Gray needed to talk about his children. He needed to debrief after the scare he'd had with Anna.

By the time she came back into the kitchen, safely covered by a tightly knotted kimono that ended well below her knees, Gray had, mercifully, pulled on jeans and a T-shirt and he was freeing the cork from a bottle.

CHAPTER FOUR

GRAY WAS EXTREMELY grateful that Holly was prepared to sit and have a drink with him at midnight.

His daughter's screams had shocked him and, even though Anna had calmed quite quickly in his arms, the experience had left him feeling shaken. Anxious.

Now, more than ever, he was aware of his lack of skills. There was so much he didn't know, didn't understand about his children. He wouldn't be able to read the experts' books on psychology and grief and yet, very soon, Anna and Josh would be completely in his care.

Suddenly, his excitement over having them back in his life was mixed with terror. All his failures came back to haunt him—all the problems stemming from his childhood that had tainted his marriage.

Hell. How could he be a good single father? How could he be a role model for his kids? He'd let his parents down, let his wife down. Would he let his children down, too?

Worries chased each other, snapping like dogs at the heels of his thoughts as he and Holly sat on the corner sofas next to plate glass windows with views of the city.

They left the lamps turned low and the curtains open so they could see the black towers of the skyscrapers dotted with squares of lemon light. From below came the non-stop honk and roar of traffic. New York, the city that never sleeps.

It was a wonder anyone could ever sleep here with that constant racket, Gray thought wryly.

Holly was now wrapped in an elegant dressing gown of jade-green silk with a pattern of graceful white cranes. She sat with her bare feet tucked to one side, slim fingers curled around her glass of wine.

'It's a Margaret River red,' he said. 'Should be good. Cheers.'

She smiled faintly as she raised her glass. 'Cheers.'

They sipped the wine and shared satisfied smiles. The wine was very good.

At first they talked about practical things, about the kinds of clothes the children would need immediately in Australia, and what could be boxed for posting. There were toys to be sorted, too—favourites to go with the children now, some to be sent to charities, others to be shipped.

'How will Anna and Josh feel about leaving their friends behind?' Gray asked.

'Their school friends?' Holly shrugged. 'I don't think that will be a problem. Little kids move on. Friends come and go.' She smiled. 'Don't look so worried, Gray. Josh is cracking his neck to get to your ranch.'

Somewhat reassured, Gray had to ask the question that really bothered him. 'About Anna's nightmares—'

'Yes?'

'Do you know why she has them? Could it be because she was with Chelsea when it…when the aneurism…happened?'

'There's a good chance.' Holly dropped her gaze to her

glass. 'Chelsea collapsed when she was in the middle of making Anna a peanut butter sandwich.'

It was almost too awful to imagine. Poor Anna. Poor Chelsea. For a moment he couldn't think past the horror of it. How helpless and terrified Anna must have felt and, quite possibly, even guilty.

He sighed heavily. 'Does Josh have nightmares, too?'

Holly's dark hair rippled as she shook her head. 'I think Josh is naturally more resilient than Anna. But he rang for the ambulance, so he knows he did everything he could. I'm sure that's helped him, even if it's only at some subconscious level.'

It made sense, and the reminder of his son's quick thinking caused a small glow of pride. But poor Anna shouldn't feel guilty. 'There must be so much I need to understand. Is there anything else you should warn me about?'

Frowning, Holly took another sip of wine before she answered. 'I actually wish Josh showed more signs of grief. He's been bottling it in and I'm sure a good cry would do him good.'

'He probably thinks crying is for girls.'

'Probably. My brothers would agree.' Holly sighed. 'He probably needs to be encouraged to talk about it.'

Gray grimaced. *Talking about feelings? Sharing emotions with others?* That was so not his scene. Weren't women supposed to be so much better at it than guys? All his life, he'd been a man of action, not words.

Watching him, Holly said, 'I guess you must be very busy running your ranch. I assume you've hired a nanny to help with the children.'

'Ah…' Gray drew a sharp breath. 'So far, I've organised a team to look after the mustering, so that frees me up quite a bit. My plan was to wait till I saw Anna and Josh—and saw how they were. I thought I'd take them home, help them to settle in first, then look around for someone suitable.'

He set his empty glass on the coffee table. 'There wouldn't be any point in hiring a nanny they didn't like.'

'No. It will need to be the right person.'

Holly looked away quickly as if she didn't want him to see her eyes, but Gray was sure he'd caught a glitter of tears and his throat tightened. He'd expected her to be anxious to be free of his kids, but was she upset at the thought of saying goodbye to them?

It was so difficult for a family to span two hemispheres. There was always someone who missed out.

She turned to him again, her eyes extra-wide. 'So will Anna and Josh be involved when you choose their new nanny?'

'They'll be consulted.' Gray thought this was only fair. 'Do you have any advice?' he added, trying to be diplomatic.

'I…I'll give it some thought.' She shifted her position, uncurling her legs.

He couldn't help watching. Her legs were long and shapely and her toenails were painted a deep sexy red. In her Oriental dressing gown, with her dark hair shining in the soft light, she made a charming picture. Like a painting.

Girl at Midnight.

He thought how perfect it would be—from his children's point of view, of course—if Holly could continue on as their nanny. She understood them so well, far better than he did, and they clearly loved her. Added to that, she had teaching skills and, with her help, the transition to Australia would be almost painless.

It would never happen, of course. Holly had already told

him she was about to start a new career in the US. Why would she give that up and go all the way to the Australian Outback?

She was a city girl. She was his ex-wife's cousin, for crying out loud. She was educated and cultured, just as Chelsea had been. If she hated his place the way Chelsea had, her attitude could rub off on his kids.

Gray realised that Holly was already on her feet.

'Thanks for the wine,' she said.

'Would you like another glass?'

She shook her head. 'I need to hit the sack. Tomorrow is another day and all that.'

Her voice was tight, so tight it almost cracked. Without another word, she set the wine glass on the kitchen bench and hurried away.

She was upset. Had she been able to tell what he was thinking?

In bed, Gray lay wide awake, his thoughts running amok, trailing through the events of the day, and inevitably through the dizzying highs and lows of his romance with Chelsea. He'd met his children's mother while she was travelling in North Queensland with a touring American dance troupe, but he'd made so many mistakes…so many wrong turns…

He'd never seen a girl so delicate and fair, so perfectly beautiful in every way. He'd never looked into a woman's eyes and fallen from a great height.

It had been a classic case of love at first sight, with all the usual symptoms—the thunderbolt to the heart, the obsession.

With the recklessness of youth, Gray had followed Chelsea back to America. In New York he'd courted her with the single-minded passion of a young man desperately in love.

A hasty engagement, a wedding in Central Park and a bliss-ful honeymoon in Paris...

Then back to Jabiru Creek Station. To the Outback.

Within the first month, Chelsea had realised her mis-take. She'd loved Gray—about that there had never been any doubt—but in the Australian Outback his precious bride had wilted like a flower without water.

His throat ached now as he remembered the tears stream-ing down her face as she'd confronted him.

We've made a mistake, Gray, haven't we? Don't you think we should separate now, before this gets too complicated? You're a good man. I should have been more honest. I didn't want to hurt you.

Of course, he should have given in then. It was so easy now to look back and to see how foolish and blinded he'd been—how he'd kissed her tears and begged her shamelessly.

You must stay, Chelsea. Please, please give it a go.

It was only a few weeks later that she'd realised she was pregnant so, of course, she'd stayed...

'You wake him up.'

'No, you.'

Childish giggling penetrated Gray's sleep. *Damn.* Was it morning already?

It had taken him hours to fall asleep and he felt absolutely stuffed, unable to move, like an elephant paralysed by a stun gun. Perhaps, if he lay very still, his children would creep away again and leave him to sleep.

Not a chance. Already small hands were poking and shak-ing him.

'Dad! Dad!'

He groaned in a low protest.

'Daddy!' That was Anna's voice, now suddenly panic-stricken.

His eyes snapped open, then he cringed from the bright daylight flooding the room. 'Good morning,' he groaned. 'What time is it?'

'It's really late,' Josh told him. 'We had breakfast ages and ages ago.'

Gray struggled onto one elbow, yawned and rubbed a hand over sleep-bleary eyes.

'Are you all right, Daddy?' Anna still sounded worried.

'Yeah, chicken. I'm fine.' He yawned again. 'Just sleepy. My body thinks it's still in Australia.'

He swung his legs over the side of the bed and sat for a minute, elbows propped on his knees, holding his dazed head in his hands. Jet lag was taking its toll.

'Holly said to tell you she's made a fresh pot of coffee,' Josh announced.

Bless Holly. Coffee was exactly what he needed. As soon as he'd had a shower.

Gray ruffled his kids' hair. 'So what have you two got planned for today?'

'Packing!' they chorused.

'You're kidding?' How could they look so excited? 'Don't tell me packing's fun?'

'Sure, Dad. It's great fun. Holly's playing a new game with us. We're putting all our toys in a magic rocket box, and it's going to take off for Australia all by itself.'

'Wow. How about that?'

Gray had to hand it to Holly. She sure had a way with his kids. Damn pity she wasn't coming home with them.

As the hot water in the shower streamed over him, he reminded himself why he mustn't put any pressure on Holly to help him out. She'd already gone above and beyond for his children, and now she had a life of her own to lead. Holly was a good sport and she would never let on that she was cracking her neck to be free of her commitments here. But he knew she must be keen to get on with her new career and to start dating again, find a new boyfriend.

He wouldn't appeal to her good nature…couldn't exploit her genuine affection for his kids by trying to talk her into coming with them. That would be nothing short of emotional blackmail.

Just the same, Gray wished he felt more confident in his ability to raise his kids.

Their education was his major worry.

For all kinds of reasons Gray's own parents had totally stuffed up his schooling. Just thinking about his lack of education triggered unwelcome memories of his parents' harsh and heated bickering. He found himself remembering his mother's fits of crying and his father's sulky, blustering anger and his innards twisted.

Truth to tell, his formal schooling had finished almost as soon as it started, around the same time as his parents' divorce. However, it was only much later in his adult years that Gray had fully understood the handicap he carried. By then he'd developed a tough veneer and he'd managed to bluff his way through most challenges, never realising that his failings would come back to bite him, that he'd let his wife down…

And now he was in danger of letting his kids down…

No. There was no way he would allow Anna and Josh to grow up with the limitations he'd endured. But if he wanted to give them the very best chance, he needed help. He needed someone exactly like Holly.

If only she was free…

* * *

We've done well, Holly thought at the end of a full day of packing and, thanks to Gray's involvement, it had been relatively painless. Gray's sense of humour—a side of him she'd never really seen before—had saved a few awkward moments when decisions over toys might have ended in tears.

And then he'd surprised her further by cooking dinner.

'Because you've been working so hard,' he'd said with an endearingly shy smile that sent her stomach fluttering. 'And only if you like spaghetti bolognese. I'm afraid there's a limit to my kitchen skills.'

Spaghetti bolognese was absolutely fine, Holly assured him. Unfortunately, anything seemed fine when he sent her those smiles.

Except she didn't want to be susceptible to his smiles, did she? She was simply grateful for the chai latte he'd brought her from the drugstore two and a half blocks away, as well as the chance to soak in the tub and change her clothes before dinner, and then enjoy a meal she hadn't had to cook.

Over dinner, Anna and Josh talked about Australia. They were very excited to hear that Gray had an airstrip on his property and that his mail and supplies were delivered by aeroplane.

'We'll fly to Normanton,' Gray explained, 'and then we'll drive home to Jabiru from there.'

We'll drive home to Jabiru...

Holly pictured Gray and his children in a big SUV, skimming over wide red plains towards a distant homestead, and she was swamped by a wave of loneliness.

What was wrong with her? She'd known all along that this would happen. But she still couldn't help feeling miserable.

Everyone who was important in her life was being taken from her—Chelsea, Brandon, and now Anna and Josh.

I'll start again and build a new life around my new job.

Right now, it was hard to feel happy about that.

Suddenly she realised Josh was asking his dad about their new school.

To Holly's surprise, Gray's ears reddened. He looked pained and cleared his throat. 'The school in the Outback is a bit different from what you're used to.'

'How different?'

'It's called School of the Air.'

'School of the Air?' This time it was Holly who butted in. She couldn't help it. Her interest was thoroughly piqued. 'How does that work?'

Gray smiled crookedly. 'It's like a normal classroom, but the classes are held over the radio. There are children living in homesteads scattered all over the Outback and each homestead has a special transceiver. They send messages back and forth. The teacher can talk to all of the pupils and they can talk to each other.' He shrugged. 'It seems to work really well.'

'School over the radio? Wow. That sounds totally awesome.' Josh couldn't have looked more excited if he'd been told there were pet baby dinosaurs at his new school.

'It sounds amazing,' Holly agreed, thoroughly intrigued. To her surprise, she felt quite jealous of the nanny who would mentor Anna and Josh as they came to grips with this unorthodox schoolroom.

She shot the children sparkling grins. 'Aren't you two lucky?'

Josh, twirling spaghetti onto his fork, nodded enthusiastically.

Anna, however, looked uncertain. She turned to Holly. 'Will you still be our nanny?'

Holly held her breath, not trusting herself to answer this question without giving her feelings away.

To her relief, Gray answered for her. 'Holly can't come to Australia, Anna. You know that. But we're going to find a nice Australian nanny.'

Anna drooped. 'I want Holly. And I like my school here. Why do you have to live in Australia? Why can't you live in New York?'

Holly saw the sudden bleakness in Gray's eyes, the wavering of his smile. Even though he'd sounded confident about finding a *nice Australian nanny,* he was obviously worried by Anna's reaction.

She'd been determined to keep out of this conversation, but her heart was melting at the sight of Gray's discomfort and she felt compelled to jump to his aid.

'How could your dad live in this apartment?' she asked with a deliberate smile. 'What would he do with all his cattle?'

Anna shrugged. 'Put them in storage?'

'As if.' Josh groaned and rolled his eyes.

An awkward hush fell. Gray continued to look worried and Anna looked as if she might cry. Her lower lip trembled.

Watching her, Josh began to look anxious, too. 'It's going to be great living with Dad,' he urged his sister softly.

'Not if Holly can't come with us.'

Holly saw Gray's shoulders stiffen at the same moment she felt her face flame.

Then Anna burst into tears.

'Hey,' Holly said, quickly drawing the little girl onto her

lap, and not daring to catch Gray's eyes again. 'How can you cry in the middle of this lovely dinner your dad has cooked?'

Anna's response was to cling to Holly tightly, sobbing louder than ever. 'Why can't you come with us?'

It was a truly difficult moment. Holly knew Gray was anxious about his ability to care for his fragile daughter and now her tearful reaction would only deepen his apprehension.

But, despite this, Holly couldn't help feeling electrified, too, as if she'd touched a live wire. Anna had innocently brought into the open the very question that had rattled around in her head all day.

The thing was—school in the US didn't start again till the autumn, which meant she could spend June and July in Australia helping the children to settle in to their new home and school, and she'd still be back in time to start her new teaching job.

And now that she'd heard about this School of the Air, the idea was especially intriguing.

Of course, it wouldn't be plain sailing. After the past hectic months she would have liked a proper vacation and, if she went to Australia, she'd still be 'working'. She'd have very little chance to catch her breath before she had to start in the new school.

Then again, she didn't have any particular plans for the next few weeks—and she certainly didn't fancy going home to Vermont, where she'd spend her time either avoiding Brandon or being showered with sympathy from family and friends. And she *was* intrigued by the set-up in the Outback—and, of course, she would love to see Anna and Josh happily settled.

The only negative factor was the silly frissons that danced

over her skin whenever Gray Kidman came too near—but Holly was sure she'd soon conquer that foolish tendency.

For heaven's sake, there wasn't any danger she'd actually fall for poor Chelsea's ex when the pain of being dumped by Brandon hadn't even healed. She planned to be mega-cautious around all men in future—especially the attractive ones.

'Why don't you tuck the children into bed and read them a couple of stories?' Holly suggested to Gray after dinner.

To her surprise, he looked unhappy, as if she'd asked him to help with some horrible chore like cleaning the toilets with a toothbrush.

'But won't they expect you to do it?' he asked.

His obvious nervousness puzzled Holly. Perhaps Anna's tears at dinner had upset him more than she'd realised. She tried to reassure him. 'Anna and Josh will love it if you read to them tonight.'

When Gray still looked worried, she added, 'They need to get used to small changes, and this would be a good first step.'

He swallowed uncomfortably. 'I guess.'

'Their favourite books are stacked on the nightstand.'

'Okay.'

As he left the kitchen, heading for the children's room, Holly saw a deep red tide that was *not* sunburn staining the back of his neck. The sight of it caused an ache right in the centre of her chest. Was he nervous about being alone with his children? Was he afraid Anna would cry again? Should she have offered to be there, too?

She almost called out to him, but there was something about the resolute straightness of his shoulders and the purposeful length of his stride that stopped her. He was like a soldier marching off to war. No, she was being fanciful.

And in the end everything was fine.

While Holly cleared the table and stacked the dishwasher, she could hear the deep masculine rumble of Gray's voice and the bell-like tinkle of the children's laughter. They were clearly having a great time.

With the kitchen tidy, she went into the living room and tried to relax, curled on the sofa with her current paperback novel. As soon as Gray was finished with the bedtime stories, she would talk to him about Australia. She only wished the thought of their conversation didn't make her feel so inordinately excited.

It was quite a while before Gray returned, however, and he was smiling, his blue eyes reflecting relief and a new contentment.

'That seemed to go well,' Holly said warmly.

'Yeah.' He stood in the centre of the room, hands resting lightly on his hips, and he grinned. 'Seems like I passed my first test as a single dad.'

'That's great. I suppose Josh pressured you into reading the pirate story.'

'No, actually. I told them a completely different story tonight.'

'Oh, right.' She couldn't help asking. 'Which one?'

Gray shrugged. 'I made one up. About Hector Owl and Timothy Mouse.' He shot her a shrewdly narrowed glance. 'Your experts wouldn't object, would they?'

'N-no, of course not. I'm just surprised. Amazed, actually. I've loved stories all my life but, even if you paid me thousands, I couldn't make one up on the spot. Anna and Josh seemed to love yours.'

Still standing in the middle of the living room carpet, Gray shrugged again and scratched at the shadow of stubble on his jaw, then he quickly changed the subject. 'Fancy another glass of that wine we opened last night?'

'Why not?' Wine might help to steady her nerves.

While he collected the bottle and glasses, Holly set her book aside and stood quickly, taking a surreptitious peek at her reflection in the long mirror on the opposite wall. It was silly. Really, she knew the neatness of her hair, the fit of her jeans or the flounces on her cream silk blouse were of no interest to Gray. But the conversation she was about to launch was almost a job interview. Checking her appearance was an automatic reflex.

'You look great,' Gray said, coming back into the room more quickly than she expected.

Flustered, she fought off a blush and sat quickly, wishing she could think of a witty retort.

'No, honestly, that new hairstyle suits you,' he said, handing her a glass of the rich Australian red.

A trip to the hairdresser had been part of Holly's post-Brandon recovery plan, but she was amazed that Gray had noticed.

'Thanks.' She raised her glass. 'Here's to settling the twins happily in Australia. May it all go super-smoothly.'

'Amen to that.' Gray settled into an armchair and stretched his long legs in front of him, crossing them at the ankles.

Holly tried not to stare, but Gray had a way of catching her eye. His jeans were soft and worn and faded, hugging his strong thighs. His elastic-sided boots were tan and clean and made of finely cut leather. Lamplight caught the dark sheen of his hair and accented the ruggedly masculine planes and angles of his face and the shadow on his jaw.

There was no denying the man was bone-deep sexy. At Chelsea's wedding, even Holly's grandmother had been all girlish and coy in Gray's presence.

Perhaps she shouldn't say anything about Australia after all. She didn't want to spend the next couple of months stealing sneak peeks at Chelsea's ex just because she was currently without a boyfriend. She was supposed to be getting on with her exciting new single life, making plans for her brilliant career.

She drank some wine, buying time to compose herself, but her brain refused to let go of one particular thought and suddenly the words just tumbled out. 'I've been thinking that you might need help with the children when you first arrive in Australia.'

Gray nodded calmly. 'I've been thinking the same thing. I wondered if I should phone ahead to an employment agency.'

'An agency in Australia?'

'Yes.'

Holly felt a surge of emotion, almost panic. 'I'm at a loose end.'

Oh, cringe. How annoying that she could say something in her head all day and it sounded fine, but now, as soon as she said it out loud, it sounded utterly dumb.

It didn't help that Gray's head snapped back as if he'd been punched in the jaw. He was staring at her as if she'd announced she was planning to fly into outer space. On a broomstick.

'How do you mean—a loose end?' he asked quietly.

'I'm free—for a month or so.'

'I thought you were starting work in a school.'

Holly's mouth was suddenly parched. She took a sip from her glass and to her dismay her hand was shaking. 'The schools here are about to close for the summer.' She wished her voice wasn't shaking as well. She cleared her throat. 'I wouldn't be expected to start in a new job until August, or possibly September.'

His eyes widened. 'So you're free through the rest of June and July?'

'As long as I'm still in phone or Internet contact. For interviews.' Seeing the surprise in Gray's eyes, Holly's nervousness accelerated. 'It's just a thought. A possible option.'

'But it's a fantastic option.' His eyes were gleaming, and his face broke into a fully fledged smile. 'You'd be perfect.'

For God's sake, stay cool.

'Do you have a passport?' Gray asked, clearly thinking more calmly than she was.

Holly nodded. She'd studied Italian at school and her parents had scraped and saved to send her on a fabulous school excursion to Tuscany. Her passport was still valid.

Gray's smile was replaced by a quick frown. 'Are you sure you wouldn't mind giving up so much time?'

'I'd be happy to come. I'm really interested in this School of the Air. I'd love to see how it works and, of course, I'd really like to help Anna and Josh to settle in.'

Gray was frowning again and he launched to his feet, pacing the room as if something troubled him. 'I promise you'd have nothing to worry about—' He swallowed and looked awkward. 'I mean—accompanying me and the kids—no one out there will jump to conclusions about us. I...I mean no one will assume we're a couple.'

Looking distinctly embarrassed, he gave a forced laugh, as if he was trying to make a joke but knew it wasn't funny.

To Holly's dismay, she felt her face flame. 'Well, that's good,' she hurried to assure him. 'And you certainly don't need to worry from my end. Romance is totally off my agenda. I've just broken up a long-term relationship, and it was harrowing to say the least, so it'll be a very long time before I start looking for any kind of—' She couldn't quite finish the sentence.

Gray nodded thoughtfully, his eyes sending a message of sympathy, and Holly felt a clear wave of relief to know that they had the ground rules sorted.

Just the same, she couldn't help also feeling the teensiest sting over Gray's mega-eagerness to make it clear that he wasn't romantically interested in her.

How crazy was that? She dropped her gaze to her wine and reminded herself exactly why she'd made this offer. Gray needed help, Anna and Josh needed a nanny, and she needed to feel she'd done everything she could for Chelsea's children.

She was the perfect person to help Anna and Josh to adjust to their new life in Australia.

'So that's definite, then?' Gray was serious again. Businesslike. 'You'll come?'

Suddenly it felt inevitable. Predestined. As if this question was always going to be asked. And the answer was always going to be…

'Yes.'

CHAPTER FIVE

GRAY WAS SURPRISED by how over-the-top pleased and light-hearted he felt now that he knew Holly would be accompanying them on the return journey.

Now, the challenge of becoming a single father no longer loomed as forbidding as Mount Everest and, over the following days as they finalised the packing, even Anna came to look on the move as a huge adventure.

By the time the foursome reached JFK Airport, they were all keyed up and looking forward to the flight.

It was while they were waiting to get through Security, with the line shuffling ever closer to the X-ray machines, that Holly received a call on her cellphone.

Gray assumed it was yet another of her many friends ringing to wish her well and he watched with a ready smile as she answered the phone. He saw the sudden tension in her eyes.

She turned away, her dark hair swinging with the movement. She pressed her fingers to one ear to block out the airport noise as she frowned and gave her caller her full attention.

Gray realised he was watching her more closely than was

polite, but he couldn't help it. Holly might not have Chelsea's beauty, but she had something else—something, he suspected, more lasting than prettiness. At times like now, when her face was animated and her dark eyes were sparkling with excitement, she looked utterly enchanting.

Snatches of her conversation drifted his way.

'Yes…yes…that's wonderful…yes. Oh, wow, thank you.' And then, 'Australia…a family commitment…just away for the summer…' She was nodding and smiling, looking flushed and pleased.

The phone call ended just as it was their turn to go through Security, so it wasn't till they'd reached the other side and had collected their watches, wallets, passports and backpacks that Holly turned to Gray with a wide and happy smile.

'So it was good news after all?' he asked.

'Yes. At first I thought it might have been Brand—might have been someone ringing to say goodbye. But it's even better than that. It looks like I've landed a job.'

To Gray's surprise, he felt a snaking of alarm. How would this affect their plans? Was Holly still free to help? 'When do you start?'

'Not till August.' Holly's smile widened into a beaming grin, then she gave a little skip and punched the air. 'I can't believe it. This is my dream job! My first choice. The school I've always wanted to teach at.'

Gray nodded, willing himself to be pleased for Holly. Judging by her excitement, this was very important. She must have been the pick of the applicants. Good for her!

It hit him then that he knew very little about her. It seemed she was very smart—an ace teacher—and his kids were lucky to have her even for a short time.

He was pleased for her. In fact, he was pleased for all of

them. Everything was working out perfectly. By August his children would be settled into their new home and school and, with Holly's help and approval, he'd have hired a new nanny. Then Holly would head for home to start this new flash job.

It made absolutely no sense that he couldn't dredge up more enthusiasm. It was sheer selfishness not to be happy for Holly.

'Fantastic,' he said and he held out his hand. 'Congratulations.'

At last, he cracked a smile.

Landing in Sydney was a total surprise for Holly.

Throughout the journey, she'd been mentally preparing herself for the Australian Outback. It was, she knew, a challenging place of wide red plains, isolation, dust and heat.

She hadn't given much thought to Sydney, hadn't expected to fly in over gorgeous golden beaches to a big and modern city heart crowded with skyscrapers. She also hadn't expected to find Gray's mother waiting to greet them at Sydney Airport.

Holly had vague memories of Sasha Carlisle from the wedding. She was tall and silver-haired, strikingly attractive and well dressed. Today she was wearing a white linen trouser suit, with sparkling jewellery at her wrist and a long black and white silk scarf draped with unfussy elegance. There was no doubt about it; she'd nailed casual chic for the older woman.

Beside her, Holly, in jeans and a crumpled T-shirt, with her hair hanging limp after more than twenty hours in a pressurised cabin, felt decidedly drab. But she soon forgot about that as she watched the greeting between mother and son.

No warm hugs. Just a cool—

'Hello, dear.'

'Hello, Mother.'

And an expertly made-up cheek held at an angle for Gray to kiss.

The tension was so thick Holly would have needed a very sharp knife to cut through it. It evaporated quickly, however, when Gray's mother turned her attention to her grandchildren.

'Sweethearts,' she cried, opening her arms to Anna and Josh. 'You remember your Australian granny, don't you?'

Fortunately, the children obliged her with warm smiles, and they submitted to hugs and kisses without complaint.

'Your granny's missed you so much.'

Brightly wrapped packages were produced from a voluminous designer handbag, and Holly was pleased to see that Anna and Josh looked quite thrilled and remembered to say thank you.

Gray placed a hand on Holly's shoulder, almost making her jump out of her skin. 'You might not remember my mother, Sasha Carlisle.'

With her shoulder still tingling from the warmth of his touch, Holly held out her hand. 'I do remember you, Mrs Carlisle. How do you do?'

Gray's mother shook hands super-carefully, as if she were afraid Holly might be grubby.

'Holly was one of Chelsea's bridesmaids,' Gray reminded her.

'Ah, yes, and now she's the nanny.'

'Holly's going to help us with School of the Air,' Josh explained importantly.

'Is she now?' Sasha's eyebrows lifted high and she shot

a chilling but meaningful glance to Gray. 'Is she properly trained?'

Bristling at being discussed as if she wasn't even there, Holly decided to speak up for herself. 'I'm a fully qualified English teacher.'

The older woman smiled faintly. 'Thank heavens for small mercies.'

What was going on here?

The chilling tension was broken by Anna, who urgently wanted to find a bathroom. Grateful to escape, Holly accompanied her and, by the time they returned, Sasha had left.

'My mother had a function she needed to attend,' Gray said smoothly. The expression in his eyes lightened and he smiled at Holly. 'Come on, let's find a taxi.'

Their evening in Sydney was fun. The four of them dined out at a fabulous Thai restaurant and then they walked back to their hotel, enjoying the mild winter night and the brightly lit streets. The children were drooping by this stage, however, and Gray had to carry Anna for the last block. She and Josh were so tired they fell straight into bed and were asleep before anyone could think of finding a story to read.

Gray stayed behind to share a nightcap with Holly in the cosy sitting room that was part of the luxurious suite he'd booked for her and the children.

They found ice and glasses and little bottles in the mini-bar and then they sat in deep comfy armchairs. Holly wasn't sure how relaxed she'd be, or what she and Gray would talk about, so she was totally thrown when he steered the conversation to her break-up with Brandon.

'What went wrong?' he asked, watching her through slightly narrowed eyes.

'Oh, the usual.' Holly had only talked about her break-up with her mom and one or two girlfriends, and it felt weird to try to explain it to a man she hardly knew. 'He was more interested in another woman.'

'So he was a fool,' Gray said sympathetically.

'Yes, he was a total idiot.' She forced a smile. 'But it was partly my fault, I guess. I moved away to New York and, in this case, absence did not make his heart grow fonder.'

Gray nodded and took a thoughtful sip of his drink. 'Don't know if it helps…but after Chelsea took off with the kids…I thought I'd never get over it, and yet, after a time, the worst feelings began to fade.'

Holly wanted to ask him what had gone wrong in his marriage, but it felt too intrusive to ask Gray when Chelsea had been so close-lipped about it.

Instead, she said, 'I guess Chelsea must have loved it here in Sydney.'

Gray's smile vanished as if someone had flicked a switch. 'I'm sure Chelsea must have told you how she felt about Sydney.'

'No.' Holly blinked. 'If she did, I don't remember. She would never say much at all about her time in Australia.'

He downed a hefty slug of Scotch and scowled into his glass, and Holly felt compelled to explain her comment. 'It's just that I was surprised to see how busy and cosmopolitan it is here. Bright lights. Masses of skyscrapers. Lots of people. So many theatres and restaurants. It's everything Chelsea loved.'

She watched Gray's mouth thin into a downward curve.

He sighed. 'Yeah, Chelsea loved Sydney all right. She used to fly down here for two or three days and stay for two or three weeks.'

'Oh.' Sensing that she'd awoken bad memories, Holly tried to make amends. 'I suppose she dropped in to chat to the dance companies here and—'

Suddenly, she wasn't sure how to finish what she'd started. She was trying to defend her cousin when she had no idea really…

'This place had *everything* Chelsea needed,' Gray said bleakly.

Holly wondered if this had been the heart of the problem with their marriage. 'Did you ever—' she began hesitantly. 'I mean, I don't suppose you…um…considered moving here? Or…or living closer…'

'No.'

There was quiet vehemence in that single syllable. Gray's face was a grim stony mask as he stared down at his almost empty glass.

'I guess it would have been difficult to move.'

She was trying to be diplomatic, but she knew she was on shaky ground. Just the same, she couldn't help thinking that if Gray had really loved Chelsea he might have been prepared to make sacrifices. Couldn't he have given up cattle farming and tried something more suited to his wife's temperament and talents?

If he'd wanted to save his marriage…

'Moving was out of the question,' he said with a marked air of finality.

Right.

It was time to drop this line of conversation. Holly wondered if stubborn inflexibility was Gray Kidman's Achilles heel.

Or was that a bit harsh? After all, her cousin had been

adamant when she married him that she was happy to give up her career to live with him in his Outback.

Whatever. It's none of my business.

To change the subject, Holly said, 'I'm looking forward to tomorrow and finally getting to see your place.'

She saw Gray's shoulders relax then, and he looked directly into her eyes and smiled slowly in a way that started her tummy fluttering. 'So am I,' he said. 'I'm always glad to get home.'

The warmth in his eyes suggested that he wasn't just voicing a cliché. He really meant it. He felt nostalgic about his home in the vast empty Outback. Holly understood this. She always felt a catch in her throat whenever she drove back to her family's farm and saw the green pastures and red barns of Vermont.

Tomorrow Anna and Josh would reach their new home. Holly hoped, for their sakes, but more especially for Gray's sake, that they liked it. Actually, it was her job to make sure that they did.

Gray couldn't sleep.

Leaving his bed, he prowled the length of his hotel room, trying to shrug off the tension that kept him awake. He'd lied to Holly tonight. He'd told her that feelings and memories faded with time but, after his mother's cool reception at the airport today, and his conversation with Holly about Chelsea, he was once again battling with the feelings of inadequacy and failure that had dogged him all his life.

As a child he'd never lived up to his mother's expectations. Hell, he hadn't even come close. He could still hear the way she'd yelled at his father.

The boy's hopeless. Unteachable. A disgrace.

Even now, the memory brought his clenched fist slamming into his palm.

Was he never going to shake off these patterns of failure? First his mother had left Jabiru, never to return, and then his wife had left, and both times he'd known he was a major cause of their problems.

If he'd been able to, he would have taken Chelsea to live in Sydney, as Holly had so innocently suggested. He would have taken her to New York or wherever she wanted to live.

But, thanks to his lack of schooling, he was unemployable in the city, and even if he'd sold his property and invested in stocks and shares to eke out a living, he would have gone mad in the claustrophobic city. After twenty-four hours, he was always chafing at the bit to get away to the bush.

He'd tried his best to love and support Chelsea at Jabiru. When the twins arrived, he'd done everything he could to hold his little family together. He'd been a hands-on father, taking his turn at bathing and changing and walking the floors with the crying infants.

But the timing had been lousy. The babies' arrival had coincided with a downturn in the cattle industry. Overseas markets had collapsed. Money had been tight and, before the babies were six months old, he'd been forced to lay off the fencing contractors and the mechanics he'd hired, and he'd taken on these jobs himself.

When these tasks were added to the usual demands of running a vast cattle property, his available time to help at the homestead had been minimal. He'd kept on his housekeeper, who'd also helped with the twins, but the toll on Chelsea had been visible.

Gray had been shocked to see her growing thin and drawn and faded, so he'd sent her to Sydney for short breaks. And, as he'd admitted to Holly, the times she'd spent away had become longer and longer.

When his wife had told him she needed to go home to New York, he'd let her go, taking the children with her, even though he hadn't been free to accompany them. By then he'd known that to try to hold her was too cruel.

When she'd rung from New York to tell him she wasn't coming back, Gray had been heartsick but not surprised. He'd agreed to the divorce, accepting that he'd had no other option.

He'd tried his hardest and failed, and he had no idea what else he could do. He would rather admit defeat than watch his wife become trapped and embittered the way his mother had been.

But his sense of failure was overwhelming, even worse now that Chelsea had passed away. He hated to think that his love had made any part of her short life unhappy and he was determined that he wouldn't fail her children as well. He couldn't, he mustn't.

These next two months were critical. He would be guided by Holly and he wouldn't be too proud to accept her advice. Sure, there were bound to be humiliating moments when his inadequacies were exposed once more, and Holly would probably be as disdainful of his home as Chelsea had been.

But he could face another woman's scorn—as long as his kids still looked up to him—and as long as he didn't let them down.

By the following afternoon, they were finally in Far North Queensland, barrelling over flat, pale grasslands in a big four-wheel drive which threw up a continuous plume of dust. The vehicle had a luggage rack on top, and bull bars protecting the engine—from kangaroos, Gray told them—and there were water tanks on board as well. To Holly it felt like an expedition.

Wide open plains sprinkled with straggly gum trees and silvery grey Brahman cattle stretched in every direction. Flocks of white birds wheeled in the blue sky like fluttering pieces of paper.

In the back seat, the children watched the panorama excitedly, waiting for their first kangaroo sighting.

'This is my country,' Gray told Holly and his emphasis on the word *country* seemed to instil it with special meaning.

Holly had to agree there was something primitive but almost spiritual about the vast stretch of empty space. She could feel an awareness of something greater than herself and, strangely, it wasn't unlike the way she'd also felt the first time she'd walked into the huge book-lined silence of the New York City Library.

Every so often their vehicle would climb over a rocky ridge, giving a view of grasslands stretching for ever. At other times the road would dip downwards to cross a single lane wooden bridge over a stream. Some creeks only had a concrete ford disappearing beneath brown muddy water.

'There's no water here at all in the dry season,' Gray told her.

They came to a wider river, so deep that when Gray pushed the vehicle through, the water threatened to seep under the doors.

He grinned at Holly. 'This is where I did my ankle in, but the creek was flowing a lot faster then, of course.'

The tops of the banks were still covered in flattened grass and the small twisted trees were all leaning in one direction, clear evidence of how high and savage the floodwaters had been.

Holly hated to think what it must have been like to try to drive through it.

'I thought you had an airstrip at Jabiru,' she said. 'Couldn't you have flown instead of driving?'

Gray shook his head. 'The ground was too boggy for a normal plane to land—and all the choppers were needed for emergency rescues. I waited for the water to go down a little, then took my chances.'

How scary. Holly shuddered, as she tried to imagine pushing a vehicle through a raging flood.

'And that was when you broke your ankle?' she asked.

'I was testing the bottom before I drove across. Foot went down into a crevice.'

'You weren't on your own, were you?'

'Sure.'

'You mean you had to rescue yourself?'

'It was either that or—' He flicked a glance over his shoulder and dropped his voice. 'Or this pair would have been orphans.'

Holly shivered, chastened to remember how she'd rolled her eyes and complained loudly when Gray had telephoned to say he was held up in Australia by floods and a broken ankle. Now that she was here, and could see where the accident had happened, she was appalled.

No wonder Gray gave off an aura of hidden toughness and competence.

As they cleared the creek and continued over flat land again, squawks from the back seat reminded Holly of her duties. Anna and Josh were pinching each other and poking out tongues. Clear signs of boredom. Very soon they'd start, *Are we there yet?*

She rummaged in her bag and produced a CD. 'This might keep them entertained,' she said, waving it at Gray.

'Good idea. What is it?'

'Winnie-the-Pooh.'

His brow wrinkled. 'Never heard of them. Are they a new band?'

She laughed. 'Oh, that's a good one.'

He turned, sending her a puzzled grin. 'Seriously, who are they?'

Her mouth dropped open. How could he ask? 'You know Winnie-the-Pooh—the children's story. You must have read it when you were little. The bear who loves honey.'

He pulled a face and shrugged. 'Whatever. We've got about three-quarters of an hour to go, so if you think it will keep the kids happy, bung it on.'

Bemused, she slipped the CD into the player and soon the cabin was filled with the storyteller's beautifully modulated English voice. The children stopped squabbling and listened. Gray seemed to listen attentively, too, and he actually chuckled at the antics of the famous characters as if the funny bits were a brand new experience for him.

How curious.

The CD hadn't finished when they turned in at big metal gates beneath an overhead sign with *Jabiru Creek* painted in white.

'We're here!' Anna cried enthusiastically. 'This is your place, isn't it, Daddy?'

'That's right, pumpkin, but we're not at the homestead yet. It's about another fifteen minutes.'

Resigned, the children slumped back in their seats.

'I'll get the gates,' Holly announced, opening her passenger door.

Gray's eyebrows shot high. 'You don't have to.'

'It's fine,' she called over her shoulder as she jumped down from the vehicle. 'I'm a farm girl.'

She turned, saw the surprise in his blue eyes.

'When were you on a farm?'

'I grew up on a farm in Vermont.'

Through the dusty windscreen she saw his smile and a new light in his eyes—keen interest, extra warmth. She blushed and felt flustered. *Idiot.* Abruptly, she turned and paid studious attention to the gates.

By the time the gates were shut once more and she'd climbed back in the cabin, Gray was closing his satellite phone. 'I let them know at the homestead that we're nearly home. Almost time to put the kettle on.'

Anna leaned forward as far as her seatbelt would allow. 'Will we see the puppies? Are they borned yet, Daddy?'

'Sorry, I forgot to ask.' Gray grinned back at his daughter. 'You'll soon find out.'

They drove on and the CD resumed, preventing conversation or questions about Holly's life on the farm. But Holly couldn't stop thinking about the surprised delight in Gray's eyes. Why should it matter where she'd grown up?

The bush was thicker now, and the gum trees threw shadows across the narrow wheel ruts that formed the rough track. Several times, Gray had to brake suddenly as a kangaroo appeared on the edge of the road, bounding unannounced from a shadowy clump of trees.

Each kangaroo sighting was a source of huge excitement for Holly and the children, but Holly could tell that the animals' sudden arrival on the track was dangerous. In the fading light they were hard to see. She switched off the CD so Gray could concentrate.

'That wasn't a bad story,' he said. Then he called over his shoulder, 'Hey, kids, what do you reckon? Is that Pooh bear almost as good as Hector Owl and Timothy Mouse?'

'Nah. Winnie-the-Pooh's for babies,' Josh replied, even though he'd spent the best part of an hour listening to the CD quite happily. 'Hector Owl's much better. Hector Owl's awesome. He killed the Bad Bush Rat.'

Holly smiled. How could poor Winnie compete with a murderous owl?

But it still puzzled her that Gray spoke as if he'd never heard of Winnie-the-Pooh. How could that be? Surely almost every child in the US and Australia was familiar with the honey-loving bear.

Should she be dreading what lay ahead? Would Gray's house be as stark and unappealing as that lonely homestead on the back of the playing cards he'd bought?

She was about to find out.

Ahead of them, the track rounded a corner and they emerged into open country once more. Holly saw tall corrals and stockyards, home paddocks fenced with timber instead of the barbed wire she'd seen everywhere else. Then, ahead, more buildings began to appear—machinery sheds, silos, bunk houses, barns, even an aircraft hangar—it was almost a small village.

Clearly Jabiru Creek Station was a much bigger concern than the farms she was used to.

'Which one is your house, Daddy?' Anna wanted to know.

'That place straight ahead with the silver roof.' Gray pointed to a long, low, white timber building surrounded by surprisingly green lawns.

To Holly's relief, Gray's home looked inviting. It was a simple homestead, but it was large and rimmed by verandas. Across the front of the house a deep shady veranda was fringed with hanging baskets filled with ferns, while the verandas on either side were enclosed from floor to ceiling with white timber louvres.

The lawns in front of the house were divided by a gravel path and on either side stood massive shade trees with deep glossy foliage.

'I can see a swing,' Anna shouted, pointing to a rubber tyre hanging by thick ropes from the branch of one of the trees.

'It's waiting for you,' Holly told her, and already she was picturing Anna and Josh playing on this smooth sweep of lawn, swinging in the tyre, riding bikes, throwing balls, chasing puppies...

The front door opened and a woman came out with a beaming smile, wiping her hands on an apron. She was aged somewhere beyond sixty and was dressed in a floral cotton dress, with wisps of grey hair escaping from a haphazard knot on top of her head.

'My housekeeper, Janet,' Gray said as he turned off the engine. 'She helped us to look after the twins when they were babies and she can't wait to see them again.'

Janet looked perfect, Holly thought, watching the woman's happy face glow pink with excitement as she waved to the children.

'Come inside where it's warm,' Janet said when they'd clambered from the car and she'd given them all, including Holly, huge hugs. 'The chill starts early on these winter afternoons, and I've got a heater on in the kitchen.'

As they followed her into the house, which was warm and fragrant with baking smells, Holly thought everything about Gray's home seemed comfortable and welcoming. Her fears, it seemed, were unwarranted.

Of course, first impressions could be deceiving. No doubt Jabiru Creek Station would soon reveal its downside. There had to be a downside. Right now Holly couldn't imagine what it might be, but something had driven Chelsea away from here.

CHAPTER SIX

THAT EVENING THE sky put on a show, as only Outback skies could. A mass of brilliant crystal stars blazed in the vast black dome that arced from one distant horizon to the other. Gray stood on the front steps, drinking in the silence and the grandeur.

After the non-stop pace of New York, the crowds in the busy airports and the bustle of Sydney, it was good to let the tranquillity of his home seep into his veins. Since Chelsea's passing he'd been on a constant roller coaster of worry and despair, but tonight he felt calmer than he had in a long time.

Behind him, in the house, Janet was pottering about in the kitchen and he could hear the clink of cutlery and china as she stowed things away in the big pine dresser. Holly was in the bedroom down the hall, putting his children to bed, calming them after the excitement of their arrival, and the discovery of a basket of tiny three-day-old puppies in the kitchen by the stove.

Gray chuckled, remembering the shining adoration in Anna and Josh's eyes as they'd knelt by the basket, begging permission to pat the little pups that wriggled and squirmed against their mother.

Of course the children had begged to be allowed one puppy each to keep as a pet, and of course Gray had said yes, they could choose their pups as soon as their eyes were open. But no, they couldn't *both* have the all black one, and if there was any fighting neither child would have a puppy.

Holly had been a major help, backing him on this ruling and then diverting the children by offering to read them one of their favourite stories about a runaway cocker spaniel.

Already, he owed a great deal to Holly.

She'd been fabulous while they were travelling, keeping Anna and Josh entertained and comfortable, and remembering to tell them what to expect on each leg of the journey. Gray couldn't help noticing that she wasn't just capable—she was genuinely fond of his children—and he was beginning to suspect that it would be a real wrench for her to finally be parted from them.

She was quite a surprise package, actually. He'd assumed she was like Chelsea, a city girl born and bred.

Today, however, in her simple T-shirt and jeans, she'd deftly unhooked the notoriously tricky rural gate, and she'd looked every inch the country girl she'd claimed to be.

He recalled the cheeky smile she'd tossed over her shoulder when she'd told him that she'd grown up on a farm. Her dark eyes had sparkled and her lips had curled and—

'Gray.'

Holly's voice brought him swinging round.

She was standing in the doorway and she smiled shyly. 'Two little people are waiting for their goodnight kiss.'

'Right.' He spoke a little too gruffly because she'd caught him out. 'Thanks.'

He crossed the veranda to where she stood, backlit by the light spilling down the hall. Her dark eyes were shining and her pretty lips were pink and soft and wonderfully inviting…

It would be so easy, so tempting to ask his children's nanny if she'd like a goodnight kiss, too. She was kissing close and she smelled of flowers and—

And the last thing Gray wanted was to start flirting with Chelsea's young cousin when she'd come to his home as an especially kind favour to his kids.

I must be one post short of a fence.

Relieved that he'd come to his senses in time, he strode on past Holly, down the passage to the room where Anna and Josh were waiting.

Holly lay snuggled beneath a soft, warm duvet in a pretty room that had one doorway leading to a hallway and another onto a veranda. She listened to the night sounds of the Outback, which amounted to silence mostly, punctuated by the occasional owl hoot or the soft, distant lowing of cattle. She thought how amazing it was that she could be so far from Vermont and still hear the same sounds she'd grown up with.

After the long journey she was dog-tired and tonight she'd broken the habit of a lifetime and left the book she was currently reading unopened on her nightstand. Right now, she simply wanted to take a moment, before sleep claimed her, to relive her first evening at Jabiru.

Already, to her surprise, she'd found much to like—this pleasant bedroom, for example, and its old-fashioned double bed with gorgeous brass ends, and the big homey kitchen filled with timber dressers and tempting aromas. The children's room was similar to hers, but was cheery with matching multi-coloured duvets, and Holly really liked the inviting verandas scattered with cane loungers, not to mention the cuter than cute puppies that had so enchanted the children.

She even liked the scents of grass and animals and dust that filtered in from the outdoors. She felt amazingly at home here and, despite the flight inland to Normanton and the long car journey, she found it difficult to remember she was miles and miles from anywhere. She'd expected to feel lonely and isolated, but she only had to look out of her window to see the lights of the stockmen's cottages twinkling in the darkness like friendly stars.

She thought about Chelsea and wondered how she'd felt on her first night in Gray Kidman's home. As a born and bred New Yorker, she might have found it all very strange. The children seemed to have settled in happily enough, however, although Gray wasn't as relaxed as she'd expected. Actually, there was something about him that puzzled her.

Most of the time, he had an air of quiet confidence and competence that was very reassuring. But every so often she caught a hint of his vulnerability, lying surprisingly close beneath his strong exterior. She'd glimpsed it at times when she'd least expected it—like tonight when she'd called him in to say goodnight to Anna and Josh.

Was he more worried about his new responsibilities than she'd realised? Was he scared that his children would soon grow tired of this place and want to hightail it back to New York?

Somehow, Holly didn't think that was likely and she would do her best to make sure Anna and Josh settled in smoothly but, after Chelsea's reaction to Jabiru, she could understand Gray's concern.

As she nestled more snugly under the duvet, she remembered there was one other thing about Gray that had bothered her—

His books.

Or, rather, the lack of his books.

Where were they?

As a lifelong lover of the written word, Holly had always found herself sneaking peeks at other people's bookshelves. It wasn't so much that she was looking for books to read—this time she'd brought a good supply and she could easily order more over the Internet—but she'd always been fascinated by what books revealed about their owners—their hobbies and interests and tastes in fiction.

For her, books had always been a kind of getting-to-know-you shortcut. So far, in Gray's house, she'd seen a few recipe books and women's magazines in the kitchen, but they were obviously Janet's. Where were Gray's books?

Perhaps he was a very orderly man who liked to keep all his reading material in one place—in his study, possibly.

Yes, his study was sure to have floor-to-ceiling bookshelves. Content with that thought, she fell promptly asleep.

Holly was in the depths of sleep when the screams started, so deeply asleep, in fact, that she almost ignored them. One part of her brain urged her to respond, but she felt drugged, glued to the mattress.

But then she remembered it was Anna who was screaming.

Fighting desperate weariness, she opened one eye and saw moonlight streaming through an unfamiliar window. For a frantic moment she panicked. Where was she?

It came in a flash and she sat up, her heart thudding as she threw back the bedclothes. Shivering in the sudden cold—it was winter here, after all—she switched on her bedside lamp, shivered again when her feet met icy floorboards. Regrettably, Outback homes did not have central heating.

But there was no time to hunt for a warm dressing gown. Anna's screams had risen several decibels and she'd wake everybody in the outlying cottages. Holly dashed from her room and down the passage to the children's room.

Gray was already there. In the dark, Holly could see him sitting on the edge of Anna's bed, trying to calm her.

'Shh, Anna,' he was murmuring as he drew the little girl into his arms. 'You're okay, baby. Shh.'

Anna continued to scream.

Holly stepped closer and, although she couldn't see Gray's face, she sensed how helpless he felt. Poor man. She knew he was horrified by his daughter's terror, and tonight he was probably also worried that the screams would alarm everyone within hearing range.

Gently, Holly leaned closer and stroked Anna's hair and her soft cheek. 'Hey, Anna,' she said in her most soothing voice. 'It's okay, honey. You've had another nasty nightmare, but it's all over now. You're okay. I'm here with you, and Daddy's here, too.'

To her relief, the screams began to subside, reducing in time to shuddering sobs.

Beside her, Holly heard Gray's heavy sigh.

'It might be best if I take her back to my bed,' she offered, knowing the strange environment would make it harder for Anna to settle back to sleep this time.

Gray didn't hesitate. 'Okay. Thanks. Let me carry her for you.'

Holly nodded, then went over to Josh's bed. 'Are you okay, champ?'

'Yeah,' the boy murmured sleepily.

'I'm taking Anna through to my room, okay?'

'Okay.'

Holly gave him a reassuring hug, loving the scent of baby powder on his skin. She tucked the duvet more closely around him, then went with Gray, down the cold passage to her room. She was shivering as she climbed into bed again—was too cold, in fact, to worry about the intimacy of having Gray Kidman in a T-shirt and striped pyjama bottoms in her bedroom.

At least Anna was calmer now. She blinked in the lamplight as Gray lowered her into bed beside her.

His arms brushed Holly's arms, electrifying her, leaving her nerve endings jangling as he straightened once more and stood beside the bed.

When Holly looked up, she saw tortured darkness in his eyes.

'Anna's all right now,' she told him.

'But is she?' he whispered, unable to hide his anxiety. 'Are you sure?'

'Yes, Gray. She'll be fine. I'm sure.'

The mattress dipped as he sank onto the side of Holly's bed and she could see his hand shaking as he stroked Anna's hair. 'I'm so sorry, baby.'

He spoke in a tight voice, as if he was somehow responsible for Anna's distress. Holly had read somewhere that parenting was mostly about guilt. Looking at Gray, she could believe it.

She wanted to reassure him that he was doing a great job with his kids, but she couldn't talk about it now in front of Anna.

'You're going to sleep now, aren't you, Anna?' she said instead as the child snuggled close.

Eyes closed, Anna nodded against Holly's shoulder.

Even though the little girl was calm again, Gray continued to sit there, watching her. Holly realised she was holding her breath. He was so close she could almost feel his body heat, and he looked so impossibly gorgeous in the lamplight, so dark and manly and—

Holly caught the tropical scents of his cologne as he leaned forward and kissed his daughter.

'Goodnight, poppet.'

His blue eyes gleamed as he smiled sadly at Holly. 'Thank you,' he whispered. 'You're wonderful, Holly. Thank you so much.'

And then, before she recognised quite what was happening, he kissed her cheek.

Her entire body flared like a freshly struck match.

Gray's kiss was no more than a friendly glancing brush, but it was positioned very close to the corner of her mouth, and her libido seemed to have developed a mind of its own, creating all kinds of pleasurable expectations.

Gray straightened and stood. 'Is there anything else I can do for you? Anything you want?'

Oh, man. Holly might have laughed if she wasn't so stunned. She might have answered if she wasn't too breathless to speak. Thank heavens Anna was there, preventing her from saying anything reckless.

'I…I'm fine,' she managed, eventually. 'Anna and I will… um…both be fine now. Thank you.'

Gray stood again, looking down at them, his eyes dark once again and serious. 'Goodnight, then.' He cracked a tiny, crooked, utterly gorgeous smile. 'I hope you both sleep well.'

Holly couldn't reply, could merely nod as she watched

him leave her room—watched his shiny dark hair, his broad shoulders, his perfect butt and his long legs disappear through her doorway.

'Josh?' Gray whispered into the darkness.

He heard the rustle of bedclothes and a sleepy voice.

'Is that you, Dad?'

'Yeah. I came back to make sure you're okay.'

Light spilling through the doorway from the hall showed his small son curled on his side, with the bedclothes tucked up to his chin, his longish dark hair framing his soft, fresh cheeks.

The boy was only six—so little—and yet there were times when Gray thought he caught glimpses of the man his son would one day become.

Cautiously, he sat on the edge of the bed, and the small mound beneath the bedclothes wriggled to make room for him. 'It's pretty scary when Anna screams like that, isn't it?'

Josh nodded solemnly. 'But she's getting better.' He sounded surprisingly grown-up. 'Holly says it'll stop eventually.'

'I'm sure Holly's right.' Gray was thinking of a conversation in New York when Holly had talked about his children and their grief. Ever since then, he'd felt guilty that he'd shied away from raising the subject of Chelsea's death with them.

If he took Holly's advice and talked about it more, he might be able to save Anna from her nightmares. Holly was in there now with Anna, soothing her, doing everything she could to help his daughter to feel safe…to heal.

But in a few weeks Holly would be gone, and it would be up to him. And for all he knew, Josh might need his help, too. At the moment the boy seemed to be coping just fine, but how much pain had he kept bottled up?

'Josh, I've never thanked you,' Gray began unsteadily, and already, just thinking about what he wanted to say made his eyes sting and his throat choke up. 'I've never thanked you for ringing the ambulance for your mom—'

He stopped, took a breath to clear the shake out of his voice. 'That was such smart thinking. I'm so proud of you, son.'

At first there was no sound from the bed. And then, 'But I didn't save her.' In the darkness, Josh's voice sounded extra-tiny and quivery. 'Mommy died.'

A sob brimmed in Gray's throat and he gulped it down. 'Sometimes we can't save people, Josh.' He took a breath. 'But the big thing is, you did your best and that's so fantastic. That's why I'm so proud of you. Your mom would have been proud, too.'

Tears threatened again and the next breath Gray drew shuddered in his chest. To his surprise, he felt two wiry arms winding around his neck, and then Josh was clinging to him, his bony head pressed hard under Gray's jaw.

'Thanks, Dad.'

Gray smelled the warm just-bathed scent of his son, mingled with a faint whiff of puppy, and he was flooded with love. Then he felt hot tears wetting his T-shirt. A beat later, Josh was crying noisily, weeping as if his heart would break.

Fighting his own tears, Gray gathered the boy in and held him close, felt his small body shaking as the grief poured out of him.

Poor little kid. Gray could remember how he'd looked when he was born—tiny, red, fists curled ready to take on the world. He pictured again the fine man the boy would grow up to be.

'I'm here for you, Josh,' Gray whispered. 'I promise. I'll be the best dad ever. No matter what it takes.'

It was some time before Josh was calm again. Worn out from crying, he finally sank back onto the pillow and looked up at Gray with tear-washed eyes.

'Dad, do you think if we'd stayed here with you that Mommy wouldn't have died?'

Gray stifled a groan of dismay. His throat closed over and he couldn't speak.

'No,' he finally managed in a tight voice. 'I'm afraid it wouldn't have made any difference, mate.'

'Why didn't we stay here?'

'Didn't—' This was so hard. 'Didn't your mom explain?'

'She just said she needed to work at the ballet.'

'That's right. Your mom's work was very important to her. She was very talented and she needed to live in New York.'

Josh nodded and sighed, then rolled sleepily onto his side. To Gray's surprise, the boy was very soon asleep, his breath falling evenly and softly.

But when he went back to his own room, he lay staring at the ceiling, thinking once again about his marriage, about Chelsea, and his wonderful kids…

His old fear returned. How he could pull off being the 'best dad ever'? He wanted to be everything Anna and Josh needed, but they needed an educated father, someone who had the right connections, someone who'd learned so much more than running a cattle station.

He thought of Chelsea again, of her growing disappointment and unhappiness. He thought of his own mother, who still to this day managed to make him feel unbearably deficient.

How long would it be—years or only months—before Anna and Josh saw through his bluff and discovered the failings he'd worked so hard and so long to hide?

'Your dinner's keeping warm in the oven,' Janet told Gray two nights later, when he arrived home after a long day of shifting cattle on his western boundary. 'I've left Holly's dinner in the oven, too. Right now, she's putting the children to bed.'

'Already?' Gray glanced at the clock on the wall in surprise. It was only ten past seven. 'The kids aren't sick, are they?'

Janet laughed. 'Heavens, no. If that pair were any fitter they'd be dangerous.'

He sent Janet a cautious glance. 'How was their first day of school?'

'I'll let them tell you.'

Her enigmatic answer caused a twinge of fear—the old fear that had haunted him as long as he could remember—but Janet was smiling, so he decided he was overreacting. He set off down the hall.

Even before he reached the children's room, he heard their laughter, but then he realised the sounds were coming from Holly's room.

His pace slowed, then stopped altogether. For the past two days and nights, he'd been dealing with images of Holly in bed—which only proved he wasn't the brightest young bull in the paddock. In the midst of his poor little daughter's distress, he'd been distracted by an overpowering urge to kiss her nanny—despite the nanny's sensible flannelette pyjamas.

It was an unforeseen problem—this tendency to find his thoughts flashing to Holly. It was the last thing he'd expected, the last thing he wanted. He had no intention of setting himself up for another romantic disaster.

A burst of laughter from the bedroom was accompanied by Holly's voice, high-pitched and squeaking. Actually, the sound was more like quacking, as if Holly was acting out a story. Gray drew a bracing breath and continued on to the doorway of her room.

To his surprise, the room was in darkness. In the dim light he could see that Holly's bed had been transformed into a tent made from sheets draped from the tall brass bedposts and joined in the middle by large safety pins. The silhouettes of his giggling children and their nanny were illuminated by torchlight inside the tent.

It looked like incredible fun.

Gray stood in the darkened doorway, watching them, hands sunk in the pockets of his jeans…moved beyond reason…flooded by memories of his own lonely childhood in this house and his parents' constant bickering and battles.

Never once had he experienced anything close to this level of fun or fellowship. Later, he'd enjoyed yarns around campfires and he'd discovered the camaraderie of the stockmen in the mustering team, but his early home life had been constantly marred by his parents' tension and deep unhappiness.

By contrast, Holly was going out of her way to keep his children entertained and happy and secure. Her generosity was a revelation to him. Damn it, he was fighting tears.

Taking a deep, steadying breath, he knocked on the bedroom door.

'Who's there?' called Josh, sounding important.

'Hector Owl,' Gray responded in his most booming voice.

'Daddy!' squealed his children, and two little faces appeared from beneath the side wall of the tent.

'Hey, there. Looks like you're having fun.'

'We're putting on a puppet show.' Grinning widely, Josh lifted the sheet to reveal Holly caught in a beam of torchlight and sitting cross-legged at the bottom of the bed. Her hand was encased in a glove puppet that vaguely resembled a duck.

She blushed when she saw Gray.

'I don't want to interrupt,' he said.

Holly shook her head. 'You're not interrupting. We were only filling in time until you got home.'

'But don't let me stop your fun. Keep going.'

She smiled shyly. 'Um…well…'

'Just tell me something first,' he said, quickly. 'How was school?'

'Awesome!' his children shouted in unison.

'Really?'

Anna's eyes were almost popping with excitement. 'It's a rocket ship school, Daddy. Me and Josh and Holly are in one rocket ship and we talk on our radio to all the kids in the other rocket ships.'

'A rocket ship?' Gray shook his head in bemusement. 'Sounds exciting.'

'It is exciting. And we've already learned all kinds of math and about wombats.'

Gray smiled at Holly—seemed he wanted to smile more and more lately. 'I'll get all the details from you later.' Already he was looking forward to their conversation.

'But you'll play with us now, won't you?' demanded Josh.

'Ah…' Gray hesitated. They were probably acting out another story he'd never heard of. An excuse—an urgent need to see a man about a dog—was ready on the tip of his tongue.

'Here, Daddy,' cried Anna bossily. 'You can have a puppet.' She held up something made of bright pink fabric. 'You can be the pig.'

'The pig,' he repeated, feeling instantly inadequate, just as he had on the night Holly had pushed him to read a bedtime story.

But, despite his misgivings, he knew he *needed* to learn how to do this stuff. For his kids' sake, he had to make the most of these next few weeks while Holly was still here to show him the ropes.

'Sure,' he said, bravely walking closer to the bed and holding out his hand for the pig. 'What do I have to do?'

CHAPTER SEVEN

'SO, TELL ME,' said Gray after he'd heard Holly's full report on his kids' first day in their new school, 'is our Outback as bad as you expected?' He was smiling but Holly thought she detected tension in his eyes, as if her answer really mattered.

'I wasn't expecting it to be bad,' she said.

'Not even after Chelsea's warnings?'

She shook her head. 'I'm not like Chelsea,' she told him bluntly. 'Chelsea was a city girl through and through—city girl lifestyle, city girl career, city girl clothes. Not that I need to tell you that.'

They were sitting at one end of the kitchen table eating their heated-up meals. The puppet play had been a great success and Gray had joined in with gusto. Now, Janet had retired to her cottage and the children were in bed, so Holly and Gray were alone in the big silent house.

Gray had showered and changed into a fresh white shirt that made the tanned skin at his throat even darker. His hair was damp and he'd shaved, and Holly could see a small scar on his jaw she'd never noticed before. She told herself this was an everyday, average evening meal and it made no sense

that she felt all fluttery every time their gazes met across
the table.

'Don't you think of yourself as a city girl?' Gray asked her.

She shook her head. 'You know what they say. You can
take the girl out of the farm, but you can't take the farm out
of the girl.'

He smiled. 'So what kind of farm did you grow up on?'

'A dairy.'

'Really?' His eyebrows lifted with surprise. 'Dairies are
hard work.'

Holly laughed. 'And your kind of farming is easy?'

'Piece of cake,' he said with a sparkle in his blue eyes that
sent her hormones rattling. 'Except for when I'm driving a
truck through floodwaters.'

'Or wrestling with crocodiles.'

'Yeah, or wrangling wild bulls.'

They shared another smile. Holly, trying to ignore another
flutter, asked quickly, 'So how big is Jabiru Creek Station?'

'Close on a million acres.'

'Wow.' She stared at him. 'I'm sure there are countries in
Europe that are smaller than that.'

Gray shrugged. 'A few, I believe.'

'But Janet told me you run this place all by yourself. She
said you've been in charge here for almost ten years.'

'I have, more or less, but I couldn't have done it without
the help of Ted. He's my manager and he keeps the books and
looks after the paperwork. I couldn't have managed without
Janet, either. She and Ted are a great backup team.'

'But you don't have any other family here?'

'No.' Gray concentrated on spearing a bean with his fork.
'As you know, my mother's in Sydney. She and my dad split
up when I was a nipper. Later, my dad's health went down-

hill, so he moved to Cairns to be closer to doctors. But he's okay, as long as he has regular check-ups.'

Gray lifted his gaze. 'Tell me about your farm. Do your parents still run it?'

'Sure—with my eldest brother's help. He and his family live with my parents.'

'Your *eldest* brother?' Now Gray looked amused. 'So how many brothers do you have?'

'Three. All of them are older.'

Smiling, he pushed his empty plate aside and leaned back in his chair in a way that somehow made his shoulders look huge. 'So you're the only girl and the baby of the family.'

'Yes.' Holly couldn't help returning his smile. 'I know, I know. I must be a spoiled princess.'

'I can't see any signs of spoiling,' he said, letting his gaze run over her.

To her surprise, a happy kind of buzz started inside her, something she hadn't felt in a very long time. 'You haven't mentioned any brothers or sisters,' she prompted. 'Are you an only child?'

'Yeah. But I can't claim to have been spoiled.'

'No,' she agreed quietly, remembering his mother's cool reception at the airport.

Setting her knife and fork neatly together, she said, 'Actually, my brothers are my stepbrothers.'

'Really?' Gray was too well mannered to ply her with awkward questions, but she could tell he was curious. She decided she wanted to tell him.

'I've never met my real father, you see. He took off when I was a baby, so my mom was a single mom, a hairdresser, and until I was five we lived in town. Just the two of us in a little flat above her hairdressing salon. Then one day this nice guy came into her salon with three young sons who needed haircuts.'

She smiled. 'Turned out he was a lonely widower, a dairy farmer. He and my mom hit it off and, when they married, we became a family.'

To Holly's surprise, Gray frowned. 'And you've all lived happily ever after?'

'We have indeed.' Sending him a deliberately light-hearted smile, she added, 'So you know the moral of that story, don't you?'

'Do I?'

'Sure. Next time you're in town, you have to keep an eye out for a friendly but lonely hairdresser.'

It was supposed to be a joke, but she could see it had fallen flatter than Kansas.

'I'm not looking for a second wife,' Gray said grimly.

Okay. Point noted.

Holly had been thinking of her stepdad and how happy he was with her mom, how happy they both were—but perhaps she'd been insensitive. She hoped she hadn't sounded as if she was pushing Gray to find a replacement mother for his kids.

It was clear she'd upset him. Gathering up their plates, she carried them to the sink, mad with herself for spoiling a perfectly pleasant conversation. For a moment there, Gray had looked as if he wanted to pack her bags and put her on the next mail plane out of Jabiru.

Knowing a change of subject was needed, she asked, 'While I'm up, would you like a cuppa?'

'Thank you.' Already, he was sounding more conciliatory. 'I'll stack the dishwasher.'

She tried to ignore the view of him from behind as he bent

over to load their plates. How could ordinary old blue jeans be so attention-grabbing?

'By the way,' she said casually as her gaze flickered to his low-slung jeans, then away. Then back again. 'I meant to thank you for letting us use your study as a schoolroom.'

'No worries.' Gray finished with the dishwasher and leaned casually against the kitchen counter, arms crossed, his eyes friendly once more. 'You're welcome to use the study.'

'It doubles really well as a school room, but I've told Anna and Josh they have to keep it tidy for you.'

He pulled a face. 'Doesn't really matter if they mess that room up. I'm not in there a lot.'

'I must admit I was surprised to find it so tidy. I thought it would be full of your books.'

Gray frowned and his eyes narrowed. 'Why?'

'Well, there are hardly any books anywhere else in the house. I thought they'd be in the study, but you obviously keep them somewhere else. I must admit I kept all mine in my bedroom in Chelsea's flat. I had them double stacked on floor-to-ceiling shelves, piled on the nightstand, on the floor—'

As Holly said this, she realised that Gray's expression had changed.

Again.

This time, however, she saw a flash of pain in his eyes. *Real* pain.

What was the matter now? What had she said wrong?

Behind her the kettle came to the boil and she whirled around quickly. Confused, embarrassed, she concentrated very carefully on pouring hot water into mugs.

When she looked back at Gray again, a cool mask had

slipped over his face and his blue eyes were almost icy. 'I never have time for reading,' he said.

Okay. So here was another subject that was a conversation stopper for this man. First, she'd upset him by asking about his former wife's preference for Sydney. Then she'd made a light-hearted comment about his marital future and hit a brick wall. Now his taste in books was a taboo topic...

Aware that the evening's lovely relaxed mood would almost certainly not revive, Holly suggested that she might take her tea through to her room and Gray looked relieved. They exchanged very polite goodnights and parted.

In bed, however, nursing her mug of hot tea, Holly couldn't help conducting a post-mortem of their conversation. She thought how much she'd enjoyed Gray's company up until the point when she'd apparently put her foot in it. Gray wasn't just a sexy dude. She'd seen glimpses of a really nice, friendly guy.

Then she'd spoiled everything. For heaven's sake, who was she to judge his reading habits? What did she know about the responsibilities involved in caring for a million acre property? Gray couldn't have been much more than twenty when he'd shouldered that responsibility, and it wasn't so remarkable that he hadn't had time to laze about with his nose in a book.

Just the same, it was clear there was more to Gray than met the eye. He might seem to be a straightforward Australian cattleman with a down-to-earth manner but, beneath the simple and sexy blue-jeans-and-riding-boots exterior, he was a complicated puzzle.

Working him out wasn't part of Holly's job description. But, if she was to leave Anna and Josh in his care, shouldn't she try to understand him?

* * *

After Holly left, Gray stayed behind in the kitchen, brooding as he stared out through the window at the dark, starless sky.

He'd been steeling himself for Holly's nosy questions. She was, after all, a teacher but, truth to tell, her question about his books hadn't bothered him nearly as much as her suggestion about his plans for the future.

Whenever he thought about the rest of his life stretching ahead into his forties, fifties and beyond, his heart felt rimmed with ice. But was he really going to close down his emotions and never look at another woman again? Was it okay if his children never had a stepmother? Weren't Janet and a nanny enough?

He'd always looked on Chelsea's arrival in the Outback as a gift from the gods, but he'd wrecked that chance.

Had it been his only chance?

What was he planning for the rest of his life? Would he simply take advantage of casual opportunities? Or would he put himself in the marketplace—like those crazy TV shows—*Cattleman wants a Wife.*

He hadn't come to terms with any of these questions yet— and he sure as hell wished Holly hadn't raised them.

By Friday afternoon, the children were well settled into their new home. The school week had gone really well and now Anna and Josh were out of the school room and playing on the swing. It was a favourite afternoon pastime that came a close second to admiring their growing puppies, which now resembled fat little sausages with lovely seal-smooth coats.

Selections had been made and Josh was the proud pre-owner of the all black male, while Anna had settled on a sweet little blue-speckled female.

From the kitchen Holly could hear the children's voices drifting through the window, squealing with delight as they pushed the swing higher.

Janet, in the kitchen, was browning chicken pieces at the stove.

'Let me help you,' Holly said. 'Maybe I can chop something?'

Janet tried to shoo her away. 'Your job's in the school room, lovey. I don't expect you to help in here.'

'But I'd like to.' Holly was thinking of all the times she'd chopped ingredients for her mom in the pretty blue and yellow farmhouse kitchen at home. For some reason she couldn't quite explain, this afternoon she was feeling homesick.

She told herself it had nothing to do with the fact that Gray had made himself scarce all week, ever since Monday night's conversation.

'Well…' Janet took a good long look at Holly and apparently made up her mind about something. 'You could chop carrots and celery if you like. I'm making chicken cacciatore.' Then she sent Holly an unsettling wink. 'It's one of Gray's favourites.'

Hmm…Gray again…

It was surprising the number of times Janet mentioned her boss to Holly. She'd even tried to suggest that Gray was happier now that Holly had come to Jabiru Creek.

But if Gray was happier, Holly knew it was because his children were here now, and it had nothing to do with her presence. Quite the opposite. Whenever she'd talked to Gray she'd pressed the wrong buttons and upset him. Ever since Monday night he'd been avoiding her and that bothered her more than it should.

Admittedly, a cattleman needed to rise early and to be

away from the house, working on his vast property from dawn until dusk. But each night, after Gray indulged in a quick after-dinner romp with his children, he took off for one of the machinery sheds, claiming he had a problem with a broken tractor.

Holly told herself that mending tractors was what men of the Outback did in the evenings instead of reading the paper, or watching TV like their city counterparts. Her father loved to tinker in his sheds, and she mightn't have minded Gray's absence so much if she hadn't been almost certain that he was dodging conversation with her.

Was he worried that she was waiting to pounce on him with more questions?

Now, at the end of a week of tractor-mending, she wished she knew if she'd said something that had really upset him, or if she was making a mountain out of a molehill. Surely her mind could be put to rest after a simple quick chat?

As she chopped carrots, she decided she would head out to that machinery shed this evening and offer Gray some kind of olive branch...

There was no helpful moonlight when Holly cautiously descended the homestead steps at half past eight, after the children were safely tucked in bed. She made her way across the paddock to the shed by the feeble glow of her flashlight.

A shadow rose from the grass beside her and large wings flapped, making her jump. With a hand pressed to her thumping chest, she thought about turning back, then told herself it was probably an owl and that crossing a paddock at Jabiru Creek was no different from playing hide-and-seek in the barns back home with her brothers.

Just the same, it felt like ages before she reached the yellow light shining through the doorway of the tall corrugated iron shed.

The sound of hammering came from inside. Or was that her heart?

A few more steps brought her through the doorway and inside the shed. She saw rubber tyres of all sizes stacked against a wall. Bits and pieces of rusty machinery. An intact tractor.

Gray—not in the expected overalls, but in his usual faded jeans and an old navy-blue woollen sweater with the sleeves pushed back and a hole at one elbow—was working at a long wooden bench. He'd stopped hammering now and was planing timber, smoothing down the edges of a very large box-shaped object.

Intent on his task, Gray turned slightly and Holly saw the strength in his hands and forearms. She could even sense the movement of his shoulder muscles beneath the thick wool of his sweater.

She turned off her flashlight and put it in her coat pocket. Her palms were sweaty, so she jammed them in her pockets too. Then, feeling like an intruder, she took a deep breath and went three steps deeper into the shed.

She felt ridiculously nervous. Any minute now Gray would look up and she would have to explain why she was here.

She tried to remember the opening she'd rehearsed. *Something about his tractor.* But he wasn't working on the tractor…

With her gaze firmly fixed on Gray, she took another step forward—and tripped on a metal pipe, sending it rolling and clattering across the concrete floor.

Gray's head snapped up and his blue eyes widened with surprise. 'Holly.'

'I'm sorry,' she cried, bending down to rub her smarting ankle.

'Are you okay?'

'Yes, I'm fine.'

He came hurrying over to her, wiping his dusty hands on an old rag. 'Are you sure you're all right?'

'The pipe's probably worse off than I am. It's okay. Really. Just a bump.'

'I hope you don't end up with a bruise.' A beat later, he said, 'What are you doing out here?' His smile was quickly replaced by a frown. 'Is something wrong? Is it Anna?'

'No, no. Nothing wrong. A-Anna's fine.' Holly's mouth was suddenly as dry as the sawdust on the floor. She tried to swallow, then remembered that she'd planned to smile to set the right mood. 'There's no problem, Gray. The children are sound asleep.'

'That's good to hear.' With hands on his hips, he studied her, a puzzled gleam lurking in his bright blue eyes. 'So, what brings you out here at this time of night? I thought you'd be curled up with your nose in a book.'

Yes...well...

Now that he was waiting for her answer, Holly felt more foolish than ever. Gray seemed totally relaxed and not at all put out by her sudden appearance, so how could she suggest there was a problem that needed sorting?

'Have...have you finished the tractor?' she asked.

'The tractor?'

'I...um...thought you were working on one.'

'Oh, yes. You've blown my cover.' Gray's eyes twinkled, and then he turned to the bench where he'd been working. 'I've been making something for Anna and Josh, actually. It's almost done.'

'Oh,' she said in a very small voice.

'Would you like to take a look? I still have to paint it.'

Without waiting for her answer, Gray went back to the bench and picked up the large boxlike frame he'd been working on. Not quite hiding his pride in his workmanship, he set it on the floor.

'Oh,' Holly said again when she saw it properly. 'It's...it's a puppet theatre.'

He was grinning. 'I made the stage high enough for Anna and Josh to stand behind.'

'It's perfect.' Holly meant it. She was amazed and she felt so silly for thinking he'd been avoiding her. She wasn't even on his radar.

'They'll love it,' she said. 'Wow. You've even made a pointy roof and a little wooden flag to go on top.'

'And Janet's making red velvet curtains.'

'Fantastic!'

So Janet was in on this, too? Holly felt as if the rug had been pulled from beneath her. Here she'd been, all week, stewing about Gray's sensitive reaction to their conversation, while he'd been busy creating a wonderful surprise for his children.

'It's a fabulous idea,' she said, running her hand over the smooth silky wall of the stage and admiring the fine craftsmanship. 'Did you say you're going to paint this?'

'I thought the kids would like something bright.' He scratched at the side of his neck. 'But don't ask me about colour schemes. Apart from painting the roof red, I'm a bit stumped.'

'You can't just nip down to a hardware store, so I suppose it depends on what paint you already have.'

'Practically every colour under the sun, actually.' He went

over to a cupboard against the wall and flipped it open to reveal several shelves lined with spray cans. 'Last year there was a ringer working here who moonlighted as a rodeo clown and I helped him to make his props.'

Holly laughed. 'So you have enough colours to make a rainbow.'

'I guess I do.'

'Rainbow walls would be fiddly, but they'd look fabulous.'

Gray considered this, a smile pulling at a corner of his mouth. 'I'm no Vincent Van Gogh.' He shot her an amused glance. 'What about you? Are you handy with a spray can?'

Holly had wielded many a spray can while making children's library displays, and she'd discovered a creative streak she hadn't previously known she possessed.

'We—I mean *you*—would need to work from the top down,' she said. 'And you'd have to use something like cardboard as a shield.'

'You'd help me, wouldn't you?'

She knew she shouldn't feel so flattered. 'I'd be prepared to give it a go.'

'Terrific,' he said, matching her enthusiasm.

And then, looking straight into her eyes, he smiled. *Oh, man.* His smile packed a wallop.

Not that she should be noticing.

It shouldn't have been so much fun—working hard and staying up till nearly midnight to get the last rainbow stripe in place. Holly enjoyed every second of the project.

Early in the evening, while the undercoat was drying, Gray boiled a billy on a small gas ring and made tea. He had milk and sugar in a battered old cooler and even a packet of cookies.

They sat on rickety camping stools in the middle of the messy shed, drinking sweet hot tea from chipped enamel mugs and eating cookies.

'Yum,' Holly said as she helped herself to a second one.

'Good to see a girl with an appetite.' Gray took a second cookie as well. 'Chelsea was always so careful about what she ate.'

'All dancers seem to diet. They're very strong-willed,' she suggested.

'Obsessed,' Gray said tightly.

Holly now knew better than to pursue this sensitive topic. After all, she'd come here to hold out an olive branch.

Smiling, she said brightly, 'So tell me, Gray, does your hat still fit?'

He looked at her with puzzled amusement. 'Last time I tried it. Why?'

'Janet and Ted have both been praising you to the skies this week and I thought you might have a swelled head.'

Looking down at the curls of shaved wood on the floor, he shrugged. 'That pair are biased.'

'Maybe, but they're not easily hoodwinked. They told me you're a brilliant cattleman, highly respected and looked up to by others in your industry. Ted said that when you took over the reins here ten years ago, you dramatically improved the carrying capacity and diversified the cattle breeds. And you placed yourself at the cutting edge of land management and water conservation.'

Gray was staring hard at his mug. 'Sounds a bit grand when you put it like that, but when I'm out, driving around, I listen to a lot of agricultural radio programmes. It's a good way to learn things.'

'According to Ted, you hoard all that info in your brilliant memory and then put it into practice.' Holly smiled. 'He also said you're fantastic with figures. He called you a human calculator.'

Gray shrugged again. 'That man has far too much to say. I'm not paying him to gasbag.' His eyes flashed a cheeky challenge. 'And why are you trying to flatter me?'

'I'm not flattering you. I'm giving you positive feedback. You can blame my teacher training.'

'Yeah, right.' He gave a smiling shake of his head. 'But shouldn't we be working out how we're going to paint these rainbow walls?'

They decided on a plan. They would start at the top with orange just beneath the red roof, then progress downwards through blue and purple to finish with green at the base.

With the plan settled and the undercoat dry, they got back to work. After a short trial run, Gray admitted that Holly could produce the most even spray paint finish, so they agreed that he should hold up the cardboard shield for her.

As they worked, she engaged him in safe topics—mostly about the twins and their first week of school. She told him that Josh was very clever at arithmetic and had developed a passion for Natural Science—particularly frogs.

'I hope you don't mind. This afternoon we converted a pickle jar into a tadpole aquarium,' she told him.

Gray laughed. 'I was mad about spiders when I was a kid. Tried to start a redback spider farm in an ice cream container.'

'Eeeeww.' Holly gave an elaborate shudder, then told him that Anna was the twin who was curious about spiders. 'She also has beautiful handwriting and a musical ear and an exceptionally vivid imagination.'

Holly enjoyed herself immensely, which surprised her,

considering that once upon a time she'd looked forward to sharing this sort of task with Brandon. She'd even been silly enough to imagine that she and Brandon would paint a nursery for their first baby, and she'd actually picked out a colour scheme of white and sunshiny yellow with a brightly coloured rainbow frieze.

How strange that this puppet theatre inspired her now almost as much as her old dream had.

On Sunday morning, Gray rose just as the screeching corellas took off from the trees along the creek bank, and he crossed the frosty grass to the shed where the puppet theatre stood in all its rainbow-walled, red-curtained glory.

He grinned when he saw it. It looked so bright and cheerful and, even if he did say so himself, very professional. Almost as good as the puppet theatre he and Holly had taken the children to see in New York.

His kids were going to love it.

All thanks to Holly, of course…

Without her, he wouldn't have known such things existed. And without Holly he wouldn't have enjoyed the final decorating tasks nearly as much. She was so easy-going and comfortable to be with.

Gray totally understood why his kids loved school when Holly was around to help make it fun.

How would they cope when she left?

Soon, he would have to seek her help in posting an ad for a replacement nanny, and then he'd also need her input when he vetted the applicants.

Right now, Gray couldn't think of a more unpalatable task, couldn't imagine another woman filling Holly O'Mara's shoes.

* * *

A movie director couldn't have created a more pleasing scene than Anna and Josh's discovery of the puppet theatre. They bounced into the kitchen for breakfast, spied the theatre positioned just outside the flyscreen door, and reacted just as Holly had hoped they would—with dancing and squealing and their eyes almost popping out of their heads with excitement.

'And it isn't even our birthday,' Josh exclaimed in grinning disbelief as he and Anna took turns to pull the cord that drew the splendid red curtains open and shut.

Anna was beaming, too. 'I can't believe we have a theatre *and* our puppies. Wow, Daddy, this is so cool.'

Together, the children squeezed inside the 'back door' and examined the stage. When they plied Gray and Holly with questions, they were stunned to learn that their dad had actually made this glorious construction with his own hands.

Holly smiled at Gray, taking in the quiet satisfaction in his eyes.

'They'll remember this day for the rest of their lives,' she told him quietly.

He merely nodded, but this time when he smiled back at her, she had to look down. The crackling *something* in the air was suddenly too much.

After breakfast, the children jumped straight into presenting their premiere puppet show on the veranda, and of course Holly, Gray and Janet were the audience, very happy to sit on a row of chairs, with the basket of puppies at their feet.

'The puppies have to watch, too,' Anna had insisted.

Naturally, the show was received with thunderous applause, and afterwards the children rushed straight off to plan their next performance.

'We'll soon be calling them Shake and Speare,' Janet muttered good-humouredly, before she returned to the kitchen to make a batch of scones for morning tea.

Holly might have followed Janet if Gray hadn't detained her with his hand on her arm. She jumped at his touch as if he'd burned her, and then she felt seriously foolish.

'Would you like to come for a drive with me?' he asked.

'A drive?' She needed a moment to catch her breath. 'I'm sure we won't be able to prise Anna and Josh away from their puppets.'

The tanned skin around his blue eyes crinkled. 'I wasn't planning to invite the children. I'm sure they'd rather stay here, and they'll be fine with Janet.'

'But—' Holly's heart gave a strange thump. 'Are you sure Janet doesn't have other plans?'

'I'm certain of it, Holly. I've already spoken to her, and she'd love to spend a day with the twins. In fact, she's already started on a picnic lunch for us.'

'Oh? I…I see.'

'You've earned a day off, and I thought you might like to see the gorge.'

It was kind of Gray to take the trouble to entertain her. 'Thank you.' Holly's voice was a shade too proper and polite. 'I'd love to see the gorge. I'll explain to Anna and Josh—'

He held up a hand. 'I can do the explaining while you get ready. You'll need sunscreen and a hat and sturdy shoes.'

She was being bulldozed—steamrollered—but for once she didn't mind.

In her room, as she grabbed her shady hat from its hook on the back of her dresser, she caught sight of her reflection in the mirror. She was, as usual, in a boring old T-shirt and jeans, with her hair tied back and a new crop of freckles on her nose.

If she was in New York, she was quite sure that if a new man invited her out for the day she would go to a great deal of trouble, hunting through her wardrobe for the perfect outfit, ringing her friends for fashion advice, going for a manicure, a pedicure, a leg wax.

It was strange to think that she was now going to spend an entire day alone with a man who was *not* Brandon, and yet she didn't feel an overwhelming urge to worry about how she looked. It was rather comforting to know she didn't have to try too hard with Gray Kidman.

After teaming with him on the puppet theatre, they'd reached a comfortable working relationship and she could save her dating charms for the new man she was bound to meet once she was back home again in the fall. The sizzle she felt around Gray Kidman was nothing more than hormones—and she supposed she should be grateful to know they were still in working order.

CHAPTER EIGHT

As Gray drove away from the homestead with a cloud of dust pluming behind his vehicle, Holly was reacquainted with how very isolated Jabiru Creek Station really was.

They'd only just passed the last outbuilding before they were once again following a faint dirt track across endless plains that stretched and stretched to the distant horizon. She saw nothing but cloudless blue skies, red dirt and dusty faded grass, with occasional mobs of silvery hump-backed cattle sheltering in the scant shade of straggly white-trunked trees.

'It must be fabulous to tear across this country on horseback,' she said, partly because she meant it, and partly because she wanted to say something positive about the monotonous scenery.

Gray turned to her, clearly surprised. 'Do you ride?'

'I haven't for ages.'

'But you know how to.'

'Sure. There was a time when horse-riding was my favourite sport.'

His eyebrows shot high. 'Why didn't you tell me?'

'I came here to be your children's nanny. Not to prance around on horseback.'

Still watching the track ahead, Gray shook his head. 'But I'm sure you could squeeze in a little riding time while you're here.'

'That would be wonderful—although I'm sure I'd be sorry when I was stiff and sore.'

His eyes sparkled as he turned to her. 'You'll soon loosen up.' A little later he said, 'I'm planning to teach Anna and Josh how to ride.'

'Oh, good. They'll love it.'

'Even Anna?'

'Especially Anna,' Holly assured him. 'She's getting more into life in the Outback every day.'

Gray smiled. 'I'll have to measure them up for riding helmets.'

After that, he seemed to lapse back into thoughtful silence, and Holly sensed his focus shift from conversation to the ancient landscape all around him.

Eventually, a red range of hills appeared, rising out of the flat land ahead of them. Holly was reminded of the backdrops of the old western movies her dad used to watch on Sunday afternoons, and she almost expected to see smoke signals puffing from the jagged ridges.

When they crested a hill, Gray braked and in front of them the land dropped away, plunging, without warning, down sheer red cliffs.

'Oh, my gosh!' Holly was glad of her seatbelt. Leaning as far forward as the belt would permit, she peered through the dusty windscreen. 'I guess this must be the gorge?'

'It's not quite the Grand Canyon.'

'But it's spectacular.' She glanced back over her shoulder

to the rear window and the view of the empty plains they'd just crossed. 'Are we still on your land?'

'Sure.' Already Gray was opening the driver's door. 'Come and take a look. I love it out here.'

Outside, the sun was scorching hot. Holly jammed her hat firmly on her head, but she wasn't keen to step any closer to the edge of the gorge. It was an awfully long way down to the glinting water of the rock pools at the bottom. After just a hasty glance down there she felt dizzy.

'Here, come with me.' Gray had retrieved their backpacks from the rear of the truck and he handed the smaller one to Holly. 'I'll show you the best way to see the view.'

She almost declined. She had quite a nice view from where she was standing, and she had a safe hold on the truck's sturdy metal bull bar, thank you very much. But Gray was holding out his hand to her, and his air of confidence was very convincing.

Summoning her courage, she managed to loosen her grip on the bull bar and his hand holding hers felt wonderfully strong and trustworthy, but she clung to him so tightly she was afraid she'd leave bruises.

To her relief, he led her away from the cliff's edge to what at first seemed like a hole in the ground, but turned out to be a man-made staircase cleverly hewn out of the rock.

'This leads down through the roof of a cave,' he said.

'Wow. Did you make these stairs?'

Gray laughed. 'No way. They've been here for over a hundred years, but my grandfather helped to carve them out.'

Intrigued, Holly allowed him to guide her down the rocky staircase. Already she could see that the cave below them wasn't gloomy or dark, but filled with sunlight. And it had a wide sandy floor, so she began to feel calmer.

By the time they reached the bottom of the steps, she looked around with amazed delight. The cave was set into the side of the escarpment and it formed a safe shelf, a fabulous, cosy viewing platform offering a spectacular view all the way down the gorge.

'Gray, it…it's fabulous.'

His blue eyes met hers, watching her closely, as if he was intensely interested in her reaction. Apparently satisfied, he smiled. 'Not bad, is it?'

'It's amazing. I think I'll sit down though, so I can take it all in.'

By this time, she'd become super-aware of their linked hands—of the heat of Gray's palm against hers, of the pressure of his fingers as he gripped her firmly and safely. To her surprise, she was incredibly reluctant to release his hand before she lowered herself to the sandy floor.

Once she was seated, Gray edged forward, closer to the mouth of the cave, and he hunkered down, taking in the view. He loved this place with its rock pools that reflected the sky and the spectacular sandstone escarpments carved out of the ancient landscape. He never failed to be moved by its grandeur.

But today he was trying to imagine how the gorge might look through Holly's eyes. He wasn't sure why it mattered so much, but he found himself hoping that she might somehow understand what it meant to him.

At least she wasn't talking non-stop. She seemed happy enough to drink in the atmosphere, or to quietly take photographs with her small digital camera.

In the languid silence Gray let his shoulders relax against a warm wall of sandstone. He heard the warbling notes of a pied butcherbird and a flock of galahs calling in the distance. Below, on the water, a pair of grebes floated.

After a while, he asked quietly, 'So, what do you reckon?'

'This is so beautiful,' Holly said softly. 'It feels almost… spiritual.'

A good answer. 'It *is* spiritual,' he said. 'At least it is for the Aborigines.'

And for me, he added silently, thinking of the many times when his life had hit rock bottom and he'd come to this place to search for some kind of peace.

Moving carefully on her hands and knees, Holly crawled a little closer, then sat cross-legged, looking out. 'It's awesome. Unforgettable.' She spoke in a hushed undertone, the way people talked in church.

She took a few more photos, then lowered her camera. 'I'm sure this gorge has been here for ever. A dinosaur could come lumbering out from behind a rock and it wouldn't look out of place.'

Her face was soft, her dark eyes luminous with wonder. And Gray had to look away, concentrating his attention on a lizard as it disappeared down a crack in a rust-stained rock.

He'd hoped Holly would like this place, but he hadn't expected her to so totally *get* its timeless mystery.

'Is it weird to feel that there's someone here?' she asked. 'A gentle spirit, looking after us?'

He had to swallow the hard lump in his throat before he could speak. 'Not weird at all. That's why I love it. Sitting here quietly, taking in the silence, always makes me feel stronger. Uplifted. The Aborigines call it "listening to country".'

He turned and saw Holly nodding slowly, a pretty smile lighting her eyes.

'Listening to country,' she repeated softly. 'I like that. I used to do a lot of that when I was growing up in Vermont. On my way to school I used to love walking over the covered bridge on Staple's Brook and along the banks beneath sugar maples and birches. *Listening to country.* I am so on that page.'

Launching to his feet, Gray moved to the very mouth of the cave, appalled to realise he'd been on the brink of tears. He'd never expected to meet a woman like Holly, someone lovely and sweet and in tune with his world. For a heady moment there, he'd almost pulled her close and kissed her, tasted her smile, her laughter.

Not a bright idea. She was here to help his children, and she was going home to America to start a fancy new job. Besides, she'd just had her heart broken by some fool of a boyfriend. Last thing she needed was her cousin's Australian ex making a move on her. Especially as that ex was absolutely useless at making women happy—or keeping them happy, at any rate.

For all kinds of reasons, he'd be a fool to start anything with Holly. Even if she did claim to love his Outback, he couldn't expect her to want to stay here. Not with him. She'd soon realise her mistake, just as his wife had.

Hell. He should wear a danger sign, warning women to keep their distance.

'This country must inspire musicians and artists,' Holly was saying. 'Or writers. I've never read any literature about your Outback, but there must be novels and poetry. Do you have any—?'

She stopped in mid-sentence and her face turned bright red, as if she realised she'd made a dreadful gaffe. 'Sorry. I know reading's not your thing.'

Gray's entire body tensed, as if the cliff had suddenly crumbled away beneath his feet. Fear knifed through him— the fear of ridicule that he'd never managed to shake off.

His only hope was to change the subject…

'I could give you a few lines of bush poetry,' he said quickly.

Anything, even the embarrassment of a recitation, was better than risking exposure of his incompetence.

'Poetry?' Holly sounded shocked, and already he was feeling foolish.

She was leaning forward now, hands wrapped around bent knees. 'Gray, I'd love to hear some bush poetry.'

Of course he was already regretting the offer. He wasn't a performer and he wished he could come up with an excuse—he'd forgotten the lines—anything. 'It's pretty basic stuff. Hardly Wordsworth or Shakespeare.'

'But the simplest things are often the truest.'

Damn. Gray knew he'd talked himself into a corner. He'd look even more foolish if he backed out now. He made a show of clearing his throat and then, keeping his gaze fixed on the gorge, he began to recite.

'I've crossed harsh country parched and red,
With ghost gums shining white,
Where sand dunes choke the river bed,
And all day I prayed for night.
I've heard that country sing to me
In the stillness of my mind,
A Dreamtime chant from rock and tree—'

Gray paused and he realised that Holly was staring at him, her eyes full of questions.

'Sorry.' He could feel his face burning. Why the hell had he grabbed onto the poem to get him off the hook?

'Don't apologise. I loved it, Gray.'

He shrugged elaborately and looked away again, down the gorge to where a mob of black-tailed rock wallabies were feeding quietly on the moist vegetation at the edge of a waterhole.

'When did you learn that poem?' she asked, with the nosiness he should have expected from a teacher.

Gray shrugged. 'Can't remember.'

'Who wrote it?'

The heat in his face deepened and he answered brusquely, without looking at her. 'It's nothing. Just something I made up.'

He heard her shocked gasp. 'You made it up?'

'Yeah. No big deal.'

'But…when did you write it?'

He gave another big-shouldered shrug. 'Years ago. I can't really remember. Beside a campfire. Sitting here. Alone.' Sure that his face was crimson now, he got to his feet and scooped up his backpack, eager to be done with this conversation.

'Gray, please don't be embarrassed, but it *is* a big deal that you've made up such a lovely poem. I'm seriously impressed.'

'Thanks.'

'Did Chelsea love it?'

Chelsea? He sighed, then stared out at the deep blue of the sky and the deeper red walls.

'I shared my poetry with her once, but she saw it as yet another excuse to plead with me to give up my cattle and head for the city. She wanted us to be artists together—she could be a choreographer in Sydney and I could perform my poetry.'

'That doesn't sound very…practical.'

'She was convinced I'd be a great hit. She was always looking for something else for me to do besides raising cattle.'

Holly made no comment, but she was frowning and then, as if she'd been struck by a bright idea, she flipped open her backpack and pulled out a notebook. 'I'd like to write your poem down.'

'Why?' Still thinking about Chelsea, Gray growled the word suspiciously.

'Because it's great. I really like it. I want to be able to read it again later, when I'm back in America.'

Already, she was sitting with her small spiral notebook in her lap, open at a blank page, her pen poised, ready to write.

Gray forced himself to relax. There was no threat in Holly's request. He actually liked the idea of her taking out her notebook when she was back in busy, bustling Manhattan, turning to his poem…reading it… Maybe she'd recall this moment. This peace.

Where was the harm in that?

Feeling self-conscious but no longer uncomfortable, he began to recite again: 'I've crossed harsh country parched and red…'

Holly's pen flew across the page leaving a neat curving script in its wake.

'With ghost gums shining white…'

She nodded enthusiastically as he continued on to the end of the first verse, then added a second stanza.

'Wow, that's fabulous,' she said when he'd finished. 'Thank you.' She spoke warmly, and her cheeks were flushed and her dark eyes were suspiciously shiny as she slipped the note-book back into the pack and closed the flap.

'You're welcome.'

'Having a copy of your poem makes this trip to the gorge even more perfect.'

He was more pleased than he should have been, but he was determined not to show it. Poker-faced, he said, 'So…would you like to keep going all the way to the bottom of the gorge?'

'Sure.' Holly scrambled to her feet and accepted his hand with almost childlike trust. 'Lead the way.'

Gripping Gray's hand once more as they made their way carefully down the rough, steep track to the bottom of the gorge, Holly discovered she was in deep, oh-my-God trouble.

She'd learned two important things about Gray just now—his soul-deep love of his land, and a strong reason for the breakdown of his marriage.

And then she'd learned something about herself.

While she'd sat in the cave in the middle of Gray's shatteringly beautiful wilderness, listening to him shyly recite his poetry, something huge had happened, something totally unexpected, something guaranteed to break her heart.

The noonday sun reached deep into the gorge, warming the wide ledge of rocks where they ate their simple picnic of egg and lettuce sandwiches on homemade bread, along with doorstop slices of rich fruity cake, and oranges.

Holly leaned down, dipping her fingers into water so clear she could see tiny silvery fish feeding on the sandy bottom.

Gray was busy lighting a fire for their billy tea and he called to her, 'Is the water cold?'

'Cool, but not freezing.'

'We could go for a swim if you weren't afraid of crocodiles.'

'Well, of course I'm afraid of crocodiles. Who wouldn't be?'

Catching his grin, she knew he'd only been teasing.

She sat up to watch him work, to watch the smooth tanned skin on the back of his neck and the damp line of sweat on his collar, the stretch of his cotton shirt over his wide shoulders, his long fingers deftly snapping twigs and poking them into the flames.

She imagined changing into bathers and swimming with him—if there were no crocodiles—and sweet shivers ran through her.

'The billy will take a few minutes to boil.' Gray's voice broke into her musings. 'We may as well make a start on our tucker.'

Holly discovered, to her surprise that she was ravenous and the sandwiches were surprisingly fresh with just the right balance of mayonnaise and pepper.

The gorge was completely silent now. Earlier there'd been bird calls but, in the midday stillness, the birds had retreated. Gray, looking very relaxed, sat with his back against a warm rock wall, his long jeans-clad legs stretched in front of him, his face shaded by his broad-brimmed hat.

Holly was quite prepared to eat her lunch in silence, lazing like a lizard in the sun and growing drowsy. And she was sure that was what Gray wanted, too, so she was surprised when he spoke suddenly.

'So…what made you decide to become a teacher?'

'Oh, that's easy,' she said. 'I was inspired by my fourth grade teacher, Miss Porter. She was lovely and brilliant and kind. And she turned our whole class onto books and reading.'

Gray nodded slowly, watching her from beneath his shady brim.

'I started out as a regular classroom teacher in Vermont,' Holly explained. 'That was fine for a few years, but all the time I was in the classroom I could feel the library calling to me, so I decided to get extra qualifications to run school libraries. That's when I moved to New York.'

'And you left your boyfriend behind.'

'Yes.' Holly waited for the slug of pain that always hit her when she thought about Brandon. It eventually came, like a delayed reaction, and it still hurt but, to her surprise, it was no longer crippling.

She realised that Gray was watching her, but he swiftly switched his gaze to the fire and the boiling billy and he lifted it from the fire, then added tea leaves and gave them a stir.

'Are you ready for your tea?' he asked after a few minutes.

'Thank you.' Gratefully, Holly accepted an enamel mug of tea that was black and sweet and hot. Sipping it helped to calm the strange new tension inside her—a tension that had nothing to do with talking about Brandon and everything to do with her present company.

'Gray—'

'Hmm?' He leaned comfortably back against the rock and sipped his tea.

'Did you have School of the Air when you were a child?'

'Do you *have* to start talking about school right now?'

'I don't suppose it's essential, but I just told you about my favourite teacher. And I was thinking about your lovely poem, and I wondered where you learned about poetry.'

'It certainly wasn't on School of the Air.'

'Did you go away to boarding school?'

This was greeted by a deep sigh. 'Can we give this a miss, Holly?'

'I'm a teacher. I can't help wanting to know these things.'

'School is not everyone's favourite subject.'

'Is this another conversation stopper?'

He frowned. 'What do you mean?'

'It seems to me that every time I have a conversation with you I run into trouble. There's always something you don't want to talk about. Chelsea, I can understand. But what's wrong with talking about school?'

'The school a person went to doesn't matter out here in the bush. We're not snobs about that sort of thing.'

'I'm not asking you to show off. I was just curious—*anything* about your school would do. Best teacher, worst teacher. Favourite subject, favourite sport—'

There was a movement on the rock beside her. A beat later, Gray was close beside her, leaning in to her, and Holly realised with a shock that he was planning to kiss her.

Small explosions detonated all over her body.

She was sure she should say something to stop him, but her brain refused to cooperate.

When Gray touched his lips to hers, her surprise melted like sugar in hot tea and—*oh, man*—she responded like a person in a dream.

His mouth was like the sun burning across the sky, moving over her mouth, inch by fiery inch, cautious at first, and testing. Holly remained perfectly still, afraid that at any moment she might wake up and feel obliged to behave responsibly.

She didn't want to behave responsibly. She was too curious initially and then she was bewitched by his totally masculine enchantment.

Already, she was melting, softening and, when her lips drifted apart, Gray accepted her invitation without hesitation. His hands cradled her head and his kiss, tasting faintly of orange and tea, became clever and darkly seductive.

She could smell the sunlight on his skin, could feel its warmth on her closed eyelids, and she was sinking beneath it. Melting beneath his persuasive lips. Melting and needy. So needy. She could no longer resist him even if she'd wanted to.

A sweet, compelling ache started low inside her, urging her to lean into him, to link her hands behind his neck and to return his kiss, to communicate with her body the shocking, thrilling impatience that had taken possession.

Oh, heavens, she might die if he stopped.

A sound broke the noonday silence—half a whimper, half a moan. Amazingly, it had come from her, but she couldn't stop to worry about decorum now.

But, to her dismay, Gray pulled away from her.

'Holly.'

Noooo. She kept her eyes tightly closed.

In the stillness she could hear the hammering of her heartbeats and the reckless pace of Gray's breathing.

He dropped a soft kiss on the bridge of her nose, then moved further away.

'What—?' she began, then had to pause to catch her breath.

His sexy blue eyes were apologetic. 'I'm sorry,' he said.

Sorry?

Oh, God. How could he share the hottest kiss of her life, possibly the most fabulous kiss since the beginning of time, and then apologise as if it were a mistake?

Distraught, Holly stared at him. 'Why are you sorry?'

'I shouldn't have done that.' His throat rippled as he swallowed. 'Please don't read too much into it.'

'But why did you do it? Why did you kiss me?'

He offered her a rueful smile. 'It seemed like a good idea at the time.'

'You kissed me to shut me up?'

Gray merely shook his head and Holly sank back against the rock in dismay.

What a klutz she was.

She'd gone into swoon mode, allowing herself to be completely carried away, while Gray had merely found a new technique to stop her from asking nosy questions.

'I'm an idiot,' she said out loud.

'No, Holly.'

'What am I, then?'

His answer was a smiling shake of his head. 'Another question? I should've known it's dangerous to kiss a teacher.'

'Yes, you might learn something,' she snapped, but her response was even testier than she'd intended. She'd never been any good at jokes, and light-heartedness was doubly impossible when she was so upset.

Damn Gray. She could still feel the warm pressure of his lips on hers. She could still smell him and taste him, could still feel the ripples of pleasure pooling low and deep inside her, like aftershocks.

But for Gray the kiss had been a game, a purely practical ploy to stop yet another annoying conversation.

Not daring to look at him, Holly jumped up quickly and, in a bid to cover up her embarrassment, she began to tidy away their picnic things.

As they took the climb back to the top in easy stages, Gray was uncomfortably aware that he'd spoiled a perfect day. He'd let Holly think that he'd kissed her to distract her and, yes, it was true. More or less. She'd pushed their conversation in a direction he had no wish to follow. She'd been holding his feet to the fire of a secret shame and he'd had to stop her.

It was a bad habit that had started during his marriage. Whenever his wife had come up with one of her grand schemes for getting them away from Jabiru Creek, he'd found it easier to seduce her than to tell her the truth—that he had no employable skills beyond running this cattle property.

But, although his initial impulse to kiss Holly had been self-preservation, everything had changed the instant their lips had touched.

A kind of spell had come over him. Admittedly, it was way too long since he'd kissed a woman, so that might explain why he'd been so totally fired up. But abstinence couldn't explain why he'd felt emotionally connected to Holly, or why there was so much that felt *right* about kissing her, so much that felt right about just being with her.

In spite of her nosy questions, she was amazingly easy company, and she was surprisingly at home here in his Outback. He found himself wanting a deeper connection with her, and his body still throbbed with a need to lose himself in her sweet, willing embrace.

It was a lucky thing that her soft needy cry had brought him to his senses. Without that warning, he might never have found the willpower to stop. But now he'd hurt Holly by once again going into defensive mode. He'd protected himself, but he'd spoiled something special.

Damn it, he should have known better.

Hadn't his marriage taught him that he was no match for a clever, educated woman, no matter how strong her appeal? Hadn't his life lessons proved that he was better on his own?

He was fine on his own.

Or at least he would be until his kids' education caught up with him.

* * *

The journey back to the homestead was wrapped in uncomfortable silence, which meant Holly had plenty of time to brood as they rumbled across the trackless plains.

She thought about the moment, while she and Gray were looking down at the gorge, when she'd experienced a feeling of true connection with him. In the same moment, she'd realised something else—she hadn't wanted to fall for Gray but it had happened, almost against her will.

Which meant he had the power to hurt her, just as Brandon had.

She shouldn't have allowed him to kiss her. Why hadn't she shown more sense? Here she was—still suffering from shell shock after Brandon's dumping—and the last thing she wanted was another romantic entanglement—especially with Chelsea's ex.

She wanted freedom, not complications. Why would she put her heart at risk when she had a fabulous job lined up to go home to?

Please don't read too much into it he'd said.

How could Gray kiss her into oblivion simply to shut her up? What was his problem? Where was the crime in asking him about his school? Or about his lack of books, for that matter.

He knew schools and books were her thing, and just because—

Oh, my God.

A sudden chill skittered down Holly's spine as all sorts of puzzling things about Gray suddenly started to fall into place.

The lack of books in the Jabiru homestead. The fact that he'd never heard of Winnie-the-Pooh. His reaction in New York when she'd suggested he should read to his children.

The way he'd waved away menus, and brushed aside the Central Park pamphlet—

Could he have literacy problems?

She stole a glance at him now…at the snug stretch of denim over his thighs to his strong, sun-weathered profile.

Gray Kidman…expert cattleman, gorgeous, take charge of anything…

Surely he couldn't be illiterate?

It was hard to take in.

But if he'd grown up out here, miles away from schools and possibly without a tutor, it wasn't too much of a stretch to believe that he might never have learned to read. He probably knew a few words that enabled him to function—Departures and Arrivals in airports, for example—but beyond that—

Holly remembered his mother's lack of warmth. What had her role been in her son's early years? Had the tension between them started decades ago? Holly knew from her teacher training that literacy problems often stemmed from emotional issues connected to early schooling experiences.

She also knew that illiterate people could still be incredibly astute and competent—and Gray was clearly intelligent and gifted. He made up poetry in his head. How many people did that? With Ted's bookkeeping help, he managed his business very successfully.

Her soft heart ached to think that a proud and capable man like Gray could have a problem he'd felt compelled to hide, managing superbly in spite of it.

Then again, she might be overreacting—jumping to totally incorrect conclusions.

The last of the daylight was turning the paddocks to pink and mauve as they pulled up outside the homestead. Crickets and katydids were already singing their dusk chorus in the trees by the creek.

Anna and Josh, freshly bathed and in their dressing gowns and slippers, came running down the front steps to greet Holly and Gray, while Janet hurried after them like a fussy mother hen.

'They've been no trouble,' Janet assured Gray. 'They've been busy in the school room for most of the day.'

'I thought they'd be playing with their puppets,' he said.

'The puppets have had a good airing, but mostly they've been doing their homework.'

'Homework?' Holly frowned. 'But I didn't set any homework.'

'Well, they've been beavering away on some kind of writing project for the puppet house.' Janet laughed. 'I'm definitely renaming them Shake and Speare.'

'We're going to have a puppet show after dinner,' Anna explained with great excitement. 'And there's a part for everyone.'

Out of the deep pockets of her cherry-red dressing gown, she pulled folded sheets of paper and, glowing with pride, the little girl separated three pages for Holly, three for Janet and three for Gray.

Each sheet was covered in photocopies of her best printing.

'You're Hector Owl, Daddy, and I'm Timothy Mouse and Josh—'

Holly didn't hear the rest. She was too busy watching Gray and the dawning horror in his eyes.

Her heart galloped as she looked down at the paper in her hand. Clever little Anna had written a rudimentary play script with a list of characters and lines of dialogue beside the characters' names.

It was the sort of creative writing exercise the twins had been encouraged to try at their progressive school in Manhattan, and Holly wanted to be thrilled for them. She *was* thrilled, actually, but she was also very worried about Gray.

Were her suspicions about his literacy correct? Was this his personal D-Day?

Judging by the sudden paleness of his complexion and the unhappy twist of his mouth as he stared at the paper, the answer was…

Yes.

Her heart broke for him as she watched him force a crooked smile.

'Wow,' he said. 'A play. Aren't you two clever?'

'You have to put on your growliest voice,' Josh informed him.

'I see.' Gray tapped the paper and blew out his cheeks thoughtfully. 'So have you changed much of my original story?'

'We've changed lots!' exclaimed Anna. 'See!' She pointed importantly to her script. 'You can read it all here. We've made up a whole new story, so we can have the owl and the mouse, as well as a frog and a wombat and a pig. There are parts for everyone.'

Gray looked decidedly ill.

CHAPTER NINE

GRAY LOOKED DOWN at the script in his hand, fighting hot panic. It was covered in Anna's childish, clever printing and, as always, he could catch a word here or there, but then the letters of all the other words blurred. He couldn't breathe. His heartbeats hammered in his ears.

I've got to get a grip. I can't lose it now.

As casually as he could manage, he said, 'But you can't have a puppet play without puppets and you don't have an owl puppet, do you? I'll have to make one before you put on the show.'

'No need, Dad,' said Josh. 'Janet's already made us an owl. She's made it out of a tea cosy.'

Gray was very familiar with the brown and yellow knitted cosy that Janet used to keep the breakfast teapot warm, and he could imagine how easily it would have converted into a perfect owl puppet.

'Your play sounds very exciting,' Holly told the children in her best kind-but-firm nanny voice. 'But, right now, your father and I need to collect our picnic things from the truck and put them away, and then we have to get cleaned up for dinner.'

Grateful for her intervention, Gray turned back to the vehicle to fetch their backpacks. To his surprise, Holly came with him.

'Organise a phone call,' she said cryptically out of the corner of her mouth.

'A phone call?'

'Yes.' Her gaze was very steady, her dark eyes huge and shining with determination. 'If one of your friends calls you straight after dinner—an important business call that you have to take in your study—you'll miss the puppet play, but the twins will get over their disappointment.'

Gray stared at her, stunned.

Holly smiled gently and placed her hand on his wrist. 'Janet and I will play puppets with Anna and Josh. We'll send them to bed happy.'

Oh, God, Holly *knew*.

She knew everything.

Gray's throat tightened on a razor-sharp knot of shame.

Holly knew. She'd guessed the weakness that hurt him so deeply he couldn't even bring himself to name it in his private thoughts.

Today he'd kissed her in a desperate bid to stop her from talking about it. Now he was in danger of being exposed in front of his children and he didn't deserve Holly's help, but she was offering him a lifeline.

'You're right,' he said, resisting an urge to sweep her into his arms. 'A phone call's a good option. Thank you.'

He spoke more gruffly than he'd meant to. Then he slammed the door on the back of the vehicle and swung his pack over one shoulder.

He couldn't look at Holly as they walked back into the homestead together. It was hard to accept that the shame he'd successfully covered up for more than twenty years was finally out in the open. Right now, he couldn't bear to see Holly's lovely eyes brimming with sympathy.

He felt like such a fraud. This evening Holly was saving his bacon, but what would happen tomorrow and the day after that? He couldn't keep hiding the truth from his children. The fate he'd always feared had now arrived, and he had no choice but to brace himself for humiliation.

Around eight-thirty, Holly tapped on the door to Gray's study.

'Who is it?' he called cautiously.

'It's Holly.'

'Come on in. The door's not locked.'

When she pushed the door open she found him sitting at his desk in a pool of lamplight. He rose stiffly from the chair, giving the surprising impression that he'd aged in the hour and a half since dinner. He had a sad and caved-in air, as if he'd received a terrible blow.

'Are the children in bed?' he asked.

'Yes, all tucked in.'

'Are they happy?'

'As pigs in mud.' Deliberately, Holly smiled as if nothing was wrong. 'They were disappointed you couldn't join them in the fun, but they understood about the phone call.'

'Thank you.' He spoke with almost formal politeness.

She felt compelled to warn him. 'Anna and Josh are treating this evening's performance as a dress rehearsal.'

'Right.' Gray's mouth twisted in a wry attempt at a smile. 'So they still plan to have a grand performance?'

'I'm afraid so. With a full cast, including the hero, Hector Owl.'

His mouth tilted again, faintly. 'When? Tomorrow night?'

'That's what they're hoping.'

He nodded glumly and looked so unhappy Holly was moved to the edge of tears.

'Don't worry, Gray,' she said quickly. 'I can help you with this. I'm actually quite good at this sort of problem.'

He shook his head. 'I'm quite sure you're a brilliant teacher, but—'

'Before you say *but,* take a look at this.' She pulled a folded sheet of paper from the pocket of her jeans and, as she handed the sheet to him, she drew a deep breath, hoping it would calm her. She was almost as nervous as he was.

Gray unfolded the sheet and swept a brief glance down the page. His mouth tightened. 'What is this?' His blue gaze flicked to her, flinty with anger and despair.

'It's your poem, Gray. I've printed it out for you.'

'My poem?' His eyes flashed disbelief, but then he looked down at the page again.

Holly held her breath as she watched him—the formidable, proud cattleman standing in the middle of his study, with photographs of prize bulls on the wall behind him and a shelf full of silver trophies that he'd won for campdrafting.

Now, with his shoulders braced, boots planted firmly on the Oriental rug, he was frowning at the sheet of paper with deep concentration…

And then…she saw his lips begin to move as he followed the words across the page, sounding out each familiar syllable beneath his breath.

I've…crossed…harsh…country…parched…and…red…

Her throat stung to see this big, capable man reduced to

small boy vulnerability. She swallowed and blinked madly, not daring to shed tears in front of him.

He continued on until he reached the bottom of the page. When he finished, he looked up, a dazed kind of hope shining in his eyes.

His throat worked and deep colour stained his cheekbones. 'I'm sorry. I should have offered you a seat.' He indicated the sofa against the wall, deep and inviting with plump vermillion and green striped cushions. 'Please, sit down, Holly.'

As she obeyed him, he returned to the chair at his desk and, almost immediately, as if he couldn't resist it, he began to read his poem again.

When he finished he looked up. 'So...how does this work? Is it like a code? If I become familiar with these words, do you think I can use them to decipher all the others?'

'That's one of the tools you can use,' Holly said. 'As for the puppets, I can easily go through the play with you, and we can rehearse your lines the way actors do. It's not exactly a three-act Shakespearean drama. Anna and Josh probably won't even notice if you ad-lib the odd line here and there.'

Gray nodded slowly, then pulled out the sheets of the play script from a drawer in his desk. A tiny spark shone in his eyes and he sent her a playful wink.

'Okay, teacher. I'm game if you're game.'

He came and sat on the sofa beside her.

It was fun—way too much fun, really. Holly loved every minute of sitting with Gray, trying to ignore the tingles his proximity caused as she read through the script with him.

It didn't take long for him to get the gist of the simple little story and his character's role, and only a little longer to learn his lines. He had an excellent, well exercised memory.

Afterwards, they sat in the late night silence, basking in a warm sense of accomplishment.

'Anna's so clever, isn't she?' Gray said, looking down at the script with bemusement.

'She's your daughter, Gray.'

'She's her mother's daughter. Chelsea was clever and creative.'

'And so are you.'

As she said this, she saw the shutters come down on his face.

'It's true,' Holly insisted. 'You're every bit as clever as Chelsea, or your children. You're missing one skill set—that's all—and I think I can help you with that.'

With a groan, he launched to his feet. Holly jumped up beside him. 'I'd be sorry to see you run away from this again.'

He sent her a sharp glance, piercing, almost venomous.

Holly stood her ground. 'You've learned your lines tonight and you'll get through the play tomorrow with flying colours. But what about all the times after that? You know there'll be more challenges.'

'I'll manage.'

'Yes, you will. You've managed very well for a long time, but you'd manage so much better if you could read and write.'

There. She'd brought the harsh truth out into the open.

A terrible sound broke from Gray as if something inside him had fractured. His face contorted with pain and Holly felt her heart stand still. The tears she'd been holding back spilled down her cheeks.

This was *so* hard for him. She had said out loud the words he couldn't bear—that he couldn't read or write.

Had she been too cruel?

She'd only spoken up because she was sure she could help

him. If she was strong enough—if they were both strong enough—she could get him through this. And then he'd be free…

Savagely swiping away her tears, she reached out and touched Gray's arm.

'Why don't we just talk about it?' she said gently.

He answered with a groaning sigh.

But Holly wasn't prepared to give up. 'I'm guessing that something happened when you were little. Can you tell me?'

He shook his head. 'What's the point?'

'It could be important. I know you're intelligent and exceedingly capable, which means there's probably an emotional reason why you didn't learn to read. Have you ever talked to anyone about this?'

'No.'

'Not even with Chelsea?'

He shook his head.

Holly wasn't surprised. She'd often suspected that her cousin had fallen in love with Gray's gorgeous looks, but had been unable to meet his deeper needs. Which meant he'd carried this burden alone for too long.

'I'm no shrink,' she admitted. 'But I think talking about it might be the first step.'

'Talking? You want me to lie down on the couch and talk about my childhood?' He stared at her, jaw stubbornly jutting forward.

Holly held her breath, and waited. Then, to her relief, she saw a glimmer of a smile.

'All right, Dr O'Mara. I may as well give it a shot.'

Gray didn't actually *lie* on the couch, but they both made themselves comfortable. He poured them both a Scotch, which Holly wasn't used to drinking but, to be companionable, she sat nursing her glass.

Gray took a gulp from his glass. 'Okay—where do you think I should start?'

'Did anyone ever begin to teach you to read?'

Gray sighed. 'My mother tried.'

Holly remembered the woman she'd met at Sydney Airport and the obvious tension she'd sensed between mother and son. 'Was she living here with you at Jabiru?'

'Yes. We had the lessons—if you could call them lessons—right here in this room. I hated it,' Gray said. 'I loved my mother, of course, but I used to dread our reading sessions.'

'Why?'

'I knew they were a chore for her, and she was always impatient. I used to panic, trying too hard to please her, but then I'd be slow and she'd get frustrated, and she'd end up in tears.'

Oh, Gray. Holly hated to think of that poor little boy trying to please his difficult mother and failing dismally.

Gray downed the second half of his Scotch and set the glass aside. 'It didn't help that my mother hated living out here. She and my dad had terrible rows almost all the time. They were heading for divorce, although I didn't realise it. Then my reading—or rather my lack of it—became a huge issue during their pre-divorce wrangling. My mother blamed my father. He blamed her.'

'They argued about your reading in front of you?'

'Sometimes,' he said bleakly. 'But even when they were behind closed doors, I could still hear their raised voices. I felt so guilty. I was the cause of all their unhappiness. I knew if I could read they'd love each other again and everything would be okay. But my mother had already washed her hands of me.'

He stood and went to pour another drink, then changed his mind and came and sat beside her again. 'No point in getting sloshed over something that happened years ago.'

'You can have mine if you like.' Holly held up her glass. 'I've only had a few sips. I'm not much of a Scotch drinker.'

He took it with a watery smile. 'Thanks.' After a sip, he said, 'You're right. I think it does help to talk about this. I've never really allowed myself to think about it.'

'I can see how the reading broke down,' she told him. 'You developed an emotional block about it.'

'My writing was just as bad. The crunch came just before my mother left Jabiru. I wanted to beg her to stay and I thought if I wrote her a letter and told her how much I loved her that of course she'd stay. No question.'

He forced a bitter laugh, but Holly could hear the terrible pain in it. She wanted to pull that hurt little boy into her arms, to hold him and comfort him.

'The letter was going to be a wonderful surprise for her,' Gray went on. 'I slipped it under her bedroom door. Worst mistake of my life. My parents had the ugliest fight over my spelling.'

Slumping back against the cushions, he closed his eyes. 'They were yelling and I heard every word. She said my letter was illegible. I was hopeless. Unteachable. A disgrace.'

Holly shuddered, but she could so easily imagine the note full of spelling mistakes. Shaky printing. Almost no punctuation. And yet it would have been a message straight from the heart of a distraught little boy. How could Gray's parents have ignored that?

'It sounds as if your mother couldn't cope,' she said. 'But surely your dad stood up for you?'

Gray shook his head. 'That was the other side of the problem. My old man never had much faith in book learnin'. That's what he called it. He hadn't had much schooling and most of his mates hadn't, either, and he reckoned they were okay. Who needed Will-bloody-Shakespeare and encyclopaedias? Books couldn't help a man to catch a wild bull, or strain fencing wire.'

Holly nodded, imagining the situation—the stubborn, uneducated cattleman married to the tense, unhappy city woman. In the next generation, history had repeated itself in Gray's marriage to Chelsea.

'Did your mother leave?' she asked.

Gray let out another hefty sigh. 'It happened a few days later. She left us and went to live in Sydney, and it wasn't long before she found a new husband. A property developer. Their son went to the best schools, and now he's a bright young investment banker.'

'And you stayed here with your father?'

He nodded. 'My education was purely practical from then on.' From beneath lowered lids, Gray sent her a lazy, lopsided smile.

Holly shivered as a wave of longing washed through her. When he looked at her like that, she could only think about snuggling up to him and running her fingers over his skin. She clenched her hands tightly to stop herself from reaching out to touch him.

'So,' she said primly, 'you didn't have a nanny, but what about School of the Air?'

Gray shook his head.

'You mean you had no schooling?'

'That's…the story, I'm afraid.'

'But how could your father get away with that? Surely there must have been someone in the Education Department asking questions about you?'

'Probably.' His shoulders shifted in a shrug. 'I think my dad made sure I was away with the mustering team whenever anyone official came snooping around asking nosy questions. He prided himself on teaching me practical skills and keeping me clear of books and schools. When I look back, I can't help thinking he kept me away from books as a reaction to Mom leaving us.'

But that's a crime! Holly wanted to shout, but she bit down on the words. Criticising Gray's father was not going to help him now.

'By the time I was old enough to understand what a handicap I had, it was more or less too late, and by then I was also too proud and stubborn.' He gave another shrug. 'As I said, I've managed.'

'You've managed brilliantly.'

'I made sure I knew how to write my name and my address, and how to fill in basic forms. If I'd really wanted to, I might have found a way to teach myself more. But I never really needed reading in my line of work. And now—' He paused and frowned at the glass in his hands.

'I'm guessing that you'd rather Anna and Josh didn't have to know too much about your lack of schooling.'

He stared at the glass. He hadn't finished drinking it, but he set it aside. Very quietly, he said, 'I can't go on hiding it from them. And I'm sure it's too late for me to start learning now.'

'I don't think so.' Holly spoke just as softly as he had.

Then, because she couldn't help herself, she leaned closer and kissed his cheek. 'In fact…I'm quite sure it's not too late.'

Their faces were only inches apart. She could see his individual eyelashes and the tiny flecks of grey floating in the blue of his irises. She felt her skin grow hot.

Her words *I'm quite sure it's not too late…* seemed to hang in the air. It was almost as if she was no longer talking about reading. Gray was looking at her with a burning intensity that stole her breath.

It would be so easy to lean closer still, to fall into his arms and invite a repeat of their kiss. She wanted nothing more.

But somehow she found the strength to move away. She had to think clearly. She had to remember that the kiss at the gorge had not been prompted by Gray's desire for her. He'd made that quite clear. The important thing now was to remember that she only had a few weeks left in Australia and she had to at least make a start in teaching him to read.

She would never forgive herself if she didn't try.

'Actually, it's probably too late to start reading lessons tonight,' she said, keeping her eyes lowered. 'But we could certainly try for tomorrow night—once the children are in bed.'

Then she looked up, she saw the shimmering emotion in Gray's eyes. He lifted a hand, as if he was going to touch her hair. She felt a hot flame rush over her skin, then he seemed to think better of it and he let his hand fall.

'Thank you,' he said simply.

'You're welcome.'

'I mean it, Holly. Thank you so much. You're an amazing girl. You have no idea—'

'But I do,' she said. 'I have a very good idea.' She forced a small smile. 'That's why I'd really like to help you.'

He grinned, looking suddenly younger, lighter, freer.

'You've done so much for me. What can I do for you in return?'

Kiss me again? Good grief, where was her common sense? 'Maybe you could organise some riding practice?' she said quickly, grasping at straws. 'Not just for me, for the kids as well.'

'I will. First thing in the morning.'

Gray sat for ages after Holly left, looking around at the four walls of his study and replaying the memories he'd bared to her. To his surprise, the unhappy recollections were already losing their power to hurt him. It was as if talking about his memories, setting them before Holly—Exhibit A, Exhibit B—had made them real, no longer private nightmares, but clues in a crime.

At some deep level, he'd always believed that the not-reading business was his fault. He'd let Chelsea walk away from him because he'd always known that he wasn't really worthy of her. But the reality was: his mother had stuffed up teaching him to read. His father had held him back from a decent education.

Okay, his dad had taught him almost everything he knew about cattle and engines and carpentry, but the world was a big and complicated place and homespun knowledge only took a man so far.

For the first time Gray felt entitled to accept that he wasn't totally to blame for his inadequacies. Then again, it *was* his fault that he'd done nothing about the problem he'd been left with. Hell, if he'd had a physical handicap, he would have sought medical help; he certainly wouldn't have tried to cover it up.

Then again, it was true that practical skills were highly

valued in the Outback. In a way his dad was right. You didn't need book-learning to ride a fleet-footed horse or to clear heavy bullocks out of the scrub, or to sell and buy cattle at an auction.

But, in the scheme of things, the Outback was a limited world and he wanted his kids to have choices he'd never had. Choices meant education.

Holly would never know how much it had cost him to admit to her that he couldn't read or write. Hell, he still flinched just saying the words 'read and write' in his head. But, thanks to her, the words no longer made him feel sick and hopeless. With her help, he was finally going to do something about it.

He felt like a man who'd been let out of jail.

He should tell Holly that some time. It would probably make her smile, and he really liked—no, he downright *loved*—to see her smile.

'Now it's Holly's turn,' Gray told his children. 'She's going to show us how a farm girl from Vermont mounts a horse.'

He'd woken them all early, declaring it was time to start riding lessons before school, and he'd brought four of his gentlest horses into the home paddock. Already, Anna and Josh were smugly sitting astride small, quiet ponies, while Gray held their reins.

Holly had hoped to get in a little riding practice without an audience, but now three pairs of eyes were watching her first attempt.

She shot them a warning frown. 'I told you it's a long time since I've been on a horse.'

'But you won't have forgotten how,' Gray assured her.

'My muscles might have forgotten.'

He grinned. 'That's defeatist talk.'

Holly knew he was probably right, and perhaps it was her attitude that brought about her problems for, no matter how hard she tried, she could *not* swing her right leg up over the saddle. After the umpteenth embarrassing try, she felt like a ninety-year-old former ballet dancer who'd insisted she could still do an arabesque.

'Here, let me help you,' Gray said, handing the reins to his children and instructing them not to move till he returned.

'I'm sure I'll get the hang of it—' Holly insisted as she began to lift her leg one more time.

Then she felt Gray's hands on her bottom. With a firm shove, he hefted her high and suddenly she was up in the air and she swung easily into the saddle.

Anna and Josh cheered.

'Thank you,' she said, but when she looked down into the smile in Gray's eyes, her breath caught. His eyes were shimmering with a special light.

Just for her.

Small fires flared in the pit of her stomach. She could still feel the warm imprint of his hands on her behind and now she was remembering the way he'd kissed her at the gorge. She was almost certain that he was remembering it, too. She'd always thought that he'd kissed her to shut her up. Now she wasn't so sure...

The atmosphere in the study that evening was different right from the start.

Gray was in high spirits after the puppet play. Anna and Josh had been thrilled with his Hector Owl rendition, which wasn't surprising considering how heartily he'd thrown himself into the role.

The children had been overexcited, actually, and they'd taken a while to settle to sleep, but all was quiet now. Janet had retired to her cottage for the night, and Holly had joined Gray in his study.

He could hardly wait to get started on the reading lessons and his eyes were shining. 'Take a look at this.'

From a drawer in his desk he produced a manila folder, letting small squares of paper flutter from it onto the desk's surface.

Holly picked up a square and turned it over to find the word 'red'.

'I recognise that printing. It's mine. Did you cut it out of your poem?'

Gray grinned. 'I photocopied the poem, then cut out all the words.' He looked incredibly proud of himself, exactly the way Anna had looked when she'd produced her play script. 'Choose any word,' he said. 'Test me to see how many I know.'

Holly hesitated. She wanted to ask if he'd had enough time to learn all these words. There were rather a lot of them, after all, but if she showed any sign of doubt, she would undermine his confidence.

'It's okay,' he said, sensing her hesitation. 'I've been practising out in the shed all afternoon.'

'Wow. That's conscientious.' She picked up a piece of paper and handed it to him.

'Dreamtime,' he said, smiling broadly. She tried another word and another and he knew them, too.

Holly grinned at him, thrilled for him, knowing how pleased he was. 'I knew you were brilliant.'

And suddenly his arms were around her and she was being squeezed against his big broad chest, and then they were dancing a crazy jig, bumping into the desk and knocking over a chair and not caring two hoots.

Breathless with laughter, they finally collapsed onto the sofa, panting and grinning stupidly. Holly was quite sure she'd never felt happier, or more uplifted and exultant.

Or more in lust.

Then Gray went very still and everything changed as the air became electrified with tension.

His tension and hers.

'Holly,' he whispered, trailing his fingers down the side of her neck to her collarbone.

She tried to reply but no sound came out. She was too aware of his body pressing against her, too aware of his arousal, and of her own desire coiling and tugging low inside her.

Heat flooded her. She struggled to ignore it. This shouldn't be happening. Wasn't she supposed to be still in love with Brandon, still pining after Brandon...?

She was super-aware of how different Gray was from her ex-boyfriend—he was a bigger, more muscular man, darker, more intense. Everything was different...the feel of his skin beneath her fingers...his breath on her neck...

And ever since he'd kissed her yesterday she'd been aching for more...

Even though he'd tried to dismiss the kiss as a mistake, she'd been yearning for the heady closeness of his lips locked with hers, of his arms about her, of his strength binding her...

She longed for his touch...couldn't bear it if he turned her away now.

'Please don't tell me this is wrong,' she whispered.

'Holly, I wouldn't dare.'

It was all the permission either of them needed. His lips

grazed her cheek, then he kissed his way to her mouth…first taking her lower lip and drawing the soft flesh between his teeth in wonderfully intimate possession.

He was an expert, she realised gratefully, and already she was kissing him back. Indeed, she couldn't stop kissing him.

As she wriggled beneath him, positioning herself against his hardness, she heard his groan and, when he touched his tongue to hers, their kiss turned wild.

Moments later, they were helping each other out of their clothing.

CHAPTER TEN

THE NEXT MORNING there was school and Holly was grateful for the routine of breakfast, bed-making and setting up the school room. Gray had already breakfasted and left before she and the children woke, so she didn't have to worry about catching his eye across the kitchen table.

That was a good thing. If he'd been there, she might have found herself blushing—and who could blame her after the sexy moves they'd made on each other last night?

Now she had a whole day to compose herself, and to convince herself that last night had been a celebration, but nothing more. They had both been thrilled about Gray's breakthrough, and then they'd experienced a kind of romantic movie moment, when they'd been a little carried away.

Well, okay, more than a little carried away.

Nevertheless, it was time to remind herself that Gray wasn't looking for a serious relationship. Last night had probably only happened because she was the only young woman within a hundred kilometre radius.

For her part, she'd decided that making love with Gray had

been a necessary step in her post-Brandon recovery plan. A healing tonic.

At least, that was what she tried to tell herself, but as soon as she'd woken this morning she'd wanted to dwell on every amorous and blissful detail of Gray's lovemaking, wanted to savour his sweet tenderness and his breathtaking passion.

But now she had to put a lid on those memories. It was time to put these last few weeks with Gray and his children into perspective.

In a month's time—maybe less than that—a new and permanent Australian nanny would arrive, and that woman would occupy the teacher's seat in Gray's study. That woman would join in the puppet plays and that woman would, no doubt, be taken to admire the beautiful gorge. She might even go horse-riding with Gray and the children.

Holly's future lay in America—in a new city and a new school. All kinds of opportunities were bound to open up for her there. Maybe even a new man.

Why couldn't she feel happier?

'I think we should agree that last night was a one-off, don't you?'

Holly had been practising this suggestion all day and, now that she and Gray were alone in his study for another reading session, she was relieved to get it out in the open—especially as the sizzle between them was even more obvious than it had been last night.

'I mean,' she said now, feeling obliged to explain her point, 'we both know we could never have anything more than a fling, and flings are—'

'Fun?' Gray suggested with a smile that was hard to read.

'I was going to say dangerous.' Holly sat primly away from

him on the sofa with her arms and her legs crossed. 'I'm your children's nanny, after all.'

'That's true,' he said, in a tone that suggested this wasn't a convincing argument.

'We have to think of Anna and Josh,' she added quickly before she tossed prudence out of the window. 'It could be disastrous if they cottoned onto any…um…liaison between us.'

'I guess you're right.' This time Gray sighed, then reached for her hand and gave it a gentle squeeze. 'Damn it. I suppose teachers are always sensible and right.'

Feeling the warm pressure of his fingers, Holly was overwhelmed by a need to throw herself into his arms. One more time.

Heavens, she was a hypocrite. Now that Gray was agreeing with her, she felt disappointed. Truth was, she'd never experienced such exciting, heart-thumping sex, hadn't known she had it in her to be so passionate.

Now, she had to forget her newly enhanced libido and she had to remember why she'd started this conversation.

'Children can't be expected to understand casual relationships. It's not healthy for them—and after everything Anna and Josh have been through—'

Gray nodded and then he frowned. 'I wish I knew what to say. Thank you sounds crass. But I have so much to thank you for, Holly.'

His smile was both sad and cute as he lifted a strand of her hair and tucked it behind her ear. 'Last night was amazing and special and unforgettable. We shouldn't look on it as a mistake.' His eyes shimmered and his throat rippled. 'We need to be friends for a long, long time.'

'Yes.' It was little more than a whisper.

'But what you're doing for my kids is more important than anything.'

Determined not to cry, she spoke without looking at him. 'My job now is to prepare Anna and Josh for their new nanny.'

She was relieved that Gray agreed. Really, she was, or at least she would be once she was back home and safely embarked on her new career.

The question of the replacement nanny came to a head two weeks later.

The day started on a high note when the mail plane landed on the dirt airstrip with its load of newspapers, letters, catalogues and packages.

Like everyone else at Jabiru Creek, Holly looked forward to the weekly mail delivery. It was a major social event and Gray, Holly and the children piled into the truck to go down to the airstrip to chat with George, the mailman, and any passengers he might have brought with him 'for the ride'.

Sometimes George had time to come back to the homestead for a cuppa and a gossipy chat, but this week he was in a hurry, with engine parts needed urgently by their neighbours at Half Moon Station.

Holly grabbed a moment for a quick word with George about an idea she'd had for a book exchange between the women she'd met via School of the Air. He thought this was a great idea and promised to spread the word.

Back in the homestead kitchen, they opened their mail. There were the usual bills and letters to be handed over to Ted, as well as books Holly had ordered over the Internet— for herself, for the children, and now, discreetly, adult literacy books for Gray as well. He was making fantastic progress.

This week there was also an unexpected package.

'What's this?' Anna cried. 'It's got your name on it, Holly.' She gave the parcel a squeeze. 'It feels like clothes.'

'Clothes?' Holly looked up with a frown. 'I haven't ordered any clothes.'

She saw a hasty, almost smug look flash between Gray and Janet.

What was going on?

With a little shove, Anna sent the parcel sliding over the table to Holly. 'Open it,' the little girl urged with a giggle of excitement.

'I don't know if I should. It might be a mistake.' Holly gave the package a tentative squeeze. It certainly felt like clothing. She double-checked the address. It was definitely addressed to her. 'This is weird.' She checked the postmark. 'It's from Melbourne.'

'They have lovely dress shops in Melbourne,' Janet remarked, staring rather fixedly at the teapot.

'I'm sure there are very nice dress stores in Melbourne, but I didn't—'

'Oh, go on and open the thing.' Gray was almost scowling at her. At least he was trying to scowl, but his eyes betrayed an ambiguous, half-amused glint. 'It's obviously for you.'

It seemed silly to hesitate any longer. 'Can someone pass me the scissors?'

Josh was closest to the old ginger jar on the kitchen dresser, where scissors, wooden spoons and other utensils were kept. Like most boys, he wasn't interested in clothing but, after he'd delivered the scissors, he hung around Holly's chair to watch her cut through the thick tape.

Everyone in the room was watching Holly, especially Gray. Her heartbeats picked up speed.

'It's wrapped in beautiful tissue paper and looks like

it must be terribly expensive,' she said as she opened the padded envelope.

She shot a shocked look Janet's way. About ten days ago, right here in this kitchen, she and Janet had been poring over catalogues together. They'd decided to order riding gear for the twins and, once that was organised, they'd idly thumbed through the women's fashion pages and Holly had gone into a swoon over the most beautiful cocktail dress.

It had just been a bit of fun. Holly had never spent exorbitant amounts of money on her clothes. Chelsea was the one who'd been fashion mad, while Holly had lashed out on books.

'Hurry up and open it.' Josh gave Holly's elbow a nudge and she opened the tissue-wrapped parcel carefully, trying not to tear the fine pearl-grey paper.

All eyes were on her.

And, suddenly, the last layer was lifted and there it was— the beautiful red wool crepe dress from the catalogue.

Holly couldn't speak. She was stunned. She shot a questioning glance to Janet, who lifted her hands in a don't-ask-me gesture and nodded her head towards Gray.

'Do you like it?' Gray asked, frowning.

'It's gorgeous,' she could only whisper.

'Hold it up,' Anna demanded. 'We want to see it properly.'

Holly pushed her chair back so she had room to stand, then displayed the dress by holding it against her. It was divine. The wool crepe was so soft and refined, the finishing was superb and the colour was strong but not gaudy.

'That red is perfect with your dark hair,' Janet confirmed.

'It looks like it should fit you.' Gray spoke casually enough, but he was watching Holly with a breath-robbing intensity.

'It does seem to be my size,' Holly agreed, checking the label. 'But…but I don't understand.'

'It's a thank you present.' From across the table, Gray's eyes gleamed. 'From all of us.'

'Oh.'

Her spirits soared for a beat and then, just as quickly, the wind dropped out of her sails. It was silly to be suddenly upset, but it occurred to her that a thank you present was more or less the same as a farewell present. Everyone here was quite calmly preparing to wave her goodbye.

Holly, on the other hand, was finding it harder and harder to think about leaving here. She loved these people. More than ever now, Anna and Josh felt like her own children, Janet was fast becoming a close friend, and Gray—well, her feelings for him were in a league of their own. But everyone at Jabiru Creek was very dear to her.

To her horror, she was struggling not to cry. How silly. They weren't about to give her marching orders.

'Thank you,' she finally managed to say. 'Thank you so much. I've never had such a lovely dress.'

'You should try it on,' Anna urged.

'Now?'

'Wear it for us tonight,' Janet suggested. 'I'll cook something special for dinner and we'll eat it in the dining room.'

'And I'll put on a tie,' Gray added with a smiling wink.

'Wow! A party!' Anna clapped her hands. 'A new dress party.'

'I guess that's better than a farewell party.' Holly couldn't help it. The comment just slipped out.

It was met by a circle of such puzzled glances that she wondered if she was reading too much into this.

She went back to her room and hung the dress on a padded

hanger in her wardrobe and decided that yes, she'd probably been jumping to conclusions about the significance of this gift. It was just a kind thought. Not a clear goodbye.

After all, there was still almost a month before she was due back in the United States.

One thing was certain: she was not wearing this elegant dress to dinner without first spending time on her grooming. She would have loved to rush out to the nearest beauty spa to be professionally made over from head to toe but, as that wasn't an option, she retired to the bathroom as soon as the children were released from the school room.

A shampoo and blow-dry, a manicure, a pedicure and a DIY leg wax—*ouch*—were all on the agenda. Holly spent ages over each task, wanting to be as close to perfect as the beautiful dress deserved.

She chose her best uplift bra and her barely-there panties and, when at last she was ready, she tried the dress on in front of the long oval mirror on her wardrobe door and she...was...

Gobsmacked.

Wow. Was the vision in the mirror really her?

She turned left and right, spun around to check out the back view. The dress was divinely cut with a deep V neckline and had no sleeves and an elegant side tie. The colour made her complexion glow and the fitted bodice and slim skirt gave her more noticeable curves and a glamour she'd never dreamed of. Even her hair looked more glamorous than usual—extra glossy and dark and bouncy.

Thrills of excitement tingled all over her. What would Gray think of his lovely gift now?

When Gray came home that evening he sensed a general air of excitement in the homestead. Delicious aromas wafted from the kitchen and from the dining room there came the tinkle of silver and glassware as Janet set the table with the best dinnerware. From the children's bathroom came the sound of taps running.

In his bedroom, he was surprised to discover that his housekeeper had taken the trouble to lay out clothes for him—well pressed moleskin trousers, a crisp pale blue shirt and his best navy-blue and silver tie.

It was clear Janet wanted this evening to be a big success. She was very fond of Holly and she'd taken a great delight in helping him to think of the right gift for her.

'That dress is perfect,' Janet had said. 'It's something Holly would never think to buy for herself.'

Gray had been worried that Holly wouldn't like something so…so dressy. He'd only ever seen her in the simplest of T-shirts and jeans. Her taste in clothes was almost the opposite of Chelsea's. His former wife had always wanted her clothing to be that little bit different from everyone else's, with one shoulder bared, or keyholes cut in the back, or frills where you least expected them.

Holly's simple styles suited her calm, warm spirit—the spirit and sense for which he was so increasingly grateful. Of course she'd been right to stop their affair before it had barely started.

It nearly drove him crazy to spend each evening working with her on his reading instead of making slow, languorous love to her. But he was grateful—or, rather, he was *amazed* at the progress he'd made. With Holly, reading had become an exciting challenge instead of a black art to be feared.

He'd wanted to thank her and Janet had convinced him that the dress was the answer.

'Holly spent ages looking at it in the catalogue,' Janet had assured him. 'And it's not frilly or fancy. It's a classic look. She'll knock your eyes out when you see her in it. Just you wait and see.'

At the time he'd almost imagined that his housekeeper was trying to matchmake, but why would she bother? She knew as well as he did that Holly would be gone in a matter of weeks. Besides, Janet had witnessed the disaster he'd made of his marriage.

He was also surprised that Janet had pushed for this dinner party. When he'd ordered the knockout dress, he'd never expected that Holly would actually parade around in it here at Jabiru Creek. He'd only ever imagined her wearing it when she was back in America.

He could easily picture her at a cocktail party—somewhere flash with marble floors and fountains and a string quartet playing beneath potted palms. She'd sip a Martini and converse with some handsome Ivy League guy about Tolstoy and Beethoven and quantum physics.

But, if Gray was honest, he should admit that deep down he also hoped that wearing the dress would prompt Holly to remember him. And his kids, of course. And the time she'd spent here.

Would she miss them as much as they were going to miss her?

Hell. Alarmed by how suddenly downbeat he felt, Gray hurried through to his bathroom to shave with extra care.

'Wow, you look awesome, Daddy!'

Anna was the first to greet Gray when he arrived in the kitchen, dressed and ready for dinner.

'You look pretty swish, too,' he said, as his daughter performed a pirouette in her green plaid party dress. 'And so do you, Josh.'

Josh, in jeans and a button-down shirt, was more interested in playing with the puppies.

Janet was busy at the stove and she was wearing an apron over her best black dress and turquoise beads, and Ted was there, too, standing in the corner, looking scrubbed and smart with his damp hair carefully combed over his bald patch.

'Don't you get paw marks on your shirt,' Janet told Josh, then she let her eyes run over Gray and gave him a nod of approval.

'Thanks for ironing these,' he said.

'I didn't want you slinging a tie on over a crumpled old work shirt and jeans.'

He grinned. 'You know me too well.' Taking a step towards the stove, he sniffed. 'Dinner smells great. What is it? Roast beef?'

'Roast rib of beef with Yorkshire pudding.'

'And your special gravy and horseradish sauce?'

'Of course.'

'Fantastic. I could eat a horse and chase the rider.'

'Daddy!' cried Anna, shocked.

Gray laughed and tickled her tummy. 'Where's Holly?'

'Still getting ready.' His daughter pulled a face. 'She's been getting ready for hours an' hours.'

'Maybe she wants to make a grand entry,' suggested Janet.

Gray shook his head. 'That's not Holly's style.'

Janet turned from the stove. 'Well…everything's more or less ready here. Why don't you pop along to Holly's room to let her know?'

Something like a bolt of lightning ripped through Gray. Going to Holly's bedroom was not a great idea, not with all the fantasies he fought off on a daily basis. He almost suggested that Anna should go to fetch Holly, but then…

His curiosity overpowered him. He was dead anxious to see her all dressed up.

Ridiculously, his throat was dry and his palms clammy as he walked down the hallway and tapped on her door. 'Dinner's almost ready,' he called.

The door opened and Holly peeped out, and the top half of her, which was all Gray could see, looked amazingly beautiful. Holly was always pretty, but tonight she'd done something special with her hair, and with her make-up.

He'd never dreamed that eye shadow and mascara and lipstick could make such a dramatic difference. Combined with the dress, the whole effect was breathtaking.

'Wow,' he whispered.

Holly rolled her eyes. 'But, Houston, we have a problem.'

'A problem?' What on earth could it be?

Of course, he'd still only seen the top half of her, but she looked sensational. 'Is there something wrong with the dress?'

Holly shook her head. 'The dress is perfect. *However*—' She gave a sheepish smile as she opened the door fully. 'Ta-da!'

The dress *was* perfect. Holly was perfect. She looked like a princess, a movie star, a fashion model. Except…

Gray's eyes travelled down to her feet.

'Not a good look, is it?' she said with an embarrassed smile.

She was wearing sneakers.

'I didn't bring anything with heels, Gray. I was coming to the Outback, you know, so I brought sneakers and walking boots.'

He felt an urge to laugh, but Holly looked as if she might tip either way—into hysterical laughter or into tears.

'It's my fault,' he said quickly. 'I should have thought to order glass slippers.'

And then, because it was the most natural thing in the world to do, he opened his arms to her.

Her hair was silky and fragrant, her skin deliciously scented, and her body felt sensational beneath the soft fabric of the dress. In a New York second, Gray was overwhelmed with the need he'd been battling since their night together.

Unfortunately, what he had in mind would almost certainly mess up Holly's perfect make-up. Her lipstick and mascara would end up all over his shirt. And then…for sure, his shirt and her dress would have to go…and…

And he dropped his hands before he weakened.

'I think these shoes are perfect for tonight,' he murmured against her ear. 'Everyone's going to love how you look.'

Perhaps it was best that Holly wasn't wearing high heels. Gray's lovely embrace had thrown her completely off balance and her legs were dangerously wobbly as they went down the hallway to the kitchen.

He'd awoken every memory of their one night together—the scent of his skin, the hardness of his body, the daring intimacy of his touch and the incredible fireworks.

Fortunately, by the time they joined the others, she'd taken enough deep, slow breaths that she was calmer. More or less.

And the sneakers provided a welcome distraction. They were greeted by smiles of sympathy, and everyone was gratifyingly complimentary about the dress. Holly was truly made to feel like the guest of honour.

The meal was superb. Holly had never eaten golden, sumptuous Yorkshire pudding with roast beef. It was delicious, and it was such fun for everyone to be all dressed up and to eat in the dining room. They were in high spirits and, even though the conversation was mostly about puppies, or the horse-riding lessons the children were about to begin, no one minded. Best of all, Holly's feet were hidden under the table for most of the evening.

Throughout the meal she was super-aware of Gray. Their glances kept colliding and, each time, tingles broke out on her skin. The warmth in his eyes seemed to suggest that he was remembering all the things they were supposed to be forgetting.

Every time she caught him looking at her, her body would flash and she'd remember the thrill of his arms wrapped around her and the seductive scent of his aftershave, his powerful body burning against hers.

It was something of a relief, at the end of the meal, to jump up and help Janet to clear the table.

Of course, Janet tried to protest. 'You don't have to help, Holly.'

'I do. You've been slaving all day, and I'm very grateful. But now I'm going to wash up while Gray tells the children a bedtime story. No arguments, please, Janet. You go off and put your feet up and read your new magazine.'

Holly didn't check to see how Gray felt about this arrangement. This evening, she didn't want to be involved in helping him with the children. She was happy to stay in the kitchen. Really. It was a matter of self-preservation.

'You're a living treasure,' Janet told her fondly. 'I must admit my bunions are killing me. But at least put an apron on.' She unhooked a long white wraparound apron from the back of the kitchen door.

Holly was still wearing this when Gray came back into

the kitchen half an hour later, just as she finished scouring the last baking dish.

Of course she looked totally unglamorous now, wrapped in the voluminous apron, with her hands in rubber gloves, her bare ankles showing and her feet in sneakers. But perhaps it was just as well, she thought. She'd had a lovely evening, and the dress had been fabulously exciting, but it was time to come back to earth.

Gray had taken off his tie and loosened his shirt collar, but nothing could dim his gorgeousness.

'You really are Cinderella tonight,' he said. 'Home from the ball and straight into the kitchen.'

Holly snapped off the rubber gloves and smiled. 'I don't mind. It's the least I could do after Janet cooked such a fabulous meal. That roast was so tasty and the lemon syllabub was divine.'

Reaching behind her, she untied the apron strings, but she felt strangely self-conscious. With the red dress about to be revealed once more, and Gray's intense gaze fixed on her, removing the apron felt as risqué as a striptease.

She concentrated on *not* blushing as she hung the apron on its hook behind the door.

'I think that dress might be the wisest purchase I've ever made,' Gray said, watching her from behind.

Holly concentrated harder on remaining calm. 'It really was very kind of you to buy me something so beautiful.' Slowly she turned around, only to find his blue eyes watching her with heartbreaking attention.

She dropped her gaze to her sneakers. Surely they would sober her.

Gray said, 'You're the one who's been kind, Holly. You've

given up your summer holiday to help the children, and now you're helping me as well—'

'It hasn't felt like I've given up anything. I love Anna and Josh and—' Holly bit down on her lower lip before she said anything dangerous that she'd regret. 'And I've had so many wonderful new experiences.'

She looked down at her hands. It had been a stroke of luck that she'd brought red nail varnish with her, especially as the colour matched the dress perfectly. But now, in the homestead kitchen, the bright nails looked citified and out of place.

Forcing a laugh, she said, 'Listen to us. We're talking as if I'm leaving already, when I still have weeks to go.'

'Yes,' Gray said, but he made an uncomfortable throat clearing sound. 'That's something I wanted to speak to you about.'

Holly felt suddenly ill. Reaching behind her, she grabbed the edge of the sink for support. 'Do you want me to leave earlier?'

'No, no. No way. You're welcome to stay as long as you like.' He let out a heavy sigh. 'But it's time I sent off the ads for the new nanny, and I was hoping you could help me with the wording.'

'Oh, yes, of course.'

It was ridiculous to feel so abruptly miserable. She knew that Gray wasn't going to take one look at her in the red dress and suddenly change his mind about never wanting another wife.

Fortunately, he'd never know that, despite her protests that they mustn't get too close and that she had an all-important job to return to, she'd still foolishly fallen in love with him.

'Of course,' she said quickly. 'I'd be happy to help you work up an ad.'

She had to keep busy—busy and businesslike.

'When do you want to start? Now? Why don't we do it here in the kitchen? There's pen and paper right here in the dresser.'

Holly was gabbling, talking to fill in gaps. Gaps were dangerous—they left room for tears.

Without waiting to gauge Gray's reaction, she retrieved the pen and paper and sat down at the kitchen table.

Gray moved more slowly, taking his time to stroll around the table and sit opposite her, leaning back in his chair, long legs stretched beneath the table.

Not wanting to see the expression in his eyes, Holly kept her gaze on the page and, when he was seated, she spoke in her most businesslike voice. 'Right. Let's see what you'll need. I imagine you'll want someone over eighteen years of age?'

When he didn't answer immediately, she shot him a sharp look. 'You want an adult to look after your children, don't you, Gray?'

'Yes,' he said, frowning and looking uncomfortable. 'Yes, sure.'

Holly began to make a list. 'And someone who enjoys and values working with children?'

Gray nodded.

She made another note. 'With a first aid certificate?'

'I...I guess that would be handy. Mostly, I want a good teacher.'

'You'd be unlikely to attract a person with teaching qualifications, but you should aim for someone who can provide stimulating activities for the children.'

'That's right.'

Oh, God. This was killing her. 'I'm sure you'd prefer someone who can produce a variety of age appropriate activities that encourage the development of life skills.'

Gray blinked. 'That sounds good.'

'And you'd want to be able to check this person's references.'

He nodded unhappily.

'What about public liability insurance?'

'We'd need to sort out something. I already have employee insurance.' Letting out a sigh, Gray reached for the salt and pepper shakers that had been left in the middle of the table and began to move them about like chess pieces.

Under the table, Holly squeezed her left fist tightly, letting her fingernails dig into her palm. The more it hurt, the better—anything to distract her from getting too emotional. 'I think this list covers the most important requirements,' she said. 'Can you think of anything else?'

'No.'

'If you tell me which newspapers you'd like to advertise in—'

'I'll get Ted to give you a list of them in the morning. And…er…I think there are sites on the Internet as well.'

'Yes, there are bound to be.'

'Ted will know.'

'Great.' Holly noted: *Internet—ask Ted.* And she pressed so hard she made a hole in the paper. She set the pen down and rubbed her arms. Now that this discussion was over, she felt a chill, as if she was coming down with something.

'I guess we won't bother with the reading tonight,' Gray said.

'That might be best.' Again, she kept her eyes on the page. 'It's been a big day. You could always read one of your new books in—' her cheeks burned '—in…bed.'

'Now that's a novel idea.'

Keep busy...

Holly rubbed at her eyes as if she were sleepy, but mostly she wanted to make sure there were no tears. Then she tore the page with her list from the notepad and got up to put the pad and pen away in the drawer. Behind her, she heard the scrape of Gray's chair on the timber floorboards.

She realised she was shaking from the effort of holding herself together. What an idiot she was. She couldn't fall apart now just because they'd drawn up an ad for her replacement. She'd always known this was going to happen. It was what she'd planned right from the start when Gray first asked her to help him out. How crazy to feel so upset. Anyone would think she'd just signed her own death warrant.

Turning back to the table, she reached for the list, but she still couldn't bring herself to look at Gray, even though he was now standing quite close to her.

She heard his heavy sigh, felt it reverberate all the way through her. What did he have to sigh about?

'I wish it could be you,' he said softly.

Holly froze.

'I know it's selfish,' he said, still in that same soft, low voice. 'But I wish we didn't have to find a new nanny.'

She allowed herself to look at him then. His eyes were extra-shiny and his mouth tight as if he, too, were holding his emotions in. He sent her a quarter smile and his shoulders lifted in a shrug. 'Where are we going to find another Holly?'

Her heartbeats thundered in her ears. Wild, extravagant hope lifted her like a high wind. She struggled to ignore it. 'I'm replaceable.'

'No, you're not.'

She gasped, had to grip the back of the chair. 'Are you saying that you want me to stay?'

'I know you can't stay. You're lined up for a fabulous new career.'

'But if you really needed me—'

His eyes widened. 'You'd stay?'

'I...I might.'

Had she really said that? Had she deliberately put herself out on a limb? Was she out of her mind?

Gray's throat worked. 'It would be perfect, wouldn't it? The kids love you. You're so good for them, Holly.' His words flowed freely enough, but he was standing to attention as if he were facing a court martial.

Holly waited for him to go on, waited for him to tell her that it wasn't only his children who needed her.

Please, please let him need me, too.

Perhaps now was the time to admit that she'd been falling steadily in love with him since she'd arrived at Jabiru. They could both admit that their night together and the closeness they'd shared on so many levels had grown into something deeper—something lasting and wonderful.

As they stood in the middle of the kitchen, Holly felt the Outback night close in around them. The only sound was the ticking of the old-fashioned clock on the wall beside the dresser. She could see the baking dishes on the drainer, shiny and silver after her conscientious scouring.

She saw Gray's hands clench and unclench. Remembered the way those strong hands had held her this evening, remembered the burning need she'd sensed in him.

Say something, Gray. I won't stay unless you want me, so just tell me the truth about how you feel. Let me off the hook, or reel me in, but don't leave me dangling.

When he didn't speak up, Holly knew she had to say something or scream.

'What about you?' Her voice sounded impossibly loud, bouncing off the walls. Then, in a more moderate tone, she asked, 'Do you want me to stay?'

CHAPTER ELEVEN

Do you want me to stay?

Gray bit back a groan of frustration. Of course he wanted Holly to stay, but how could he ask that of her?

It meant asking her to give up *everything*—her job, her home, her country. It meant asking her to commit to *his* lifestyle, *his* family, *his* country. And it meant taking their relationship to a whole new level, a committed level.

He'd vowed he'd never take that risk again.

Chelsea had quickly come to resent this place, just as his mother had. They'd been miserable here. He couldn't bear to make Holly unhappy.

Okay, it was true that she seemed to like the Outback. And if he'd been looking for a wife and had made a wish list of qualities he needed, Holly would score a tick in every box.

She was fun to be with. She fitted into Jabiru as if she'd been raised in the Outback. His kids adored her. Janet and Ted adored her.

And he owed her so much. She'd lifted such a burden from him, and she'd shown him that his future was not restricted by his past. But beyond all that she was so sweet and sexy and she was—*Holly.*

She'd wound her way around his heart. He wanted her—wanted her kisses, her warm sexy body. Tonight, seeing her in the red dress and keeping his distance had been torture.

His imagination kept playing scenes in his head of peeling the lovely red dress from her, slowly, slowly… And, as each inch of her soft, silky skin was revealed, he'd shower her with kisses until they were both almost blind with wanting, and then he would make love to her. Tenderly or passionately.

Her wish would be his command.

But he couldn't indulge his selfish fantasies. He had to be practical and clear-headed, had to remember that where women were concerned he'd fooled himself too many times. Holly was an educated city woman—like his mother and Chelsea. Eventually, her enjoyment of his isolated lifestyle would begin to pall and she'd long for her old life.

He had to be strong, and his task was painfully clear. He had no right to keep Holly here. He had to set her free. Now. Tonight. He had to send her back to the brilliant career and the secure future that awaited her in America.

Hands plunged in his pockets to stop himself from weakening and touching her, he gave her the only possible answer. 'I can't ask you to stay, Holly.'

Her head jerked up and she opened her mouth as if she was about to speak, but he held up his hand.

Now that he'd started, he had to get this out.

'I know my children are very important to you, and I know you'll miss them and they'll sure as anything miss you. But I'll do my best for them, Holly. You've shown us the way.'

He had to pause to swallow the brick that had wedged in

his throat. 'I…I think we'll be okay from now on. We'll always be incredibly grateful to you.'

Holly's lips trembled and Gray felt his courage failing. 'You have a wonderful job to go back to,' he said quickly, before he changed his mind. 'A great life in America. You know I couldn't possibly ask you to give that up.'

She stood very still, not meeting his gaze, with her arms wrapped over her stomach as if she were nursing an ache.

'You have your wonderful family there, too,' he added. 'And I know how important your new job is. I've never seen anyone as excited as you were when you got that phone call at JFK. Your face lit up and you punched the air like you'd won a gold medal.'

Her eyes widened with surprise, as if he'd reminded her of something she'd forgotten.

'You need to go home, Holly.'

'You want me to go.' It was a statement rather than a question.

'I don't want you to be trapped here.'

Her intelligent gaze narrowed and for a moment he thought she was going to debate this final point, but then her mouth twisted into a grotesque attempt at a smile. She snatched up the piece of paper with the list she'd made for the ad, turned and almost ran from the room.

Gray watched her red dress and sneakers disappear and his heart was as heavy as a stone.

Holly reached her room without crying, but she was trembling all over. In all her life, she'd never felt so filled with despair. Worse, she wasn't even sure how she'd reached this point.

Until this evening, she hadn't realised how very badly

she wanted to stay at Jabiru. Now she knew she wanted it so desperately she felt as if her happiness depended on staying here. But she could only stay if Gray felt as strongly about her as she felt about him. Tonight, he'd only talked about his children's needs.

Couldn't he guess she needed him?

She loved him.

Oh, help. That was the truth of it, although she had no idea when it had happened. Was it tonight when Gray had held her? Or at the point when she'd picked up the pen and paper to make the fateful list? Or had it started at the gorge?

Perhaps she'd been changing from the moment Gray had walked into the apartment in New York?

Oh, God, why hadn't she been more careful? She'd known all along that Gray would never risk a second marriage—especially to another American—and if he'd asked her to stay he would have felt obliged to marry her.

How could she let this happen to her again—this cruel, unbearable pain? This cold ache in her heart was so much worse than after the break-up with Brandon. When she left Jabiru she would leave part of her soul behind.

It was ages before she rose from the bed and super, super-carefully took off the lovely red dress and hung it back on its hanger. Then she changed into her pyjamas and went through to the bathroom to take off her make-up, telling herself that the routine would help.

It didn't.

When she climbed into bed and opened the book on her nightstand, she knew she had no hope of reading herself to sleep. She lay there, replaying every painful word of the night's terrible conversation.

When she finally turned out the lamp, she buried her face in her pillow and let her tears fall...

'You're so comfortable and capable with your children now,' Holly told Gray several evenings later. 'Those riding lessons have made such a difference. They're proper little Outback kids now and you're going to manage just fine on your own.'

'I don't think I'm ready to fly solo yet.'

'Of course you are,' she said with necessary briskness. 'You've made great strides with the reading, and it's just a matter of practice now. You should read to Anna and Josh. They'll love it.'

The suggestion seemed to please him and he grinned, looking unbearably cute, like Josh. 'I have to admit I feel as if a huge burden has rolled off my shoulders.'

'I'm glad.' Ignoring the sudden nervous tumble in her stomach, she said, 'Actually, as things have turned out, you'll have to manage on your own quite soon.'

Gray frowned. 'How have things turned out? What do you mean?'

'I've had an email from the principal at my new school and she'd like me to start work earlier than we'd originally planned.'

He stared at her, shocked. Then his blue eyes narrowed suspiciously, as if he sensed something wasn't quite right about her claim.

The tumbling in Holly's stomach intensified. Could Gray guess that she'd engineered this new development?

She'd felt so despairing and heartbroken that she'd had to do something. Staying at Jabiru Creek had become the worst form of self-torture. Each bird call, each sunset, each family meal, each evening session alone with Gray reminded her of everything she was losing. In desperation, she'd written to the principal, advising that she was available to start sooner, if it suited them.

'What's the rush?' Gray asked, so quietly Holly could only just hear him.

'A benefactor has died and left a large sum of money to the school library, so they'd like me to start early, buying in new books for the new school year.' She flashed a falsely bright smile. 'A spending spree. Lucky me.'

He sank back in his chair, his expression gratifyingly sombre, but Holly no longer fooled herself that his gloominess was of any special significance. Her early departure would be an inconvenience, but Gray would manage. Anna and Josh would manage, too. They had a father who loved them, who would do anything for them.

The advertisement for the new nanny had been sent to several newspapers and Internet sites, so that ball was rolling. Until the nanny arrived, Janet could be taught how to set up the School of the Air each morning and the teacher would take it from there. Meanwhile, for Holly, leaving early had become an increasing necessity, a sanity saver.

'When do you have to leave here?'

'I thought I'd get a lift on the next mail plane.'

Shock flared in Gray's eyes. 'But that's only three days away.'

'Yes.'

He launched to his feet, ploughed a frantic hand through his hair. 'What about the children? They'll get such a shock.'

'Not really. They've known all along that I was eventually leaving and I've already been preparing them for their new nanny.'

He came to an abrupt halt with his hands sunk in his pockets, his cheeks leached of colour. 'They'll still be shocked. When will you tell them?'

'I was hoping we could both tell them together, tomorrow morning.'

This was met by stormy silence.

'You'll do that, won't you, Gray? You'll back me up?'

It was ages before he answered. But, to her relief, he finally nodded, said very quietly, 'Yes, of course.'

The only good thing about the next three days was that they were incredibly busy. Suddenly there was so much for Holly to organise—flights home, a hotel booking in Sydney, detailed notes for the new nanny and farewell emails to all the Outback mothers, teachers and governesses she'd met via School of the Air.

She spent as much time as she could with Anna and Josh, and of course there were weepy moments and lots of questions and reassuring hugs.

'You'll come back to us, won't you?'

Holly couldn't answer this. 'I'll see you when your daddy brings you to America to your grandma and grandpa,' she said instead.

She set them up with email accounts, so they could write to her when she was back in the US.

There were no more reading lessons with Gray. The evenings were taken up with farewell activities. Janet insisted on a party and she invited everyone on the property, including the ringers. Holly really liked these easy-going, laconic men and partying with them reminded her of how much she was going to miss their dry jokes and colourful stories about mustering and droving.

On the last night Gray made a campfire down on the riverbank and he roasted freshwater crayfish that he'd caught in the river that afternoon. They ate out under the stars and the food was delicious, the evening magical. The children danced their own version of an Aboriginal corroboree around the fire and Gray told another Hector Owl story. Holly had no idea how she held back the tears.

The actual farewell the next morning was the worst moment, of course. No one—not even Gray—could pretend to be cheerful, and down at the airstrip, the children clung to Holly, tears flowing.

'I love you, Holly,' Josh whispered.

'I love you, too, darling.'

Anna cried. 'I don't want you to go.'

'I know, but you have Daddy now, honey. And you remember what we said? You're going to be brave, aren't you?'

Holly was sure she could actually feel her heart breaking. These gorgeous children had lost their mother and now they were losing her. She wasn't going to be like her own mom who'd married a lonely widower to become his cherished wife and his children's dearly loved stepmom.

She was flying out of their lives.

Janet was too grim-lipped to speak. She gave Holly a fierce, silent hug.

But it was the bleak look in Gray's eyes that almost burst Holly's floodgates.

'All the best with the new job,' he said gruffly, hugging her close so that she felt his heart thundering before he stepped quickly away. 'I hope that school knows how lucky they are to have you.'

By a minor miracle Holly managed not to cry, but the worst was yet to come—climbing into the tiny plane and taking off, watching the homestead and the outhouses and the tiny figures beside the airstrip growing smaller and smaller until they were no more than dots...

The pilot sent her a sympathetic smile. 'You'll be back,' he said.

Holly shook her head. She would write emails and letters and make phone calls to Anna and Josh, and she would see them whenever they came to the States, but she wouldn't come back to Jabiru Creek.

She couldn't bear to be received as a visitor, an outsider, in the place where she'd left a huge chunk of her heart.

They were asleep at last.

Gray held his breath as he closed the story book and backed out of the children's room.

Contrary to Holly's predictions, Anna and Josh had reacted rather badly to her departure and he expected them to wake again at any moment. For now, thank heavens, they were sleeping like baby angels.

He tiptoed down the hall to his study, steeling himself for the empty space on the sofa. Even so, Holly's absence hit him like an icepick in the chest.

He'd done the right thing by letting her go, but he couldn't believe that doing the right thing could feel so bottom-of-the-pit bad.

How amazing that one girl had made such a difference in the lives of all of them here. Everyone at Jabiru loved Holly. They'd all been cheered by her sunshiny personality. They'd respected her knowledge and skills, and they'd appreciated her genuine interest and desire to help. With her latest book-swapping scheme, she'd even begun spreading the goodwill further to women in outlying properties.

Gray didn't dare—or, rather, couldn't bear to list his private reasons for missing Holly.

He *might* have felt better about waving her off if he'd been confident that she was happy to go. But that was the killer, the worry eating away at him now like a worm in an apple—Holly had been a different girl these past few days.

She'd put on a brave face, smiling her way through all the farewell activities but, although she'd laughed and said how wonderful it all was to have so many great memories to take home, Gray had been watching her closely and he'd seen her frightening fragility. He'd seen the tremble in her smile and the new cautiousness, as if she was scared she might crack like an eggshell unless she was very, very careful.

He'd been so sure he was doing the right thing in sending her away, but now he felt sick and uncertain. And bloody lonely.

'You're a sight for sore eyes,' Janet remarked the next morning when Gray came into the kitchen, yawning.

'Anna had a nightmare last night,' he said, rubbing a hand over his unshaven jaw. 'I took her in to sleep with me, and then I couldn't get back to sleep.'

Janet paused in the process of stirring scrambled eggs. 'That's the first nightmare Anna's had for ages, isn't it?'

He nodded as he poured himself a mug of tea.

'Gray, you know what's caused it, don't you?'

'I guess she might be missing Holly.'

His housekeeper shot him a look that made it clear she considered him one sandwich short of a picnic. 'Of course the poor little lamb is missing Holly.' Turning the gas beneath the saucepan down, Janet came over to him and lowered her voice. 'Where are the children now?'

'They're still getting dressed. They slept in. Why?'

'I've got something to say to you. Unfortunately, I had to wait till Holly was gone before I thought you'd be ready to listen.'

His housekeeper studied him, and then she nodded smugly. 'You're in a bad way, aren't you? Can't sleep, face like a dropped meat pie.'

He began to make excuses. 'But Holly was—'

'You've realised you made a big mistake, letting Holly go.'

Gray almost denied this, but what was the point? 'I had to.'

'Forgive me for saying this, Gray, but that's rubbish. That wonderful girl loved living here, and she was perfect for Jabiru in every way. If you think she's cut from the same cloth as your former wife, then you're thicker than two short planks.' Janet leaned closer. 'And the really terrible thing is Holly *loves* you, Gray. You must know she's mad about you. She loves all of us, bless her tender heart. She loves this place. But even a blind man could see how she feels about you.'

The kitchen swam before Gray. His throat stung. 'But her job—'

'Do you really think Holly would care two hoots for that job if she thought she could be here with you?'

He had to set his mug of tea down before it slipped from his shaking fingers.

'Have I been a coward, Janet?'

'Lord love you, no. You're just a man, after all.' Picking up a corner of her apron, Janet dabbed at her eyes. 'And I understand you're scared you'll be hurt again.'

'I'm not, actually. Not with Holly. It's *her* happiness I'm worried about.'

'Then you should stop worrying right now and do something about it. If you let Holly get all the way back to America, I might never forgive you.'

'But she's already on her way home.'

Janet shook her head. 'She has a two-night stopover in Sydney. Thought she might as well see a little more of Australia before she leaves.'

'Two nights.' Gray's heart swooped high, then took a dive. 'But she only has one night left. How the hell can I get to Sydney by tonight?'

Janet smiled and patted his cheek. 'Where there's a will there's nearly always a way.'

Sydney was a beautiful city. Holly woke to a sunny and dazzling winter's day—and where better to spend it than out on the Harbour?

She walked to Circular Quay and took a ferry ride, cruising beneath the famous coat-hanger bridge and past the dramatic sails of the Opera House, stopping at a five star seafood restaurant right on the sparkling waterfront.

She tried to enjoy herself. Honestly. But it wasn't easy to have fun when her senses were completely numb.

This stopover in Sydney was so different from last time, when she'd first arrived here with Gray and the children, all excited about their new adventure. It felt like a lifetime ago. Was it really only a month?

In the evening, she forced herself to go out again. She'd bought a pair of snappy high heels to wear with the red dress. Why waste it?

After a toss-up between a musical, a play or a movie, she opted for the play because one of her favourite actresses was in the leading role. It was rather embarrassing, though. She cried rather noisy buckets in the third act—which was all very tragic—and people around her stared.

She managed a little make-up repair in the Ladies room and then treated herself to coffee and dessert at a trendy little wine bar. Normally, a chocolate soufflé would lift her spirits, no matter how low they'd been.

Not tonight.

Gray paced the hallway outside Holly's hotel room, his stomach bunching with nerves. It was past eleven and she still wasn't back. How much longer could he wait before he was accused by a hotel employee of stalking?

Everything had been going his way until now. It was quite amazing the way fate had smiled on him this morning when he'd rung an old mate, a charter pilot, on the off chance. Luckily, Jack had been willing to juggle schedules just to get Gray to Sydney on time, and Janet had been able to tell him where Holly was staying.

The only spanner in the works was Holly, who was clearly spending a night on the town.

Gray patted his jacket pocket and felt for the small rectangular envelope, and the knots in his stomach pulled tighter than fencing wire. A hard lump filled his throat. Could he do this?

He'd left messages on Holly's phone, but if she got back very late there was every chance that she wouldn't bother to check them.

Could he follow through with his alternative? Could he risk the pain that had haunted him all his life and leave this note under her door?

Memories crowded in—awful, sickening memories of the one other time he'd tried such a desperate measure—his plea to his mother to stop her from leaving Jabiru.

The stress of repeating history brought him out in a cold sweat. This time he had everything to lose.

And everything to gain.

His hand was shaking as he took the envelope from his pocket. It was such a small piece of paper, so few words. Such a simple task to slide the note through the narrow crack below the door. Such a small window of opportunity in which to convince Holly.

As he knelt in the empty hallway, his mind flashed an image of a heartbroken boy, trembling with hope as he slipped a note beneath his mother's door.

Was he mad to try this again?

After her coffee and dessert, Holly wandered back to her hotel but she felt lonelier than ever. The streets were *full* of couples—couples holding hands and laughing, couples with their arms around each other, couples kissing in shadowy doorways.

It was a relief to reach her hotel. The girl at the front desk sent her a smile when she came in, but Holly thought she saw sympathy in the girl's eyes, as if she was sorry for her—all dressed up and on her own. She hurried into the elevator and whizzed up to the nineteenth floor.

As the elevator doors opened and she stepped out into the carpeted hallway, she saw her reflection in a gilt-edged mirror hanging above an elaborate flower arrangement.

Her red dress looked as gorgeous as ever. In fact it looked even better now—she'd lost weight in the last week and she'd acquired cheekbones and a tragic air. Like a heroine in a sad love story.

Ha, ha. Not funny.

She continued down the hall to her room, slotted the key in the lock, heard its click and the door swung silently open. So much for her last night in Australia.

CHAPTER TWELVE

THERE WAS A white envelope lying on the carpet just inside the door. Holly saw it, but she knew it would be her bill and she was too weary and despondent to worry about it now. Stepping over it, she told herself she would deal with it first thing in the morning when she checked out.

She went through to the luxurious bathroom with its gorgeous plunge bath and gold taps and rows of pretty little bottles. A warm bath with fragrant oils might help her to sleep.

Sitting on the edge of the bath, she started the water running and unscrewed the lid on one of the bottles. She poured the liquid, inhaling the scents of jasmine and rose but, as she watched it swirl then foam and turn into bubbles, something tugged at a corner of her mind.

Something about that white envelope—

Perhaps she should take another look at it.

Leaving the bath running, she went back to the little entrance hallway. Her name was on the front of the envelope and it was handwritten, or rather printed in an unskilled hand. Picking it up, she felt a nervous flurry in her chest. Then shivers ran down her arms.

Her heart began to race.

Stop it. Calm down.

It wasn't a hotel bill. It was the last thing Holly had expected—something she'd never thought she'd see in this lifetime—a note handwritten in familiar shaky printing. Her legs were so weak she had to lean against the wall as she read it.

The message was perfectly simple.

Please stay. I love you. G xxxxxxxxx.

A sob broke from her and her hand flew to her mouth. Her vision blurred and her heart pounded like a marching band.

She could scarcely see the note for her tears. Her mind was a whirlpool of disconnected thoughts. How had the note got here? Where was Gray?

But, before she could begin to think about answers to these questions, she heard an ominous trickling sound. *Oh, God.* The bathwater was overflowing.

As she dashed into the bathroom to turn off the taps, the phone beside her bed began to ring.

'I'm sorry, sir. There's still no answer from Room 1910.'

Gray muttered his curt thanks and prowled back to his post on the far side of the hotel lobby. It was close to midnight now and he wasn't sure how much longer he should pace the hotel's marble floors.

Once or twice he had ducked outside to stroll along Castlereagh Street for a breath of fresh air, but he'd always checked back with the concierge desk on his return. He was sure he hadn't missed Holly, and this last call to her room had still brought no answer.

Where was she? He was fast losing hope.

Tired of pacing, he sank into the leather armchair and

thought about ordering another coffee. But he'd consumed so much caffeine tonight, his eyes would soon be out on stalks.

'Sir?'

A voice at Gray's elbow brought him leaping to his feet.

The uniformed concierge, a man of around fifty with a florid face, smiled. 'Mr Kidman?'

Gray's heart thudded. 'Yes.'

'Miss O'Mara has returned. She telephoned the desk and left a message for you.' He handed Gray a folded piece of paper.

Gray opened it, and died a thousand deaths.

It was a handwritten note, not printed, but written in a spiky script with curls and flourishes disfiguring the familiar shape of the letters. He hadn't a hope of deciphering it.

Already the concierge was returning to his desk. Gray hurried after him.

'Excuse me.'

The man turned, eyebrows raised. 'Can I help, sir?'

Gray's face burned crimson. His throat closed over and he wanted to turn and run for the hills. In the past he would have found any excuse to avoid this embarrassment. He would have given up and walked away rather than expose his shame.

Now, his hand shook as he held out the note. 'Would you—' he began, but his voice was hoarse and choked. He tried again. 'Would you mind telling me what this note says?'

The concierge covered his surprise quite creditably once he got over his initial jaw-drop.

'Of course, sir,' he said super-politely. 'Perhaps I should apologise for my handwriting.' He cleared his throat. 'The note says: *Sorry I missed your calls. I'm in my room now. Please come up.*'

* * *

Holly was waiting by the door, and she opened it at the first knock.

Gray was dressed in a dark jacket and tie, and he looked more heartbreakingly handsome than ever. She wanted to hurl herself into his arms; she'd been bursting with excitement since she'd read his note.

But she didn't move. She was worried that she might have somehow misread his message—although how could you misinterpret *I love you?* There was always the chance that it didn't mean quite what she'd instantly hoped. Tonight she couldn't risk taking anything for granted.

'I know it's late,' Gray said. 'But I had to see you.'

Despite her wildly thumping heart, she tried to speak calmly. 'I've been out. I went to a play.'

'How was it?' He looked and sounded as nervous as she felt, probably because he could see how red and swollen her eyes and nose were.

'The play was fabulous.' She waggled her fingers at her puffy face. 'Sorry about this damp look. I'm okay, really. Just being a girl, as my brothers would say.'

He looked worried. 'It must have been a sad play.'

'Yes, it was a tragedy.'

'Can I come in, Holly?'

'Oh, yes, of course. Sorry.'

Dizzy with excitement and fear, she led him down the little hallway that opened into her room which was dominated by a very large king-size bed.

There was only one chair, a pretty pink upholstered armchair in the corner beside a standard lamp.

'You take that,' she said, pointing to it and feeling uncomfortably like a movie director trying to direct a scene without having first read the script. 'I can sit on the bed.'

'I'd rather not sit.' Gray's wide shoulders and height seemed to take up a great deal of space in the middle of the room. His blue eyes shimmered. 'You got my note, didn't you?'

'Yes, it was such a surprise.' *Understatement of the century.*

'I kept it brief. Less risk of getting the spelling wrong.'

'I thought it was very brave of you,' she said, knowing what it must have cost Gray to repeat an action that held so many sad memories.

He shook his head. 'I shouldn't have left it so late.'

'Well, no, you shouldn't. It's after midnight.'

He reached for her hands and her whole body flamed at his touch. 'I should have spoken up before you left. I should have thrown myself in front of the plane.'

'Maybe I should have been brave enough to tell you I didn't want to go.'

He smiled. 'Really?'

'Of course. Leaving Jabiru was the hardest thing I've ever done.'

'I was so worried that I'd trap you if I asked you to stay.'

'I know. You're worried because of Chelsea.'

'I always felt as if I failed her. Our feelings for each other weren't enough to bridge the huge gaps between us. I didn't want to fail you, too, Holly.' He gave her hands a gentle squeeze. 'But you've taught me something important—to stop dwelling on the failures of my past.'

Looking down at her hands, he rubbed the backs of her knuckles with his thumbs. 'I was fooling myself when I said the kids and I could manage without you.' He smiled crookedly. 'We tried. We tried playing with the puppets, we tried reading stories and lighting a campfire down by the river. But none of it was any fun without you, Holly.'

She was starting to feel giddy with relief.

'There's so much about you that I've missed,' he murmured, reaching out and tracing her cheek with his thumb.

A tremor of happiness ran over her skin.

Gray smiled, then he let his hand drop and he was looking serious once more. 'But we need to talk about this job of yours. I know how much your career means to you and—'

Holly silenced him with a shake of her head. 'The job is just—a job, Gray. When I applied for it, there were at least sixty other people after it.'

'Which means?'

'Which means that one of those sixty can have it.' She smiled into his eyes. In the lamplight they were as blue and bright as the skies above his home. 'I'm a farm girl from Vermont, remember. I love your Outback and, better still— I grew up in a patchwork family.'

'So you did. I'd forgotten that.'

'The only job I really want is the one I left behind at Jabiru.'

Gray laughed, then he gathered her in for the most tender and gorgeous and earth-shattering kiss of her life. She never wanted it to end.

When he finally released her, he said, 'There's still one really important thing that I haven't told you.'

'What's that?'

As if he couldn't bear to not be touching her, Gray picked up her hands again and began playing with her fingers. 'The thing is that now, thanks to you, I know how to study and get new skills and a different job.'

'Why would you want a different job?'

'I would if you wanted me to.' He lifted her hands to his lips and began, very gently, to kiss her fingers. 'If it made you happier, I'd study, take a course. If you wanted to live in New York I'd learn how to be a fireman—whatever.'

'Wow. A New York fireman. Now, that's a tempting option.' To Holly's surprise, Gray didn't show the slightest double take, and that was when she knew for sure that they were going to be all right. His willingness to walk away from the security of Jabiru Creek Station was a bigger gesture than any avowal of love, written or spoken.

'I happen to be in love with you exactly the way you are,' she assured him. 'But I'm very honoured that you'd be willing to change your life for me.'

'I want us to be together for a very long time.'

'That happens to be my personal fantasy.'

She smiled again, letting the brilliance of her happiness show. Then, lifting her face, she brushed her lips over his. 'I'm a girl with simple needs. Truth be told, *this* is what makes me happy.'

With another brush of her lips, their kiss became even more spectacular and glorious than the last one.

Then, with one arm around Holly's shoulders and another beneath her knees, Gray scooped her into his arms.

'Wow,' he breathed.

'I know. I'm heavy. Sorry.'

He laughed. 'Not that. I've just noticed your fabulous new shoes.'

'Oh, yes.' Floating with happiness, Holly lifted her legs high, in a move that might have impressed dancers at the Moulin Rouge. Now they could both admire her slender black patent shoes with pointy toes and follow-me-home heels.

'I'm glad you like them,' she said. 'I think they go really well with this lovely dress, and they're a definite improvement on the sneakers.'

'They're very elegant,' he murmured sexily in her ear. 'But I love you in sneakers. I might have to ask you to wear them for our wedding. What do you reckon?'

She grinned at him, more gloriously happy than she'd ever thought possible. 'If we're married out at your beautiful gorge, I might need sneakers.'

Gray smiled into her eyes. 'That sounds like a plan.'

'An absolutely perfect plan,' Holly agreed.

* * * * *

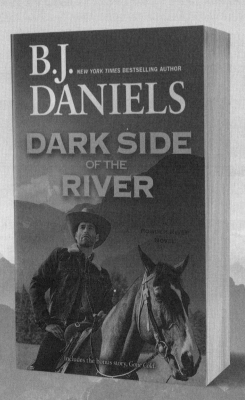

Subscribe and fall in love with a Mills & Boon series today!

You'll be among the first to read stories delivered to your door monthly and enjoy great savings.

WE SIMPLY LOVE ROMANCE

MILLS & BOON

JOIN US

Sign up to our newsletter to stay up to date with...

- Exclusive member discount codes
- Competitions
- New release book information
- All the latest news on your favourite authors

Plus...
get $10 off your first order.
What's not to love?

Sign up at **millsandboon.com.au/newsletter**